About the A

Laura Martin writes historical romances with an adventurous undercurrent. When not writing, she spends her time working as a doctor in Cambridgeshire, where she lives with her husband. In her spare moments Laura loves to lose herself in a book and has been known to read from cover to cover in a single day when the story is particularly gripping. She also loves to travel – especially to visit historical sites and far-flung shores.

Regency Whispers

Regency Whispers:

Scandalous Matches

LAURA MARTIN

MILLS & BOON

First Published in Great Britain 2024
By Mills & Boon, an imprint of HarperCollins*Publishers* Ltd,
1 London Bridge Street, London, SE1 9GF

www.harpercollins.co.uk

HarperCollins*Publishers*
Macken House, 39/40 Mayor Street Upper,
Dublin 1, D01 C9W8, Ireland

MIX
Paper | Supporting
responsible forestry
FSC™ C007454

This book contains FSC™ certified paper and other controlled sources to ensure responsible forest management.

For more information visit: www.harpercollins.co.uk/green

Printed and Bound in the UK using 100% Renewable Electricity at CPI Group (UK) Ltd, Croydon, CR0 4YY

A MATCH TO FOOL SOCIETY

To the many inspirational female mentors I've been lucky enough to have in life. Your time and encouragement have always made a difference.

Chapter One

'I do declare, it has been a thoroughly successful year,' Lady Mountjoy said to the group of women gathered round her. 'And we have still got the main round of balls and events ahead of us.'

'How many matches have you secured?'

'Four. Four out of five of the debutantes I brought from Somerset are now married.'

Jane took a step back, wondering if there was any way she could fade into the background. Never was there a time she liked to be the centre of attention in a ballroom, but right at this moment she would have been happy to blend into the wallpaper. If any of the women in Lady Mountjoy's circle turned and saw her, there would be exclamations of pity and reassurances that she too would find her match. Even though that would be painful, it wouldn't be as bad as Lady Mountjoy's eyes turning to her in that affectionate but calculating way.

'What about number five?' one of the companions asked.

Number Five took a step to the left, wondering if

she might make it to the door without attracting any attention.

'Miss Ashworth is a fine young lady and I have no doubt that we will see her happily married before the Season is out.'

Shuffling her feet, Jane inched towards the door and freedom from the inquisitive stares. None of this had seemed so bad when her friends had been there to experience everything with her, but now she was alone and exposed to the glare of curiosity without anyone to shield her.

Jane continued to shuffle, all the time wondering if she would be better to stride away, then all the group of matriarchs would see would be her squared shoulders and head held high.

Nearly at the door, she risked a look back, catching a snippet of the conversation.

'The quiet, mousy ones...'

For a moment she stiffened, allowing the frustration to course through her, revelling in the fire it stoked deep inside her, before she took a deep breath and banished the defiance that burned bright. Turning, she made the last two steps to the door quickly, already rejoicing in her smooth escape as she rushed through, looking over her shoulder to see if anyone had noted her exit from the ballroom.

Her body collided with something solid and, before Jane could even look round, she flew back through the ballroom doors, her arms spread wide, trying to grasp on to anything she could. There was a moment when she thought she might regain her equilibrium and keep her feet, but it was short lived, and instead she slipped anew on the shiny floor and landed with a hard bump on her bottom.

Every pair of eyes in the ballroom turned to her. Hands raised to mouths and smiles were suppressed. No doubt there were even a few genuine gasps of sympathy.

Quickly Jane leaned to tug down her dress. It had puffed up as she had tumbled backwards and the hem now sat just below her knees, giving everyone a glimpse of her practical white stockings.

Hating the way the blood rushed to her cheeks and the tears pooled in her eyes, threatening to spill out onto her lashes, Jane pressed her lips together in an attempt to maintain her composure.

'My apologies,' a deep voice said, stepping into her line of vision and offering her his hand.

Jane regarded the man for a moment, realising this was the solid form she'd so disastrously bounced off. He was smiling, although she didn't get the impression he was laughing *at* her, as many of the other guests were.

There wasn't anything to do but take his hand and allow him to pull her to her feet. She stood quickly, a little too quickly, and her body bumped against his before she could take a step back and put some distance between them.

'Are you hurt?' His concern seemed genuine, although the hint of a smile was still tugging at the corner of his lips.

'No,' Jane said abruptly. She turned to move away, surprised when the man caught her hand, stopping her from fleeing.

'You're in a hurry, Miss…?'

'Ashworth. Yes, I am.'

'Miss Ashworth,' he said, looking her over appraisingly. 'So, where is the guest of honour of tonight's ball running off to so fast?'

Closing her eyes for a moment, Jane tried to ignore the sideways looks they were getting from a group of young ladies Jane vaguely knew. Silently she dug her fingernails into her palms and summoned a tight smile. It was no use trying to flee now anyway. All eyes were on her. She had missed her opportunity to slip away unnoticed.

'Ah, Miss Ashworth, I wondered where you had got to. Did you injure yourself in your fall?' Lady Mountjoy hurried over and Jane turned to the older woman. Despite her penchant for match-making the countess was kind, warm and motherly and Jane knew her concern was real. 'Whatever happened?'

Jane's eyes flicked to her companion, wondering if he would let it slip that she had been fleeing the ballroom.

'Carelessness on my part, I am afraid, Lady Mountjoy,' he said, inclining his head in greeting. 'I wasn't looking where I was going and barrelled into Miss Ashworth.' He smiled at her and Jane felt the full force of his charm. 'A thousand apologies, Miss Ashworth, please forgive me.'

'Of course,' Jane murmured.

'Have you been introduced to Mr Stewart? No?' Lady Mountjoy beamed, and Jane felt as if a lead weight was sitting in her stomach. 'Miss Jane Ashworth, this is Mr Stewart. Mr Stewart, this is Miss Ashworth, one of the young ladies who accompanied me to London this year.'

'Delighted to make your acquaintance.' Something sparkled in his green-blue eyes as he looked at her and Jane got the impression he found everything in life a little amusing. There was a certain warmth to his smile that sought to draw one in and an air of merriment she hadn't come across often.

'We are honoured to have you attend tonight, Mr Stewart, I have not seen you at one of these events for a long time.'

Jane's curiosity was momentarily piqued, and Lady Mountjoy must have sensed it, for she propelled Jane forward a few steps with a light touch on her lower back.

'Miss Ashworth is free for the next dance if you would care to take to the dance floor.'

'Miss Ashworth?' Mr Stewart murmured, showing no chagrin at having been so deftly manoeuvred into offering a dance.

'I have somewhere…' Jane began, choking back the response as Lady Mountjoy elbowed her gently in the ribs. 'I suppose a dance would be pleasant. Thank you.'

With an amused expression on his face, Mr Stewart held out his hand and led Jane to the dance floor where the other couples were beginning to assemble. As the music began for the dance, Jane sent up a silent prayer of thanks that it wasn't a waltz. She wasn't the most skilled at dancing, but the lively steps of a quadrille or cotillion were much more forgiving to disguise the odd misstep or stumble.

'You are frowning, Miss Ashworth, do you not like the dance?'

Jane looked up and missed a step, grimacing as she planted her foot on Mr Stewart's toes. He barely reacted, and his face remained impassive, but he couldn't suppress the flicker of surprise in his eyes.

'I like the dance,' she said, focussing on the numbers in her head as she counted her steps.

'Perhaps it is the company you find taxing?'

She stumbled again and Mr Stewart effortlessly caught her elbow and whisked her into the next turn. A chain of uncharitable thoughts started to run through Jane's head and she had to swiftly silence them. It wasn't Mr Stewart's fault he was attractive, charming and good at dancing. Some people were blessed in the endeavours that society found important, others were not. Usually it did not bother Jane that she found the idle chit-chat at balls difficult to engage in, and that her dancing wouldn't have anyone madly clamouring to partner her, but today she wished she had just a little more grace.

'I have to count my steps,' she said through clenched teeth. 'And I frown when I concentrate.'

'Ah. What happens if you don't count your steps?'

'I wouldn't be able to dance.'

'I don't believe you.'

'You think I'm here counting steps and treading on your toes for fun?'

Mr Stewart laughed, throwing his head back and letting the laugh rip through him. Jane looked around uncomfortably. People were beginning to look. Nothing about this evening was going to plan and Mr Stewart was not helping.

'Come,' he said, waiting for her to meet his eye once he had stopped laughing. 'Clear your head of all those numbers and all the nonsense your dance tutors taught you and feel the music. Feel how it flows through you and then put your trust in me.'

'I barely know you. Why would I trust you?'

'I am asking you to trust me with a dance, Miss Ashworth, not your life.'

She grumbled under her breath but realised the quickest way to get rid of Mr Stewart and his enthusiasm was to play along. Soon the dance would be finished and, if at that point he realised what a truly terrible dancer she was, she was hopeful he would leave her alone. Then she would find a way to slip away and find some peace in the rest of the house.

'Fine. My head is clear.'

'You're lying.'

Her eyes shot up to meet his and she saw the determination there underneath the sparkle of humour.

Leaning in closer, he spoke quietly, his breath tickling her ear and sending shivers down her spine. 'I can see your lips moving.'

It took all of her self-control not to clamp her lips tightly together.

'Close your eyes, empty your head of all your thoughts and trust me.'

'Fine.'

They covered a few feet of ballroom floor before Jane panicked about the lack of control she had over her movement. In the same instant, her feet became tangled and she fell forward, this time thankful for Mr Stewart's solid form to stop her from tumbling from the floor.

'Whoa,' he said softly, allowing her to recover her own balance. Jane looked around, realising many of the people gathered around the dance floor were watching them, and that she had brushed far too close to a man she did not know.

Thankfully the musicians quietened, the couples stopped their lively movements and Jane was spared any further embarrassment.

'Thank you for the dance,' she said quickly, turning away before Mr Stewart had time to answer. She doubted he would ask her for another, not unless he secretly enjoyed getting his toes stomped on.

'Setting your cap a little high, aren't you, Miss Ashworth?' Mrs Farthington said as Jane hurried past. Mrs Farthington had started the year with Jane as one of Lady Mountjoy's debutantes, but had recently married the insipid Mr Farthington. Jane still thought of the woman as 'snide Miss Huntley', and found it difficult to believe she was now married. It was an odd match, with Mr Farthington rather in awe of his young bride. He boasted a fortune and a kind heart, but was rather a hapless soul, and nowhere near sharp enough to keep up with his fiancée. Even now he hovered close by as if not sure whether to stand with his new wife or not.

'I'm not setting my cap at anyone,' Jane snapped.

'*Everyone* saw that not-so-subtle stumble into his arms. I'm not sure you're his type, though.'

'I'm not trying to be his type.'

'Good. I hear he has a wicked reputation.'

Jane glanced back over her shoulder, catching a glimpse of Mr Stewart's dark hair as he bowed over a young lady's hand. He was attractive. Even she could not deny that. He had an air of confidence about him that seemed to pull people in, to make them want to be part of his circle. Then there were his eyes, that deep mix of blue and green that was adept at making you feel as if you were the only person in the room.

'Enjoy the ball, Mrs Farthington,' Jane said as she swept away, the effect rather ruined as she tripped on her hem and stumbled, but thankfully this time did not lose her footing entirely.

Chapter Two

Tom pulled the covers over his head and groaned, trying to remember where he had ended up the night before. The evening had started respectably enough at Lady Mountjoy's ball. There weren't many society events he attended throughout the Season, but Lady Mountjoy was a distant cousin of his mother and had always been kind, even indulgent with him, so he had dropped in on the way to his club.

After the ball had come far too many drinks with an old friend, and he had vague memories of ending the evening in his friend's tavern on the other side of the river, but had no recollection how he had got home.

The knocking on the door started again and Tom threw off the bed clothes in frustration. It was far too early for visitors—far too early for anyone honest to be out and about. Even his footmen were taking a while to get to the door, which meant either they were still in bed or at the very least downstairs taking an early breakfast.

He rose, moving to the window to see if he could catch a glimpse of who thought it was acceptable to wake a man with a hangover when the sun was not yet peeking over the horizon.

Whoever it was had positioned themselves too close to the door for him to see, and with his head pounding he decided to let his footmen sort it out and collapsed back into bed.

Two minutes later, there was a light tap on the door.

'Excuse me, sir.' Upton's voice came through the thick wood. 'You're needed downstairs.'

His servants normally required very little guidance. He paid well and ensured his staff were happy and motivated in their jobs. It meant he didn't need to worry about any of the day-to-day running of his household and made his life so much easier. It was unusual for one of them to seek him out to deal with something, and as such Tom knew it must be important. Even so, it was still a struggle to drag himself out of bed.

'Come in, Upton,' he called, pulling on a nightshirt and then lifting his dressing gown from where he had thrown it the night before.

'Very sorry to disturb you so early, sir, there is someone downstairs you need to see.'

It looked as though the footman had thrown on his livery, and as Tom peered at the clock on the mantelpiece he realised it was only a little after six.

'At this hour?'

'They insisted, sir.'

Tom raised an eyebrow but didn't argue further, deciding instead to hurry downstairs and sort out whatever misunderstanding had caused someone to knock at his door at such an unsociable hour. By the time he reached the bottom of the sweeping staircase, his mood had not improved, and he threw open the door to the dining room.

All the bluster was knocked from him by the sight that met his eyes. Sleepily curled in an arm chair was a young boy with a shock of dark hair. His eyes flickered open as Tom entered the room, but it was too much of an effort, and after a moment's assessment he closed them again.

Sitting next to the boy was a woman of middle age. She was wrapped up against the cold, the hood of her cloak still pulled up over her hair, and her cheeks rosy from the bite of the winter wind.

'Who are you?' If he was honest with himself, Tom knew without having to be told at least who the boy was, but his mind was struggling to wade through the shock of seeing the child here.

'My name is Alessia Endrizzi. You do not know me, but I promised a dear friend to undertake a journey for her, and she assured me we would be well received when we arrived.'

Tom felt his throat closing up and reached to loosen his collar, only remembering he was in his night clothes when his hand touched the soft cotton of his nightshirt.

'Your friend…?'

The woman smiled kindly and Tom saw the hint of sadness.

'I have a letter. Perhaps it would be best if you read that first.'

Tom nodded, taking the letter but unable to bring himself to open it for a minute. He stood by the fire one of the servants must have hastily lit when the guests had arrived and stared into the flames, trying to summon the courage to tear open the envelope.

My dearest brother,
How long it has been since I set eyes upon you.
Often I think of home, of those childhood days we
spent playing together. Always you could make
me smile and laugh, even in the most dire of cir-
cumstances, and I will be thankful for ever for
your love and companionship.

Next comes an apology. I am sorry I left it so
long to contact you. I know you would have wor-
ried about me, and if I had been a better sister I
would have returned sooner, but in truth I have
been happy here hidden away in rural Italy. I
know you would never have reproached me for
my choice and I hope this will make what I ask
easier for you.

My husband, my dear Giovanni, passed away
three years ago. He has no surviving family and
although I am surrounded by good friends I can-
not ask of them such a momentous favour.

I am dying. The doctors cannot tell me exactly
what is wrong, but I have a large growth in my
belly. It is eating away at my life force and soon
there will be nothing left of me. I do not have the
strength to make the journey home even though
I wish I could hug you one last time.

My kind friend, Alessia, offered to bring Ed-
ward to you. I am so sorry I did not send advance
warning of their arrival, but things are happen-
ing so quickly. I know it will be a shock, but I beg

of you to look after my darling boy for me. Love him, cherish him, tell him about his mama and how much he was loved by both his parents.

Edward is six. He is kind and loving and intelligent and funny. I know you will provide everything he needs, because I know the kind of man you have grown in to, but I beg you to love him as well. You know as well as I do what it is like to go through childhood without love, and at least we had each other.

I will bid you farewell now and hope one day we will meet again in heaven, and there you can tell me all about my wonderful son.

All my love
Rebecca

For a long moment Tom couldn't think of anything but his sister's sunny smile and he felt a searing pain shoot through him at the realisation he would never see her again. It had been twelve years since she'd left. For twelve long years he'd missed his childhood companion, but he'd always imagined one day they would be reunited. As always when he thought of Rebecca he felt a horrible mass of guilt and regret pushing down on him. He had not done the best by his sister, having abandoned her to save his own sanity, and he had never forgiven himself.

He glanced at the boy sleeping in the arm chair, noting the familiar curve to his lips and the shock of dark, curly hair, identical to Rebecca's when they had been children, impossible to tame.

'This is Edward?' It was a wholly unnecessary question, but Tom didn't know what to say. Never had he imagined he would start the day today with his nephew in the house. A nephew he hadn't even known existed.

'This is Edward,' Alessia said softly.

A kindness radiated from her and Tom could see why his sister had entrusted her son to this woman.

'The journey has been long, and he is very tired.'

'You must be tired too. Shall I ask one of the servants to show you upstairs to a bedroom to rest?'

'I cannot stay.'

'You've only just arrived.'

'Our journey was plagued by delays.' She smiled kindly at him. 'I have been away from my family for a long time already and I need to get back to them.'

'Do you have children?'

'Six. They are with their grandmother, but I must return as soon as possible.'

'Surely you have time to rest for one day?' Tom wanted to hear about his sister, about her life in Italy and the years during which she had disappeared.

'I have booked a passage on a ship that sails later this morning.' She paused and then reached out, took his hand and squeezed. 'You look just like her.'

'Was she happy?'

Alessia nodded. 'Very happy. She loved Giovanni very much and he worshipped her. Of course, when Giovanni died she was heartbroken, but her love for Edward helped her through.' Gesticulating to the hall, she continued. 'She wrote more letters, letters for Edward but also some for you. She had time to prepare. Her decline was gradual but steady and she wanted to leave something for Edward to remember her by. All the legal documents are in the bundle as well.'

'Thank you for bringing them.'

'I am sorry I cannot stay. I had planned to remain for a few days before returning, but as I say, it is impossible. I am happy to write, once you have read the letters, if you have any questions.'

Tom ran a hand through his short hair, enjoying the bristly feeling on his fingertips. Part of him wondered if he was in some terrible dream fuelled by too much alcohol the night before. Perhaps in a few minutes he would stir, woken by a sound in the real world.

No such relief came.

He could not force Alessia to stay, and understood the sacrifice she had made already in fulfilling her friend's last request. Even so, as the kindly Italian woman stood he felt a wrench of panic.

'He likes stories and make-believe, long hugs and to be sung to sleep at night,' she said, as if reading his mind.

'Thank you for everything you have done for them both. Can I give you something to pay for your passage?'

'No. I couldn't do much for Rebecca, but I could do this.' She leaned over the sleeping boy and kissed him tenderly on the cheek. Edward stirred but did not wake and, with one final caress of the sleeping boy's cheek, Alessia left.

Staggering a little, Tom sat down, the reality of everything he had just been told starting to dawn on him. His sister was dead, and now he was guardian to her son, a vulnerable young boy who had lost so much already.

'I'm not the person you need,' he murmured as he

looked across at his nephew. He knew nothing about children. Over the last decade he had steadfastly refused even to contemplate courting a woman with a view to settling down. He didn't want to continue the family line and had no intention of ever being anything but a happy bachelor.

A wave of panic washed over him, building gradually until he thought he might be crushed under the weight of responsibility. Tom pulled at his collar, feeling as though something was tightening around his neck, but there was only the loose fabric of his shirt.

He felt the sudden and overwhelming need to get out of the house. The walls were closing in around him and he needed to suck in the fresh air, to remind himself there was a whole world out there.

'Mrs Hills,' he called, certain his steadfast housekeeper would not still be abed, with all the commotion going on.

She appeared from the hallway instantly, her face drawn with worry but softening when she saw the sleeping boy.

'This is my nephew, Edward,' he said, the words feeling foreign on his tongue. 'He has had a long journey and I expect will sleep a while. Is there a bed for him?'

'The blue room is aired and ready.'

'Good. I will carry him upstairs. I want someone to sit with him in case he wakes. No doubt it will be disturbing for him to be in an unfamiliar house.' For one dreadful second he wondered if the boy spoke only Italian, then dismissed the idea. Surely Rebecca would have wanted to teach her son her language, to share that part of her with him? 'I will be back in an hour, maybe two. There are some things I need to arrange.'

'Of course, sir. I will ask Hetty to sit with him. She has half a dozen younger siblings and is wonderful with children.'

'Good.'

Tom hesitated before walking over to his nephew and threading his arms underneath the sturdy little body. The boy was warm and snuggled in to Tom's embrace as he lifted him, exhaling a soft breath and murmuring something inaudible. Something clenched in Tom's chest and he felt the flicker of recognition. It was as if he were holding his sister in his arms, picking her up when she had scraped her knee or fallen from a tree in one of their games.

Forcing his legs to move, he took one step and then another, moving slowly so not to jolt Edward awake.

As he placed his nephew into the soft double bed in the blue room, the young boy's eyes flickered open for a second, settling on Tom's face. He smiled, wriggled down under the sheets and promptly fell back asleep.

Chapter Three

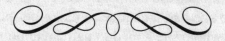

Jane was glad of the darkness as she drew the hood of her cloak over her head and slipped out of the back door. It was a route she had taken many times now and she knew which floorboards to avoid and how to twist the key in the lock to prevent it from making a horrible screeching sound. She wondered if some of the servants were aware she sneaked out like this, choosing to keep quiet rather than inform their mistress, deciding it was none of their business what a country girl from Somerset was doing, creeping about London at all hours.

Outside the morning was misty and cold and a persistent drizzle fell from the sky, soaking her in minutes. It was mid March and sometimes in Somerset the spring flowers would be blooming, but this year the cold temperatures had delayed the first signs of spring. At this time, she knew she would have to walk a fair distance before there would be a hackney coach to hail. It was too early for most people wealthy enough to want a carriage for hire to be up and about.

She walked briskly, head bent against the weather, the package she carried held tightly to her body.

It was barely better in the hackney, once she found one. She was so wet from the walk that she shivered the entire way, feeling her damp skirts clinging to her legs.

Self-consciously she tried to smooth down her hair, telling herself it wasn't about appearance, but also aware that if she looked too bedraggled she would be thrown out before she had a chance to make her point to the man with whom she hoped to gain an appointment.

Jane watched the streets of London pass by, feeling a heaviness in her stomach as they crossed the river. Even country girls like her knew Southwark was not a place for gently bred young ladies. She might not be wealthy, but she had been raised in a certain way.

The carriage slowed and Jane peered out, suddenly unsure now she was so close to her destination.

'I can't take you no further, miss,' the driver said, jumping down. 'Streets are too narrow.'

A heaviness settled in her stomach and part of her wanted to stay in the relative warmth of the coach and tell the coachman to take her back home. With a glance down at the package she held close to her chest, she rallied. *This* was the whole reason she was here in London, the whole reason she had endured months of balls, dinner parties and trips to the modiste.

'Thank you,' she said as she stepped down, handing the fare to the driver. 'Can you direct me where to go on foot from here?'

'Down that street there, take the second left and you'll come into a courtyard. The address you want is somewhere there.'

'Thank you.'

Jane wished it was a little later in the morning. Although the sun had risen, the streets were still dark and a thin fog curled around her ankles. For a moment she didn't move, her eyes darting left and right, taking in the drunken man sprawled in a doorway and the two young children working up the courage to poke him with a stick. In the distance a group of women bustled through the streets, calling to each other, already well into their day, but here it was quiet.

The sound of the rolling of the carriage wheels beside her made Jane start and she had to move away quickly to avoid being splattered with mud and whatever other filth ran through the streets.

'Come on, Jane,' she muttered to herself, raising her chin and straightening her back. This had been her dream for so long. She wasn't about to give up now.

Blinking as he stepped into the bright sunlight from the gloomy interior of the tavern, Tom grimaced. Southwark wasn't his favourite place to visit at any time of day, but in the dim morning light one saw it for what it really was without the forgiving shield of darkness. The houses were built too close together, overflowing with families too large for the rooms they lived in. Worse still were the people who no longer had a roof over their heads, their eyes filled with despair when they managed to look up.

'Little slice of heaven my lord?' a woman called half-heartedly, as if she knew already her offer would be declined.

When he'd left his house a couple of hours earlier, he

hadn't planned to traipse so far, but his feet had moved of their own accord and he'd found himself crossing the river into the less salubrious part of town.

'Remember that moment of pure dread just before the cavalry charge?' Western said as he followed Tom out of the tavern. The man was huge in stature, a giant of a man who took pride in having the deadliest punch in London.

'I remember,' Tom said quietly.

'If you could survive that, you can survive this.'

Without another word, Western gave him an almighty slap on the back, enough to have made Tom stumble if he hadn't braced himself, and then turned and went back inside the tavern.

Western might look as though he would be at home running a gang in the slums of St Giles, but his solid reliability and staunch friendship made Tom feel more grounded. He'd walked into the tavern a mess, his thoughts racing, jumping, not able to settle on what must be done about the surprise arrival of his nephew, the boy he was now charged with looking after. Western had succinctly told Tom to focus on the practical and everything else would fall into place in time.

'The practical,' Tom murmured to himself. If only he knew something, anything, about children.

He looked around, taking in the bustle of the street, wondering if he would be able to find a carriage for hire to take him back home, where he could start making his plans.

At first his eyes skimmed over the well-dressed young woman walking hesitantly down the street, but after a moment he registered how out of place she looked, and his gaze darted back to her.

Her dress was covered with a dark cloak, the hood pulled up over her hair. There was nothing ostentatious about her clothes, but there was a quality about the fabric that one did not normally see in Southwark. For an instant the young woman turned her head and Tom caught a glimpse of her face. It looked familiar, although she had turned away so quickly he couldn't quite place her.

It was none of his business what this young woman was doing in this part of the city, but his protective instinct had been sparked, and he glanced around, seeing that he wasn't the only one who had taken note of the woman's fine clothing.

Making a decision, he started to cross the street, meaning to intercept the young woman and ensure she did not need any help, but before he could approach she moved way, walking briskly into a dark alley.

Cursing, Tom followed her, expecting to see her ambushed at any moment. She hurried along, looking up at the buildings as she went as if she was unfamiliar with this part of town. Not once did she look behind her and Tom marvelled at her lack of awareness of the danger she could be in. The alleys were narrow and dark, the buildings leaning inward and blocking out much of the light. Filth ran beneath his shoes and the stench was awful. He couldn't imagine what would induce a well-dressed lady to come to this part of town.

After a moment, she turned into a side alley, disappearing from view for a few seconds. Tom moved faster, darting round the corner. As he did, a fist came out of the shadows, connecting with his jaw and snapping his head to the side. It wasn't a particularly hard punch, but it had taken him by surprise and it took him a moment to recover. He did manage to dodge the second punch, the follow-through with the other fist, catching the hand in his before it made contact with his face.

The skin under his fingers was soft and the hand delicate so it was no surprise when it was a woman he drew out of the darkness. The hood of her cloak had fallen back and, as the light hit her face, he drew in a sharp breath of surprise.

'You?'

She frowned in recognition.

'Miss…' He fished around in his brain for the name from the ball the night before. 'Miss Ashworth.'

'Mr Stewart.'

'What are you doing lurking in dark alleys, punching people?'

Miss Ashworth spluttered. '*I* was doing nothing of the sort. I was going about my business, walking down the street, when you decided to follow me.'

'It's a dangerous part of London.'

'Hence why I darted into the alley and punched the man who was following me.'

Tom suppressed a smile at her defiant tone. 'I am sorry if I scared you. That was never my intention. I was concerned that you may not be aware of the dangers of walking alone in Southwark.'

Her fingers twitched in his and he realised he was still holding her hand. Quickly he released it and Miss Ashworth took a step back.

'What are you doing here?'

She hesitated. 'I have an appointment with someone.'

'In Southwark?'

'What are you doing here?' she fired back.

'I was visiting an old friend.'

He saw her raise an eyebrow, knowing the direction of her thoughts, but didn't disabuse her of the notion. People didn't understand the friendship between Western and himself at the best of times. It wasn't something he was about to try and explain in a dark alley to a woman he barely knew.

'You have a good punch,' he said, rubbing his jaw.

'Thank you.'

'I can't just leave you here, alone and unchaperoned, Miss Ashworth,' he said slowly. There was a flare of defiance in her eyes.

'I have not asked for your protection Mr Stewart.'

'Yet I am honour-bound to give it.'

'Go home, or back to whatever warm bed you've hopped out of, and forget you ever saw me.'

'You know that is not possible. What if you were set upon by a band of thieves, or worse?'

'I can look after myself.'

Tom rubbed his forehead on either side with his thumb and forefingers. He was developing a headache and Miss Ashworth's stubborn arguments weren't helping. He needed to go home to start organising whatever it was six-year-old boys required in life, not stand in an alley in the cold, arguing with a woman he had met only once before.

'How about I make you a deal?' he said, trying to keep the frustration from his voice. 'You allow me to escort you wherever it is you need to go, and ensure you get back home to Lady Mountjoy's house safely, and in return I will not tell anyone where you have been or what you are doing here.'

Miss Ashworth opened her mouth to argue but before she could speak Tom ploughed on.

'It is a good deal, Miss Ashworth, and I do not have the time or the inclination to negotiate. The alternative is I bundle you into a carriage, take you back to the Mountjoys and tell them where I found you.'

'Fine,' Miss Ashworth said after a couple of seconds. 'Keep up.'

Reaching down, she picked up a package Tom hadn't even realised she had dropped then spun on her heel and marched off down the alley, taking a couple of turns until they came out into a dreary courtyard. The buildings huddled around a cobbled square, ramshackle and grimy, the upper levels accessed by a set of rickety wooden stairs that looked as though they would barely hold a man's weight.

Miss Ashworth, who until this moment had managed to keep up at least a façade of confidence, faltered.

'Not what you were expecting?'

She ignored him, looking up at the doors on the upper level, turning in a circle as she did.

'Would you like me to go first?'

'I can manage from here.'

Despite her protests, Tom followed her up the stairs carefully, spreading his weight evenly so as not to crash through the rotting wooden planks.

Up close the upper level was even worse. The windows were covered in a thick layer of grime and some of the doors were rotting on their hinges.

'Are you sure you're in the right place?' Most of the buildings looked abandoned and beyond repair.

Miss Ashworth paused outside a door that looked as though it had been once painted dark green. She bent down, looked at a scuffed plaque on the door and then straightened with a grimace.

Tom stepped closer and peered at the sign, surprised by what he read: *William Highbury, Book Publisher.*

'A publisher?' Now he was even more confused than before.

She knocked.

'What do you want with a publisher?'

Ignoring him, Miss Ashworth stepped to the side and squinted through the window.

'What do you want with a publisher in Southwark?'

'That is absolutely none of your business.'

'There's no one here. These buildings are not fit for anyone to live in or run a business in.'

Miss Ashworth knocked again, this time louder and more insistent.

'There's no one there, love,' a voice from below called up.

They both moved to the edge of the upper walkway and looked down to the courtyard below.

'Do you know where Mr Highbury is now?'

'Dead. Buried two years ago.' The woman was already starting to walk away, a basket under her arm and a young child trailing in her footsteps.

'And his business—did anyone take it over?'

'He had no children. He had no one,' the woman shouted over her shoulder before disappearing into the alleyway.

Tom watched as Miss Ashworth closed her eyes and let her shoulders sag, unable to comprehend what could have been so important to cause her such disappointment now the chance was gone.

'What did you want with him?'

Miss Ashworth shook her head, glancing down to a bulge beneath her cloak. He remembered the package she had retrieved from the floor after dropping it to punch him.

'What is in that package?'

'It is none of your concern.' She gave an exasperated exhalation. 'In fact none of this is any of your concern. Good day, Mr Stewart.'

'We made a deal, Miss Ashworth,' he said, easily keeping up with her as she started to climb back down the rickety steps.

She turned to glare at him and in doing so her dress caught on a protruding nail on one of the wooden planks. As she turned back, the fabric snagged, pulling and causing her to stumble.

With a little cry she managed to regain her balance, just as Tom lunged forward to grab hold of her, but both their combined weight on one rotten wooden step was too much and there was an ominous crack.

They were only four steps from the ground and, preferring a twisted ankle to a flesh wound from the splintered wood, Tom jumped, grabbing on to Miss Ashworth's arm and pulling her with him. They landed heavily, their bodies crashing into one another. Tom could see he had sent Miss Ashworth reeling so, trying to correct his mistake, he reached out again, ensuring they fell together, and he cushioned the landing.

As he made contact with the cold, wet cobbles, he felt the jarring impact travel through his spine, made worse when Miss Ashworth's body landed squarely on top of his, pushing the air from his lungs.

For a moment neither of them moved, both too stunned to do anything but catch their breaths.

'What did you do that for?' Miss Ashworth asked after a few seconds. She was looking at him as though he were a maniac.

'The wood was splintering! Get cut by a piece of filthy wood, and at best you could lose your leg, perhaps even your life. I chose not to risk it, for either of us.'

Miss Ashworth looked over at the collapsed bottom portion of the staircase, some of the indignation ebbing out of her expression.

'Filthy perverts, it's broad daylight,' a voice shouted from the end of the alleyway leading into the courtyard. 'Go somewhere private or at least wait until after dark.'

With horror Miss Ashworth looked down, only now realising the position they were in. Tom was lying on his back on the stone cobbles with Miss Ashworth straddling his hips. It wasn't comfortable, and no one in their right mind would choose this filthy location for getting intimate, but he could see from a distance, and in the right light it might look as though they had been overcome by lust for one another.

Quickly Miss Ashworth scrambled to her feet, backing away to put as much distance between them as possible. Tom took a little longer to get up, his back protesting after the jolt it had taken as they'd fallen.

'I'm going home,' Miss Ashworth declared.

'First sensible thing you've said all morning,' Tom muttered.

Either she didn't hear him or chose to ignore him as she stalked back through the alley to the wider streets. It didn't take too long to find a carriage for hire to take them back to Mayfair. Miss Ashworth seemed to relax a little once the wheels were moving and they wound their way back towards the river and the more familiar parts of London.

They sat in silence for the journey. Normally Tom would have found a way to charm the serious young woman sitting across from him, but today he was too distracted. His mind was already back home, on the little boy with the dark hair and long eyelashes who was now completely reliant on Tom for everything with which a parent should be providing him.

'Can you tell the driver to stop at the end of the street?'

'Why?'

Miss Ashworth rolled her eyes and leaned out of the carriage window, shouting up to the driver. She looked satisfied as a carriage rolled to a stop and went to open the door.

'Thank you for a diverting morning,' Tom said dryly.

'Let us hope our paths do not ever need to cross again.'

She hopped down and without a backward glance began to stride along the street. Tom could probably have stayed in the carriage—it was well past nine o'clock and the streets were busy. It was only a couple of minutes' walk to Lady Mountjoy's house and Miss Ashworth had bowed her head in the drizzle and was making fast progress. Still, he knew he wouldn't feel easy if he didn't see she got safely indoors, so he followed her out of the carriage, quickly paid the driver and walked after her.

He wasn't all that surprised when Miss Ashworth eschewed the front door, instead slipping round the side of the house and into the garden, no doubt to enter the house via a back door, hopefully unnoticed.

'Strange morning,' he murmured, shaking his head. It had been one of the most bizarre mornings of his life.

He paused outside of the Mountjoy house, looking up at the windows, and then turned to leave.

'Mr Stewart! Mr Stewart!' a voice called.

With a sinking in his stomach, he slowly turned back. Lady Mountjoy was standing just outside her front door, waving over to him.

Chapter Four

It was far too early for visitors, but Lady Mountjoy was well known for her hospitality, and taking in those members of her circle who didn't have anyone else to turn to, so the servants didn't blink when she asked for tea and toast to be brought up to the drawing room.

'I just happened to glance out of the window and saw you standing opposite the house, and I thought you had the look of a man who does not know what to do,' Lady Mountjoy said as she poured the tea. 'It is early for visiting, but I am sure Miss Ashworth would be amenable to coming down, seeing as it is you.'

'Miss Ashworth?' Even as the words left his mouth, he knew his tone was a little too sharp, a little too defensive.

'She is the reason you are here, is she not? You two did dance beautifully at the ball last night.'

Tom closed his eyes. Lady Mountjoy, consummate match-maker, thought he was a possible suitor for her last remaining debutante. His instinct was to rush in, to put her right immediately, but he was aware he needed to step carefully. As much as he didn't want to become embroiled in one of Lady Mountjoy's match-making schemes, equally he knew he couldn't betray why he had really been outside the house. Miss Ashworth might have been foolish to travel to Southwark for her mystery mission, but it wasn't his place to tell her temporary guardians.

'You have it wrong,' he said quickly. 'Pleasant as I am sure Miss Ashworth is, it wasn't her I came to see.'

'Oh.'

'I need your help. It is a delicate matter, but I thought you may be able to advise me.'

The older woman sat back in her chair, resting her tea cup in her saucer, and motioned for him to go on.

'I am sure you remember my sister, Rebecca.'

'Of course.'

'The official story my father liked to tell is that she married a foreign count.'

'Yes, I remember.'

'It was nonsense, of course. My sister fell in love with an Italian, but he wasn't a count, he was a musician.'

'She married him?'

'I don't know. She left with him quietly. My father was not a reasonable man, and if he'd had any notion of what was about to happen he would have locked her up and sent her away.'

Lady Mountjoy nodded thoughtfully. 'That cannot have been easy for you.'

'I loved my sister dearly, and missed her terribly, but I do not begrudge her seizing a chance of happiness. She would have been married off to one of my father's old friends and been under the control of another vindictive old man had she stayed.' He didn't speak of the guilt he felt every morning for the decision he had made at eighteen to leave her behind. It still plagued him, how quickly he had signed up to join the army, how quickly he had moved on with his life whilst she'd still been made to endure a thousand tiny psychological tortures every day from their father.

'You speak of her in the past tense.'

'I learned recently that she passed away a few months ago.'

'I am sorry, my dear.'

Tom nodded, feeling the prick of tears in his eyes. Throughout his childhood he had been schooled that gentlemen did not show their emotions and, although over the last few years he had been trying to do exactly the opposite of many of his father's lessons, showing true emotion was still difficult.

'I can trust your discretion, Lady Mountjoy?'

'Of course.'

'She and her husband left behind a son, my nephew. He has just been delivered into my care and, I have to be honest, I have not the slightest idea what to do with him.'

'Oh my. What a responsibility,' Lady Mountjoy said, reaching across the divide between them and touching him briefly on the hand.

'I know nothing about children. I have never had any desire to father a child of my own. My lifestyle is not conducive to raising a six-year-old.'

'Yet here you are, with a young boy waiting for you to step up.'

Tom closed his eyes. 'I do not have any close relatives.' He grimaced. 'And my friends are mainly men who live their lives in the same manner I do. I thought...' He trailed off, looking across at the older woman with anticipation. It might not have been the true reason he had come to the Mountjoy residence today, but he *did* need help, and Lady Mountjoy was not known as society's favourite matriarch for nothing.

'You thought I might be able to offer some advice?'

'Yes.'

Tom could see the countess was formulating an answer when the door flew open and Miss Ashworth burst into the room. She had changed. Her dress was clean and dry and her hair was pulled into a neat, low bun, although if he looked carefully he could still see some loose damp strands curling at the base of her neck.

'Mr Stewart,' Miss Ashworth said, her tone accusatory.

Tom stood. Even though he had spent less than an hour in total in her company, he knew she was going to make assumptions that were not true and likely expose both of them to unnecessary scandal.

'Good morning, Miss Ashworth, I trust you enjoyed the ball last night?' he said, trying to convey a sense of calm.

'How could...?' She faltered as she registered his calm tone and serene smile. 'Yes...yes, I did. Thank you.' She glanced at Lady Mountjoy, who was looking at her curiously. 'It is rather early for a visit, is it not?'

'I apologise,' Tom said. 'I have had a lot on my mind and I thought it later than it is. Lady Mountjoy, generous hostess that she is, was too polite to turn me away.'

'Mr Stewart, if you would wait a moment whilst I find my address book, I have a few contacts that could help you.'

Before Tom could answer either way, Lady Mountjoy had risen and swept from the room, leaving him with Miss Ashworth.

'What are you doing here?' Miss Ashworth whispered as soon as she could be sure the older woman was out of earshot. 'You weren't meant to follow me in. Why are you interfering with everything?'

'Calm down.'

It was the wrong thing to say. The young woman pressed her lips together until they were almost white and colour flooded to her cheeks.

'So far today you have stalked me through the streets of Southwark, injured my hand, drawn lewd comments from the local residents and now you're here to betray me.'

'You're being melodramatic. And wrong.'

'What are you doing here?'

'Firstly, I wasn't stalking you. I was concerned for your welfare. Secondly, you hurt your hand by *punching me*. Thirdly, you were the one who stomped down the rotten staircase and made us fall into the grime of the Southwark streets.' He paused, glad to see some of the defiance had left her. 'And fourthly, I wanted to check you got home safely, but Lady Mountjoy spotted me outside. I have told her I was here for another reason. I have not even mentioned you at all.'

'Oh.' She hesitated. 'Thank you.'

'Here we are,' Lady Mountjoy said as she breezed back into the room. 'I have written down a few essential contacts. There is an agency that provides nursemaids and nannies, the details of a couple of tutors and three tailors that are wonderful with children.'

'Thank you,' Tom said, taking the piece of paper and getting to his feet. He was ready to leave the events of this morning well behind him.

'You have younger siblings, don't you, Miss Ashworth?'

'Yes, five younger sisters.'

'Good. Tomorrow Miss Ashworth and I will call on you and if needed provide some practical and emotional support. You will get through this, Mr Stewart.'

He bowed, eager to get out of the house before he had to impart any more details of his personal life to either of the two women in front of him.

'Thank you for all your help, Lady Mountjoy. Have a pleasant day, Miss Ashworth.'

'Why don't you see Mr Stewart to the door, Miss Ashworth?' Lady Mountjoy said with a twinkle in her eye. 'My hip is paining me all of a sudden.'

Tom left the room, waiting for the footman to bring him his coat and hat before he stepped out through the front door. To his surprise, Miss Ashworth followed him, pulling the heavy wooden door closed behind her and accompanying him onto the steps in front of the house.

'Is something the matter?'

'I should thank you,' Miss Ashworth said quietly. 'For not giving me away. I know you didn't have to lie for me.' She didn't meet his eye as she spoke but her words were clear.

'It is not my place to inform Lady Mountjoy what you

have been doing, but a word of advice—she is a sharp woman, *very* hard to deceive. I doubt she is completely in the dark as to what you are doing, even though I have not a clue.'

Miss Ashworth nodded slowly then turned to go back inside. 'I didn't know you had children, Mr Stewart,' she said over her shoulder.

'I don't.'

'But Lady Mountjoy said…'

'It is for my nephew. He has recently come to live with me. And now I must get back to him.'

Tom bowed, turned and took the steps two at a time, not stopping to look back over his shoulder. Enough distractions. Now he needed to get home and work out how he was going to cope with his life being turned completely upside down.

Chapter Five

'He is not going to want me bursting into his drawing room at a time like this,' Jane protested, even though she knew it was futile.

'Nonsense, the man has just become guardian to a young child he barely knows. He will be glad of any and all support offered.'

'Surely he would rather have privacy and solitude in this difficult time?'

'If that was what he wanted, would he have come to call yesterday?' Lady Mountjoy asked, and Jane quickly dropped her protestations. It was too late anyway, they were already drawing up to an impressive house on Grosvenor Square.

'Lady Mountjoy,' Jane said, knowing this might be her only chance to talk in private with her benefactor, 'Please promise me you are not going to try and match me with Mr Stewart.'

'Why do you ask, Jane? He is lovely, isn't he?'

'No.' She said it far too quickly and loudly, taking hold of her emotions and toning down her vehemence as she repeated the word. 'No. I mean, I am sure he is a perfectly pleasant gentleman, but on the couple of occasions we exchanged words there was nothing between us.'

'Really? I thought I saw a spark. That first flare of interest.'

'No.' Jane felt her heart sinking. Lady Mountjoy was thinking of pushing her and the irritating Mr Stewart closer together. 'I can promise there was nothing between us.'

'If it is meant to be, it is meant to be,' Lady Mountjoy said cryptically.

There was no time for any further argument as the carriage door was opened by the driver and Lady Mountjoy hopped out, spritely in step and not showing any hint of the hip pain she had complained of the day before.

Jane wondered about staying in the carriage, knowing it was pure fantasy to think she would escape this visit. With a groan she stepped down and followed the countess in through the front door.

A footman led them through the hall to a room at the back of the house, bypassing the grand drawing room. Instead they were shown into the library, where Mr Stewart and a young boy with the same shock of dark-brown hair and long eyelashes were poring over an atlas together.

For a moment the man and boy didn't realise they were being observed and they continued to talk in low voices. Then the child looked up, confusion on his face.

'Lady Mountjoy and Miss Ashworth to see you, sir,' the footman announced.

'Thank you. Would you see to it tea is served in the drawing room?'

He stood, motioning for his guests to go ahead whilst he turned and spoke to the boy next to him. The boy nodded, but looked crestfallen at having his uncle taken away.

'How is he settling in?' Lady Mountjoy enquired as they sat down in the drawing room.

Mr Stewart grimaced. 'He cried for his mother all last night, which is hardly surprising.'

'Poor child,' Jane murmured. She was lucky enough to have both her parents still alive, but she had lost her twin sister a few years earlier, and she still mourned Harriet every day. Losing someone you loved was terrible, but it was even worse for someone as young as Mr Stewart's nephew.

'This isn't the right place for him,' Mr Stewart said, running a hand through his hair, and for the first time since meeting him Jane saw his vulnerable side. Normally he was all glib comments and perfectly timed quips. Now he looked as if he was about to be bested by a six-year-old boy.

'Of course it is. You're his family,' Lady Mountjoy said.

'I know. And I know it is my responsibility to look after him but this house, this life in London, it isn't the right environment for him.' He motioned around the room. 'I have no toys, no books, nothing to interest a child. For the last hour we've been looking at atlases to see which route his ship took from Italy to here, but I cannot stretch out that activity any longer.'

'He's too young for school,' Jane said quickly, knowing it wasn't her place to tell Mr Stewart how to organise his affairs, but unable to stop herself.

'Why do you say that?'

Jane felt the force of his stare on her, as if he were probing her mind to see what secrets lay there. She thought of the day her parents had sent Harriet and her off to school, convinced they were doing the right thing by their daughters, furthering their education so one day they might become governesses or music teachers. In principle, it *had* been the right thing, but Jane would never forget the coldness of the teachers or the hostility from some of the other girls. She'd missed her family, missed her home, and she had been fourteen years old. She couldn't imagine being sent away at the tender age of six.

'He's young, and he's just lost everything and everyone he knows and cares about. Sending him to school before he can feel he has a home to come back to would be devastating for him.'

'It is early yet to make such decisions. Things will get easier,' Lady Mountjoy said. 'Did you have any luck with the agency that employs nannies?'

Mr Stewart grimaced. 'Three weeks is the soonest they can have someone available. Apparently it is a very busy time for them.'

'That is a long time,' Lady Mountjoy murmured. 'But perhaps we can help. Miss Ashworth is wonderful with children, and she is always complaining that I drag her to too many society events. Perhaps a couple of times a week she could come and spend some time with your nephew.'

Jane looked at Lady Mountjoy, completely stunned. She had anticipated some subtle manoeuvring, gentle suggestions that might place Mr Stewart and her together on a few occasions, but not to be volunteered for a job as part-time nanny to a boy she didn't know.

'I could not ask that,' Mr Stewart said quickly, and Jane would have been offended by the alarm in his eyes if hers had not reflected the same sentiment.

'Nonsense. Miss Ashworth loves children, and I am sure she would rather that than I line up a parade of suitors for her.'

Jane thought of her relative freedom in the Mountjoy household, the way she was able to take time to write in the afternoons, and her trips across London to visit various publishers in a bid for one of them to read her work. The last thing she wanted was to be under Lady Mountjoy's constant scrutiny, to be the one on whom the countess focussed her match-making eye.

'It is such a pleasant afternoon,' Jane said quickly. 'Perhaps we could go for a walk, Mr Stewart, and discuss the idea. Your nephew could come too, of course.'

Mr Stewart looked surprised, and after ten seconds hadn't answered when Lady Mountjoy clapped her hands. 'What a wonderful idea. I would accompany you, but did I mention my hip is paining me?'

'It is raining,' Mr Stewart said.

'Mere drizzle.'

'And the wind is whipping up.'

'A little gust of wind never hurt anyone.'

'And there is talk of snow.'

'I am sure your nephew would be delighted to see snow.'

'Fine,' Mr Stewart said. 'As you are so enthused. Shall I see Miss Ashworth home after?'

'That is most kind of you, Mr Stewart,' Lady Mountjoy said. 'Perhaps you have a maid who could act as chaperon?'

Twenty minutes later they stepped through the gates of Hyde Park, their heads bowed against the wind.

'Is it always so cold here?' Edward asked, his voice quiet as it was whipped away by the wind.

'Not always, and certainly not normally in March,' Jane said, trying to inject a note of cheerfulness into her voice. 'I expect you are used to much warmer weather in Italy.'

He nodded and shivered. Jane crouched down in front of him and adjusted the boy's coat. It was thin, not made for an English winter, and already looked to be getting too small for him. To combat this, he had two scarves wrapped around his neck and a pair of over-sized gloves on his hands that kept slipping off. Pulled down over his ears was a warm woolly hat, also a few sizes too big.

'Mama said England was beautiful.' He screwed up his nose and looked at the bare trees and muddy grass. 'It doesn't look beautiful.'

'Not now,' Jane said, squeezing his hand. 'But just wait until it is covered in a thick layer of snow, everything white and fresh. Then it will look beautiful.'

'Will we have snow? Really?' His face lit up.

'Yes, without a doubt. If not this year then certainly next winter. And you will be able to throw snowballs and go ice-skating, and perhaps even go sledging.'

'I will be the best at throwing snowballs,' Edward

said, becoming animated. 'I always play catch with Roberto and Michel.' Suddenly his face dropped.

'It is hard leaving people behind, isn't it?'

He nodded and Jane felt her heart squeeze for the little boy. Children were resilient. He would settle in his new home, and in a few years there would be no outward signs of missing what he'd once had, just an inner longing, a feeling of not being quite complete.

'Lady Mountjoy was right—you are good with children,' Edward said as Jane straightened up to continue their walk.

'It is not hard. You merely talk to them as another human. So many people think they do not understand enough to hold a conversation, but they are wrong. Children see everything and hear everything, even if they might sometimes need help interpreting what they have taken in.'

Mr Stewart was silent for a few minutes, his eyes locked on his nephew as they strolled through the park.

'I had an ulterior motive for agreeing with Lady Mountjoy that we should take a walk together,' Jane said as they rounded a corner and came out into a wide-open grassy area. There was no one else about so she could be sure they wouldn't be overheard.

'Go on.'

For a moment she hesitated, unsure as to how to continue now she had broached the subject.

'I am not looking for a husband,' she said, wanting to claw back the words when Mr Stewart's eyes widened in horror.

'And I am not looking for a wife,' he said quickly.

'Of course not,' Jane snapped. 'That is not what I

meant. Be quiet and listen for a moment.' Her embarrassment made her speak sharply, but it had the desired effect; Mr Stewart remained silent and motioned for her to go on. 'I am not looking for a husband, but it is Lady Mountjoy's greatest wish to pair me off with some suitor. She feels everyone is happier when matched with someone else.'

'Yes, she does have a certain reputation for match-making.'

'I respect Lady Mountjoy greatly, but I do not have the time or energy to fend off her match-making efforts. She started with five debutantes, and everyone else is married. All she has left is me.'

'I can see why you would feel nervous,' Mr Stewart murmured.

'I have…things I need to be doing. Until now, I have enjoyed a modicum of freedom, but I can feel that slipping through my fingers.'

'Things?'

'Yes, *things*,' she said, refusing to elaborate. He didn't need to know about her dreams, that this was her one chance to make everything she had hoped for and worked for a reality. 'I cannot spend every waking second of my day being paraded in front of an endless line of dull gentlemen who are never going to be interested in me anyway.'

'What is it you think we can do for each other?'

'If Lady Mountjoy believes there is a chance we are falling for each other, then she will leave me in peace when it comes to other suitors.' She risked a glance up at Mr Stewart and saw that so far he wasn't convinced by her plan. 'You need help with your nephew and, whilst I am no nursemaid, I enjoy the company of children. I would be happy to visit a few times a week, to take Edward on trips to the park or read with him quietly in the library.'

Slowly Mr Stewart nodded. 'You help me with Edward, and in doing so Lady Mountjoy assumes the reason you are so keen to spend time with me is because we are falling for one another.'

'I am sure we can be civil to one another in company and perhaps even attend a few of the same events to build the illusion.'

'What about at the end of the Season?'

'At the end of the Season I will return to Somerset and you will have your nanny and will have settled into a routine with Edward.' Jane risked another glance at the man beside her. He hadn't dismissed the idea outright so she was hopeful he might see the merit in it.

'I cannot see the harm in trying the idea, as long as we are both completely honest with one another. If an attachment begins to form...'

Jane laughed and then realised he was serious. 'Do women fall for you that easily, Mr Stewart?'

He shrugged.

'I promise I have no feelings for you except a mild gratitude that you might save me from the match-making machinations of Lady Mountjoy.' She held up her hand so he didn't interrupt. 'And I promise that if I find your... *charm*...so irresistible I will immediately let you know and we can sever our arrangement.'

'Then I cannot see a problem.'

'I will inform Lady Mountjoy that I wish to help you

and Edward, as was her suggestion, and we will take it from there.'

Jane held out her hand and waited for Mr Stewart to shake it.

'I do have one condition, though,' he said, holding her eye.

'Name it.'

'You tell me what it is that is so important that you were sneaking around Southwark yesterday morning, and why you are eager for Lady Mountjoy not to scrutinise your every move these next few weeks.'

Jane held his eye, wondering if it would be the final straw if she shook her head and refused to answer him. For so long, her writing and her ambition had been private, something she had held close to her and hadn't let anyone see. She thought of Mr Stewart's steely determination when he had followed her the morning before and, even though she didn't know him well, she could tell he was a man used to getting what he wanted.

She paused, looking down and scuffing her shoe on the path.

'I write,' she said finally. 'And draw—illustrations for the stories I write.' Quickly she glanced up to see his reaction. It was unheard of for a woman of middling social status to have ambitions that stretched beyond marrying well and supporting her husband in his endeavours.

'What do you write?'

She frowned. She hadn't expected his interest to be beyond the superficial. She'd thought, one he found out her secret, he would immediately dismiss it as the dream of a naïve young woman.

'Stories for children.'

'And you draw?'

'Yes. And paint.'

He nodded slowly. 'You're looking for a publisher. That's what you were doing in Southwark.' He paused. 'Surely there are more reputable places to find a publisher than an alley in Southwark?'

Jane wondered what it must be like to be born into a life of privilege, a life where everything fell at your feet. Her family wasn't poor, but they did not have connections outside Somerset, and even if they had she wouldn't have had access to them as a woman.

Slowly he shook his head. 'I suppose you have tried them already?'

'They will not even meet with me when they find out I am a woman.'

'Ah.'

It was not an unexpected turn of events. She had known it would be difficult, perhaps even impossible, to get her stories published, but she hadn't expected everyone to refuse even to look at her work.

'I am not afraid of rejection,' she said quietly. 'I know my stories and illustrations may never be published, but I wish they would be judged on merit, not on who has written them.'

'I could…'

She held up a hand to stop him. 'No. Whatever you are offering is kind, but I need to do this on my own. I do not want to succeed because I have passed my work off as someone else's.'

'I was merely going to suggest an introduction or two.'

'And have my stories published out of some favour

someone owes you? No. Again, thank you for your kindness, but I if I do this it will be on my own.'

Mr Stewart looked as though he was going to say more but thought better of it.

'Can we go and see the ducks?' Edward asked, pulling on Jane's hand.

'Yes, let's see if we can spot any swans or geese too.'

Chapter Six

'Where is he?' Miss Ashworth asked as she burst into the house. She was trailed by a weary-looking maid who Tom didn't envy, it would be quite a job to keep up with the energetic Miss Ashworth, acting as chaperon as she raced around the city.

'He's upstairs in his bedroom,' Tom said, feeling a deep relief that someone else had arrived to share in his panic.

Miss Ashworth rushed towards the stairs and then caught herself, turning back to face him.

'Tell me exactly what happened.'

'I am told he woke in the night and started calling for his mother. The maid who has been sleeping in his room tried to comfort him, but he became more distressed and asked for me. I was…' He fell silent, the guilt of not being where he'd needed to be almost overwhelming him. 'I was not there and he has been inconsolable since.'

'Where were you?' Miss Ashworth asked, and then quickly shook her head. 'I do not wish to know the answer to that question.' She started back towards the stairs and Tom followed, feeling out of place in his own house.

The heart-wrenching sound of sobs led Jane along the upstairs hallway to a room at the end, and softly she knocked on the door. There was no answer, but she hadn't expected one, instead waiting for a moment before going in.

Edward was on the floor next to his bed, hugging his blanket as if it was all he had in the world. His face was tear-streaked and blotchy and his hair looked tousled.

Jane felt a rush of affection for the little boy and rushed to him, wondering if it was too familiar to scoop him up in her arms. She thought of her little sisters at six, at what comfort they'd got from a loving touch or cuddle, and she quietened her doubts and cradled the little boy in her arms. His sobs grew louder as he buried his head into her chest, as if he were overcome with emotion and finally allowing himself to let it out.

She sat there for a long time, holding him tight, one hand gently rubbing his back, occasionally dropping a kiss onto the mop of dark hair. She let him cry, let him rid himself of all the overwhelming emotion, and only when his body had stilled and his sobs quietened did she try and speak to him.

'Did you have a bad dream?'

He nodded, a minute movement of his head against her chest.

'Did you want to tell me what it was about?'

'I can't remember.'

'Sometimes when I have bad dreams I just want to have a cuddle with someone.'

'I wanted my mama,' Edward said, his voice breaking and the tears starting again. 'I want my mama.'

'I know you do, little one,' Jane murmured, stroking his hair. She sang to him, a song she had sung hundreds of times before to her little sisters whenever they had scraped a knee or bumped a head.

'Lavender blue, dilly-dilly...'

Finally, after what felt like thousands of repeats of the gentle lullaby, the little boy's body grew heavy in her arms and his breathing deepened. Jane stayed in the same position for a while longer, ensuring he was deeply asleep before she set him down on the bed and tucked him in.

Mr Stewart shifted by the door and she realised he had been there the whole time.

'How did you do that?' He was looking at her in awe.

'He's a child. He needs comfort and security and someone to hold him tight and make him feel as though they will protect him from the world.'

'It's not me that he wants to do that.'

'Of course it's not. Edward wants his mother, but she isn't here, and you are.'

Mr Stewart closed his eyes and shook his head, as if trying to rid himself of the morning's events.

Jane knew she shouldn't push the man. He had suffered the bereavement of his sister and taken in his nephew, but even though she didn't know him well she thought he was capable of more for the child.

'Do you want children, Mr Stewart?'

'Good lord, no,' he said quickly as they walked side by side down the hallway.

'Any reason for the vehemence of your reply?'

He shrugged. 'It isn't in my plan for my life.'

'May I enquire what is in your plan?'

He paused and turned to her, and Jane felt the full force of his charm. He smiled at her and for a fraction of a second she saw what gave him the reputation of a rake. The women in ballrooms whispered about him whilst biting their lower lips and looking on longingly. It was ridiculous, but she could see the basis of their infatuation. Mr Stewart was an attractive man, with his dark hair and green eyes, but it wasn't just his appearance that made him so popular. There was something about his smile, the way he looked at you, something that made you want to be in on the joke he was telling or the tale he was spinning.

Quickly she caught herself. It was superficial, the gift of a charmer and no more.

'To stay blissfully free and single and unencumbered.'

'No wife, no children?'

'Are you volunteering yourself again, Miss Ashworth?'

'No. I'm just surprised. You are a wealthy and influential man. I thought the ambition of all wealthy and influential men was to marry a submissive young lady and then ensure their house is filled with enough heirs to carry on the family name.'

Leaning in a little closer, he smiled. 'You may be right that is the wish of many gentlemen, but I have no title to pass on, no inflated sense of my family name. I am quite content with living *my* life to the full rather than ruining another generation.'

'You are dedicated to a life of pleasure, then?'

'Is it so surprising?' They had reached the stairs and he spun to face her. Jane felt a rush of anticipation, as if she were being swept into his confidence. 'What other purpose do we as humans have? We are born, we work and then we die. Surely the only way to make a life worthwhile is to enjoy it to the full for the few short years we are here?'

'Some people would argue that dedicating your life to others, through charity or good deeds, is a more worthwhile way to spend a lifetime.'

He shrugged. 'It is exactly the same. People do the things that make them feel good. Yes, for some there is also an element of sacrifice, that decision to put someone else's happiness first, but in the end *that* makes them feel worthy.' He paused and searched her eyes with his own. 'The only difference is I can admit my life is about seeking pleasure.'

Jane regarded him for a long moment. It was an interesting concept and, although she didn't entirely agree, she did see his idea had merit.

'Yet you have kept Edward here with you,' she said quietly.

'I'm not a monster. The boy has lost everyone he loves.'

'If you were truly dedicated to your own pleasure then you would have sent him away. I would wager you have a country residence tucked away somewhere, a comfortable house you could have sent him to with a couple of servants to keep him safe and looked after.'

'Is that what you think I should do with him?'

'No,' Jane said quickly. 'That would be devastating.

You know that, and you are putting his needs ahead of yours.'

Mr Stewart gave her a quick smile. 'I said I seek pleasure, not that I am selfish.'

Together they walked downstairs, and Jane paused in the hallway. She knew she should leave. Her maid was peeking out from the door that led to the kitchens and it would be most appropriate if she returned home now Edward had settled.

'Stay,' Mr Stewart said. 'Stay until Edward wakes.'

'I could,' Jane said slowly. 'But I wonder if it would be better if he woke and you were sitting beside his bed.'

Mr Stewart didn't argue, watching her silently as she ushered her maid into the hallway and to the door.

'I thought of taking Edward to Astley's later. Perhaps you would like to come?'

Jane hesitated. She had thought of trying to slip away that afternoon to visit some of the publishing houses she had been to when she had first arrived in London, hopeful and inexperienced. They had refused to even admit her then, but she was getting better at the patter that would gain her an audience with the right people.

'Astley's sounds lovely.'

'Bring whoever you would like as a chaperon.'

'Thank you.'

'Shall I pick you up at four o'clock?'

She felt a frisson of excitement. When she had agreed to come to London with Lady Mountjoy for the winter months leading up to the Season, her focus had been entirely on trying to find someone to publish her stories. But, as the weeks had passed and her friendship with the other debutantes had blossomed, she had begun to enjoy all the new experiences. Not so much the balls and the dress fittings, but the trips around London, the visits to Vauxhall Pleasure Gardens, the strolls through the park. Jane was well aware that after these few months she would return to Somerset and might never leave the county again. It was a long way from Bath to London, and a journey her family could ill afford.

Astley's was another place she had heard much about, and she reasoned one afternoon away from her mission wouldn't hurt.

'Thank you.'

She turned to go, a footman opening the door for her, but before she could step outside Mr Stewart caught her hand. Jane felt a jolt of energy pass through her, making her skin prickle and burn as if it were on fire.

'Thank you for coming this morning,' he said quietly, sincerely.

Jane managed to nod, feeling her heart pound in her chest, and forced herself to pull her hand away and break contact. Out on the pavement she risked a glance back, feeling the breath being pulled from her body as he gave her one last smile.

'Stop it,' she muttered to herself. Mr Stewart was a consummate charmer, a man she tolerated for the convenient agreement they had made, and for the sake of his sweet nephew. She would not allow herself to succumb to the allure of his smile. She was stronger than that, shrewder than that.

'This is all very mysterious,' Lucy said, and Jane had to pull herself away from the window to reply.

'There is nothing mysterious at all about it.'

Lucy raised an eyebrow. 'A man with a reputation as a notorious rake has invited you to Astley's for the afternoon. I only moved out three weeks ago, and before that I am quite sure you had never once mentioned a Mr Stewart.'

'I didn't know him then.'

'How *do* you know him?'

'We were introduced—at Lady Mountjoy's ball. The one you were meant to come to, but were caught up in wedded bliss so missed it.'

'I have apologised a thousand times!' Lucy grinned. 'But when you marry…'

Jane snorted.

'*When* you marry I am sure you will understand how time slips away from you.'

'How is the delightful Captain Weyman?'

Lucy had married her childhood sweetheart three weeks earlier after an agonising wait whilst he'd been abroad with the army. Jane liked to tease her friend but was beyond ecstatic that Lucy had finally married the man she loved, overcoming all the hurdles that had been placed in their way.

'Very well. We are thinking of returning to Somerset soon to see if we can start to repair the relationship with his father. William will get his orders in the next couple of weeks, but we are hoping his next posting will be closer than his last.'

'Don't go yet,' Jane said quietly. 'I would miss you too much, and you don't want to start off your married life with the sourness of his family seeping into your happiness.'

'Perhaps we will wait until the summer. I do love

Somerset in the summer months.' She smiled at her friend, looking pointedly at the window again, and Jane made an effort to pull herself away.

'Mr Stewart recently became guardian to his nephew, a lovely young boy who is six years old and called Edward. Being a man who has never spent any time around children, he claims he is out of his depth with Edward, although it would be unfair to say he is completely useless with him.'

'I hope you don't use such encouraging words with him.'

Jane smiled, pleased to have her friend back even if it was just for the afternoon.

'So how have you become involved in Mr Stewart's situation?'

'Lady Mountjoy suggested I might help him, as I have so many younger siblings and am used to the company of children.'

'Ah.'

'Ah indeed. She has this gleam in her eye.'

'She does have a nearly perfect record. Out of the five of us she brought to London, you are the only one unmarried.'

'Don't remind me. I don't wish to disappoint her. She has been more than generous with her time and money and affection, but she is not going to see me married.'

'Not even to the charming Mr Stewart?'

'Certainly not to him.' Jane felt the heat on her cheeks and hated that this line of questioning was making her blush.

'Let me see if I have this right. Lady Mountjoy wants to pair you with Mr Stewart, even though he has a reputation as a rake who has no intention of settling down. She has volunteered you to assist with his nephew and you are just going along with all of this?'

'If it isn't him it'll just be someone else. At least I can be sure he harbours no interest in me and I know I have no interest in him. His nephew is adorable, and if I manage to avoid an endless parade of suitors then I can tolerate a few hours a week spent in Mr Stewart's company.'

'You discussed it with him?'

'Openly. He agreed.'

'What is in it for him?'

'I spend some time with his nephew whilst he waits for the nanny the agency have promised him.'

Lucy pondered for a moment. 'Not a bad plan in theory,' she said after a minute. 'But what if one of you starts to develop feelings for the other? You will be in close proximity for a while.'

'That will never happen. Mr Stewart is a man who prefers his liaisons without emotional attachment, and I have absolutely no interest in any romantic relationship.'

Lucy looked as though she was going to protest further when Jane saw the carriage pull to a halt outside.

'Miss Jane!' Edward shouted with glee as she climbed up into the carriage, darting forward off the seat where he sat with his uncle and into her arms. 'We're going to see the horses and the acrobats. Zio Tom said there are trapeze artists and tightrope walkers.'

'How wonderful,' Jane said, laughing as she got caught up in the young boy's enthusiasm. 'I have never seen a tightrope walker before.'

'Good afternoon,' Mr Stewart said, lifting his hat as Lucy stepped up.

'This is my dear friend, Mrs Lucy Weyman,' Jane said quickly. 'This is Mr Stewart and his nephew Edward.'

'Lovely to meet you,' Lucy said as she took her seat, grabbing hold of Jane as she almost overbalanced as the carriage started to move away.

The streets were busy on the journey to Lambeth, even more so as they approached Astley's amphitheatre. Jane craned her head out of the window, hoping to catch a glimpse of the theatre, awed by the size of the building they were approaching. The crowd was all heading in the same direction and there was a buzz of excitement and anticipation for the afternoon's entertainment.

Once their carriage finally found a spot to pull over to allow them to disembark, Mr Stewart hopped down and offered his hand to Jane, Lucy and finally Edward.

'Keep your coin purse hidden and anything of value secure,' Mr Stewart said as a merry group of women jostled past them. 'It is not quite the same clientele as you get at the opera.'

Mr Stewart seemed unperturbed by the mixed group of people flooding along the pavement and joining the queue to get into the theatre. Jane remembered her encounter with him in Southwark and wondered if his life in pursuit of pleasure took him to other less salubrious areas of the city.

They joined the queue, Mr Stewart paying for the tickets and leading them up the stairs to a box that overlooked the circular level stage.

Already there was a man juggling brightly coloured balls as he walked around in a circle, every so often doing a high throw or spinning before he caught the balls and continued. Edward's eyes fixed onto the juggler immediately and he was smiling by the time he had taken his seat.

'Have you been here before, Mr Stewart?' Jane asked as he courteously helped her arrange her chair so she could see well.

'Yes, many times. I had a hankering to be a horseman when I was a boy. Whenever we were in town, my sister and I would always sneak off and come to watch the show.'

Jane caught the hint of sadness in his voice at the mention of his sister.

'Did you never decide to pursue it as a career?'

'Actually, I did, although in the only way that was open to me. I was in the cavalry division in the army.'

'Did you serve for a long time?'

'Six years. Then I was injured and it took me a long time to recover.'

Jane looked at him with interest. He had no outwardly visible evidence of a bad injury. He didn't limp or walk with a stick, like many of the men who returned from war. There was no scarring on his face or his hands, and he moved quickly, agilely. She desperately wanted to know what happened to him but knew it was rude to ask outright.

Fidgeting, she tried to focus on something else.

'You can ask me,' Mr Stewart said as he leaned in closer. Jane felt the heat of his body as his arm brushed against hers for a second. 'I can see you want to.'

She'd always thought she wasn't that easy to read, and the idea of this man being able to tell what she was thinking by a quick glance at her expression or posture was unsettling.

'How were you injured?'

'I was thrown from my horse and trampled by the rest of the regiment.'

'Surely you couldn't survive that?'

'I was very lucky.' He flashed her a smile, 'Or extremely unlucky, whatever way you look at it. I was bedbound for nine months, and they tell me unconscious for the first few weeks of that.'

'Nine months!' she exclaimed, and the people in the next box turned to look at her.

'It's a long time, isn't it? At least, that's what I'm told. To me it seemed like only a few minutes had passed. The days blurred into one. I think there was an element of delirium.'

There were so many questions Jane wanted to ask. It was incredible to think he had survived such a grievous injury and she wondered if that had influenced his desire to live to indulge his pleasures.

Mr Stewart chuckled at her expression. 'This is why I don't tell anyone. Their reactions vary from disbelief to pity.'

'It is rather extraordinary. What happened to you whilst you were injured?'

'On the battlefield, a good friend scooped me up and took me to back to our camp. The doctor set the broken bone in my arm and told him that if I woke up in the next twenty-four hours I might have a chance at survival.'

'Do you remember nothing?'

'Nothing at all. I stayed in the medical tent in the camp for two weeks. I am told they managed to get some water into me, but my body was wasting away. When they thought I was hours from death I opened my eyes for the first time. From there it was a long road home, a long road to recovery. It took three months to transport me.'

'It must have been strange to wake up after so long unconscious.'

'It was. The first few days were a blur of confusion and pain, but I know I am lucky to be alive. Many of my regiment did not survive.'

'Did it take you long to recover, once you woke up?'

He grinned at this. 'Have you ever seen a baby deer, with gangly legs, all bone and no muscle?'

Jane nodded, thinking of the forest a few miles away from her home where they would go on picnics in the summer months.

'My muscles had wasted away to such a degree that I could not stand. I could barely raise a glass to my lips. I was much like a new-born fawn, stumbling around even after a few weeks. I did not start to recover until I was home, able to work on building my strength day by day, but even then it took a long time.'

It must have taken a lot of determination and work to have built himself up, and Jane felt a new respect for the man. He had no outward signs of his injuries, although she did wonder what hidden scars they had left.

'Didn't you want to return to the army after that?'

'I considered it, but I had been away for so long, and then it took months and months of work to get my fitness back to what would be required...' He shrugged. 'It was felt best I didn't return.' There was a glint of regret in his eye and Jane got the impression someone else had made the decision for him. She was about to try and probe further when there was a long blast on a trumpet and an excited gasp ran through the crowd.

Edward turned to her and grabbed her hand, his eyes shining with excitement.

'Do you think the acrobats will come first, Miss Jane?'

'Perhaps. Or maybe the trapeze artists.'

Jane felt the energy in the audience as a well-built man stepped out into the ring, raising a top hat and welcoming them to the show. He promised wonders such as they had never seen before, and as he spoke a group of performers tumbled out from back stage and began the first routine.

For an hour and a half Jane sat on the edge of her seat, enthralled by the performance, but also by the look of wonder on Edward's face. She often liked to watch her younger sisters when they tried something new for the first time, enjoying that expression of sheer magic on their faces.

In time the show neared its climax and four horses broke into the ring, galloping in a circle, hooves thundering in time, and Edward let out a squeal of delight. Jane found herself leaning forward in her chair, and next to her she felt Mr Stewart shift as well. Glancing up at his face, she saw an expression that mirrored his nephew's as he watched the acrobats standing astride the horses, swinging themselves down to the ground and back up in a show of excellent muscle control and perfect timing.

Gently she touched Mr Stewart on the arm, not wanting to spoil his enjoyment, but keen he should share it with his nephew. She motioned for them to swap chairs so he was sitting next to the young boy, and after a moment she saw Mr Stewart bend his head towards his nephew's and begin to point out something that was happening below them. For half a minute, Jane watched them together, uncle and nephew brought together by their love of horses.

Chapter Seven

'It was lovely to meet you, Mrs Weyman,' Tom said as Jane's friend bid him good day. He was sitting in a comfortable arm chair in the Mountjoys' townhouse, feeling the most content he had in days. Despite the difficult night, with Edward's nightmares and struggle to settle without his mother, it had turned into a successful day. The trip to Astley's had been enjoyable and the moment his nephew had gripped his hand when one of the horsemen had flipped himself underneath the galloping horse, excited and anxious for the man's fate at the same time, he had felt as if maybe one day things with Edward would settle.

He knew much of the success today had come from the woman sitting opposite him.

'What are you looking at me like that for?' Miss Ashworth looked relaxed, as if she wanted to kick off her shoes and curl up in the comfortable arm chair. It was strangely comforting to see her like this, prim and upright as she normally was.

They were alone together in the drawing room now

Mrs Weyman had left, although Lady Mountjoy was next door in the library with Edward, and Lord Mountjoy a little way down the hall in the study. The door was open, so there could be no suggestion of impropriety, but Tom had the sense of intimacy. It was as though he had been permitted to enter the private family cocoon and, although it wasn't something he was used to, right at this moment it felt quite comforting.

'Thank you,' he said softly.

'What for?'

'For today. For earlier this morning and for the trip to Astley's.'

'I didn't do anything this afternoon. I should be thanking you for inviting me.'

'You have a way with Edward. It makes everything easier.'

Jane smiled and he could see she was pleased with the compliment.

'I am grateful. I know you refused the other day, but my offer to help you find a publisher still stands. You are doing so much for me.'

Jane looked sharply at the open door and he realised quite how in the dark Lady Mountjoy was about Jane's ambition to get her work published.

'No,' she said quickly. 'That won't be necessary. All I need from you is what we originally agreed.'

He inclined his head. He wasn't sure why she was quite so reluctant to accept help, especially when it seemed her search for someone to publish her work wasn't going very well. They hadn't discussed details, but it was already mid March. She could only have a few more months in London until she returned home, losing her opportunity to wander the London streets with the package she was hopeful someone would take a chance on one day. Still, it wasn't his place to push the idea. He had put forward his offer to help twice now. She would ask him if she did want any assistance.

With a surreptitious glance at the door, Jane stood and moved closer to him, crouching down next to his chair and leaning in.

'We should ensure our deception is believable, though. Visiting Astley's was a good start, but perhaps we can endure a ball or two to make Lady Mountjoy really think she does not need to start parading me in front of other suitors.'

'Do you find balls something to be endured?'

'Don't you?' She looked up at him, her eyes wide under the dark eyelashes, and he felt something stir inside him. He realised he'd never properly looked at her before, never noticed the clarity of the green of her eyes or the fullness of her lips. Her skin was smooth, marked only by the few freckles dotted over her nose.

Tom frowned, wondering why he hadn't noticed her this way before. It was true he tried to steer well clear of gently bred young women. There was no point even considering a dalliance when he was not interested in marriage, but still, he normally noticed an attractive young woman.

His eyes drifted from the top down, noting the severe way she parted her hair in the middle and pulled it back from her face and the dress that was too big and shapeless on her form. Miss Ashworth was hiding and doing it quite successfully. Thrown into a world where all the other debutantes wanted to shine, wanted to be noticed, Miss Ashworth was doing her best to fade into the background.

He had the urge to reach out, to run a finger over her smooth cheek, to draw her closer and get her to spill all the secrets she was holding deep inside. She intrigued him, with her obvious dislike of social events and single-minded focus on her aims.

'I don't go to many,' he murmured. 'The privilege of answering to no one but yourself. I can choose what I attend and what I do not. It means the few I do attend I quite enjoy, but only because they are a rarity.'

Miss Ashworth let out a little sigh and then bit her lower lip. It was mesmerising to watch this close up, and Tom was well aware he was staring. Luckily, Miss Ashworth seemed preoccupied with the idea of doing exactly what one wanted and had a dreamy, faraway look in her eye.

'What do you say, then?' she said, snapping back to reality. 'Will you attend a few balls with me, dance a couple of dances?'

'Of course, it is the least I can do. I shall send you details of what events I am free to attend. Perhaps you might like to accompany me to Lord and Lady Parson's dinner party tomorrow night?'

'That sounds like a good idea. I shall check with Lady Mountjoy if we have been invited.' She looked up at him, seeming to realise for the first time that she was leaning in so close. He expected her to jolt away but he saw her hesitate for just a moment, tucking a stray strand of hair behind her ear.

'Your nephew has quite outfoxed me playing draughts,' Lady Mountjoy said as she breezed into the room, stopping abruptly as she saw Miss Ashworth crouching by his chair, her face angled up towards him.

It looked intimate, there was no denying it, even though they had only been talking about society events.

Lady Mountjoy coughed to hide her surprise and then he saw her work very hard to suppress the smile of satisfaction that was trying to work its way across her face.

Miss Ashworth rose to her feet, colour flooding to her cheeks.

'We were discussing balls,' Miss Ashworth said as she rushed back to the seat she had been sitting in originally.

'Of course, of course,' Lady Mountjoy said quickly. 'Will you be attending Lord Framlingham's ball on Friday?'

There was no reason he couldn't. He hadn't made any plans with friends on Friday, and he wasn't quick enough with a deception to lie convincingly.

'Yes,' he said, telling himself it was only fair. *This* was how Miss Ashworth was asking him to support her—he needed to step up and do as she asked. Even if it meant society thinking they were romantically inclined.

He shuddered at the realisation of the impact of this agreement. Even when it became apparent he and Miss Ashworth were not heading for marriage, his reputation as a man with no interest in settling down would be rocked. No longer would the debutantes and their mothers avoid him completely.

'We can share a carriage, if you would like,' Lady Mountjoy offered.

It was an ingenious ploy on the part of the older woman. There was no good reason for him to refuse.

His residence was not far from hers and they were going to the same destination, but it did mean he and Miss Ashworth would be seen arriving together, which would set tongues wagging. Added to that, it would be harder for him to leave after an hour or two. Politeness would oblige him to stay until the ladies were ready to depart.

He smiled, impressed with her skill. If he and Miss Ashworth had not been playing a part, if there'd been a flicker of true attraction between them, he could see how Lady Mountjoy and her little tricks would go about fanning those flames.

'That is most generous,' he said. 'What time will you be leaving?'

'Why don't we call for you en route?'

'Thank you.' He hesitated, wondering if organising two events in one conversation would look too keen, but he caught a glimpse of Miss Ashworth's encouraging look and forced himself to speak. 'I have been invited to Lord and Lady Parson's dinner party tomorrow night. I wonder if you and Miss Ashworth will be in attendance?'

Lady Mountjoy looked as though it was Christmas morning and she had just received the most fabulous gift. 'Yes, we will be. I shall have a word with Lady Parson, speak to her about the seating arrangement.' She clapped her hands in excitement. 'How fabulous.'

Tom gave an unconvincing smile and nodded, glad when Lady Mountjoy turned her attention away from him.

'Now I must see what book Edward has chosen to take home with him. We have such a collection of children's books sitting unread in the library. I said he must choose one.'

The countess glided out of the room and for a long moment both he and Miss Ashworth sat in silence.

'I'm sorry,' she whispered after a moment, 'I never meant to push you. A dinner and a ball all in one week. I'm sure you have other more exciting plans.'

'I am looking forward to it.'

Miss Ashworth scoffed. 'Do not go too far, Mr Stewart. We all know it will be a bore, but I am grateful all the same.'

'I will make you a promise,' he said, leaning forward in his chair. 'If you give me your word you will be open to enjoying yourself at the ball later this week, I promise you I will make it fun for you.'

'At a ball? With everyone watching our every move?'

'Do you not believe my reputation?'

She shifted in her seat, glancing at him and then quickly looking away.

'Go on, what do people say of me?'

She shook her head.

'I will not be offended, Miss Ashworth. I know very well people's opinions on me.'

'They say you are a rake. A man devoted to the pursuit of pleasure. They say you will often shun polite company in preference for less desirable companions.'

'There must be more.'

'I can't repeat it.'

'Of course you can.'

'They say you leave a trail of broken hearts behind you…that you must hypnotise the women you conduct your affairs with because no one you are close to has a bad word to say about you, even though you are obviously a sinner.'

'What do you think?'

She looked over at him and shifted in her seat. For a long while she was silent and he thought she might not answer at all.

'I think so many people believe that living a life of pleasure and indulgence means you cannot be a decent person. They think only those who are outwardly pious or charitable can be good. Of course, that is not true— we've all heard of the charitable patron swindling the poor or the vicar dipping his fingers into the collection pot.'

Tom liked how much thought Miss Ashworth put into her answers. He never knew what she was going to say, but he knew she would never stick to the merely superficial.

'In the same way, they think a man who has lots of affairs, lots of mistresses, a man who refuses to play by the rules of polite society, must be inherently *bad* in some way. They're wrong, of course. You can make questionable choices but still be a good person.'

Raising an imaginary glass, he grinned. 'To questionable choices.'

'I am quite interested in seeing if you are viewed as a reformed character when you do start to socialise more.'

'The gossips love nothing more than a story of salvation.'

'You will be in demand, no doubt.'

'But I only have eyes for you.'

She laughed at this, and Tom saw her finally relaxing in his company. Miss Ashworth worked hard to keep up her wall of defence. She scared people off with her severe expressions and frumpy way of dressing and styling her hair. She worked hard to exude an air of bookishness, to ensure people thought she would not be fun company, but when you dug down beneath all of that there was so much more underneath.

Miss Ashworth was quick-witted and sharp. She had views on things other than the latest fashions or society gossip and was a keen observer of human nature. It had never featured in his plans to pretend to be courting a debutante this Season, but if it had to be with anyone he was glad it was Miss Ashworth.

'I will show you a ball can be enjoyable, if only you keep the right company.'

'I will look forward to it.'

Chapter Eight

It was at moments like this that Jane missed the protective shield the other debutantes had provided before they had all married, when they'd gone out in a gaggle to dinners and balls. She stood out, alone with Lord and Lady Mountjoy, and it felt as if all eyes were on her.

'Good evening,' their hostess said as she welcomed them into the drawing room where there was already a crowd of people.

'What a lovely group you have here,' Lady Mountjoy said. 'Thank you for the invitation. Your dinner parties are always a highlight of the Season.'

'You are too kind, Lady Mountjoy.' Lady Parson lowered her voice a little and leaned in, as if imparting a secret. 'Mr Stewart has not arrived yet, but I have arranged the seating so he and the young lady will be next to one another.'

'Thank you. I shall not forget this, Lady Parson.'

Jane almost rolled her eyes at the hushed voices of the two older women and quietly excused herself, stepping in to the room and seeing if there was anyone she recognised.

With a groan, she saw too late the closest person was Mrs Farthington with her hapless husband. Jane wondered whether it was too late to quietly back away, but as she took her first step Mrs Farthington turned and caught sight of Jane. Knowing she could not show any weakness, Jane summoned a smile.

'Miss Ashworth, you look…' Mrs Farthington trailed off as her eyes flicked up and down, taking in Jane's pale-green dress and simple hairstyle. 'Well. You look well.'

'As do you, Mrs Farthington. Lovely to see you, Mr Farthington.'

Her gaze darted around the room as she spoke, wondering if there was someone else she knew, someone to latch on to so she didn't have to spend her time talking to the woman in front of her.

Mrs Farthington was having none of it. She linked her arm through Jane's and started to stroll leisurely around the room as if they were old friends. Her husband trailed behind, carrying his wife's glass of wine.

'You are a secretive little mouse, aren't you?' Mrs Farthington said. 'When I teased you the other day about pursuing Mr Stewart as a possible suitor, I really was joking, but I hear he has agreed to come to this dinner party because of you and insisted you sit together.'

Jane closed her eyes for a moment, wondering how gossip and rumour spread so easily throughout the *ton*.

'Is it true, then?' Mrs Farthington probed. 'How interesting. I wonder what he wants from you.'

Jane knew it was an insult, as were most things coming from this woman's mouth, but she needed to keep her composure and not let anything slip.

She shrugged. 'I'm sure I do not know.'

'You do know his reputation?'

'Yes. I know what people say about him.'

'He doesn't really attend society events, not beyond one or two balls a year. He's handsome, of course... You can see why all the ladies sigh as he walks by, and I hear rumours he is a magnificent lover.'

'Mrs Farthington, I must protest,' Mr Farthington said, trying to insert himself next to his wife, but she flicked him away with a dismissive hand.

'I hear he has the choice of partner and I can only wonder what he wants with you.'

'Perhaps he enjoys my scintillating conversation or my impressive wit.'

Mrs Farthington laughed.

'I understand why you are suddenly so eager to capture yourself a husband, Miss Ashworth, with Miss Greenacre and Miss Stanley married to lords and Miss Freeman now a captain's wife.' She paused and by the glint in her eye Jane knew the next barb was going to be particularly sharp. 'But a little friendly advice—perhaps you should lower your expectations a little.'

'Or perhaps not,' Jane murmured as Mr Stewart walked into the room. All eyes were drawn to him as he greeted their host and hostess and then made his way directly to her. He was attractive, Jane couldn't deny it, and he had a presence that commanded attention.

'Miss Ashworth, it is a pleasure to see you again.' His eyes flicked over Mr and Mrs Farthington, and he nodded in greeting, but Jane was glad to see he did not seem inclined to stay and talk.

'Please excuse us,' he said with a blinding smile. 'I have the urge to speak to Miss Ashworth alone for a moment.'

Without waiting for their answer, he whisked Jane away.

'Thank you,' she murmured as they paused on the other side of the room.

'You looked uncomfortable.'

'Mrs Farthington is not a pleasant person. She was one of the debutantes Lady Mountjoy brought from Somerset. The other three were absolutely lovely, but she has always been cruel.'

'What did she say to you?'

'She was curious as to why you would suddenly be interested in me.'

Mr Stewart frowned, glancing over at the young woman and her husband on the other side of the room.

'Apparently you could have your pick of women, debutante, married or widowed. She does not see what would ever induce you to pick me.'

'I am sorry, Miss Ashworth,' he said, shaking his head. 'Some people baffle me in how they come out with such rude things. I particularly dislike bullies, and Mrs Farthington is a bully.'

'I suppose she is right, in a way, but there is no need to say it.'

'She's not right,' he said quietly, waiting for Jane to look up at him. 'Believe that. You are not worth less than I am—if anything I think you are probably worth more. It is just some people judge by the wrong standards.'

'I know.' Jane thought back a few years, to the time when her twin sister had been alive. Harriet had been beautiful, with dark-brown eyes and blonde hair. Her lips had been full and rosy and her skin soft and clear. They'd not been identical twins, and when they'd been young Jane had often wondered how two sisters born minutes apart could be so dissimilar.

They had done everything together, but even from a young age Jane had seen how they had been treated so differently. Things had been easier for Harriet—people had wanted to help her more, wanted to give her more. Not once had Jane begrudge her sister the benefits of being attractive, but Jane had learned as a child she was going to have to work twice as hard to achieve the same, being *the plain sister*.

She often wondered if it was this that had encouraged her to pursue her writing and illustrating, this need to stand out in some way against Harriet's superior looks and grace. Then her desire to write and paint had only intensified after Harriet's death as Jane had looked to find something to focus on outside her own deep grief.

As always when she thought about Harriet, she felt the sadness threatening to pull her down and she quickly supressed it, grasping instead for one of the happy memories of her sister.

'Everyone is going through to dinner. Shall we?' He offered her his arm and together they walked through the double doors to the resplendently decorated dining room.

Tom was actually enjoying himself. Dinner was delicious, and he reminded himself to accept more invitations when he was in want of a fancy meal. Now the sweet course was being served, and the steamed pears with cinnamon smelled divine.

He had been seated in between Lady Mountjoy and Miss Ashworth, but at the beginning of the meal Lady Mountjoy had leaned in to him and whispered that she was going to break all the rules of dinner party etiquette and focus on talking to the man on her left so Tom need not worry about conversing with her. Instead, he could focus on Miss Ashworth. He had to applaud Lady Mountjoy's commitment to her cause as she was sitting next to Lord Willoughby, a notoriously dull man who only liked to talk about his time in the army forty years earlier.

Miss Ashworth was a delightful dinner companion, especially after a little coaxing and few glasses of wine. They had spent much of the meal with their heads bent together, discussing the other guests. Her observations were sharp and witty, and he was surprised that underneath her meek and mild exterior there was a woman who would be able to run rings around most of the other distinguished guests here tonight.

'That is incredible,' Miss Ashworth said, tasting a mouthful of the steamed pears.

Tom had been around far too many women who were so preoccupied with their figure that they would have refused pudding along with half the meal. Miss Ashworth had committed to enjoying every bite. She was slender but not skinny, although it was hard to tell under the loose dresses she wore. He got the impression she was trying to hide her figure, trying to stay as invisible as possible, and he wondered why. Now was not the right time to ask. They did not know each other well enough for a question like that, but perhaps one day he would work it out.

'Thank you for joining us, Mr Stewart,' Lady Parson said from the head of the table, catching his attention with a wave of her hand. 'It is wonderful to see you at an event such as this. I wonder, with you attending more society events, are we to assume you are looking to find a wife and settle down?'

Tom cleared his throat, having to resist the urge to glance at Miss Ashworth. He needed to tread carefully. He couldn't laugh at the notion and destroy the carefully curated picture he and Miss Ashworth were trying to build, but equally he didn't want to confirm the rumours and be besieged by debutantes thinking they might be the right match for him.

He gave his most charming smile. 'Who amongst us knows what the future holds, Lady Parson?'

'Indeed.' Sensing she wasn't going to get the answer she wanted, Lady Parson moved on, dropping the subject.

'Very diplomatic,' Miss Ashworth murmured as he turned back to her.

'I didn't think the truth would help our deception,' he whispered.

'The truth?'

'That I will never marry.'

'"Never" is a long time.'

'It is, Miss Ashworth.'

She looked at him curiously, but thankfully didn't push him to explain why he was so adamant. Some things were too private. Tom had decided long ago he would never marry, even before his accident. He couldn't trust himself with another person's happiness, another person's wellbeing.

For a moment he closed his eyes and pictured his sister. She looked young in his mind, just seventeen years old. That was the last time he had seen her, the last memory he had of her. After years of aggression and cruelty from their father, Tom had joined the army as soon as he'd turned eighteen. He had done it to escape, to rid himself of the feeling he was always doing wrong in his father's eyes. He'd always been afraid of angering him. He had joined the army and breathed a sigh of relief when he'd been sent away to fight. Of course he had thought about Rebecca, but the urge to escape had been too strong, and he had bought a commission even though he knew it meant leaving Rebecca behind with their father.

When she'd disappeared, the guilt he'd felt had been overwhelming. The situation must have been so bad to make her leave with nothing more than the clothes on her back. For years he had carried the guilt and self-recriminations. He knew he couldn't be trusted to put someone else's needs before his own, so he had vowed to never marry, never be in the situation where someone was reliant on him.

After his injury, he had become more determined, deciding to live every day as if it were his last, but to keep to his pledge of not developing any lasting connections.

It had all been going so well until Edward had turned up on his doorstep.

Thankfully, the conversation around them had moved

on, and as everyone finished their pudding the gentlemen all settled down for drinks whilst the ladies withdrew to the drawing room. As Miss Ashworth stood, eyeing the other female guests warily, he caught her eye and winked, feeling inordinately happy at the momentary smile this elicited. Then the doors to the drawing room closed and he was swept into a world of business deals, estate management and parliamentary matters.

Chapter Nine

Jane touched her hair self-consciously as the carriage rolled to a stop outside Lord and Lady Framlingham's house. She had asked her maid to try a different style, something a little less severe than the centre parting she normally opted for. The curls that bounced around her face felt foreign and distracting, but when she had looked in the mirror before leaving she had felt a flush of pleasure in the change in her appearance.

'Shall we?'

Mr Stewart was sitting opposite her and jumped agilely down from the carriage as it rolled to a stop. As usual he looked devastatingly handsome with his dark hair swept across his forehead and his clothes cut to display his enviable physique.

The house was grand, even by London standards, situated out of the centre with more land around it. It meant it was larger than many of the townhouses Jane had visited in her time in London, many of which had to make do with throwing open the doors of the drawing rooms and dining rooms to make space for a ball.

As they walked inside Framlingham House, it was apparent no expense had been spared for the evening. Candles flickered inside glass lanterns to line the route up to the house and inside the decorations continued. Fresh flowers had been placed in every possible location, giving off a beautiful aroma and making the guests feel as if they had stepped into a painting of spring time. Despite it being mid March the weather this year was far too cold for these flowers to be blooming naturally and Jane wondered how they had achieved such an effect.

They were greeted by their hosts and guided to a magnificent ballroom with walls painted in light-blue and gold. A magnificent chandelier sparkled above their heads and already the musicians were playing gentle music to welcome the guests.

'All very civilised,' Mr Stewart murmured in her ear, and Jane had to press her lips together to stop a laugh bursting out.

She felt giddy and a little reckless tonight, very unlike her usual self. She knew part of it was because of the man holding her elbow, the man she realised was slowly becoming her friend.

Throughout all the balls, dinner parties and the operas she had disappeared into the background, overshadowed by the three other beautiful debutantes Lady Mountjoy had brought to London. Jane knew it was mainly her own doing—she hadn't wanted to be centre of attention and had done everything to ensure she wasn't the first to be asked to dance or the one the gentlemen clamoured to sit next to at dinner. Until recently she had still managed to enjoy a few of the events, swept along by her friends but, with Lucy and Eliza happily settled with their husbands, it had been looking like a grim few months as the Season started properly, observing solely from the edge of the room.

With Mr Stewart by her side it felt as though someone was seeing her, truly seeing her, for the first time. It felt thrilling to know that later on he would ask her to dance and she would actually enjoy the experience.

'Go, go,' Lady Mountjoy urged as she waved to an acquaintance across the room. 'You two young things take a walk around the room and enjoy yourselves.'

'She's planning the wedding already,' Mr Stewart murmured in Jane's ear as they obeyed, slipping into the crowds of the ballroom.

'I think she had it all planned out the moment you visited her drawing room after the last ball where we danced together.'

'A big celebration or a small family affair?'

'A big celebration, certainly. I am the fifth and final debutante she sponsored for the Season. She would want a party to match the scale of her achievement.'

'St George's?'

'Without a doubt, with a gathering after in the gardens of the Mountjoys' townhouse.'

'A fair engagement, then, for a summer wedding?'

'These things can't be rushed. Not when it should be the wedding of the year. Mr Stewart, the infamous rake, and the woman who finally enticed him to settle down.'

They both laughed and Jane saw a few people looking in their direction.

'Good evening, Mr Stewart,' a pretty young woman said as she glided up to them, resplendent in a dark-blue dress that draped beautifully about her shoulders, making her look like a Grecian goddess.

'Mrs Harper, lovely to see you. Are you well?'

'Quite well, Mr Stewart. Although surprised to see you here tonight.'

'May I introduce Miss Jane Ashworth, a friend of mine?'

'Delighted to meet you, Miss Ashworth.'

'And you, Mrs Harper.'

Mrs Harper's eyes raked over Jane and Jane had to resist the urge to pat her hair and smooth her dress. Instead she adopted a serene half-smile that she hoped gave her an air of confidence she didn't quite feel.

'How is Mr Harper?' Mr Stewart asked, and Jane thought she saw a darkening of the other woman's eyes.

'His gout ails him this evening. He has stayed at home.'

'Please send him my best wishes.'

Mrs Harper reached out and touched Mr Stewart's hand. 'You've always been so considerate. Do let me know when we can welcome you at our home again.'

'Was that a little strange?' Jane said as the slightly older woman smiled and walked away. 'It felt a little strange, although I don't think she said anything outrageous.'

'It was a little strange.'

Jane followed the pretty young woman with her eyes and then gasped. 'She's one of your mistresses!' It sounded so dramatic, but she couldn't believe the realisation had only just occurred.

Mr Stewart grabbed her hand and pulled it down from where she was covering her mouth.

'That is how rumours start,' he muttered.

'Is she not one of your mistresses?'

He coughed uncomfortably.

Jane felt a surge of envy and quickly tried to suppress it. It was absolutely none of her business if Mr Stewart had a dozen mistresses dotted about London. Still, she looked after the beautiful and confident young woman who had melted into the crowd and felt a stab of sadness that she would never have that confidence.

'But she's married.' Quickly Jane held up her hands. 'No, no, no. It is not my place to judge. You have always been very open about how you conduct your life and your philosophy for how you live it.'

'Stop. Please,' Mr Stewart said, again taking her wrists and lowering them to down, his fingers lingering on her skin for just a second more than they should have. With a glance over his shoulder he guided Jane to a quieter area of the ballroom where they were shielded from the view of most people by some well-placed arrangements of flowers.

'You don't need to explain yourself to me.'

'I know,' Mr Stewart said, but continued on anyway. 'I knew Mrs Harper before she married her second husband. She was widowed young and spent a year or two enjoying the new-found freedom of being wealthy and independent and allowed to make her own decisions for the first time ever.'

'And she chose you?'

'We spent a little time in one another's company.'

'She seemed very keen to renew your acquaintance.'

Mr Stewart sighed and swept a hand through his hair. 'I don't have many rules in life, but I do refuse to dally with innocent young women and married women. There is no need. There are plenty of people unattached and eager for a liaison outside of those groups.'

'The beautiful Mrs Harper doesn't have the same rules, I assume?'

'She married a much older man and I can only assume he can't keep up.'

Jane glanced up, seeing Mr Stewart's wicked smile, and thumped him on the arm.

'You're trying to embarrass me.'

'You look so pretty when you blush.'

'Hasn't anyone told you it is wrong to corrupt the minds of innocent debutantes?'

'But it is so much fun.'

'If you don't behave, I will find Mrs Harper and tell her you will climb through her bedroom window in the small hours tonight.'

'A threat indeed. Come, Miss Ashworth, we should return to the main area of the ballroom or someone will think I'm ravishing you behind here.'

This did make the blood flood to Jane's cheeks, as she couldn't help herself from imagining Mr Stewart's lips on hers, kissing her until she didn't know who she was any more. Quickly she tried to push the thought aside, but the image had become lodged in her mind, and she found it impossible to look at her companion without being drawn to his perfectly shaped lips.

'Would you give me the honour of the first dance?' Mr Stewart asked as the pace and volume of the music the musicians were playing changed, indicating the couples should take to the dance floor.

'Of course,' she said, and then hesitated as she realised it was a waltz. 'Or maybe we can sit this set out and try in the next one.'

'Don't you like to waltz?'

'Do you remember our last disastrous dance?'

'It wasn't disastrous.'

'I can just about make it through a quadrille or cotillion,' Jane said, wondering why they were still heading to where all the couples were assembling. 'But a waltz is so much harder.'

'You've just never had the right partner.'

'It's nothing to do with my partners. *I* can't dance it. My feet get all in a muddle, then I overthink it and end up stumbling. You *do* remember the last dance we had together?'

'Do you trust me?'

Slowly she nodded, realising that even though their acquaintance was short she was starting to trust him.

'Then give me one more chance.'

For a long moment she didn't answer. It was foolish. She was going to end up in a tangled mess with the whole room staring at her, laughing that, not only did she think she could have a chance with a charming and handsome man like Mr Stewart, but she couldn't dance a simple waltz either.

'Fine. But if I fall you will have my eternal embarrassment on your conscience.'

She allowed him to lead her to a space in between the other couples and tried not to look at all the people gathered around the edge of the dance floor.

'Relax,' he said, slipping a hand around her waist. Jane shifted, aware of the heat of his skin through the thin material of her dress.

'I'm trying to.'

'People trying to relax do not clench their jaws.'

With a gargantuan effort Jane relaxed her jaw and let out a deep breath.

'Better... Now make your grip a little looser. It'll be nice to leave the ball this evening with a few of my fingers still attached.'

He was smiling at her, and Jane felt some of the tension ebb away.

Leaning in, he dropped his voice so only she could hear. 'Do you know the best way to forget you're nervous?'

She shook her head.

'Imagine everyone around you has come to the ball in their underclothes.'

A laugh burst from Jane's lips at the absurdity of it.

'Go on, try it. I promise it'll work. How about Mr Leggety?'

'Stop it,' Jane said as they started to move.

'Or Mrs Waterbeach.'

'Don't, this is cruel.'

'To them or to you, having to imagine it?'

'Both.'

'What about Lord Penrose?'

Jane laughed again and then looked down, realising that they were waltzing and had been for some time.

'It's working, isn't it?'

She panicked, not knowing what beat she was on, and tried to start counting.

'Stop,' he said firmly. 'You do not need to count. You are dancing beautifully.'

She stumbled again as she glanced down at her feet.

'Look at me, Miss Ashworth.'

She did, feeling the pull of his dark eyes and feeling a shiver run down her spine as he leaned in closer to her.

'If it helps, imagine me in my underclothes.'

Jane spluttered, even though she hadn't been about to say anything.

'Oversized bloomers, double layer of vest, perhaps even a thick nightshirt.'

'You don't wear any of that, do you?' she managed to say, aware her eyes were raking down his body, trying to imagine exactly what was underneath the well-tailored jacket and trousers.

For a long moment Jane thought he wasn't going to answer and then he leaned in even closer so his lips were almost up against her ear.

'Nothing at all.'

He spun her, whisking her round and round, his eyes locked on hers as if she were the only person in the world.

Jane had no idea how long the dance lasted. It felt as though everything else had faded away into nothing. Even the music was a faint melody in the background. When Mr Stewart stopped moving, she stood for a moment, completely still in his arms, her chest heaving from the exertion and the heightened awareness.

'Thank you for the dance, Miss Ashworth,' he said, and Jane managed to mumble something as they stepped away from the dance floor.

'You look a little flushed. Would you like a glass of lemonade?'

She nodded, glad of the suggestion. She needed a few

minutes alone, a few minutes to reason with herself, to try and claw back some of her sanity.

As Mr Stewart left her, Jane stayed still for a few seconds, and then as he disappeared out of view she let out a deep exhalation and turned to leave. She planned to find a quiet corner, perhaps on the chairs set out for chaperons and spinsters, to get her breath back and reset her equilibrium.

Instead she barrelled right into a tall man. Apologising quickly, she rushed away, not even looking the man in the eye.

Feeling as though the crowd of people was closing in, she decided she needed some air and hurried towards the ornate glass doors that led onto the terrace.

Outside the air was cold and the sky was a deep inky black. There was no moon and no sign of any stars to illuminate the gardens below. The candlelight from the ballroom spilled out onto the terrace, but a few feet from the doors everything was plunged into shadow.

It was quiet on the terrace, with two couples strolling arm in arm along its length, but no one else venturing out of the heat of the ballroom so early in the night.

Closing her eyes, Jane leaned on the stone balustrade, glad of the darkness so no one could see her expression. She was still shaking, still hadn't recovered from the dance with Mr Stewart. It had started so well, with him distracting her, making her laugh even, and then twirling her until she'd felt as though she were dancing on thin air, floating above the floor of the ballroom. Then he had looked at her with those dark, enticing eyes and invited her to picture him without his clothes on.

Even now Jane got a flush of heat flood through her body as she thought of it.

Do not do this, she ordered herself. It was not a helpful reaction to have to the man who was assisting her. She needed Lady Mountjoy to believe in their fake attachment for one another, not to build it up herself into something that it wasn't. *He is doing you a favour.*

Mr Stewart was kind and generous, more so than he liked people to know, but she knew there was no way he would ever be attracted to her.

Even as she shook her head to try and rid herself of the images, another flooded her brain—the picture of Mr Stewart wearing very little, leaning in as if he were about to kiss her.

She spun abruptly, startling a couple that was walking arm in arm along the terrace behind her. Managing a smile she hoped didn't look too deranged, Jane hurried further away into the darkness at the end of the terrace, breathing a sigh of relief when the cold night air became too much for the other people who had ventured outside. Finally alone, she closed her eyes and took a few deep breaths.

Soon she would have to return to the ball, to Mr Stewart and his charming smile. She would have to pretend nothing had changed, to laugh, talk and dance as if her whole world hadn't just shifted under her feet.

Don't be so dramatic, she told herself. It was a flicker of desire no more. Objectively, anyone would have to admit Mr Stewart was an attractive man. It was not remarkable to feel a pull, a desire, to be close to him. Perhaps it would be stranger if she didn't feel anything at all.

Knowing she had to return to the ballroom, Jane was about to step out of the shadows at the end of the terrace when the door opened once again, momentarily making the volume of the music flare for a few seconds. It was a young couple with their heads bent together and their voices lowered to breathy whispers.

Not wanting to intrude on an intimate moment, Jane went to step into the light, but before she could move she saw the woman reach up and pull the man into a deep kiss. Jane froze, not knowing what to do for the best. The couple must have thought they'd snatched a rare moment of privacy and surely would be mortified to be caught like this.

For a moment she wondered if they were married, but the furtive way the young woman kept glancing at the door to the ballroom made it obvious they were not. Jane felt paralysed, knowing that every second she remained hidden, the more she would see, the more the couple were compromising themselves, but already feeling it was too late to stroll out of the darkness and announce her presence.

As the couple continued to kiss, Jane spun, wondering if there might be another way. The glasshouse sat at the end of the terrace and there was a door right behind her. Perhaps if it was open there might be another route into the main house and no one need ever know what she had witnessed.

Almost crying with relief as the door shifted, Jane slipped inside, closing it silently behind her. The air was warmer in there and a little humid despite the cool, crisp conditions outside. At first it was hard to see anything, and the darkness seemed all-consuming, but after a few seconds her eyes began to adjust and she could begin to make out the outlines of things. Much of it still looked unfamiliar, but Jane reasoned that was probably because the glasshouse was filled with exotic plants and flowers. Carefully she felt her way through the foliage, trying to be as quiet as she could.

The glass house was massive, three long interconnecting buildings attached to the edge of the main house. There was a sickly sweet smell pervading the air and Jane realised this must have been where all of the flowers for tonight's ball had been grown.

She had just stumbled her way through the first glasshouse when she heard the unmistakable click of the door opening and closing and then the giggle of the young couple who had been outside.

Jane stiffened, unable to move, surrounded as she was by the leaves of a palm tree. Even the tiniest movement made the fronds rustle and would give away her presence immediately.

Cursing her poor judgement for not stepping out of the shadows as soon as the young couple had ventured outside, she closed her eyes and waited, listening as the couple giggled and crept through the glasshouse. At one point they passed right by her, the young woman in touching distance.

For a moment she thought they might carry on all the way through the glasshouse, perhaps seeking the door Jane had thought to use at the other end, but nothing was going in her favour tonight and they paused a few feet away from her and began to kiss again.

Ever so slowly, Jane started retreating, feeling out

each step as she did and barely breathing until she felt the cool glass under her fingers.

Before she could open the door and slip out to freedom, she looked up, surprised to see a figure approaching the glasshouse, relieved beyond words when the familiar features of Mr Stewart came into focus.

'What...?' he began, his voice booming through the quiet night air.

Jane grabbed the handle to the door, pulled it open and pressed a hand to his lips.

His lips were soft beneath her fingers and for a moment she was distracted, unable to think of anything but how they would feel trailing across her skin.

'There's someone in there,' she whispered, 'Well, two people.'

Mr Stewart glanced over her shoulder, his frown deepening. 'What are you doing in there?'

'Trying to avoid them.'

'By joining them?'

'No,' Jane said, a little louder. 'Don't be ridiculous. We need to get back to the ballroom. I'll explain once we're in there.'

Mr Stewart looked as if he was going to protest, but with one last glance over Jane's shoulder he nodded.

Jane stepped forward, glad to be out of the heat of the glasshouse, and dreading what a state she must look after panicking for ten minutes in the humid air. She had only taken one step when the door to the ballroom opened again and a group of women flooded out onto the terrace.

'What do we do?' Jane felt the evening couldn't get any worse. Here she was standing in the shadows with a notorious rake, probably looking dishevelled and as if she had been up to no good for the last half an hour. Mr Stewart hesitated, looking her up and down. He must have come to the same conclusion, for he groaned quietly and pulled her back into the glasshouse.

He shut the door gently behind them and then gripped her hand, leading them away from the windows so they would be less likely to be observed.

'Stay quiet,' he murmured in her ear, leaning close so his voice was just audible. Jane felt the heat of his body and had to resist the urge to reach out and touch him.

They were standing behind a raised bed, planted with exotic flowers, the petals bigger than anything Jane had ever seen before. It would be a fascinating place to see in the daylight, but right now she wished more than anything to be back in the safety of the ballroom.

'We'll be out of here soon,' Mr Stewart whispered, misjudging the distance between them and brushing his lips against her ear. A shiver of anticipation ran down Jane's spine and she found herself recklessly reaching out into the darkness. Her hand found his shirt and she felt his muscles tense as he became aware of the contact. She was surprised when he didn't move away. Instead, he shifted his stance just a little so he could rest his hand on the small of her back.

Jane felt all the breath leaving her body. It felt exquisitely intimate, standing here in the darkness with Mr Stewart, his fingers tracing gentle circles on her back, separated only by the thin fabric of her dress. She wanted more than anything in that moment to tilt her chin up and seek out his lips with her own.

Trying to banish all thoughts of kissing Mr Stewart,

she shifted again, a small gasp escaping her lips as her hip bounced off the raised flower bed and the ricochet pushed her further into the arms of the man behind her. Glancing up, she could only see his silhouette in the darkness, but she had the impression he was feeling the same pull, the same attraction she was.

'Jane,' he murmured, one hand pressing into her waist and pulling her tighter to him. She wasn't sure if it was the darkness, the heat or the heady scent coming from the flowers but she felt as though reality was being swept away and she was floating into a place where anything could happen.

Jane raised herself up on her tiptoes and at the same moment Mr Stewart lowered his head, seeking out her lips in the darkness. The kiss was gentle, so full of promise that Jane yearned for more. His lips were like velvet on hers and as he kissed her she felt her body surrender and melt into his.

They both stiffened as the door to the glasshouse opened and light flooded inside. Quickly, they moved apart as much as they were able, but Jane's body was still pressed against Mr Stewart's in the confined space. For a long moment Jane could think of nothing but how right it had seemed, being in his arms, and then the reality of their situation came crashing down upon her.

'This is my pride and joy,' the voice of their hostess, Lady Framlingham, rang out clearly. 'Of course, it is better viewed in the daylight, but I do often walk through here at night, marvelling at the flowers and the exotic plants.'

'It has the feel of a jungle,' another woman said as the group entered, closing the door behind them.

'Over the years we have collected more than four hundred different exotic plants. I would wager we have the most comprehensive collection in England.'

Jane wondered if they might pass by into the second of the interconnecting buildings, allowing Mr Stewart and her to slip out. As much as she secretly yearned to be kissed again, the sensible part of her knew it would be disastrous to be caught by the group of matrons traipsing through the glasshouses. It would mean certain ruin for her and, even though she did not plan to marry, she did not want to be sent home from London in disgrace and shunned evermore by polite society.

The group of women took their time admiring the flowers by lantern light. At one point one of the ladies moved closer to where Jane and Mr Stewart were standing, hidden by the drooping leaves of some exotic plant. Jane felt Mr Stewart's arm tighten around her and pull her closer, as if instinctively trying to protect her, but thankfully the woman moved away before they could be discovered.

'We need to get out of here,' Mr Stewart whispered into her ear as the ladies moved further into the glasshouse.

Jane nodded, looking over at the door. It was no distance away, really. Perhaps twenty long strides and they would be out in the air.

Carefully they picked their way back through the plants, stopping every few seconds to ensure Lady Framlingham and her friends were still occupied elsewhere.

They were almost at the door, almost to freedom, when Jane felt her nose begin to itch. There was a lot of pollen in the glass house, and she must have brushed up against one of the flowers. The urge to sneeze was overwhelming, and despite her best efforts Jane could not hold it in.

She sneezed. The sound was so loud it was as though someone had let off a gunshot in the enclosed space.

Mr Stewart didn't lose a second. He grabbed her by the hand and pulled, running out of the glass house and along the terrace. Whipping open the door to the ball-room, he stopped only to release her hand and place it lightly on his arm, and then, as if they had been doing nothing more than strolling on the terrace, he escorted her inside.

Jane felt a mess. Her hair was flattened to her head, damp with the moisture from the glasshouse, and she knew her skin would be flushed. If anyone took a closer look at them, it would quickly become apparent some-thing untoward had happened.

'Ah, it's our second dance, Miss Ashworth,' Mr Stew-art said, calmly leading her to the dance floor.

'We're dancing? Now?'

'It's a quadrille,' Mr Stewart said, the pleasant smile not dropping from his lips. 'By the end, every dancer will be gently perspiring and we will not look so out of place.'

The had taken their first steps when there was a commotion at the door leading to the terrace from the ballroom. Jane tried her hardest not to look, not want-ing to catch anyone's eye. A murmur of excitement was slowly spreading through the ballroom as Lady Fram-lingham imparted her news.

'Don't look,' Mr Stewart instructed, 'But Lady Mount-joy is waiting for us to finish dancing.'

'Oh no, what have I done?'

'No one could have seen us. Perhaps Lady Framlingham caught the other couple you heard in the glasshouse.'

'Why would Lady Mountjoy want to talk to me so urgently if that was the case?'

'You must hold your composure.'

'So must you,' Jane shot back, irritated he thought she would be the one to let something slip she shouldn't.

'You do not need to worry about me.'

'Nor you me.'

He gave her a long, hard stare.

'Don't look at me like that. I will have you know I can lie very well.'

'Hmm.'

'I would wager I am a much more believable liar than you.'

'I doubt it,' he said, the easy smile returning to his lips. 'I've had a lot of practice.'

'We should talk about…' Jane trailed off, knowing she should not even mention the kiss they had shared in the glasshouse.

'Yes,' Mr Stewart said, his eyes searching her face. 'A moment of madness?' He phrased it as a question and Jane felt a mild pang of disappointment in amongst the relief.

'A moment of madness,' she agreed.

There was no time to discuss it further as the dance ended and the couples thanked each other, but she promised herself she would revisit the subject later, once Lady Mountjoy had been dealt with.

'Have you heard?' Lady Mountjoy said with no preamble as Mr Stewart escorted Jane from the dance floor.

'Heard what?' Jane tried to make her voice nonchalant, her whole demeanour relaxed.

'Lady Framlingham was giving a tour of her famous glasshouse to some of her friends and they disturbed a couple in there.'

'No!' Jane gasped and felt Mr Stewart exert a little pressure on her arm. Perhaps she was overdoing the enthusiasm. Normally she would say she didn't have any interest in gossip or something similar. 'Who was it?'

There was a long pause whilst Lady Mountjoy scrutinised Jane and Mr Stewart. 'No one knows,' she said eventually. 'Yet.'

'What a thrilling mystery,' Mr Stewart said quietly.

'Indeed. You were out on the terrace, were you not?'

'A while ago,' Mr Stewart said, 'But we were back before the quadrille was called and didn't see anyone heading into the glasshouse.'

Lady Mountjoy was silent again, searching them both with her eyes for some weakness.

'What's this?' she asked, leaning forward and looking at a tiny mark on Jane's dress. It was from where some pollen had rubbed against the fabric, a miniscule brown mark on the bodice, something anyone less observant would have easily missed.

'I don't know,' Jane said, trying to feign lack of interest. 'I am sure Mary will be able to get it out. She managed to make my dress look as good as new when

I threw lemonade all over it at the Osbornes' dinner a few weeks ago.'

'Did you hear?' A woman bustled up to them, grasping Lady Mountjoy by the arm. 'They found a woman's glove in the glasshouse. It is only a matter of time before it is matched to the owner.'

In unison Lady Mountjoy and Mr Stewart looked down at Jane's hands where they rested by her side. Feeling some of the panic leave her, Jane smiled serenely as she lifted her arm to tuck a stray strand of hair behind her ear. Both her hands were encased in delicate satin gloves, the fabric covering her forearms and buttoned at the elbow.

Lady Mountjoy gave a suspicious tut.

She leaned in towards Jane and Mr Stewart. 'Best behaviour,' she said firmly. 'Everyone will be watching everyone else. It will be like a chapter in one of those awful crime stories Lord Mountjoy likes to read.'

'Best behaviour,' Jane promised.

'I wouldn't dream of anything else,' Mr Stewart said.

Lady Mountjoy tapped him on the chest with the end of her fan. 'You may be charming, Mr Stewart, but remember you are an honourable man as well.'

The countess spun and walked away.

'What did she mean by that?'

Mr Stewart shook his head. He had lost his smile and looked a little worried.

'What did she mean?'

'I do have honour,' he said quietly, 'And that means if we had been caught...' He trailed off.

'You would have done the honourable thing,' she finished for him.

He shook himself, as if trying to rid his mind of that terrible thought.

Chapter Ten

'I'm not cut out for this,' Tom murmured as his nephew burst into tears at the sight of him. He had been playing a game with one of the maids, some complicated version of hide and seek, where Edward seemed to be at once both the person who hid and the person who searched. There had been squeals of joy and laughter, but as soon as Tom had entered the room and suggested they get some fresh air, mostly out of concern for the exhausted looking maid, his nephew had started crying.

He would have to remember to pay his staff extra this week. They had all quite happily taken on extra duties to help him with Edward, not once complaining about the work involved, and he knew he had to show his appreciation. He was a fair and generous employer, but he didn't want any of his servants leaving because they felt their extra efforts were going unappreciated.

Pressing one hand against his eye where the first pulses of a headache was brewing, he took a moment before he crouched down, bringing himself to Edward's level.

'It's such a lovely afternoon, I thought we might go to the park. We could take your sailing boat and try it on the Serpentine.'

There was no response from Edward, only a continuation of the tears.

'I don't mean to interfere, sir,' Hetty, the young maid who had been playing with Edward, said. 'But I don't mind playing with the young master.'

'You're good to say that, Hetty.' He hesitated. The boy was his responsibility, but his head was starting to throb, and he had an overwhelming sense of being trapped. He needed to get outside, to gasp in lungfuls of cool air, and arguing with Edward until he was ready to come wasn't going to speed things up. 'I'll be back in an hour or two. Be good for Hetty.'

With a mounting feeling of guilt, as if he were abandoning the boy for good, he grabbed his coat and hat and quickly left the house. He walked briskly, as if he were being chased, only slowing when he had put a good distance between himself and home.

Forcing himself to try and forget all the troubles that were plaguing him, he tried to focus on the things he could see and hear. It was a trick taught to him by an old army friend during his recovery from the head injury. Then the frustrations of the slowness of his recuperation, the mountain of effort it had taken even to take a few short steps outside the front door, had been overwhelming. He had been on the verge of giving in to the melancholy and despair that had threatened to consume him when this old friend had suggested he try looking outside of himself, even just for a moment.

Now he made himself slow down and empty his

mind of everything except what he could see, hear and smell right at that moment. He let the noises of the street wash over him, the clatter of carriage wheels and the clopping of hooves, the chatter of groups of women as they passed him and the excited whoops of joy from children out with their nannies. Slowly he felt his heart rate slow and some of the stress seep from his body.

'Mr Stewart!' a familiar voice called.

He wondered whether he could get away with ignoring it, pretending he hadn't heard. All he wanted was to be alone now, to have a few minutes of peace before he allowed himself to start thinking of the future, to decide what he needed to do with his nephew.

It was Lady Mountjoy, and he knew she wouldn't let him slip away, pretending he hadn't heard. He glanced up and had to suppress a groan. Walking beside her was Miss Ashworth, looking poised and serene, and actually smiling at him as if pleased to see him. It had been a week since he had last seen her, sending a note and telling her it might be best for him to keep his distance after their near miss at the Framlingham ball.

Now a week had passed, there would be no harm in being seen strolling together out in public, chaperoned by Lady Mountjoy. Suspicion had never really fallen on them anyway, but he had needed a few days' space to try and work out what exactly had happened in the glasshouse. There had been one moment, no more than a few seconds, when Miss Ashworth's body had been pressed against his. He had been able to feel her heart hammering in her chest and the heat of her skin through the fabric of her dress. She'd looked up at him and in that moment he had wanted nothing more than to kiss her, to claim her as his own.

It was not the first time he'd felt attraction for an unsuitable young woman, but it was the first time he'd acted on it. Normally he had complete control of himself, complete restraint, but there in the glasshouse he had been unable to do anything but brush his lips against Jane's. He should be thankful that the group of ladies had entered when they had or who knew what could have happened?

These past few days he had kept his distance, fearful of what he might feel when he saw her, even though he knew he was being ridiculous. It had been circumstance, nothing more. A combination of the dark, exotic atmosphere in the glasshouse and the thrill of almost being caught.

'Good afternoon,' he said, turning to face the two women, trying to summon a smile.

'Good afternoon. Is something amiss, Mr Stewart?' Miss Ashworth asked, her forehead crinkling with concern. 'You look pale.'

He cursed himself for being so easy to read and gave a nonchalant little shake of his head.

'I came out for an afternoon walk. It seemed a shame not to get out in the sunshine.'

Miss Ashworth and Lady Mountjoy both glanced up at the sky dubiously. It was grey and overcast with only one or two small breaks in the clouds where weak rays of sunshine were managing to filter through. Hardly a day that would inspire a spontaneous need to get into nature.

'How fortuitous! Miss Ashworth has been eager to

get out for some fresh air all day. I said I would accompany her, but my hip is starting to pain me again.'

Miss Ashworth gave the older woman an incredulous look and then flashed an apologetic smile at Tom.

'Perhaps you could escort her for a short stroll whilst I rest a while on one of the benches in the park?'

'Of course. It would be my pleasure.'

They walked together into the park and found a suitable bench for Lady Mountjoy to sit and observe them from as they then carried on along the path.

'She only ever seems to complain of her hip when you are around,' Miss Ashworth said when they were far enough away from Lady Mountjoy so the countess would not hear the comment. The younger woman studied him for a moment. 'Something is wrong. You look like you haven't slept for a month. Is it what happened in the glasshouse?'

'No,' he said a little too quickly, forcing himself to slow down and summon a more serene expression. 'Although I am tired. It is Edward.' He grimaced. Sleep had been hard to come by these last few days.

He was finding the scent of lavender coming off Miss Ashworth's hair every time she turned in his direction distracting. It made him think of the night in the glasshouse and stirred something deep inside him.

'Is he unwell?'

'No, but he is not happy. I fear I am not doing the right thing by him.'

'Why do you say he is not happy?'

'Take today—I suggested we go for a walk and he burst into tears. There are a hundred instances like that throughout the day from when he wakes up until when he goes to bed.'

'What was he doing before you suggested you go for a walk?'

'Playing hide and seek with one of the maids.'

Miss Ashworth shrugged. 'There it is, then. It has nothing to do with you.'

'What do you mean?'

'What do you enjoy doing most in the world?'

He hesitated for a moment and Miss Ashworth looked at him, eyes wide.

'No, perhaps don't tell me,' she said quickly.

'I was trying to choose between riding and driving my curricle,' he said with a smile, his spirits already lifting a little in Miss Ashworth's company. 'My mind clearly isn't as corrupted as yours.'

'I am an innocent debutante.'

'Clearly not in mind,' he murmured.

'Imagine you are riding your horse,' she ploughed on, resolutely looking ahead. 'Enjoying yourself in the great outdoors, and then suddenly without warning someone comes and tells you instead you need to dismount and you are going to the opera.' She paused to see if he was following her, glancing up at him with her lips pursed. 'It isn't that you dislike the opera, or that you don't want to go with the person who is suggesting it, but in your mind you are focussed on the thing you are enjoying in that moment. For someone to come along and tell you to stop immediately, even for an adult, is a bit frustrating. For a child, it makes them feel as though they have no control over their lives.'

Tom considered Miss Ashworth's words for a long moment.

'Is there a better way of doing it?'

She shrugged. 'Watch the nannies and nursemaids in the park. The ones with happy, contented-looking children lay out their expectations. They tell them even before they get to the park that they can stay and play for half an hour, walk around the Serpentine and feed the ducks. After that, they will return home.'

He nodded slowly. It made sense, and he couldn't really understand why he hadn't realised it himself. It was obvious when he thought about it, but in the moment when Edward had started crying, and Tom had felt as though nothing he could do was right, it had been so hard to be logical.

'It may be worth trying to give him time to get used to an idea before saying you are leaving immediately.'

'I'm no good at this.'

'You are.'

He shook his head. 'I'm not. *You* are good at this. You will make an excellent mother, but I am not a fit guardian for Edward.'

'You're talking nonsense,' Miss Ashworth said, and Tom couldn't help but smile even though he still felt morose. Miss Ashworth, the woman dismissed by most of society as a quiet little mouse, didn't tiptoe around but instead said exactly what she was thought. Everyone else's opinion of her was so wrong, it was laughable.

'If you did these things—upset him and then didn't worry about it—then you would be entitled to question if you were a fit guardian. The very fact that you are out here, feeling awful and wanting to do better, shows you are exactly the right person to be looking after him.'

'Hmm.'

'When is the nanny due to arrive?'

'Ten more days.'

'That is no time at all.'

'He's so distant much of the time. I feel awkward around him.'

'Most people do around children other than their own,' she said with a shrug.

'Do they?'

'Think about it. Your own child, you know from a little baby. You learn what they like and what they don't like, how they respond to you, how to handle them, through every stage of childhood. Edward has just appeared in your life. You need to give it time.' She smiled at him, and Tom felt some of the self-doubt ebbing away.

'I would love to see him again,' she said. 'I know we were keeping our distance so society doesn't suspect we were in that glasshouse, but I haven't heard our names attached to any of the rumours circulating. I think we are safe.'

For an instant she glanced up at him and he saw a flicker of remembrance in her eyes. As she bit her lower lip, he knew in a flash that she had felt that same pull he had, that same flare of attraction. The same thing he was trying to deny every time he looked at her.

Clearing his throat, he nodded. 'Of course. I was going to take him riding, or at least introduce him to some horses. Perhaps you would like to accompany us tomorrow?'

'That would be lovely.' She smiled at him again and her eye held his just a fraction too long before she looked away quickly. He knew he had flustered her but he was too preoccupied with his own interest in this serious young woman to try and put her at ease.

'I will take you back to Lady Mountjoy. No doubt she is getting cold sitting for so long in this weather.'

They walked in silence back to the countess, Tom quickly taking his leave and heading out of the park.

It was late and Tom knew he had consumed far too much alcohol for one night. He gambled like most men in his social circle, but had a hard rule that he never did so after more than five drinks. He had seen too many men ruined from their lack of self-control at the gaming tables, forced to sell their homes or go begging to wealthier relatives to cover their debt.

Tonight, though, he had been close to breaking his rule. He'd thrown back whisky after whisky and had then been tempted to linger at the tables.

'Leaving so soon, Stewart?' Lord Rowlinson called as he pushed back his chair and bid the people at the table good night.

'My skill is no match for yours but I do at least have the good sense to know when I am beaten,' Tom said, reaching for his coat.

He was drinking to forget, gambling to forget, and that could be dangerous. Stepping out into the cold night air, he hesitated, first turning left and then shaking his head and reversing his decision. A month ago he had made the acquaintance of a beautiful young actress who had given him a key and an open invitation to join her in her rooms any night he desired company. It would be another way to forget the thoughts that plagued him, to lose himself in carnal pleasure, but he knew it was the wrong decision tonight, so instead he slowly made his way over the river to Southwark.

Even the streets here made him think of Miss Ashworth, of following her into the dark alleyway and being punched in the jaw, and then her desperate attempts to find the long-dead publisher. He quickened his pace, as if trying to outrun his own thoughts, and almost burst through the door of The Hangman's Noose.

'You being chased or just eager to see me?' a tall, slim woman called out to him from behind the bar.

'You know I can't keep away, Mrs Western.'

'Come on over and pull up a chair. He's changing the barrel but he'll be up in a minute.'

She poured him a beer, the liquid a deep amber and the top frothing, setting it down carefully on the bar in front of him.

'You look awful, Tom.'

'We can't all be radiant all the time, Mrs Western.'

'Stop flirting with my wife, you scoundrel, I can hear you from down here.' Western's voice came from somewhere behind the bar, making Tom smile.

'Is it the headaches?'

He shook his head. 'They haven't been too bad. Only had one in the last few weeks.'

'Your fancy doctors still haven't got to the bottom of it?'

'No. I stopped going to see them when they suggested leeches again.' They both shuddered at the thought.

'You've visited us twice in a fortnight. We are blessed,' Western said as he emerged from the cellar, wiping his hands on a cloth. 'You're right, he does look awful,' he said, turning to his wife.

'It'll be a woman,' Mrs Western said as she started to wipe down the bar.

'No doubt some poor girl has fallen in love with him and he's feeling the pressure of letting her down.'

'I can hear you,' Tom murmured, although he didn't mind their gentle teasing. It felt familiar and comforting and some of his troubles lifted from his shoulders as he watched his friends smile at each other.

'Is it a woman?'

'No,' he said a little too quickly, trying unsuccessfully to push the image of Miss Ashworth from his mind.

'Your nephew, then?' Western asked.

'He deserves better.'

'Nonsense,' Mrs Western said, motioning out to the street. 'Those children out there, the ones forced to work from the age of five climbing chimneys or worse—they deserve better. The ones so hungry their bellies hurt and their teeth fall out—they deserve better.'

'I can't argue with that,' Tom said quietly.

'What did you have as a child?' Western said, coming round the bar and sitting next to him.

'A mother who died when I was a baby and a father who was cruel and controlling.'

'Look at you—a bit rough around the edges with

some questionable decisions behind you, but all in all you've turned out all right.'

'Don't feed my conceit too much, Western, I might get too confident.'

'You're already too confident by half.'

'He's got a good home, a warm bed, plenty of food, people to take care of him and the chance of an education,' Mrs Western said, her voice a little softer, 'And an uncle who loves him.'

'Not like a parent would.'

Western clapped him on the back. 'Drink up and I'll pour us a whisky.'

'I don't even think it is your nephew you are feeling morose about,' Mrs Western said, eyeing him with a probing look on her face. 'It *is* a woman, isn't it?'

'Who is it this time? An actress? An opera singer? One of those widows that seem to be so eager to get to know you intimately?'

'There is no one.'

'I don't believe you,' Western said as he reached for the bottle of whisky and poured them both a glass.

'Perhaps it is something a little more than that,' Mrs Western said, motioning to a new customer that she would be along in a moment. 'Are you thinking of finally settling down, Tom?'

'Good Lord, no,' he said, throwing back the whisky and then wishing he hadn't. 'Let's talk about something else. The horse racing, business—even the damn weather. I don't care as long as it isn't about the women in my life.'

'I think you touched a nerve, my dear,' Western said

to his wife while clapping Tom on the back. 'I'll wager there will be wedding bells within the year.'

'I thought a tavern was somewhere a man could come to get peace.' Tom growled, standing and grabbing his coat.

'Come back and see us soon,' Mrs Western called from the other end of the bar. 'And bring your lady friend, whoever she may be.'

Chapter Eleven

The morning was cool and crisp as Jane hurried into the park, but there was a hint of warmth when the sun shone making Jane wonder if spring might be just around the corner. Her maid was shivering beside her despite the thick coat she wore and had already asked three times how long they would be out.

Not for the first time, Jane silently cursed the rules of society that meant she couldn't walk alone through a park or go for a ride with a gentleman without having another woman with her. It seemed ridiculous, especially in a public space. Luckily, her maid was open to a bribe if the price was right, and on more than one occasion Jane had paid the young woman to allow her to slip away when she was meant to be accompanying her.

Today, though, there was no need for a bribe as she was going for an innocent ride with Mr Stewart and his nephew. Refusing to acknowledge the thrill of anticipation that flooded her body as she thought of Mr Stewart, she started to walk even faster, revelling in the burn in her lungs and her calves. Today she would not be overcome by foolish desire and she would remember the sensible young woman she really was. She didn't swoon at the first provocation, she didn't partake in the gossip of the ballroom, and she most certainly didn't lose her head over a man, even if he was ridiculously attractive and too charming for his own good.

The last thing she was going to think about was the kiss they had shared in the glasshouse at the ball. If Mr Stewart could act as if it had never happened, she would too.

'Miss Jane,' Edward shouted as he spotted her, running towards her at full speed and flinging his arms around her in a show of affection.

'How are you, Edward? Excited to see the horses?'

'Zio Tom said he has an extra-special surprise for me.' He lowered his voice. 'I think maybe he will let me do acrobatics, like we saw at Astley's!'

'Have you ridden before?'

'Our neighbour had a donkey called Ranuncolo who she would sometimes let me ride.'

'Never a horse?'

He shook his head.

'Then this is an exciting day.'

Hand in hand, they crossed the grassy area to where Mr Stewart was waiting, discussing something with a groom.

'Miss Ashworth, thank you for coming.'

'I would not have missed this for the world.'

Mr Stewart looked a little dishevelled this morning, as if he had not slept well, but still there was a sparkle in his eyes, something Jane found drawing her in.

'Ah, here they come,' he said, turning away.

Jane turned to see three horses being led across the grass by a groom. One was large and sleek, its coat a shiny mahogany colour. The second was lighter in colour and a little smaller, whilst the third was a little pony, trotting along happily to keep up with the two bigger horses.

'This is Sapphire,' Mr Stewart said, and Jane watched as the young boy's eyes lit up.

'Hello, Sapphire,' Edward said solemnly, waiting for the little pony to stop moving before reaching a tentative hand up to stroke her. He was gentle and Jane could see from that very first moment he was in love.

'I am told Sapphire is very good for first-time riders. Do you think you would like to ride her?'

'Yes, please.'

'Let me help you.'

Jane moved so she was standing to the front of the pony, stroking the animal's soft nose whilst Mr Stewart crouched down and adjusted his nephew's coat to make him more comfortable.

'It will feel strange the first time you sit in the saddle. Remember to sit straight, but relax as much as possible, and do not hold the reins too tight.'

Edward nodded seriously as he absorbed the instructions.

'Someone will be holding Sapphire all the time, so there is no reason to worry about her bolting, but if you are afraid at all, you tell me.'

Lifting his nephew off the ground, Mr Stewart settled the young boy into the saddle, helping him adjust his position until he was comfortable. A wide grin spread across Edward's face and Jane felt her heart squeeze with affection. She might only have known him for a short time but the little boy had made an impression on her.

'Shall we go for a walk?'

'Yes, Zio Tom.'

Jane stayed where she was, watching uncle and nephew walk in a large circle, the little boy relaxing more with each step.

'You're a natural, Edward,' Jane said as they looped back round.

'This is wonderful.'

After another loop, Edward looked much more confident as Mr Stewart brought him to a stop.

'What do you think about going for a ride with Miss Ashworth and me?'

'Will someone be leading Sapphire?'

'Of course.'

The groom stepped forward and took hold of the leather strap Mr Stewart had been using to lead the little pony.

'Can I help you mount?'

Jane eyed the side-saddle and swallowed hard. She had ridden before, dozens of times, but only once in a side-saddle. Her parents hadn't had enough funds to own and house their own horse as Jane and her sisters had grown older, so the opportunities to ride were few and far between. The last time she had ridden side-saddle, she had fallen from the horse, but that didn't mean it would happen this time.

Mr Stewart stepped close behind her and for a moment all thoughts of being thrown from a galloping horse and breaking her neck disappeared. He boosted her up as if she weighed nothing at all, standing close until he was sure she was settled in the saddle.

He looked at ease as he mounted.

'Your injury didn't put you off riding?'

'No, I got back to riding even before I could walk properly,' he said with a grin. 'Nothing could keep me away from Rupert here.'

'Rupert?'

'I named him after a friend. Everyone ready?'

They set off at a very sedate pace and soon some of the anxiety Jane had felt when she'd first mounted subsided. The side-saddle was not the most comfortable way of riding, but she didn't feel as precarious as she had feared she would.

'We'll head down to the Serpentine and back. That will probably be enough.'

For a while they rode in silence, both Jane and Edward focusing on their horses, and Mr Stewart seemingly happy in their company.

'You can relax your grip a little. Your horse is very well behaved,' he said quietly, leaning over towards her after a few minutes.'

Jane looked down and saw her knuckles were white on the reins where she was clutching them so hard. Making a conscious effort to relax, she loosened her grip and lowered her hands a fraction.

'Do you get to ride much in Somerset?'

It was the first time Mr Stewart had asked about her life back home and she felt a sudden pang of homesickness. When Lady Mountjoy had given her the opportunity to come to London, she had quickly accepted, but with mixed feelings. She'd wanted the chance to come and find a publisher, to see if this dream of hers was ever going to be achieved, but equally she had dreaded the social events she would be forced to attend.

'Not much. We don't own a horse,' she said, wondering if he would find that strange. Mr Stewart might not be an earl or a viscount, but he was from a very wealthy and influential family who would likely have had a stable full of horses.

'Shame. I bet there are some beautiful places to ride.'

She nodded, thinking of the rolling hills behind their house, the gentle countryside always so lush and green. A lump formed in her throat and she was surprised to feel the sting of tears in her eyes.

'Is something wrong?'

Shaking her head, she sniffed and wiped away the tears.

'I never thought I'd miss home as much as I do,' she said quietly. 'Before I left, I didn't even think about it, I didn't even consider I might feel a pang of sadness when I thought of snow on the hills or the way the sun lights up the countryside as it is setting.'

'Is it your family you miss too?'

'Yes. Our house is chaos with my five younger sisters. It feels like there is never a moment of peace, never a place to think or be quiet.' She shook her head, 'I even pine for the noise and the disorder.'

'Do you have someone close to you age in amongst your sisters?'

'No. I had a brother, born two years after me, but he died of a fever when he was very young. My parents didn't think they would have any more children after that.' She closed her eyes and thought of Harriet, her twin, the person she had been closest to in the world. She wasn't quite ready to tell anyone about her yet.

'I am sorry.'

'Meredith, the next oldest, is ten, Abigail is nine, the twins Caroline and Elizabeth are seven and Sybil is three.'

Mr Stewart raised his eyebrows. 'No wonder you are so good with Edward.'

She glanced over to the young boy who was sitting happily in his saddle, every so often getting up the courage to lean forward and give the pony a hug around her neck.

'You seem more relaxed with him,' Jane said.

'I went to see a friend last night, the friend I told you about in Southwark. His wife has never been afraid of speaking her mind and I think this time some of her words actually got through.'

'What did she say?'

'She told me Edward may miss out on certain things in life but so many children have it harder. He has a warm bed to sleep in at night, food on the table and will get an education to allow him to make the most of his future.'

'You're forgetting something,' she said quietly.

'What?'

'Someone who loves him.'

With a glance at the young boy next to him, Mr Stewart nodded, and Jane saw true affection in his eyes. She had known it was there, right from the start, but it was wonderful to see this man allowing himself just to be with his nephew, to slowly build that relationship.

'He's lucky to have you.' She waited for Mr Stewart

to look at her so he could see the sincerity in her expression. 'You may not have much experience with children but you have a good heart, Mr Stewart, and that is more important than anything else.'

'I have been complimented on one or two things before,' he said, looking across at her with a spark of mischief. 'But never has anyone taken any notice of my heart.'

'More fool them,' Jane murmured.

Her eyes flicked up to meet his and for a long moment she couldn't look away. There was an intensity there like never before and she felt as though her body might catch alight. His eyes were always bright, but today they seemed even brighter, and Jane felt their hypnotic pull.

They were almost at the Serpentine and thankfully Mr Stewart had to look away so he could instruct the groom where to lead Edward's horse on the trip back. Jane took advantage of the lull in Mr Stewart's attention to spur her horse forward a few steps so she could have a minute to herself. As she did, there was a shout from a hundred feet away, and then a few seconds later a brown furry animal came dashing towards them.

It was a large dog, running at such speed it looked like a blur until it got closer. It was barking and showing no signs of slowing down.

'Hold Sapphire,' Mr Stewart said, his voice calm but with a commanding edge to it. Jane glanced back and saw the groom take hold of Sapphire's bridle and start to stroke the horse whilst murmuring soothing words. The little pony didn't seem overly fazed by the approaching animal.

Jane turned back round just in time to see the dog hadn't stopped and was now running fast towards her horse. She froze, not knowing whether to lean forward to try and comfort the animal and risk losing her precarious balance in the side-saddle or stay still and hope the dog came under control.

Out of the corner of her eye she saw Mr Stewart dismount quickly and run towards her, but it was too late. The horse panicked, taking a few quick steps backwards, and then reared up, kicking out its front legs. The dog barked even louder and then the horse bolted.

Jane tensed every muscle possible, clinging on tightly and wondering why she hadn't hit the ground yet. The cold air whipped against her face and pulled her hair loose so it was flying out behind her, streaming across her shoulders.

At first she squeezed her eyes shut, not wanting to see the world spin as she tumbled to the ground, but after a few seconds, when she realised she was somehow still in the saddle, she quickly opened them again. The world was travelling by in a blur and she wasn't even sure what direction she was going in. Every time the horse's hooves hit the grass, Jane felt a jolt travel through her body and push her a little further out of an ideal riding position. A hundred more feet and she would be holding on with her hands alone.

The horse showed no sign of slowing and she was not experienced enough to know what to do for the best. Her heart was thumping in her chest and she could even feel the pulsation in her temples.

A flash of dark brown caught her eye and she risked turning her head a fraction, regretting the move as she slipped a little more in the saddle. Tom was galloping up beside her, although she didn't know what he planned to do other than pick up her broken body once she fell from the horse. He was gaining ground and then suddenly he was beside her, picking up the reins from where she had dropped them and pressing them into her hands.

'Gentle pressure,' he shouted across at her. 'You need to show the horse you are calm and in control.'

It was hard to resist the urge to pull on the reins with all her strength, but she managed to follow the instruction, exerting a firm but steady pressure on the reins. The result was almost instant. The horse did not stop, but Jane could feel some of the panic ebbing away, and gradually the gallop became a canter and then the canter became a trot.

When the horse had slowed enough, Mr Stewart leaped from his saddle and took hold of the bridle, holding the animal steady and placing a calming hand on his neck.

'I've got him…you can come down.'

'I can't,' Jane said.

'Are you stuck?'

She nodded and Mr Stewart took a moment to look her over to try and assess what was preventing her from getting down.

'You're not tangled. You should be able to slip down.'

'I can't,' she repeated.

He started to speak again and then went still, his eyes meeting hers and understanding blossoming in them.

Jane took in a ragged breath as he stepped towards her and placed his hands on her hips.

'You're safe,' he murmured, smiling at her softly in reassurance. 'I've got you.'

Gently he lifted her down, holding her as he placed her feet on the floor, as if knowing her knees would buckle underneath her.

'You're safe,' he said again, and this time Jane felt it.

For a long moment they stood body to body with his hands on her hips and then he reached out, placed a finger on her chin and tilted her face up towards him.

Jane felt an overwhelming surge of desire and as she looked up into Mr Stewart's eyes she knew he was feeling the same. In that moment she didn't have the ability to question it. All she knew was she wanted to be kissed more than she had ever wanted anything else before.

Slowly, as if savouring the moment, Mr Stewart moved towards her and then his lips were on hers. At first he was gentle but, as Jane moaned and swayed into the kiss, he gripped her tighter and kissed her harder.

Jane felt as though her knees might give way again, but Mr Stewart's strong arm around her waist held her up, pulling her even closer. She felt the irresistible draw of his body and without thinking pressed herself against him. He groaned and tangled his free hand in her hair.

Jane never wanted this moment to end. She pushed away all rational thought, refusing to allow any thought of consequence or scandal cross her mind. Instead, for perhaps the first time in her life, she allowed herself to be ruled by her desires.

Suddenly Mr Stewart pulled away and Jane felt herself almost topple. She felt naked, empty, as if half of her had been ripped away.

For a long moment they stood face to face, just looking at one another. Jane saw the panic in his eyes, the uncertainty, the regret and all the warmth from a moment before left her. He looked horrified to have kissed her.

'I'm sorry,' he said, taking another couple of steps away, only realising he was tethered in place by the reins he was holding on to when they went taut. 'I'm sorry,' he repeated. 'I shouldn't have done that.'

She wanted to scream at him, to tell him she had been as much to blame as him, to do anything to wipe the look of horror from his face. Surely kissing her hadn't been all that bad?

He looked around, as if only just remembering they were standing in a public place, that anyone could have seen them. Jane did the same, noting thankfully that the relatively early hour meant this part of the park was deserted and no one could have witnessed their indiscretion.

'I'm sorry.'

'Stop saying you're sorry,' Jane snapped.

For a long moment he gave her an assessing look and then turned away, ostensibly to see to the horses.

Panicking now, Jane tried to stop the thoughts racing at speed through her mind and allow a little space for something rational to materialise. She knew she was so unsettled because she *wasn't* sorry. For the past couple of weeks, an undeniable attraction had been building, and after their kiss in the glass house she had craved another, wanting it more than anything else.

'We were flustered,' Jane said slowly. 'Shaken by the shock of the horse bolting. I have heard people do irrational things when emotions are heightened.'

'Always so practical,' Mr Stewart murmured. For a moment something flared in his eyes and Jane wondered if he was thinking about kissing her again.

'We should return to Edward and the servants and pretend this never happened.' It hurt her to suggest it, but she knew it was the only thing to do. Especially given Mr Stewart's reaction to kissing her. She wouldn't let him see how much his immediate regret had upset her.

'Yes, good plan.'

He took hold of both sets of reins and began leading the horses, turning back when he saw she wasn't following him.

'Are you hurt?'

'No,' Jane said, forcing herself to move.

At home, in the privacy of her room, she would take the time to understand the roiling emotions inside her, but right at this moment she needed to act as though nothing was phasing her.

Chapter Twelve

'Jane, come sit with me. I am so excited about the show tonight. I can't believe after all these months in London we are finally going to the theatre.'

Jane squeezed through the crowd and took the vacant seat next to Lucy, taking a moment to look around her. It had taken weeks of persuasion to convince Lady Mountjoy that a trip to the theatre in Islington would not tarnish their reputations. They had attended the opera many times, but at first Lady Mountjoy had been resistant to a night at the theatre, saying it just wasn't a thing well-bred young ladies did.

'Where is Mr Weyman?' Jane strained her neck to see if she could catch a glimpse of Lucy's husband, but if he was close he was hidden by the bodies of all the people present.

'He suggested we might like a drink whilst we watch the performance. I'm sure he will be back soon.'

After weeks of making plans, Lady Mountjoy had finally given in and allowed Jane to go and see a play tonight in the company of Lucy and her new husband.

'I love that as a married woman you are enough of a chaperon for me,' Jane said as she shuffled closer to her friend. 'It is so freeing to be able to be out with you and you alone.'

'It's strange, isn't it?' Lucy said, smiling broadly. 'So much has changed now that I am married. I do like the freedom of it.'

'I am pleased you find marriage freeing. You chose well, Lucy. Captain Weyman is a wonderful man and he seems to be happy to give you more trust and freedom than many men do their wives.'

'I wonder if it is because we have known each other for such a long time? I couldn't imagine him telling me what to do, even though he is quite used to ordering the men in his regiment around.'

Captain Weyman appeared through the crowd, smartly dressed for the evening, his lips set into a broad smile. It was impossible not to like him. He was affable and relaxed and never had a bad word to say about anyone. He and Lucy were so well-matched, Jane thought theirs must be the happiest marriage of the decade.

'Miss Ashworth, you are looking radiant this evening. I am delighted you could join us.'

'Thank you for inviting me. I know you are not in London for much longer and time with Lucy is precious.'

'Three more weeks,' Lucy said, suddenly looking sad. 'But I suppose this is the reality of being the wife of an army officer.'

'It will feel like no time at all, and I will be back again,' Captain Weyman said, but Jane could see there was sadness in his eyes too. 'Ah, I see Potters and Gillespie. I won't be a moment, my dear, but I had better go and say hello.'

Excusing himself, Captain Weyman sidled along past the other people sitting nearby to the two friends he had spotted, leaving Jane alone with Lucy.

'So, tell me, how are things going with the delectable Mr Stewart?'

'Stop,' Jane said, feeling a blush start to bloom on her cheeks despite her best efforts to maintain a nonchalant façade. 'There is absolutely nothing to tell because there is nothing going on with him.'

'I don't believe you. Look at how much you are blushing.'

'I'm not blushing.'

'It is no use denying it.'

Jane shook her head. 'Perhaps I should just tell you the truth,' she said slowly.

'This sounds intriguing.'

'Mr Stewart is helping me, and I him. We have made a mutually agreeable deal. I assist him with his nephew, accompany them on a few days out, provide a little advice until his nanny from the agency arrives...'

'And what do you get in return?'

Jane hesitated. Lucy knew that she drew and painted— they had shared a home for months and Jane would often cloister herself away in her room with her paintbrushes. What she had never confided to any of her friends was her ambition, her desire to see her work published, to try and make a living out of the stories she wrote and the pictures she painted to accompany them.

'Have you ever wondered why I decided to come to London?'

'Once or twice,' Lucy admitted. 'You never seemed that interested in the balls and the dinner parties and have expressed your reluctance to find a husband more than once.'

'It is not an environment I feel comfortable in. I don't have Eliza's easy charm, or your amiable nature, or Charlotte's good looks. I am not made to be a debutante.'

'Did your parents push you into it?'

Jane shook her head. 'No. Although they were delighted when I suggested I might approach Lady Mountjoy and see if she might consider me as one of her debutantes. With five younger sisters at home, I think they despair as to what might happen to us.'

'So, why then?'

'I wanted to come to London...' She looked around and then lowered her voice. 'I have a dream. Over the last few months I have been visiting publishers and printers to see if any might consider my work.'

'Your painting?' Lucy looked a little confused.

'I write stories to go with them. Children's stories.'

'Jane, that is wonderful, but how have you kept it secret all this time?'

'I didn't know if there was something worth pursuing with it but, now I have nearly exhausted all of the publishers in London and none will even give me an audience, I am close to giving up.'

'You can't give up, not if this is something you're passionate about.' Lucy shook her head vehemently. 'What I don't understand is what this has to do with Mr Stewart and your deal with him.'

'He caught me visiting one of the less desirable areas of London whilst I was searching for a publisher's shop.

He escorted me home and Lady Mountjoy now thinks there is something between us. We agreed to use that, to allow me some freedom from her match-making efforts, to give me more time to work on finding a publisher.'

'That is quite a scheme, Jane,' Lucy said, puffing out her cheeks as she sat back in her chair and considered all she had been told.

'So you see, there really is not anything between me and Mr Stewart.'

'I understand how this began,' Lucy said slowly, dropping her voice as someone came and took one of the seats directly behind them. 'But that does not mean feelings cannot develop.'

'You're as bad as Lady Mountjoy.'

'Would it truly be that terrible if you were to fall in love?'

Jane closed her eyes for a moment, remembering the way his lips had felt on hers, the soaring of her heart as their bodies had come together. In those moment she had allowed herself to wonder, but it had been a short-lived fantasy both times.

'Perhaps one day it might happen,' Jane said, wishing the play would hurry up and start. 'But Mr Stewart has a certain reputation. I am not one to believe every titbit of gossip that comes my way, but he is a very charming man, and I have no doubt he could have his choice of women.'

'You're putting yourself down again, Jane. *You* are marvellous. You are interesting and quick witted, you're funny and a joy to be around. You're talented and beautiful…' Lucy stopped as Jane scoffed.

'I am well aware of my talents and my shortcomings,' Jane said quietly. 'And I have made my peace with them.'

'You are beautiful.'

She thought of the flare of attraction in Mr Stewart's eyes, the way she had felt when she had seen desire in his expression. It was the first time in her life she had wondered if she was more than a plain young woman, the least desirable of the debutantes, the one always left to one side at the ball. She knew much of it was her perpetuating the cycle. She felt plain, so she dressed in a way not to draw attention to herself—that way she could pretend it was because she didn't want anyone to notice her. It was a way of protecting herself.

Jane shook her head. She desperately wanted to confide in Lucy about the kisses, but she hadn't been able to get the sequence of events straight in her own mind, let alone work out what any of it meant. Every time she thought of it, she felt something stir deep within her, a desire to be back in that moment, to enjoy again and again the kisses they had shared. Her only kisses. Then she thought of Mr Stewart's reaction after the kiss in the park and she felt a deep embarrassment, as though she had somehow got everything so wrong. How could she crave another kiss when he seemed so aghast about the last?

Thankfully the hum of chatter in the theatre started to settle, the last few members of the audience took their seats and the curtain at the front of the stage began to move.

'We will continue this conversation later,' Lucy whispered as she settled back into her chair, smiling over at her husband as he reappeared.

The play was entertaining and had Jane laughing out loud through much of it. This was one thing she loved about her stay in London—getting to experience things she otherwise wouldn't have in her sleepy Somerset village.

'That was *exactly* what I needed,' Jane said as the actors and actresses came out onto the stage to take a bow to a rousing round of applause. For two blissful hours she hadn't thought about anything but what she was watching. It had been wonderful not to obsess about the kiss, not to worry about the next time she saw Mr Stewart, not even to feel down about her dwindling chances of getting her children's stories published.

'It was entertaining, wasn't it?' Lucy said, smiling back.

'Shall we let a few people leave so we're not in the press of the crowd?' Captain Weyman suggested. They remained in their seats for a few minutes as some of the audience slowly drifted away, standing once the auditorium was half-empty.

As they made their way out of the theatre, Jane looped her arm through Lucy's.

'Thank you,' she said, leaning her head in to speak to her friend.

'You're welcome. It has been a lovely evening.'

Jane was about to say more when she glanced up and felt her whole body stiffen. Ahead of them, walking directly towards them, was Mr Stewart. He noticed her a second or two later and Jane could see the surprise on his face. No doubt he thought himself safe from bumping into her here, in his world. The theatre wasn't a hotbed of scandal, but the audience was mainly made up of smartly dressed middle class people, not the small group of the wealthy and titled that made up the *ton*.

Jane's eyes flicked to his and she saw a flare of panic before he quickly recovered his composure. On his arm was a beautiful young woman with striking red hair and deep-blue eyes. She was dressed in a flowing emerald-green dress that fitted her body perfectly, showing off every curve without offending the more conservative of theatregoers.

She hated the flare of jealousy she felt as she saw how this woman turned to Mr Stewart with a question in her eyes, placing a hand on his arm as if to claim him. At the same time, Jane caught a glimpse of the shapeless lilac dress she had chosen for the occasion, choosing comfort over style when she had dressed a few hours earlier.

'Mr Stewart,' Lucy said, filling the silence that stretched out. 'How wonderful to see you again.'

'And you, Mrs Weyman, you look well.'

'May I introduce my husband, Captain Weyman?' Lucy waited as the two men stepped forward. 'William, this is Mr Stewart, a friend of Jane's.'

'A pleasure.'

There was a pause as they all looked expectantly at Mr Stewart, waiting for him to introduce his companion.

'This is Mrs Catherine Burghley,' he said eventually. The young woman glanced at Mr Stewart, as if surprised at his reluctance to introduce her, and then cast a brilliant smile over the group.

'How lovely to meet some friends of Mr Stewart's. Did you enjoy the play?'

'It was fantastic,' Lucy said after a moment when it became apparent Jane wasn't going to answer.

Jane felt as though her tongue had become stuck to the roof of her mouth. She couldn't tear her eyes away from the intimate way Mrs Burghley stood with her hand resting on Mr Stewart's arm. Inside was a bubbling mix of jealousy she had no right to feel and shame at allowing herself to succumb to such an ugly emotion. Mr Stewart had never promised her anything. On the contrary, he had been very open about the sort company he preferred. Never had he denied his reputation as a rake. Never had he pretended his life was about much more than seeking out pleasure.

For a moment Jane closed her eyes. This shouldn't even be an issue. She and Mr Stewart were at most friends—friends who had shared two incredible kisses, but friends all the same.

She tried to give a friendly smile, but as Mrs Burghley recoiled she realised it had been more like a grimace.

'I'm a little warm,' she managed to mutter. 'Lovely to meet you, Mrs Burghley. I think I'll meet you outside, Lucy.'

Without waiting for a response, she turned and fled, darting through the groups of people still lingering in the foyer of the theatre.

As soon as she had taken her first few steps, she knew she was heading in the wrong direction. The main entrance was back the way she had come, back past Lucy and her husband, back past Mr Stewart and the stunning Mrs Burghley. In her haste to get away from everyone, she had chosen the wrong way, and now she was striding through the narrowing corridor towards areas where the public wasn't allowed.

'Miss Ashworth.' Mr Stewart's familiar voice came from behind her, close enough for her to know he had followed her. 'Miss Ashworth, stop.'

Determined not to obey, she pushed through the doors to the backstage area, surprised by the darkness. There were a few steps leading down to a narrow corridor which looked as though it ran the depth of the stage before turning abruptly at the end. There were voices in the distance, but no one visible. Jane hesitated, and at that moment Mr Stewart pushed through the doors behind her and caught hold of her wrist.

'Jane,' he said, his voice dropping now he had her to himself. It was the first time he had called her anything other than 'Miss Ashworth', and Jane felt a shiver of longing course through her body. She frowned to hide it, wishing her subconscious would behave itself.

'You followed me.'

'You looked upset.'

She shook her head, wondering exactly what she was going to say to make him believe she hadn't been fleeing from the sight of a beautiful young woman and him arm-in-arm.

'I'm not upset.' She found it best to be brief, abrupt even, in this sort of circumstance. Silently she grimaced, realising how ridiculous her thoughts were; she had never been in a situation even vaguely similar before in her life.

For a long moment neither of them spoke. She felt his eyes on her, searching her face, but she refused to look up. She was afraid if she did he might see something in her eyes, something to confirm what he was thinking.

'We never discussed our kiss,' he said after a minute. His voice seemed loud in the darkened corridor, echoing off the empty walls.

'Which one?'

'Either. Both. We need to talk about them.'

'Don't shout about it.'

'There's no one here, Jane.' There it was again, his use of her first name and the illusion of closeness it summoned.

'Someone could burst through those doors at any moment.'

'Fine,' he said, lowering his voice to a theatrical whisper. 'We never discussed our kisses.'

'What is there to discuss?'

He cleared his throat, looking uncomfortable.

'I didn't know if you were upset tonight because you saw me with another woman...' He trailed off.

Doing her best to channel the new Mrs Farthington, the haughtiest woman she knew, she raised an imperious eyebrow.

Mr Stewart was a hard man to unsettle, and he looked back at her with a raised eyebrow of his own.

'You thought I would be upset to see you with another woman, even though we agreed it was a silly mistake, nothing to ever be repeated.'

'We did agree that.'

'Yet you think I am not capable of moving on, of accepting it meant nothing?'

'I just thought...'

Jane held up a hand, hating how cold her voice

sounded but knowing she could not let him see how un-settled she really was. She didn't want to feel this way. She didn't want to have a longing to reach out, wrap her arms around his neck and kiss him until she was ruined, but it wasn't something under voluntary control.

'The kisses we shared,' she said, hoping she could maintain her composure as she spoke, 'Were perfectly pleasant, but they were both at moments of high drama. People do reckless things when they have been in dan-ger, and that was all there was to it.'

'Perfectly pleasant,' he murmured, frowning, as if no one had described his kiss as 'perfectly pleasant' before.

'We had an agreement, Mr Stewart,' Jane said, press-ing on. 'I promised you I would tell you if I started to fall for your charm.'

He nodded, his eyes all the while searching hers.

'I do not break promises lightly, and I have no qualms in telling you that I do not have feelings for you, past perhaps the developing of an unlikely friendship.' She looked at him directly now, willing herself to stay strong. 'I like you, Mr Stewart, more than I ever thought I would, but my regard for you stops there. There is no ulterior motive in wanting to spend time with you. I have no desire to ensnare you into marriage.'

The silence stretched out between them before fi-nally Mr Stewart nodded, satisfied. 'I like you too, Jane.' He said it so softly, so gently, that all of her re-solve was almost dashed in those five little words. She felt her heart squeeze in her chest at the prospect of what could be before she could harden it. Mr Stewart might have kissed her, but his reaction immediately after, and his presence at the theatre with a stunning young lady, showed her there was no chance of anything more be-tween them.

For her own self-preservation, she needed him to be-lieve she was as uninterested as he was. Shaking her head, she told herself again she *wasn't* interested. Mr Stewart had no place in her life's plans. She wanted nei-ther a husband nor a lover. For so long she had strived for something more, something she could call her own. She wanted to achieve something more than getting married and pushing out babies every year or two for the next twenty years.

'I'm sorry,' he said, waiting for her to look up again. When she didn't, he stepped forward, placed a finger under her chin and tilted it ever so gently. Jane felt as though everything around the faded away and it was just the two of them suspended in the darkness together.

She swallowed, wondering if he could hear the pounding of her heart, and cursing how her body was betraying her after she had given such a convincing speech.

'I'm sorry,' he said again. 'I shouldn't have doubted you.'

He paused and for a moment Jane thought he was going to kiss her again.

'Will you grant me a favour?'

She nodded, her chest feeling as though it were being squeezed from the inside out.

'Call me Tom. I hate the formalities of society.'

'Tom,' she said softly.

'Good. We should get back before anyone finds us here. Then we really would be in trouble.'

They both moved at the same time, her body crashing into his, and as he reached out to steady her his hand brushed against her breast. Jane inhaled sharply and looked up into his eyes, wondering if she imagined the flash of intense longing before he quickly turned away.

Chapter Thirteen

'Captain Weyman and Mrs Weyman have been kind enough to invite us for drinks,' Mrs Burghley said as Tom strolled back into the rapidly emptying foyer of the theatre.

He felt his heart sink a little. This evening had not gone to plan. Mrs Burghley had been introduced by a mutual friend and he couldn't deny she was beautiful and superficially charming. Tom had been cajoled into inviting her to the theatre as a favour to this friend, who had told him she was in need of company after being dropped by the group with whom she used to socialise after her late husband's money had started to run low. From the hints she had been dropping all evening, she was looking for a protector, a man to swoop in and save her from the precarious position she was in.

Normally he would have given the widow more of a chance, but today everything she did seemed to grate on him. Even her laugh had annoyed him, and he had quickly stopped the wandering fingers she had placed on his leg as everyone's attention had been directed towards the stage at the start of the play. He wanted to go home to bed and forget about Mrs Burghley.

Glancing at Jane, he felt that same thrum he had every time he looked at her now. He didn't want to admit this was one of the reasons he had found Mrs Burghley's company so trying this evening, but he knew his mind was distracted by Jane.

At this moment, she was trying her hardest to be inconspicuous, as he had seen her do many times before. Even so, he couldn't rid himself of the memory of their kisses. He found himself thinking about it at inappropriate moments, then having to spend time and energy chastising himself for making such a big deal out of it.

He had kissed dozens of women in his life. There was no reason for him suddenly to obsess over these two kisses with a perfectly ordinary woman.

He grimaced, admitting to himself that Jane was not perfectly ordinary. Perhaps that was the reason he was dwelling so much on the kiss; he had allowed himself to like her, to think of her as a friend, before he had kissed her. Normally he didn't let the women with whom he conducted his liaisons to get too close, showing them only his superficial self. Jane had crept under his defences, becoming his friend.

'Enough,' he murmured to himself. She had assured him that to her it was nothing more than a mistake. He needed to forget their kisses too. 'That is very generous of you. I would not wish to impose.'

'Nonsense,' Mrs Weyman said, her eyes sparkling. 'The evening is young and it would be our pleasure to entertain you.'

'Thank you.'

'I'm sure we can squeeze into our carriage,' Mrs Weyman said, motioning to a carriage as they left the theatre. 'It'll be a little tight, but it is not far.'

'A little tight' was an optimistic way of putting it and for a moment, as he climbed into the carriage, he doubted whether they would all fit. It required a great deal of shuffling until they did, and when they finally lurched forward as the carriage departed Tom was sitting squeezed in the middle of one seat with Mrs Burghley to his left and Jane on his right.

'This is fun,' Jane murmured in that dry way of hers.

He had to suppress a smile but didn't dare move to see her expression lest he upset their precarious balance.

Thankfully the journey was short, as promised by the Weymans, and in five minutes the carriage slowed. It took a little manoeuvring to get everyone out but finally they were all standing in front of a smart house with black metal railings outside.

'Oh, how pretty,' Mrs Burghley said. 'I used to live not too far away, and I've often walked past these houses and thought how well positioned they are, overlooking the park.'

'It isn't big,' Mrs Weyman said with a contented expression on her face. 'But for now it is a very pleasant home. We're renting it for a few more weeks until my husband gets his orders.'

Inside, the Weymans led the way into a comfortable drawing room and a maid bustled around, ensuring the fire was well stoked and drinks poured. Captain and Mrs Weyman excused themselves for a moment, leaving their guests to make small talk in their absence.

'Tell me, how do you know each other?' Mrs Burghley

asked, her eyes flicking between Jane and Tom, seated on opposite sides of a low table.

For a moment he thought about saying something shocking and provoking. Perhaps that Jane had punched him in an alley in Southwark and their friendship had blossomed from then.

'Oh, you know,' Jane said with a dismissive flick of the hand. 'The usual mutual friends, attending the same social events.'

'I thought you said you didn't attend many events of the *ton*.' She turned to him with confusion in her eyes.

'I don't. I met Miss Ashworth at one of the few I do attend.'

'I would wager Mr Stewart is a fine dancer. Am I right, Miss Ashworth?'

'Alas, I am not the right person to ask. I stumble at even the easiest of dances,' Jane said. He remembered the waltz they had shared, that wonderful feeling of gliding around the ballroom together. 'He is very much in demand on the dance floor, though, so I think you are right. How do you know each other?'

Mrs Burghley shifted a little closer to Tom. He was powerless to move away, pressed up against the arm of the sofa.

'We were introduced by a friend,' the widow said, looking up at him with a seductive smile. 'They thought we would enjoy one another's company.'

'Mrs Burghley, I wonder if I could have your opinion in the dining room?' Mrs Weyman said as she bustled back into the room. 'Your dress is exquisite and I have a few samples of fabric I am struggling to choose between. Perhaps you might be able to help me.'

Tom and Jane watched as Mrs Burghley left the room, throwing him a glance filled with both regret and promise as she exited.

'Fabric?'

Jane snorted. 'Lucy normally is more subtle than this.'

'What does she have to be subtle about?'

Jane gestured at the space between the two of them. 'No doubt she is hoping to return to us cinched in a passionate embrace.'

'She knows?' He hadn't meant to exclaim in such horror.

'Of course she doesn't know we kissed,' Jane snapped. 'I'm not an idiot.'

'What *does* she know?'

Jane looked at him without speaking for thirty seconds then must have decided to put his mind at ease.

'She is aware of our little arrangement.'

'Fine,' he said slowly, nodding his head. 'That's not disastrous.'

'But she is under the impression that our agreement does not preclude us developing feelings for one another.' She sighed and slumped back in her chair. 'I do wish you weren't so damn attractive.'

This made him smile. He loved how she spoke her mind, often the words flowing out before she had a chance to consider the impact of them.

'It is a burden I have to bear,' he murmured.

Her head snapped up. 'I'm not saying *I* find you attractive,' she said quickly. 'Just that objectively you are attractive, and that means everyone thinks I must be falling for you.'

'Objectively I am attractive,' he mused, trying his hardest to look puzzled rather than amused. 'So does that mean you do find me attractive or you don't?'

Jane opened her mouth to speak and then pressed her lips together so hard, they turned white.

'We don't need to have this conversation.'

'I think we do,' he said, unable to stop the grin spreading across his face.

'Stop it.'

'Stop what?'

'Looking so pleased with yourself.' She let out a long-suffering sigh and gave a dismissive wave. 'It is how people describe you. You are Mr Stewart, the charming and handsome bachelor who has no plans to settle down.'

'Is that what people say about me?'

'Yes. As if someone can be summed up in a mere sentence.'

'What do they say about you?'

She pulled a face and shook her head. 'I don't know. Probably something along the lines of Miss Ashworth, the dull and plain debutante who has no interest in society.'

'Don't be ridiculous.'

'I'm not. Society likes to put people in their boxes. I am an unattractive woman destined to be a spinster.'

'You are not.'

'I don't have any plans to marry.'

He waved a dismissive hand. 'You're not unattractive. You're not even plain.'

A hand flitted to her hair, where she had it pulled back into a tight bun.

'You may try to look plain, so you can fade into the background,' he said quietly. 'But you do not succeed.'

She scoffed and he saw the disbelief in her eyes.

'You believe it, don't you?' he said, realising now that she didn't choose the unflattering dresses and hairstyles solely to remain unnoticed. 'You believe that you're not beautiful.'

'No one, ever, has thought I am beautiful,' she said, her chin jutting out in defiance.

'That's why you do it, why you choose clothes that don't fit that well and have your hair in such a severe style.'

'Enlighten me,' she said softly. 'Seeing as you are suddenly the expert on my innermost feelings.'

'You truly believe you are plain, and you think if you made an effort it would show you care. It is about preservation, at not having to listen to anyone laugh because you tried to be more than you think people expect.'

She shrugged but Tom could see he had got to the core of it.

Knowing he should stay in his seat, he stood, hating how Jane had wrapped her arms across her chest protectively. With a glance at the door, he came and crouched down in front of her, taking both her hands in his own.

'You're beautiful, Jane Ashworth.'

At first she wouldn't meet his eye. Instead she shook her head and kept looking down at her lap.

'Look at me.' He waited, the seconds stretching out until finally she lifted her head a fraction and looked him in the eye. 'You are beautiful.'

'No. I'm the plain one, the clever one, the dull one.'

He frowned, wondering who it was she was comparing herself to.

'You are clever, I am not denying that, but you are so much more than those three words. You are witty and sharp, you are kind and generous, you are beautiful… and you are a hundred more things.'

Knowing he was on dangerous ground, he reached up and trailed a finger down her cheek. It was intimate, far too intimate, for a couple who only an hour earlier had agreed there was nothing in the kiss they'd shared, but he did it all the same.

Jane took a sharp breath and he saw her eyes darken as she looked at him.

'Beauty is not just about the thickness of a woman's hair or the clarity of her skin, it is about so much more,' he said softly. 'But, even if it were based purely on the physical, you are an attractive woman, Jane, even when you try so hard not to be.'

For a long moment she looked into his eyes and he felt as though he might be getting through, then she gave a violent shake of her head and stood abruptly, almost knocking him over, fleeing from the room out, of the glass doors into the garden beyond.

Tom stood, debating whether to follow her. It was a cold night, but he doubted the Weymans' garden was large, and she could return whenever she wanted. She would probably tell him she wanted solitude, but he couldn't bring himself to leave her out there alone, believing the lies her own mind told her.

With a cursory glance at the door to the hall, he satisfied himself no one was returning to the drawing room yet, and dashed out into the garden to follow Jane.

It took him a few seconds to adjust to the moonlight, but after a moment he saw Jane's figure in the corner of the little garden.

'Go back inside,' she said as he came and touched her gently on the arm. Already her skin was cool to touch, and he quickly shrugged off his jacket to drape around her shoulders.

'No.'

'If we're found out here together…' She trailed off, leaving the consequences to his imagination.

'All the more reason for you to tell me what has upset you and how we can fix it.'

She shook her head.

'Who were you comparing yourself to, Jane?' he asked, watching as her eyes flicked up in surprise at the question. 'When you said you were the clever one, the plain one, the dull one?'

'It doesn't matter.'

He reached out and ever so gently took her hand, hearing her sharp intake of breath. A spark passed between them, setting his skin on fire, and Tom desperately tried to ignore it. Nothing good could come out of this attraction he was feeling, and he had resolved to think of Jane as a friend. If one of his other friends were having a crisis of confidence like this, he would calmly but firmly help them through it.

'It's my sister,' Jane blurted out, her eyes darting up to meet his. 'Harriet.'

'Harriet?'

'I didn't mention her before. She was my twin. She died a few years ago. I find it difficult to talk about her.'

'I'm sorry. It must be difficult to lose someone so close.'

'She was beautiful with such a gentle temperament.'

Tom stayed quiet, allowing Jane to talk now she had started to open up.

'Everyone would joke she had stolen all the gifts when we were in the womb. She was beautiful whilst I was plain. She was kind whilst I was spiky...'

Slowly he began to see what this would have done to a little girl, raised to think she was not convention- ally attractive or worthy.

'I didn't mind,' Jane said in a voice that hinted she had minded, at least when she'd been young. 'I deter- mined I would play to my talents. Beauty might be the most treasured attribute in a young woman, but I would not dwell on the fact I had not been blessed. Instead I would look for another way to make those around me proud.'

'Was it your parents who made you feel second best?' Tom felt a sudden flare of anger that anyone could do this to a young child.

'Not directly. No one was ever cruel to me, no one came out and told me I was ugly or lacked charm.' She shrugged and Tom squeezed her hand. 'It was more sub- tle than that. People from the village would stop and make a fuss over Harriet and say how lovely she was, then they would turn to me and purse their lips, and ask me if I was a good girl and helped my parents as I should.' Jane pulled away, shaking herself a little, as if ashamed to have indulged in so much self-pity. 'I should be thankful, really. It made me realise when I was young the conventional path of marrying a man who could provide for me might not be open to me.'

'So you started to explore your other talents.'

'Yes, my writing and my painting.'

'I think I understand,' Tom said, choosing his next words carefully. 'It is all nonsense, of course, but I understand.'

'Nonsense?'

'I did not know your sister, so I cannot comment on her appearance, but I do know you. Shall I tell you what I see when I look at you?' Tom didn't wait for her to answer before pressing on. 'I see a perfectly shaped face with striking high cheekbones and gently arched brows. I see full, rosy lips and eyes that are deep and intelligent. I see thick, shiny hair, even when it is pulled back into the most severe of buns. I see you.'

For a moment he thought she was going to launch herself at him, fling her body into his arms and take advantage of the darkness.

'It is kind of you to say,' she said eventually, her voice even and under control. 'And I dare say it is true that beauty is subjective—although I am sure, if you were to be completely truthful, you would choose a woman who looked like Mrs Burghley over a woman who looked like me every time.'

Tom couldn't deny that normally the women with whom he conducted his affairs did often have certain physical attributes in common, but he was acutely aware of the attraction he felt towards Jane.

He stepped forward and took her into his arms, looking into her eyes before he lowered his lips to hers. He kissed her gently, tasting the sweetness of her lips and enjoying the way she melted into him after a few seconds. Pushing away all the self-recrimination, the voice that told him this was beyond foolish, he kissed her, loving the way she pressed her fingers into his back, not caring in that instant if they were found.

In his rational mind he knew this was reckless, needlessly so. He didn't want to marry Jane, he didn't want to marry anyone, yet here he was kissing a young woman who would be ruined if they were found. All of this he knew. He'd told himself again and again.

Normally he didn't have a problem with keeping his impulses under control. He might dart through life in search of the next pleasure, but he did it mindfully, never dallying with anyone who wasn't as free and enthusiastic as himself. Yet here was Jane, the young woman no one seemed to take any notice of, and he couldn't keep his hands off her.

'What are you doing?' Mrs Burghley's voice rang out clear and loud through the darkness. 'You're kissing *her*?'

They sprang apart, Jane knocking into the wall behind her and bouncing back off again into Tom's arms. Carefully he set her right and then stepped away, trying to form a useful thought instead of the pure panic that was threatening to consume him.

'Mrs Burghley…' Jane started to say, but was interrupted by the widow.

'I am not talking to you. I am talking to Mr Stewart.'

He saw Jane recoil and knew it would take a lot for her to hold her tongue.

'What is happening?' Mrs Weyman said as she stepped out from the drawing room. He watched as her eyes roamed over their positions in the garden before widening in surprise.

'Why did you invite me tonight?' Mrs Burghley asked, taking a few steps towards Tom in the darkness. He didn't answer immediately, knowing his future was now in this woman's hands. He doubted Mrs Weyman or her husband would do anything that might tarnish Jane's reputation, but he barely knew Mrs Burghley, and couldn't rely on her discretion.

'Lord and Lady Otterby thought we might enjoy one another's company,' he said, taking a few slow steps towards the widow. 'And I thought we would both enjoy a night at the theatre.'

'Then what is this?' She gestured at the Jane and him, a look of disbelief still on her face.

'Shall we all go inside?' Mrs Weyman said, clutching her husband's hand as he stepped out of the drawing room. 'It is a very late and I am sure some of our neighbours are asleep.'

'You invite *me* to the theatre, set up hopes there may be something between us, and then kiss *her* in the darkness?'

'He kissed you?' Mrs Weyman sounded shocked, a hand flying to her mouth.

Tom felt as though his head was spinning and about to explode from his shoulders. He had the urge to run, to push through the Weymans and Mrs Burghley and flee into the night. Every muscle in his body was tensed, preparing to flee, and then he caught sight of Jane's panicked face, her eyes darting everywhere. As much as he didn't want to be forced to marry her, she didn't want to marry him either.

'Perhaps we can all go inside and sort this out,' he said, hoping the uncertainty in his voice was audible only to his own ears.

'Forget it,' Mrs Burghley said, spinning on her heel and pushing past the Weymans. 'Goodbye, Mr Stewart.' Her words sounded ominous, like a threat, and he heard Jane gasp from behind him.

The front door slammed and for a long moment no one moved.

'I think we'd better go inside,' Captain Weyman said eventually, ushering his wife in ahead of him. Tom waited for Jane, but as she moved past him she wouldn't meet his eye.

'Sit down,' Mrs Weyman instructed gently. Tom sat on one side of the room, Jane on the other, and he was glad when the Captain placed a generous glass of whisky in his hand. 'Now, tell me everything and we will see if we can work this out.'

'What am I doing here?' he murmured and leaped to his feet, throwing back the glass of whisky. 'I will go after Mrs Burghley,' he said, addressing Jane. 'I will ensure she sees sense.'

Before anyone could voice a word of protest, he was out the door, following in Mrs Burghley's footsteps from just a few minutes earlier. With luck he might catch up with her. She would be on foot for at least the first part of her journey, until she found a carriage for hire to take her home.

It was imperative he caught her and implored her to keep what she had seen to herself. Otherwise the repercussions did not bear thinking about. Either Jane would be ruined or he would have to marry her.

Chapter Fourteen

'Calm down,' Lucy instructed, rubbing Jane's back. 'It's not worth your tears.'

Jane sniffed, trying to regain her composure. Very soon she would have to return to Lady Mountjoy's and face the questions of the older woman, enquiring how her evening had been. Any hint of redness around her eyes and Lady Mountjoy would spot it and soon prise the story out of her.

'It's late,' Jane said, glancing at the clock on the mantelpiece for the hundredth time. 'Why isn't he back yet?'

'There are a hundred reasons,' Lucy said soothingly.

'He's run away.'

'No, I'm sure that's not true.'

'Perhaps he is on board a boat to France as we speak. Better to flee the country than be saddled with a dull spinster for a wife.'

'Oh, Jane. You care for him, don't you?'

'No. Not one bit.'

It was clear from Lucy's expression she didn't believe her, but thankfully she dropped that line of questioning.

'What happened in the garden?'

Jane buried her head in her hands, trying to work out the chain of events that had led to them kissing again.

'I was unsettled,' she said slowly. 'I made an offhand comment about being a plain spinster and Tom... Mr Stewart...told me I was beautiful.'

'Was he trying to seduce you?'

'No.' She shook her head slowly. 'He's not like that.'

'He does have a certain reputation, Jane.'

'Not with debutantes.'

Lucy considered for a moment and then seemed satisfied. 'Do you love him?'

'No,' she said a little too quickly. 'No, it was a mistake, a collision of bodies in the darkness. In any other circumstance, nothing would have happened.'

Lucy fell silent and Jane considered her own words. She had been trying hard not to think about anything but the possible consequences. Grave as they were, they didn't scare her anywhere near as much as the feeling she got when she allowed herself to relive their kiss. She had felt as though she were finally alive, finally allowing that spark of joy to run free within herself. It was frightening, and she knew she had to push the feelings away.

'We need to get you home,' Lucy said decisively. 'Act like nothing untoward has happened.'

'You don't think he is coming back?'

'It is almost midnight. Maybe he thought it better to discuss things in the morning.'

Lucy was right, he wasn't coming back. Perhaps he would send a note in the morning, perhaps he wouldn't. She didn't think he would abandon her to face the gossip alone, but how well did she really know him?

'Yes,' she said wearily. 'I shall go home.'

Going off to find her husband to accompany them on the short walk back to Lady Mountjoy's house, Lucy pulled the door closed behind her, giving Jane a few minutes of much-needed privacy. She slumped back in her chair, allowing her mind to wander, to remember the heat of their kiss. She hated that her subconscious mind was still yearning for Tom, that the rebellious part of her wasn't scared or nervous, but hopeful that this could be the beginning of something wonderful.

'He doesn't want this,' Jane whispered to herself. 'And you don't want him like this.'

None of this had been planned. She didn't think he had ever set out to seduce her, just as she hadn't expected to feel an attraction to the Season's most notorious rake.

With a burst of resolve, she checked her reflection in the small mirror hanging over the mantelpiece. Carefully she smoothed her hair, glad of its simple style which allowed her to fix the stray strands of hair easily. Her eyes looked a little red but hopefully the cold air on the walk back would make her cheeks flush too and she could blame the chill breeze.

'Come on,' Lucy said, re-entering the room with Jane's coat draped over her arm. 'Let's get you home and you can have a good rest. Things will seem better in the morning.'

Jane buried her head under the covers as the maid bustled across the room, lighting the fire for the new day. She hadn't slept at all, tossing and turning through the night with her mind whirring with all the possible consequences of the night before. This morning she was no closer to having things worked out and her head was pounding. She hated that her fate was in another person's hands—really all she could do was wait to see what Mrs Burghley decided to do.

The maid finished with the fire and quietly left the room, and Jane considered pleading illness and hiding from the world in bed all day. Quickly she dismissed the idea. The last thing she needed was more time to worry about what the future would hold.

Instead she rose, pulling on her dressing gown to ward against the chill in the bedroom, and crossing to the desk to take out some papers. She was working on a story about three little field mice trying to outwit an owl, but couldn't quite get the owl's eyes right in the pictures she was creating to accompany it. For a while she sketched, trying one thing after another, enjoying the simplicity of her task, which forced her to concentrate but did not need her to be well rested or overly alert.

After about half an hour she sat back in her chair, satisfied. She had changed the shape of the owl's eyes and added some tiny tufts of fluffy feathers. Later she might try adding some colour to the picture with her paints, but at this moment it was a big improvement on what she had managed before.

There was a soft knock on her door and then Lady Mountjoy poked her head in.

'You're awake. I wasn't sure if you would be after your late night.'

'I'm awake,' Jane said, tidying up her papers and stashing them in a drawer.

'Have you looked out of your window?'

Jane shook her head then moved to the window, pulling back the curtains.

Outside the street was buried under a thick layer of snow and delicate snowflakes were still falling from the sky.

'That's fallen quickly,' Jane said, surprised. It had been after midnight when she had walked home with Lucy and Captain Weyman and although it had been overcast there hadn't been any hint of snow. Lord Mountjoy had been predicting more snowfall for weeks despite the colder months supposedly being over and she knew he would be pleased his predictions had come true.

'I do love the snow,' Lady Mountjoy said, coming in and perching on the cushions of the window seat. 'Years ago, Lord Mountjoy and I considered spending a prolonged period abroad. One of the things that made us decide to stay in England was the way the countryside looked in the snow.'

'A snowy day in London is a little different, I suppose,' Jane said. They'd had some snow a month or so earlier, a few days where the rivers had frozen over and the streets had been treacherous in the ice. At the time Jane had been focussed on finishing the book she'd been working on and had ventured out only once or twice.

'It does not hold a patch on Somerset in the winter,' Lady Mountjoy said with a smile. 'But London does have charms of its own. Perhaps Mr Stewart might take you to experience some of them.'

Jane looked up sharply, knowing Lady Mountjoy was not aware of anything that had gone on the night before, but feeling her cheeks burn all the same.

'I expect he will be busy with Edward.'

'Of course, it will probably be Edward's first time in the snow.'

Jane nodded, trying to ignore the ache inside that made her yearn to be there with them. This was an unacceptable feeling. Pure desire, physical attraction, she could dismiss as something primal and subconscious, something she was not in control of. Admitting that there was anything more than the physical was far too perilous. She shouldn't even have had a flash of an image of Tom, little Edward and her cocooned together as a happy family.

'You could offer to accompany them on whatever outing they decide,' Lady Mountjoy said, trying to look nonchalant.

'I wouldn't want to impose.'

'I doubt it would be an imposition. Mr Stewart seems to enjoy your company.' Lady Mountjoy paused, as if considering whether to say any more. 'You mustn't fear his reputation, Miss Ashworth. Mr Stewart is a good man, one of the best, despite the awful example his father set for him.'

Jane knew she shouldn't pry, knew that if it was something Tom wished her to know he would have divulged it himself, but she was intrigued by Tom's past, by his background.

'Was his father that terrible, then?'

'He's always kept the details close to his chest, but the Stewarts are an incredibly wealthy family,' Lady Mountjoy said, gazing out of the window. 'Yet at the first opportunity Rebecca Stewart elopes and is never heard from again and Thomas Stewart joins the army. He's the only son, in a family richer than most of the titled aristocracy, yet he goes and risks his life unnecessarily.'

'I can't imagine wanting to get away so badly.'

'No,' Lady Mountjoy agreed. 'Even when Mr Stewart was injured his father visited only once, I am told.'

'No wonder he isn't keen to tread the traditional path of marriage and family.' Jane's eyes widened as she realised what she had just said. Lady Mountjoy was an astute woman; it would only take one slip for their whole deception to come crashing down.

Trying not to overreact, Jane threw a cautious glance at the countess and gave a silent groan as she saw the quizzical look on the older woman's face.

'Has he told you that?'

Jane shook her head. 'No, but it is what everyone says about him. They tell me he is a rake, a man who does not care for the niceties of polite society, yet he is still accepted into the ballrooms and dinner parties with open arms. He is forgiven his sins because of his charm and his easy smile.'

'And what do you think?'

'He's not a rake,' Jane said thoughtfully. 'Not in the traditional sense. He knows what he enjoys, and allows himself to indulge in that enjoyment, but never if it would hurt someone. The sins that people whisper about, they aren't real, that is why he is so easily forgiven. There is no one he has wronged, no one to hold a grudge.'

'I think that is a very astute observation, Miss Ashworth. You obviously know him well.'

Jane thought of the way their bodies had swayed together in the darkness, the softness of his lips on hers.

'I know him a little, but what I do know I like.'

'And I can tell he likes you,' Lady Mountjoy said.

Looking away, Jane tried to stop the tears forming in her eyes. She knew he did like her. She could tell it by how easy they were in each other's company. They could talk for hours, debate the issues that interested them, speak more gently about personal matters. She also knew that he desired her from the flare of passion in his eyes, the firm way he had grasped her and the pure hunger in his kiss. Even though she couldn't quite understand it, she knew it was true.

He might like her, might even desire her, but Jane knew it wasn't enough. From the very start he had made his priorities clear, and a few fumbled kisses he probably already regretted would not change that.

'I do not know the intricacies of your family's situation,' Lady Mountjoy said slowly. 'But I am aware you are the eldest of six girls and there are likely some hopes you will make a match. You may not be searching for a wealthy husband, Miss Ashworth, but perhaps you are searching for a good man. Do not discount Mr Stewart because he happens to be wealthy. One does not preclude the other.'

Lady Mountjoy stood and crossed the room, pausing by the door. She motioned at the small desk in which Jane had secreted her pictures and writing. 'Some places of business may end up closing early if the snow really becomes a difficulty. Maybe you can take one day to enjoy the company of a man you admire.'

Jane blinked, unable to do anything but look open-mouthed after the countess as she left the room. Although she knew Lady Mountjoy was sharp, with friends everywhere, she had been convinced her search for a publisher had gone unnoticed. She had shared so much of her life with Lucy and the other debutantes over the past few months yet even they had been unaware of her secret mission.

If Lady Mountjoy knew… Jane shook her head, unable to comprehend the enormity of her realisation. These last few months, she had truly believed no one had known her secret, and here was Lady Mountjoy announcing calmly that she was aware of Jane's ambition.

Pulling out the drawer, she looked at the bundle of papers, and then carefully took them out of their dark hiding place and set them carefully on the desk. Maybe it was time to stop sneaking around. She lovingly ran a hand over the topmost of the papers, scrutinising the picture with an artist's eye.

She had received her first box of watercolour paints when she'd been eight years old and at first not paid them much attention. Only after she and Harriett had both been sick in bed with measles had she taken them out, eager for anything to assuage her boredom. Jane had found she was talented, able to study something and quickly create its likeness, and from there her love of painting and drawing had been born.

For once she had been the one receiving praise. Harriet had found the intricacies of creating something beautiful with the paints too laborious and had quickly given up. It meant, for the first time in her life, Jane had emerged from the shadows and in this one thing had outshone her beautiful and graceful sister. She didn't like to admit that had been one of the main reasons she would take out the paints at first, but as the months had gone by the satisfaction she'd got from creating something from nothing had been motivation enough.

The stories she wrote to accompany the pictures had come later, but her first love had been drawing and painting to create the pictures that now made the stories come alive. With a nod of satisfaction, she shut the drawer, leaving the pile of papers on the desk.

Chapter Fifteen

'I want to go sledging and ice-skating and build a snowman and have snowball fights,' Edward said with the enthusiasm of someone experiencing his very first snowfall.

'We can do all of those things,' Tom said as he squeezed his nephew's hand. The little boy was wrapped up against the cold in bulky layers, happily skipping along beside him. Tom had been out late the night before, trying to find Mrs Burghley, and then spending some time attempting to persuade her to keep quiet about what she had seen. When he had returned home, Edward had been curled up in his bed and the maid had apologised, saying it was the only way she had been able to settle him. Tom had carried the little boy back to his own bed and had sat with him a while, glad of the distraction of Edward's rhythmic breathing.

'Miss Jane promised she would come with us,' Edward said. 'She lives in the countryside and she knows how to go sledging.'

For an instant he allowed himself to indulge in the

image of Jane hurtling down a hill, hair streaming behind her, wild whoops of joy coming from her mouth.

'In a few minutes you will be able to ask her if she would like to accompany us.'

'Of course she will,' Edward said with a small smile. 'She likes you and she likes me even more.'

Tom wasn't sure how he would be received this afternoon at the Mountjoys' house. So far he hadn't heard of any rumours circulating about an illicit embrace between Jane and him in a darkened garden, but without a doubt Lady Mountjoy would be the first to hear of any whispers. He might already be unwelcome in the smart townhouse he was approaching…unwelcome or expected to prepare a proposal.

As he knocked on the door he felt his stomach flip, a sensation that only settled when they were shown into the drawing room without any fanfare.

'What a lovely surprise,' Lady Mountjoy said as she glided in to greet them. 'Edward, you must be so excited about the snow.'

Tom watched as the older woman ushered his nephew over to the window and she was soon listening intently to all the things the boy was planning to do in the snow for the first time.

'Mr Stewart.' He hadn't even heard Jane enter the room and spun suddenly at the sound of her voice. She looked tired, her skin pale and her eyes without their normal sparkle. Immediately he felt a cad. He could have sent word somehow to let her know the outcome of his talk with Mrs Burghley. Even though there wasn't a conclusive answer as to what she might do, he could imagine Jane had spent an unsettled night, kept in the dark, left only to speculate as to her fate,.

'Good afternoon, Miss Ashworth,' he said, trying to read her expression. 'Edward reminded me you promised to accompany us to the park in the event of snow.'

'Yes, Miss Jane, please say you will come,' Edward said, dashing over and giving Jane a big hug.

'Of course I will come,' Jane said, dropping a kiss on the little boy's head. For an instant Tom had a vision of what his future could be like. It involved Jane doting on Edward, a life of comfortable routine.

'Is something amiss, Mr Stewart? Are you unwell?' Lady Mountjoy enquired.

He shook his head, unable to speak. Suddenly his cravat was awfully tight around his neck.

'Do you need a glass of water?'

Again he shook his head. Jane moved closer, peering at him in concern. 'You're making strange noises,' she whispered.

He tried to smile but by the reaction of everyone else in the room the result could not have been very reassuring.

'I do not know who will be free to chaperon me,' Jane said, flashing a concerned look in his direction. He was grateful she was trying to move the conversation on.

'I am sure a maid will be a satisfactory chaperon. You will be out in public and accompanied by Edward. It is hardly a scandalous outing,' Lady Mountjoy said after a moment's thought.

'Would you like to join us this afternoon, Miss Ashworth? I do not know how long the snow is due to settle for.'

'Of course. Let me gather my hat and gloves and change my dress for something more suited to a spell outside.'

Tom marvelled at how quickly Jane was able to change and collect the things she needed. Many women he knew took hours just to select the right outfit, but in a mere fifteen minutes they were standing on the pavement outside Lady Mountjoy's house with a frowning maid a few feet behind them.

'Come, let us walk to the park,' Jane said, taking hold of Edward's hand. She glanced over the young boy's head to Tom, and he could see she was eager to hear his news, but unsure what to ask in front of Edward.

'I am sorry you did not get home until late last night,' Tom said, knowing that at six Edward might not understand everything they talked about, but was very capable of taking it in and repeating it at inopportune moments.

'I understand you also had a late night,' Jane said, looking pensive, then shaking her head. Tom felt a rush of relief. No doubt she only meant to delay their conversation until they reached the park, but it gave him a few minutes' respite.

They walked slowly. The snow had been fresh in the morning, but over the course of the day the pavements had become slippery and in places treacherous. It was a relief to go through the gates of the park and step into the thicker, fresh snow covering the grass where no one else had set foot.

Edward was off immediately, running over the snow and marvelling at his footprints.

'Come and play!' he shouted, whooping with joy.

Jane turned to him and Tom felt as though he were on unsteady ground. He didn't want to jeopardise what they had, didn't want to tear her out of Edward's life by his mistakes.

Slowly she shook her head, her eyes following Edward. 'He's been waiting for this since he arrived in England. Whatever it is we need to say to one another can wait.'

Tom nodded slowly. 'Are you sure?'

'Completely.'

He felt a rush of relief and, even though they were in the middle of the park, he reached out and grasped her hand as she went to move away. For a long moment they both looked down, staring at where his fingers entangled hers, both encased in thick gloves.

'You're a good person, Jane Ashworth,' he said quietly. 'We're both lucky to have you.'

'Come on!' Edward shouted again and after one final moment Jane pulled away, running in the direction of the little boy and leaning down to talk to him. Tom hurried over, but before he could get close two perfectly round snowballs came whizzing towards him. One fell short but the other hit him squarely in the chest before crumbling and falling to the ground.

'I'm going to get you,' he called, gathering up a handful of snow.

It was not a fair fight, two against one, although his aim was true on a few occasions. Jane had a surprisingly strong arm and was merciless in her attack, and before long she and Edward were giggling with laughter as they hit him over and over again.

Changing tactics, Tom made a run for them, gathering a squealing Edward up in his arms and running off to a safe distance.

'Help me, Miss Jane!' Edward giggled.

Now he was under attack from two sides. Retreating from the relentless snowballs from his nephew, he ran back towards Jane as she tried to dart away, laughing.

'Don't even think about picking me up like you did him!'

'Now, that is an idea,' Tom murmured, lunging towards her.

'No!' she shrieked, dodging away. 'Think about the consequences, Mr Stewart.'

'I can only see benefits. One, I would lift you away from your endless supply of ammunition. Two, I could pin your arms to your sides and you wouldn't be able to launch any snowballs. And three...'

He trailed off, knowing he couldn't say three out loud.

'Three?'

Luckily they were both distracted by Edward barging in, screaming and throwing snowballs as if he were in the final charge of a battle.

'I surrender,' Tom called from under the barrage of snowballs.

'Do we let him surrender?' Jane crouched down to confer with the little boy. Finally, she nodded. 'We accept your surrender on two conditions.'

'What are they?'

'You donate your gloves to Edward—his are completely soaked through.'

'Gladly, and the second?'

'You take us to see the sledgers.'

'I know the perfect spot.'

He took a moment to adjust Edward's outer layers, ensuring his nephew was still warm despite the freezing temperatures, and then took off his gloves and handed them over.

'Your prize,' he said, helping Edward slip them on.

With his nephew skipping on ahead, Tom offered Jane his arm. The maid who was chaperoning them trailed behind, looking more and more unimpressed with her job out here in the snow, when the other maids were working in the warmth of the Mountjoy household.

'What did she say?' Jane asked when she was sure Edward was far enough ahead not to hear. 'You never came back. I didn't know if that meant good news or bad news.'

'I'm sorry, it just got so late. It took me ages to find Mrs Burghley. She was almost home by the time I caught up with her.' He passed a hand over his brow, trying to rub away the headache that was threatening to return. 'She was angry.'

'She thought there was going to be something between you?'

'I think she may have got the wrong impression. The friend who introduced us thought we might be a good match for one another. She is looking for a...protector.'

'And are you looking for a mistress?'

'Good lord, no.' He shook his head. 'I think Mrs Burghley is short on funds after her husband's death and hoped I might be the one to save her from having to rethink her current lifestyle.'

'So what did you say to her?'

'I apologised for behaving poorly towards her and

explained what she had seen was a mistake. I begged her to think of your reputation.'

Jane looked up at him and he felt awful that he couldn't guarantee Mrs Burghley would stay quiet.

'She said she was tired, and needed time to think, and asked me not to contact her again.'

Jane bit her lip, her expression troubled.

'It doesn't seem terribly promising.'

'At least she didn't say outright she was going to tell everyone what she saw.'

For a moment their eyes met as they remembered the kiss and then Tom quickly looked away. He knew he needed to put an end to the inappropriate thoughts he kept having about Jane. It might have already ruined both of their futures. He couldn't allow himself to slip up again. If by chance they managed to get away with Jane's reputation intact, he could never do anything again to jeopardise it.

'So what do we do?'

'I suppose we wait.' He shook his head, knowing how unsatisfying that was as an answer. 'I lay awake last night and tried to think through all the possible solutions.'

'Did you come up with anything else?'

'I could try to bribe her,' he said, frowning into the distance. 'She is struggling financially and may be open to a payment or two to keep our secret.' He shrugged. 'It isn't as though it would need to be for ever. In a couple of months you return to Somerset, and I might take Edward to the country for the summer, so I don't think I would need to pay her more than once or twice.'

'It sounds like you don't think it is the best idea.'

'No, I worry it might be a misstep. Although she does need the money, I wonder if a bribe will seem too dirty, too offensive, and then she will feel it is her moral obligation to tell society about what she saw.'

'It's a nightmare.'

'I know.'

'Miss Jane, look. There are children sledging over here.' Edward ran back and grabbed hold of Jane's hand, pulling her with him across the snow.

Tom watched as they hurried in front of him and wondered if things would be terrible if the rumours started and he had to make things right with Jane. Edward would have someone to look after him, someone else to love him, and he would get Jane. Shaking his head, he knew that couldn't happen, but perhaps there was a way he could continue with his normal life and preserve Jane's reputation. A marriage in name, a marriage to provide Edward with a mother figure. For an instant, he wondered if he could ever keep to an arrangement of convenience like that—whether he would be able to keep his hands off Jane if she was his wife, looking up at him with yearning in her eyes.

Quickly, he shook himself. Anything else wasn't an option. It wasn't what he wanted from his life, the quiet domesticity of a married man. After his accident he had promised himself he would live every day for pleasure, for seeking out the different, the unknown. He wasn't made for a life spent with one person day in, day out. He didn't want the responsibility of someone's love, someone's trust. He wasn't a good enough man for Jane, a selfless enough man. If things went wrong between them... He shook his head, hating the idea he could ruin her life the way he'd ruined his sister's.

'Come on, Zio Tom,' Edward called over his shoulder and Tom tried to push the thoughts out of his head. At this moment the only decision he had to make was whether to try offering Mrs Burghley a bribe or not. Everything else was a mess of *what if*s and uncertainty. It was no use debating what his marriage to Jane would be like when hopefully nothing would force them into making that decision.

'He is so keen to join in,' Jane said as they watched Edward inch forward, eager to be whizzing down the hill with the older boys they were observing.

'He hasn't mixed with other children since he arrived.'

'That will come in time,' Jane said, placing a hand on his arm. 'Perhaps in the summer, when you take him to your country residence, he will get to know the local children in the village.'

'Perhaps,' Tom said.

They stood watching for a moment and then Jane stepped forward and grasped Edward's hand. 'Come with me,' she said, gently guiding the young boy behind her.

As he watched them, Tom saw Jane approach one of the older boys in the group and speak to him for a minute before Edward stepped forward. To Tom's surprise, a minute later Edward was speeding down the gentle hill on the back of the sledge, whooping in delight.

After a couple of runs down the hill, Jane slowly retreated until she was back standing next to Tom.

'I know how lucky we are to have you,' Tom said quietly. 'When you suggested this little arrangement, I had my doubts. I thought it would benefit you more than me, but it has been the opposite. I don't think Edward would be nearly as settled as he is now if you weren't in our lives.'

Jane smiled at him, but it didn't quite reach her eyes.

'I wouldn't let a scandal ruin your life, Jane,' he said softly.

'It may not be in your hands.'

'I agree I may not be able to control whether Mrs Burghley starts any rumours, but I would not leave you to face them alone.' He shook his head to try and emphasise his point. 'I am not that sort of man, and I respect you far too much for that.'

She looked at him, her eyes wide and her cheeks flushed, although he couldn't tell whether it was with emotion or the cold.

'What are you saying?'

'I would marry you, if needed.'

'If needed?'

He heard the slight change in pitch of her voice and tried to work out why she was getting upset over this.

'If there is a scandal, I will marry you.'

She turned to him fully. 'You would ask me to marry you?'

'Yes.'

'I might not accept.'

'You would be a fool not to.'

'I could just return to Somerset.'

'You could, but gossip has a long reach.' He shrugged. 'Hopefully it won't come to that.'

'Hopefully not.'

They stood in silence for a while, watching Edward

speeding down the hill, laughing with his newly made friends.

'I should go,' Jane said after a few minutes.

'I've said something wrong.' He searched her face, trying to work out exactly how he had offended her. Neither of them wanted to get married, that much he knew, but he thought it might alleviate some of her worries to know he wouldn't leave her to face the potential scandal alone.

Jane took a shuddering breath and then turned fully to face him. 'No, you haven't. It's just been a long day and I worry about the future.'

He had the sudden urge to reach out and cup her face. The feeling was so strong, he had to take a step back to make sure she was out of reach, otherwise he couldn't trust himself not to do it.

'Go home,' he said, suddenly. 'Rest. I am sure everything will look a bit better after we have both had some sleep.'

Giving a short, sharp nod, she called over to her maid, who had been loitering twenty feet away, and then hurried over to say goodbye to Edward. Tom watched her leave, wondering why he felt as though he had handled the situation badly, not knowing what to say to make it right.

Chapter Sixteen

'It's quiet in here tonight,' Tom said as he took a seat at the bar.

'The locals all know Rose has her night off on a Thursday. It makes me wonder how many come in here just to see her.'

'You do have a beautiful wife, Western,' Tom said, taking another gulp of his drink.

'I know. I'm a lucky man. Rose doesn't let me forget it.'

Tom trailed a finger around the top of the glass. His head had been pounding most of the afternoon, and he had even tried to go to bed soon after Edward had collapsed into an exhausted slumber, but he had felt the pressure building as he'd lain there between the sheets. Instead he'd opted for fresh air and had taken the route across the river to see Western.

'You look like you've been dragged to hell and whipped by the devil himself,' Western said as he looked Tom up and down.

'Thanks,' Tom murmured.

'Is it a headache?'

'Yes. They've been coming more frequently these last few weeks.'

'The doctor told you to avoid any unnecessary conflict, didn't he?'

'It is hardly anything I can avoid. Anyway, the doctor also told me I would never walk again. I don't place much faith in him.'

'By rights you shouldn't be walking. I saw that head of yours get trampled. Any other man would be dead.'

'I've always had a thick skull.'

'And the luck of the devil.'

Tom grimaced. 'A lucky man would never have been trampled in the first place.'

'True.'

Western moved away for a moment to serve two men at the other end of the bar, chatting with them easily whilst he poured their drinks.

'Why are you looking so morose?' Western asked as he returned.

'I upset someone today. I said something I perhaps shouldn't have, but I don't understand why they were quite so upset.'

'Does this person matter to you?'

'Yes.'

'A woman?' Western shook his head. 'Damn it, Rose is always right. She will be gloating about this for weeks.'

'What is she right about?'

'She was convinced you have a woman, someone special you weren't telling us about.'

Tom let his head sink into his hands.

'Smith,' Western called to the young man clearing tables at the other end of the room. 'You're in charge of the bar for ten minutes.' Leaning under the counter, Western brought out a bottle of whisky and two glasses and motioned for Tom to come into the private room at the back of the tavern.

As Tom sat down, Western poured out two glasses of whisky and pushed one towards Tom. 'Drink that down and then tell me everything. Maybe we can work out a solution before your head explodes.'

'Cheery thought.'

Western shrugged. 'You'd better start your story, then.'

'You remember when I came here a few weeks ago, early in the morning, the day Edward arrived?'

'Of course.'

'When I left, I bumped into a young woman I recognised from a society event. I was worried that she was out alone in Southwark so offered to escort her home.' Even though it was only a few weeks ago, it felt much longer. So much had happened between then and now. 'She accepted but we were spotted by the woman looking after her whilst in London. She has the idea we will be well suited.'

'Surely it is a simple matter to disabuse her of this notion?'

'Since that day, Jane has been helping me with Edward. She's good with children, and I have been helping her dodge too many engagements with other potential suitors.'

'It sounds a dangerous game. The young women do see a certain charm in you, and if she is spending that much time with you surely there is great potential for something to go wrong?'

'We kissed,' Tom said, dropping his voice until it was barely more than a whisper.

'And is she insisting you marry?'

'Good lord, no. Jane isn't like that. She does not wish to marry anyone, but there is a certain attraction between us.'

Western stayed quiet, waiting or Tom to get to the crux of the matter. Tom sighed, not sure how to put the complicated mess of emotions into words.

'We were seen when we kissed. A widow I was meant to be escorting for the evening caught us in a darkened corner. I don't know yet if she is going to expose our secret to the world or keep quiet.'

'And if she does expose you to the world?'

'Then I'll marry Jane.'

Western puffed out his cheeks and leaned back in his chair.

'I can see why you're so worried.'

Tom shook his head. 'It might not happen.'

'Is there not another way? You've always been so against settling down. You've never wanted that life of humdrum routine.'

'But maybe it wouldn't have to be,' Tom said slowly. 'Maybe we could agree on a different arrangement.'

Western scoffed. 'What? You continuing on your life as a happy bachelor in all but name whilst this woman looks after your home and your nephew?'

'It doesn't sound good when you put it like that.'

'It's not the way I'm phrasing it that's the problem.'

Tom threw back his whisky and poured himself another.

'She might not even accept my proposal.'

'I doubt she's that much of a fool.'

Tom fell silent, remembering the hurt look in Jane's eyes that afternoon when he had mentioned marriage. He knew he hadn't handled it well, but it was hardly a normal situation. He'd never had to deal with anything like this before. How did you say to a woman, a friend, that you would marry them if necessary without making it sound as if you were reluctant to do so?

'Ah, I made a mess of it,' he said, frustrated.

'It *does* all sound a mess,' Western murmured.

'When I told her I would marry her if necessary, I don't think I looked too thrilled.'

'So now she thinks you would only marry her out of charity.'

'That's not good, is it?'

Western shook his head and Tom pressed his palms into his eye sockets. The pressure felt good.

'I can't see anyone taking it as a compliment, but perhaps it is for the best.'

'What do you mean?'

'This woman… Jane, is it?' He waited for Tom to nod before he continued. 'She clearly has something about her to make you break your rules. You've always said no married women and no debutantes. It is important to you, and in all the years I've known you I don't think you've ever broken them. Until now.'

Tom thought back over the years and the liaisons. Western was right—never before had he even kissed a debutante or a married woman. It wasn't worth the hassle, but more than that it wasn't worth the guilt that accompanied it.

'I need to make things right with her, don't I?'

'Don't do anything stupid,' Western said, pouring him out another glass of whisky. 'I would love to see you settled down and happy, but I wouldn't want you to be forced into it.'

For a few minutes they drank in silence, Tom considering his options but not able to come to any conclusion.

'I think I'd better go,' he said eventually, standing and stumbling. He grabbed hold of the wall, steadied himself and blinked half a dozen times until the world looked straight again.

'How much have we drunk?'

On occasion, he and Western would share part of a bottle of whisky as they laughed and talked and reminisced through the night into the small hours, and normally he could handle his liquor well. It must have been the speed at which he'd gulped back the four large glasses combined with not eating for most of the day that affected him tonight.

'Are you safe to get home or do you need an escort?'

'I can manage. Give that beautiful wife of yours a kiss from me.'

Western scowled at him and Tom grinned as he weaved his way back through the main room of the tavern and out into the street.

Chapter Seventeen

Jane awoke with a start, finding it hard to shake off the last remnants of a dream and for a moment feeling disorientated in the darkness. Only as her eyes adjusted did she remember where she was and allow herself to sink back down into the pillows. She closed her eyes but a few seconds later there was a light tap on the window. For an instant, her body stiffened as she listened, but there was nothing further for at least a minute. Forcing herself to relax again, she looked at the ceiling for a while and then sat bolt upright as there was another tap.

She debated whether to hide under the covers or stride boldly over to the window and pull open the curtains.

'You're on the second floor,' she muttered to herself. 'Don't be ridiculous. No one is going to be outside.'

All the same, she crept over to the window and braced herself before wrenching open the curtains.

Of course there was no one there, no flying monster ready to chase her, not even a confused bat knocking into the window. Jane was about to pull the curtains closed and return to bed when she glanced down.

At first she wondered if she were still asleep, still dreaming a bizarre dream. It would be more plausible than what she saw happening for real.

Standing on the lawn was the outline of a man, a man she knew was Tom, even in the darkness. He was throwing little pebbles at her window, but either he was a very poor sportsman or he was inebriated, as his aim was truly terrible. A pebble skittered across a window further along the house and Jane sent up a silent prayer of thanks that Lord and Lady Mountjoy's rooms were on the first floor.

Quickly she pushed up the window and leaned her head out, sucking in a quick breath as the icy air whipped at her face.

'What are you doing?' she whispered as loudly as she dared.

'Jane!' Tom shouted.

He waved and swayed. Definitely inebriated, Jane thought, unable to fathom why he was in the Mountjoys' back garden in the middle of the night.

'Be quiet,' she said, leaning out a little further to check there was no movement at any of the other windows.

'Jane, I'm down here,' Tom called.

'I can see you. Wait there. Don't move.' She knew she should send him away but she didn't want to have a conversation out of the window. Every shout from Tom seemed to cut through the air and she was worried soon the whole neighbourhood would be awake.

She had the forethought to pull on her dressing gown and slip on some shoes before descending the stairs, listening every few steps to see if anyone was stirring in the rest of the house.

It was with a flood of relief she reached the back door that led out into the garden. The keys were on a hook next to the door and carefully she inserted the key into the lock and turned, slipping out through the open door into the night.

'I had to see you,' Tom said as she stepped out onto the patio. His words were a little slurred, and Jane could see he was trying really hard to be quiet, but his mouth wasn't quite cooperating.

'It's the middle of the night.'

'You look lovely,' he said, taking a step back to take all of her in. Jane pulled her dressing gown across her chest a little tighter.

'Go home. We can talk tomorrow. Or any other time.'

'I think I said the wrong thing earlier.'

'It doesn't matter,' Jane said, reaching out and turning him so he faced the garden gate. 'Go home and we will talk tomorrow.'

'I'll go,' he said, even taking a step in the right direction. 'Tomorrow we'll talk.'

'Yes, tomorrow. I promise.' She felt relieved he was leaving so easily. In two minutes Tom would be on his way home and she would be safely ensconced back in her bed.

'Goodnight, Jane,' he said, half-turning back to her and giving her that smile of his.

'Goodnight, Tom.'

Before he could take another step, there was a scraping noise from above. Jane stiffened, unable to move. She knew it was a window opening and knew that at any moment she would be caught in the garden with a notorious rake. There would be no saving her reputation after this.

Even though he was inebriated, Tom moved quickly, lunging forward and grabbing hold of her, deftly spinning her round and through the open back door. Their bodies were pressed together, with his back against the wall, and hers pinning him in place. With one hand he reached out and pressed a finger to her lips, silencing the exclamation of surprise and lingering for a moment as his eyes sought out hers.

Jane felt the beat of his heart even through the layers that separated them and was sure hers was beating exactly in time.

They heard the creak of the window a few floors up and Jane hoped the open back door wasn't visible from above. Slowly she extricated herself from Tom's arms and inch by inch eased the door shut. For half a minute they stood completely still, listening to the faint noises of the house at night, and then with a sense of impending doom they heard the opening of a door and the patter of faint footsteps.

'We need to move,' Tom whispered, his breath tickling her ear.

Jane nodded, wondering if this situation could get any worse. From the position of the window opening, she knew it must be one of the servants, but if they had heard anything they would be sure to come to investigate. Quickly she locked the back door and replaced the key on the hook and then, grabbing hold of Tom's hand, pulled him along the narrow corridor that led to the main hallway. She paused by the servants' stairs, listening again, only to feel the solid thud of Tom's body careening into hers. It took a moment to steady herself, but in that time she was convinced she could hear the soft creak of wood signalling someone coming down the stairs.

It was a gamble to head to the main staircase with Tom in tow. If she had misjudged the situation, if it was in fact Lord or Lady Mountjoy who had woken and were coming, then it would be an utter disaster. She and Tom would be caught and there would be no explaining away this scandal. Jane just had to hope it was a servant and they had subconsciously chosen their habitual route downstairs, using the narrower servants' staircase.

Silently they climbed the stairs. Jane's heart pounded even harder every time there was a creak, and a couple of times she thought her chest might explode from the awful anticipation of being caught. They made it up past the first floor, circling round and continuing up the second staircase to the second floor.

Jane didn't pause at the top of the steps, entwining her fingers through Tom's and pulling him into her bedroom. Quickly she closed the door behind them and turned the key in the lock.

She rested her head on the cool wood for a few seconds, unable to believe what she had just done. Eventually she turned to find Tom right behind her.

'What were you thinking?' she whispered, wishing she could see him better in the darkness.

'You were upset earlier,' he said, reaching out and placing a hand on her arm. 'I didn't want to leave things badly between us.'

'So you thought you would pay me a visit in the

middle of the night and force me to sneak you into my bedroom.'

He shrugged, looking around, as if only now realising that he was in her bedroom.

'I didn't think that far,' he said simply. 'I knew I wanted to see you, but I didn't think about the practicalities of it.'

'You didn't think about the practicalities?' Jane repeated, still unable to take in the enormity of the mess they were in. 'What are we going to do, Tom? If you are found here, it won't matter if Mrs Burghley says anything or not. We'll be marched down the aisle as soon as Lady Mountjoy can persuade the archbishop to give us a special licence.'

She was glad to see a flicker of a reaction in his eyes, then he shrugged again and moved away, flopping down in the chair by the writing desk.

'You're going to sit down? At a time like this?'

'Someone in this house is awake,' he said, sounding a lot more sober than he had outside. 'But it is after midnight and I doubt they will be awake for long. I suggest we sit quietly for half an hour, maybe an hour, and then I will slip out and no one will be any the wiser.'

Jane opened her mouth to protest and then closed it again as she considered his words. This was far from the ideal situation but, now they were in it, perhaps he was right. Perhaps they needed to sit it out and then hope they could slip Tom out of the house when everyone was back asleep.

She looked around for the best place to sit, but with the chair occupied there weren't many options. The window seat was far too cold at this time of night, so it only left the bed. At first she perched on the edge, feeling fidgety and jumping at even the slightest sound.

'You can sit back,' Tom said, observing her through heavy-lidded eyes.

'I don't want to get too comfortable.'

'We're hardly likely to fall asleep, are we?'

He had a point. Jane felt so on edge, so nervous, she doubted she would sleep for three days.

'I am sorry,' he said, as she plumped up the pillows and then positioned herself so she was sitting up against the headboard, her legs stretched out before her on the bed. 'It was stupid to come here.'

'Why did you come here?'

'I couldn't stop thinking of the look on your face yesterday, whilst we were watching Edward sledging.'

'I didn't have a look on my face.'

'You did after I said I would marry you.'

She felt herself bristle and stiffen again. It was something about the phrasing, the way he'd made it sound as if he'd be doing her a favour by saving her reputation if needed. Not that it wasn't true, but she hated being made to feel that way.

'It came out wrong, and I'm sorry. Any man would be lucky to have you as his wife.'

Jane snorted, allowing herself to slip down a little further on the cushions to get comfortable.

'They would.'

'Apart from you,' she said quietly. 'For you it would be an obligation.'

There was a long silence and Jane had to peer through the darkness to see if he had fallen asleep. When she was satisfied his eyes were still open, she returned to staring up at the canopy of the four-poster bed stretched above her.

'I don't think I've ever told you exactly why I have never wanted to get married,' he said eventually.

'I know about your desire to enjoy every moment of your life, after the accident.'

'Yes, that is much of it,' Tom said quietly. He sounded pensive, as if working out how to phrase the next statement. 'I had a very unhappy childhood, Jane. My father was cruel. He took pleasure in finding little ways to make our lives miserable, my sister's and mine.'

Jane turned a little to face him, wondering why such people became parents.

'Outwardly he did all the things he was supposed to as a parent. We were clothed and fed, I was sent to a good school, Rebecca had an expensive governess.' He fell quiet.

'Being a parent isn't just about fulfilling the most basic of needs, though,' Jane said softly.

'He was a clever man, and he used that intelligence to torment us. Mainly in small ways—pitting us against each other for snippets of affection, warping our perception of what was normal.' He shuddered, and Jane wanted to reach over to him and pull him into an embrace, but she kept still, knowing it would make tonight even more difficult. 'Then I left. I bought a commission in the army and I went away without ever looking back.'

'Your sister was still at home?'

'She was. Every day I hated myself for it, but I couldn't spend another month in that house—it was suffocating.' He paused, and in the moonlight Jane could see the angst on his face. 'I left her behind to save myself.'

'You can't have been very old.'

'I was eighteen. Old enough.'

'What happened to her?'

'We wrote, a lot. She begged me not to blame myself, begged me to go out and live my life without the shadow of our father hanging over me. And then she disappeared.'

'She disappeared?'

'I was away at the time, but when I returned home the servants said one day she was acting normally, going about her daily routine, and the next she was gone. She didn't take a single thing with her except the clothes she was wearing.'

'You must have been so worried.'

'My father paid for investigators—not out of concern for Rebecca, you understand, but because he hated not being in control. They uncovered nothing.'

'What did you do?'

'When I returned to London I met with some of her friends and one told me she had fallen in love. This friend informed me she had no clue who the man was, just that he was foreign. Rebecca had gone, vanished, and left no trace behind her.'

'Did you feel guilty?'

For a long moment Tom remained silent, his lips pressed together and a frown on his face.

'I should never have left her. It was selfish. I put my own future, my own chance of happiness, above hers.'

'You were eighteen, barely more than a child yourself. A child who had lived through a whole lifetime of cruelty. Subject a hundred people to that, and show me anyone who wouldn't have taken the opportunity to escape as you did.'

'I loved my sister more than anyone in the world,' he said, shaking his head. 'But I still put myself first.'

Realisation slowly dawned on Jane. 'That is why you don't want to get married. You don't feel you would be good enough, selfless enough.'

'I can't trust myself to put someone else's needs ahead of my own. I didn't do it before, and no one deserves that in a husband.'

It was as if the final piece of the puzzle had fallen into place. She had always wondered if there was something more to his adamance that he would not marry. The pursuit of pleasure was one thing, but she had wondered what would happen if he ever fell in love. Now she understood he wouldn't let himself fall in love for exactly this reason.

'I searched for her. I spent a lot of money trying to find her, but I never did. She had hidden herself too well.' He shrugged. 'At least I know now she had a good life, a kind husband, a beautiful son. All the things she always dreamed of.'

'All the things you deserve too.'

He shook his head and ploughed on, as if needing to get everything off his chest now he had started. 'Then I had my accident and when I woke up I realised how lucky I was to be alive. It took a long time to learn to walk again, to be able to concentrate for more than a few minutes without getting a blinding headache, but I made progress month by month. When I was fully recovered, I decided I would dedicate my life to finding pleasure. That way I wouldn't hurt anyone. I wouldn't betray anyone like I had my sister.'

He fell silent and Jane wished there wasn't such a distance between them. She wanted to pull him into her arms, to smother him with love, to make him see that he was more than worthy.

'Now you see,' he said after a long silence. 'I can't marry, not unless the alternative is much worse.'

The pain in his expression made her heart break and all Jane could do was nod silently. Nothing she could say tonight was going to change his mind. He'd held on to this belief for over a decade. It was firmly entrenched in his mind.

They sat for a long time, completely quiet, the only sound their rhythmic breathing. Jane couldn't stop thinking of the heartache Tom must have carried round, the burden of guilt pressing down on him over the years. Nothing could change how he had acted when he had fled at the tender age of eighteen, but she wondered if there was some way to make him see he'd not been the same man then as he was now.

Chapter Eighteen

Tom shifted, wondering why he was quite so uncomfortable. He reached back to pull a pillow into place but his hand grasped only air.

It took a moment for him to remember where he was, his eyes shooting open and taking in the darkness in the room. He breathed a sigh of relief. It was still dark. Hopefully he had merely dozed off, not slept half the night in Jane's bedroom, chaste though the experience had been.

He stretched and reached for his pocket watch, patting himself down for it, cursing when he realised he must not have brought it out with him the night before. Slowly, working out the stiffness in his muscles as he went, he levered himself up from the chair, pausing as he caught sight of Jane on the bed. Her hair was loose, fanned out on the pillows, one arm thrown up over her head in a casual manner. She still wore her dressing gown, tightly secured, but it had risen up a little, exposing the creamy white skin of her legs.

He shook his head in disbelief. Over the years he'd

had liaisons with the most desired courtesans, dallied with women said to be the most beautiful in Europe, but here he was, unable to draw his eyes away from Miss Jane Ashworth's ankles.

'Jane,' he whispered, aware that he needed her to accompany him downstairs to lock up after he had sneaked out through the back door.

'No,' she murmured, not opening her eyes and turning away from him.

Smiling into the darkness, he tried again. 'Jane, you need to wake up.'

This time she flopped an arm over her ear so she wouldn't have to listen.

Gently he laid a hand on her shoulder and gave her a shake. 'Jane, you need to let me out before anyone wakes up again.'

He didn't think she was going to rouse, but after a few seconds his words seemed to sink in and she remembered their predicament. She sat up so fast, they almost banged heads, leaned over her as he was. Luckily he moved quickly, taking a step back and avoiding a sore head for them both.

'What time is it? Did we fall asleep? This is a nightmare.'

She had leapt out of bed and was already pacing the floor, her words delivered in a low whisper. Tom spotted the clock on the mantelpiece and went over to look, an icy flood of horror spreading through him when he realised it was much later than he had thought. Far from dozing for a few minutes in the chair, he must have been asleep for hours.

'It is a quarter to seven.'

Jane let out a panicked squeak, a hand flying to her mouth.

'Cook will be up. The maids will be up. Any moment one of them will be coming in to light my fire.'

'Can we sneak past them?'

Jane paused for a moment and then shook her head. 'To get to the back door, you have to go straight past the kitchen.'

'How about the front door?'

'I don't have a key and there isn't one kept anywhere accessible.'

Tom ran a hand through his hair, aware of the minutes ticking away. Every second they wasted standing here, debating the best way out instead of moving, increased the chance they would be found and if they were found there was no way he was getting out of marrying Jane.

He glanced over at her, taking in the way her hair was ruffled and loose, flowing over her shoulders. There was a beautiful pink glow to her cheeks and a brightness to her eyes. Perhaps it wouldn't be so bad waking up to Jane every morning. Or tumbling into bed with her each night.

Silently he reprimanded himself. *If* they got caught he would, of course, do the right thing and marry Jane, but that didn't mean it would be a conventional marriage. Already, sometimes when he looked at her he saw a flash of true affection in her eyes. He couldn't risk that growing any more. Their lives would have to be separate, a marriage in name only, for he knew if he spent even just one night in her bed he would never be able to leave her behind. There was a primal pull between them, something he couldn't quite describe... something that was very hard to fight.

'I can't just stay here,' he said. 'We'll have to risk the kitchen door.'

'There's too many people. There is a door leading onto the patio in Lord Mountjoy's study. The key is in his desk. We might be able to sneak in there if the maids are upstairs lighting the fires.'

'Good. Let's go.' He paused for a second and then turned back to Jane. 'I'm sorry I came here last night and put your reputation in danger. It was beyond foolish to get that inebriated and allow my head to follow my heart.'

She looked up at him with her big green eyes and Tom got the overwhelming urge to kiss her. He wanted to fold her in his arms and kiss her until the whole household was hammering on the door, demanding to know what was happening inside the room.

'I forgive you,' she said with a little half-smile. 'Now, wait here whilst I go and fetch a glass of water from the kitchen and see where everyone is positioned. If a maid comes in...' She trailed off, glancing at the wardrobe behind him.

'You want me to hide in the wardrobe.'

'It's better than under the bed.'

'Be quick,' he instructed her, watching as she adjusted her dressing gown and smoothed down her hair. It was nice to see her this early in the morning, to see the version of her only her husband would see in the future.

Jane slipped out of the door, clicking it closed behind her, and he slumped back in the chair by the window. He felt drained, probably hung over, but also emotionally drained from being so honest the night before.

Not completely honest. The thought popped into his mind. He had told her everything about his past, all the reasons he could not marry, but he had not told her how much he was tempted to throw all of that to the wind. *She* tempted him. Every night he fell asleep with her face in his mind, he dreamed of her body pressed against his. Never before had he felt an infatuation like this, the need to be close to her.

Looking down, he noticed a sheaf of paper half-sticking out of a closed drawer in the desk. There was a flash of colour on it, a beautiful golden yellow, and immediately it piqued his interest. Aware the drawer was closed and private, he reasoned he would open it, ensure the piece of paper was undamaged and place it more carefully back inside.

As he opened the drawer he felt a flicker of surprise. On the piece of paper was the most beautiful painting of three little field mice hanging on to sheaves of golden corn. The detail was exquisite, down to the miniscule whiskers on their faces, and it felt as though you were just about to step into a real farmer's field.

He picked up the piece of paper, unable to quite believe the quality of the painting.

Underneath was a page of writing, and then sticking out from under that he could see another painting. Knowing he shouldn't, he picked up the paper with the writing on and looked at the picture under it. This one was of an owl, tawny brown and looking fierce as it stretched its wings to fly.

He longed to read the writing that accompanied it,

but knew he had already pried too much. When she was ready, maybe Jane would let him see it, let him read the entirety of her work.

Carefully he placed the papers in the drawer and pushed it closed. As it thudded shut, the door opened, and for a second he felt as though his heart had stopped beating.

Jane slipped inside, closing the door softly behind her.

'Cook is busy in the kitchen,' she said. 'I can hear the maids on the first floor, probably seeing to Lord and Lady Mountjoy's fire. I think if we are going to move it needs to be now.'

He stood, moving swiftly to join her, and then taking her hand in his own. She looked up at him and he saw the worry on her face, hating that he was the cause of it.

'If anyone spots us, the scandal will be of gigantic proportions. Whether we are holding hands or not won't even feature.'

'That is very true.' She took a shuddering breath and then smiled up at him. 'Let's go.'

With her heart pounding in her chest, Jane opened the door and stepped out into the hallway. There was no one in sight. She knew their best chance was to move quickly, but she had an overwhelming urge to creep quietly rather than rush. Thankfully, Tom gripped her hand a little tighter and together they hurried forward.

Never before had she realised quite how big the Mountjoys' townhouse actually was. There was the second-floor hallway to navigate, then a sweeping staircase down to the first floor, where anyone might be coming out of a room and spot them on the stairs. After they had navigated that gauntlet, there was the final grand staircase to the ground floor. This would deposit them in the wide hallway where there was nowhere to hide until they dived into one of the downstairs rooms.

Without looking round, Jane hurried to keep up with Tom, feeling as though her feet were barely touching the stairs as they raced down them. In no time at all her toes were on the cool marble of the downstairs hall. They both froze for a second as voices approached and Jane was certain they were about to be caught. Tom lunged through one of the doors, pulling her with him and closing it with a quiet click. Her back was pressed up against the wall and Tom's body was firm against hers. For a long moment, neither of them moved, and then Tom dipped his head just a little. Jane longed to reach up and kiss him, to abandon herself to the red-hot desire that was burning inside her. She wanted to loop her legs around him, to pull him to her and forget where they were.

She almost gave in, pushing herself up on her tiptoes a fraction, but then she thought of Tom's words the night before. His anguish had been so raw, even all these years later. It was not merely a story, an excuse for not getting married. She could see he truly believed every word he had said. He didn't think he could trust himself to put another's needs above his own.

Jane knew this was nonsense. Time and time again over the last few weeks Tom had made sacrifices for both his nephew and her without being asked, without really thinking about it, because it was the right thing to do. He had a strong moral compass, a sense of right and wrong, and even if it did not match up with the strict rules of society it didn't mean it wasn't a good way to live his life. She might know it was nonsense, but Tom believed it.

Slowly she sank down from her tiptoes, a flood of disappointment flowing through her as her heels touched the floor.

'I'll get the key,' she said, her voice sticking in her throat. She wriggled out from her spot against the wall and walked over to the desk, telling herself that soon she would be back home in Somerset. Soon she would be far away from Tom Stewart and his alluring smiles.

Lord Mountjoy's desk was meticulous. Everything was neat and ordered and had its place. It made finding the key easy, kept as it always was in the bottom drawer in a little container at the back left. Her fingers gripped it and she pulled it out triumphantly, wondering for the first time whether they might actually get away without being caught.

Tom crossed the room in four strides, joining her by the desk, relief blossoming on his face too. Quickly Jane moved to the glass doors that led out to the patio area beyond and inserted the key into the lock. She had opened the door a few times before, and knew it was stiff, so set about jiggling the key to try and get the mechanism to work.

With a start she felt Tom's fingers on her hand, gripping her wrist. Voices were approaching and she watched in horror as the door handle began to move. There was nowhere to go, nowhere they could hide in the time it would take to open the door.

Jane let out a little whimper, hating the feeling of

helplessness, the feeling her entire future was about to be decided for her.

Tom looked at her, and in the moment before the door opened he smiled. There was no dread in his eyes, no recriminations, just pure reassurance. Jane felt her heart constrict and knew in that moment that she was in love with him.

'I'll clean out the fire in Lord Mountjoy's study,' one of the maids said as she pushed the door half-open. 'Then I will be down to help with heating the water for bathing.'

The door was open wide enough for someone to see in, but the maid was looking back over her shoulder at her companion and hadn't yet spotted Jane and Tom. The companion must have said something for the maid paused and then sighed.

'No, of course that is fine. I'll get to the fire later this morning.' Without even looking into the room, the maid shut the door again with a click.

'What just happened?' Jane whispered, unable to believed they were still undiscovered.

'I think we have tested our luck enough,' Tom murmured, reaching for the key in the lock and giving it one final jiggle. The door opened and quickly he stepped out, pausing for a moment on the threshold. 'Get back to bed,' he said with a grin. 'I'll call on you later. I am sorry for all of this.'

Before Jane knew what was happening, he leaned forward and kissed her quickly but firmly on the lips, then turned and hurried down the side of the house.

Too stunned to move for a moment, Tom was already around the side of the house before Jane had recovered.

Her fingers were stiff and fumbling as she locked the door and returned the key to the drawer. It only took a few seconds then to sneak out of the study and hurry upstairs, her heart still racing even though she knew the worst of the danger had passed.

Once inside her room, she collapsed into bed, unable to believe Tom had spent the best part of the night in her bedroom and they had got away with not being caught.

She had barely pulled the bed covers up to her chin when one of the maids bustled in, ready to set her fire for the morning. Jane wasn't quick enough to close her eyes and pretend to be asleep, but the maid seemed happy enough to chatter as she worked, holding both sides of the conversation, except for the occasional murmur of agreement from Jane.

'Will you stay in bed a little longer, Miss Ashworth?' Dorothy asked as she finished with the fire. 'Shall I bring up your morning tea?'

'That would be lovely.'

Dorothy darted round the room for another minute, tidying anything out of place. As she reached the chair by the window, the one on which Tom had spent an uncomfortable night, she paused. Jane's eyes darted to where she was standing, taking in the silky fabric of Tom's cravat hanging over the back of the chair.

'Do you like it?' she said, forcing her voice to remain calm and nonchalant.

Dorothy's eyes darted to hers. 'It's a cravat, miss.'

'I know. One of Captain Weyman's. He hates the colour, so Lucy has given it to me to cut up and make ribbons.'

She couldn't tell if the maid believed her, but at least

it was a passably plausible story, something hopefully the maid would file away and not think about further. Jane did her best not to stare at the young woman, knowing acting out of the ordinary would make the implausible story even less believable.

'It is a lovely colour, miss. It will make beautiful ribbons.'

It was all Jane could do not to let out a huge sigh of relief. Instead, she leaned back on her pillows and closed her eyes. Perhaps today would be a little less stressful.

Chapter Nineteen

The snow was beginning to melt, turning into a dirty grey sludge underneath her feet, and Jane was glad of the thick-soled boots she'd brought from the country for occasions such as this. They were not the most elegant boots ever but it hardly mattered with them hidden under her dress with only the toes visible if she took a particularly big step.

'Where are we going?' She pulled her cloak a little tighter around her ears, shivering at the cold whip of the wind. It made her clench her jaw and sent an ache all the way from her ears to her chin.

'I don't know,' Lucy said, giving her friend's arm a squeeze as they walked along side by side. 'I had my instructions to bring you here for two o'clock, so that is what I am doing.'

It was all very mysterious. Jane had spent the morning restless and unable to settle, flitting from trying to read a book to taking out her watercolours, but not able to paint anything, to aimlessly staring out of the window. She'd felt as if she was waiting for something to happen although she wasn't quite sure what.

'I haven't heard any whispers,' Lucy said, lowering her voice. 'Although I will admit I haven't been out much in the last few days. I didn't want to be anywhere someone could stop me and question me if Mrs Burghley had spilled her secret.'

'You are too good, Lucy,' Jane said, leaning in to her friend. 'Perhaps she won't tell anyone. The waiting, the not knowing, is so hard. I wish I could hunt her down and just ask her. It is awful, waking up each day and not knowing whether your whole world will come crashing down.'

'It must be. I do not envy you that, Jane.' She shook her head as they waited for a carriage to trundle past before crossing the road. 'Have you seen Mr Stewart since that evening?'

Closing her eyes for a moment, Jane thought of waking up this morning with Mr Stewart gently shaking her arm. For an instant she had allowed herself to believe that that was their life, and she had awoken with a contented feeling before the panic of reality had crashed back down on her.

'Yes. We took Edward sledging yesterday.'

'Did he…?' Lucy trailed off, looking as if she didn't know how to phrase the question without causing upset.

'He proposed.' Jane scoffed and corrected herself. 'No, that's a lie. He didn't propose. He said if things went badly, of course he would marry me.'

'Did you want him to propose? Properly, I mean?'

Jane couldn't bring herself to look at Lucy, knowing her friend's expression would be one of complete concern and affection. She felt the prick of tears in her eyes and tried to suppress the wave of emotion that threatened to overwhelm her.

Taking in a deep, shuddering breath, she nodded, feeling relief as she finally admitted it.

'Yes,' she said quietly. 'More than anything else, and that scares me so much.'

'Why does it scare you?'

'I hate how easily I have given up my promises to myself.'

'To focus on your work?'

'Yes.'

'Marrying Mr Stewart wouldn't mean you would have to give up your ambitions. I know many men would not want you to continue with passions that might take your focus away from looking after the home and any children you might have, but I don't think Mr Stewart would be one of them. He seems to be very relaxed. I think he would make a wonderful husband for you.'

'He doesn't want to get married. He has his reasons, reasons he thinks are very valid. He isn't going to move away from his beliefs unless we are forced into it.'

'Do you think his reasons are valid?'

'No, at least I do not believe the worst in him, as he does himself.'

'Oh, Jane, what a mess.'

It was so frustrating, knowing the future was out of her hands. She knew if she looked at things rationally the best thing would be for Mrs Burghley to keep quiet and for Tom and her to move on with their lives. She didn't want him to be forced to marry her, even if she did want to be with him, and she knew the option she dreamed of, the option where Tom suddenly realised he was deeply in love with her and *wanted* to spend the rest of their lives married, wasn't going to happen.

They splashed through some deep puddles, both having to lift their skirts to avoid getting completely soaked. Already the hem of Jane's dress was wet and grey in colour, soaking up the moisture from the melting snow.

'There he is,' Lucy said, pausing as they rounded a corner. 'Perhaps you should tell him, Jane.'

'What?'

'Tell him how you feel about him. Tell him you love him. I wager you haven't been truthful with him yet.'

Jane thought of the kisses, the surge of emotion that had passed between them. He knew she desired him, that she enjoyed his company, but she had never really let him see the depth of her feeling.

'It wouldn't change anything,' she said quietly. 'It would only serve to make things more difficult between us.'

They fell silent as Tom spotted them and raised a hand in greeting.

'Thank you for coming today, Mrs Weyman,' Tom said, taking her hand and bowing over it. 'I know it was short notice.'

'I do not mind at all. In fact, I am intrigued as to the secrecy of where we are going.'

'Are you well, Miss Ashworth?' he enquired, sounding as if he didn't have a care in the world, but Jane knew he was really asking if everything had been calm after his departure from the house that morning.

'Very well, thank you, Mr Stewart.'

'I have done something I think you are going to be annoyed about, Miss Ashworth, but I hope with time you will be able to forgive me.'

He was smiling at her, but she could see the earnest expression on his face. She felt a roiling of nerves in her stomach. Tom had sent a note this morning, inviting her for a walk and telling her that there was a new book publisher opening up close to Bond Street. He suggested she bring her manuscript and illustrations so she could see if the publisher would grant her an audience. The heavy packet of papers was tucked under her arm.

'You're making me nervous.'

'There is a shop I am going to take Miss Ashworth into, Mrs Weyman. I know the weather is cold, but I don't expect us to be more than a few minutes. There is a little shop that serves tea across the road you could wait in. Is that acceptable?'

'Of course,' Lucy said, pulling Jane in as Tom stepped away a few paces. 'Maybe he's going to buy you a wedding ring.'

'Don't be ridiculous,' Jane whispered, hating the trickle of hope that ran through her.

'Are you ready, Miss Ashworth?'

Jane stepped over and took his proffered arm, looking up at the signs that hung above the shops. It wasn't a part of London she knew well, but she never had been one to enjoy shopping, tolerating the trips to the modiste with gritted teeth and a book stowed in her bag for the quieter moments.

'Where are we going?' Jane murmured as they walked a little way down the street. Out of the corner of her eye, she saw Lucy crossing the road and escaping from the cold into the little shop.

'Did anyone notice anything was amiss this morning?'

'You left your cravat.'

'Did someone see?'

'The maid found it, I invented some story about it being Captain Weyman's and said Lucy had given it to me to make into ribbons.'

'Quick thinking,' he said, nodding in approval. 'I must have removed it as I was dropping off last night.' He gave her a rueful smile. 'In the panic this morning, I didn't even notice. I am sorry I put you in that position. I don't know what came over me last night.'

'You were inebriated.'

'It's no excuse. I shouldn't have let myself get like that to begin with. I'm far from a man obsessed with sobriety, but I do normally know my limits.'

Tom slowed his pace and then exerted a small amount of pressure on her arm, indicating they should stop. Jane glanced around, wondering where he was taking her with such secrecy, but before she could work it out Tom pulled her attention back to him.

'You might not forgive me so easily for this.'

She frowned, not understanding him.

'This morning, whilst you were checking the coast was clear downstairs, I saw a piece of paper sticking out of one of the drawers in your desk. It had the most wonderful painting on it.' He held up his hands as if to defend himself. 'I didn't look further than the top two sheets, and even that I know is a gross invasion of privacy.'

Jane felt the blood flood to her cheeks. Even though she dreamed of being published, she hated showing people her work. It was unusual for a woman to have such ambition, to want to strike out on her own and pursue her talents beyond using them to amuse herself and her close friends and family. Hardly anyone except her younger sister had ever laid eyes on the pictures she painted, and the stories were guarded with even fiercer need for privacy.

'You shouldn't have…'

'I know. Believe me, I know, but once I had seen them I couldn't stop thinking about them.'

Jane spun round, finally realising where they must be.

'There is a man I know from my school days. I have requested an appointment with him.' Tom reached out as if to take her hand and then seemed to remember they were on a public street. 'I have told him there is someone I would like him to meet, someone who's work I think merits his attention, but I have not told him anything else.'

Jane looked over her shoulder. It was not a publisher she had been to before, although the name was familiar. When she had first arrived in London, she had begun by writing to a few of the more prestigious book publishers rather than traipsing round to their shops. It had not been very successful, but she did recognise the name above the shop here as one who had at least replied and told her gently they were not accepting new manuscripts at present.

'The man who owns the business is Richard Hambly. As I said, I know him from school, but we were not close. He was older than me. He owes me nothing and the courtesy he does me is just for a meeting. If anything comes of this, it will be because of you, not because of me.' He paused, looking at her earnestly. 'I think your work has merit, Jane, and sometimes we have to take the small advantages granted to us in life.'

For a long moment Jane's eyes flicked between Tom and the bookshop and then finally she nodded. Doing things her way hadn't achieved anything so far. Perhaps having someone who was open at least to viewing her work was what she needed.

'Good, come on. I will introduce you.'

They entered the shop and Jane paused for a moment, overwhelmed by the volume of books on display. They were beautifully bound and lined on the shelves with precision and care. Some had little stands that allowed the books to be displayed open, with their innermost secrets on show to the world. The shop seemed to stock a mixture of adults' and children's books and for the first time in a long time Jane felt a frisson of excitement. There was a reason this had originally been near the top of her list of publishers she wanted to approach.

'Mr Stewart, good morning,' a young man said as he stepped out of the room behind the counter. There was another man there, a clerk, who moved aside and busied himself with arranging a new stack of books on the shelves.

'Good to see you again, Mr Hambly,' Tom said, taking the other man's proffered hand and shaking it. 'May I introduce a good friend of mine, Miss Jane Ashworth?'

'Delighted to meet you, Miss Ashworth. Why don't you come through to my office and we can talk?'

He led the way through the door at the back of the shop to a neat office beyond, motioning for them to have a seat. There were some crates piled high in one corner and it looked as though he was still unpacking.

'Sorry for the mess. I moved in here six months ago and I still haven't got the room how I like it.'

'It is a lovely shop, Mr Hambly,' Jane said, trying to suppress the nervousness she was feeling.

'Yes, I'm rather pleased with it. I moved from a few streets away as this is more prominent and gets more passing trade. I kept the old shop for all the printing equipment, but I do miss the whir and bang of the printing press as I work.' He leaned back in his chair. 'Mr Stewart said you have some work you would like me to consider.'

Jane picked up the packet of papers from her lap and slid out the manuscript she had spent so much time on. The paper felt heavy in her hands and she hesitated before handing it over.

'I write children's stories, Mr Hambly, and draw and paint the illustrations for them.'

The publisher leaned forward in his chair and took the proffered bundle.

Her heart was fluttering in her chest, feeling like a butterfly that was fighting to break free. Although she had been visiting publishers for the last few months, this was the first time that anyone had actually invited her to sit down and show her work. It felt like a momentous moment, although Jane was acutely aware any rejection now would be a direct response to her work.

'What age group is this for, Miss Ashworth?'

'For slightly older children, although I think younger

children would enjoy the stories if read to them by some-one else. I often read my stories to my younger sisters before bed and they enjoy them.'

He nodded, turning over the first page. Jane watched him carefully, seeing his eyes widen at the beautiful illustration she had chosen to be included on the title page. It showed the three field mice dashing through the cornfield with the owl swooping down behind them, wings spread wide.

'Did you paint this?'

'Yes.'

'It is beautiful. With just one picture I feel I am al-ready inside your story.'

A warm glow swept through Jane and she felt the first flickering of hope.

'Are there more pictures like this?'

'Yes, a lot more.'

'Good.'

He settled back to read, turning the pages slowly and spending a long time scrutinising the pictures. It was the most agonising half hour of Jane's life, watch-ing him read and form a judgement on her manuscript. She struggled to sit still, having to lace her fingers to-gether to stop them from tapping on the table or play-ing with the fabric of her dress.

Finally, Mr Hambly looked up, placing down the last of the sheets of paper in the pile. For a long moment he did not speak, as if formulating a response in his mind. Jane felt her hopes crashing down. Surely if he loved it he would come out and say so straight away?

'Do you have more?' he asked eventually.

'Yes. Five completed manuscripts.'

'All illustrated?'

'Yes.'

'All in a similar theme?'

'Yes.'

'You have talent, Miss Ashworth. When I first looked at the illustrations, I thought of inviting you to work as an illustrator for some of the other children's books I am publishing, but your stories are charming and unlike anything I have come across before. Uniqueness is a good thing in our business.'

Jane couldn't quite believe what she was hearing. She glanced across at Tom, and saw his encouraging smile, before turning back to Mr Hambly.

'I would really like to see the rest of your work, but I think you have real promise, Miss Ashworth, and I would like to work with you.'

For a moment Jane couldn't react. She felt stunned and realised she had never truly believed she might ever get to this point.

'You want to publish my book?'

'Send me the rest of your work, and if you would grant me a few days to think things over I will come back to you with an offer within the week.'

He stood and Jane scrambled to her feet as well.

'I will send the manuscripts over later today.'

'I will treat them with the utmost care. I am looking forward to working with you, Miss Ashworth.'

Unable to believe what was happening, Jane let Tom escort her out of the shop and a hundred feet down the road before stopping and turning to him.

'Did that really just happen?'

'That really just happened.'

'He liked my work.'

'He loved it, Jane, and who can blame him? I only managed to read some of it, upside down as it was, but you have real talent.'

She beamed, looking up at him. All her worries seemed insignificant now. The only thing she could think of was what the future might hold.

'Jane,' Lucy's voice called out, and they both spun to face her as she hurried across the street. There was a look of alarm on her face and she was moving quickly, far quicker than was deemed appropriate for a young lady when out in public.

'Is something amiss, Lucy?'

'I was enjoying a cup of tea, watching the world go by, when I was approached by an acquaintance, a woman I do not know well. She is the wife of another captain in the army who my husband knows a little.' Lucy paused, taking in a deep breath before continuing. 'She asked me about the rumours surrounding you and Mr Stewart, dropping in she knew we were friends.'

'Rumours?' Jane felt all the elation of a moment ago being sucked out of her.

'I was a bit sharp. I was taken by surprise, and said I knew of no rumours,' Lucy said, a look of deep concern on her face. 'I should have questioned her more, found out what it was she had heard and who she had heard it from, but then I saw you two out here on the street alone together and thought it more important you did not appear to be without a chaperon.'

Next to them, Tom let out a sharp exhalation and began to shake his head. 'I thought we were safe.'

Jane had allowed herself to hope so too when they

hadn't been assailed by gossip on the first morning after Mrs Burghley had witnessed the illicit kiss. Glancing around, wondering if everyone was looking at them, Jane suddenly felt self-conscious.

'We need to get away from here and find out what has been said.'

Lucy looked at her and must have had the same thought at the same moment, for together they said, 'Lady Mountjoy.'

'She will know,' Tom agreed. He leapt into action, guiding them round to his waiting carriage and helping them inside.

They travelled in complete silence. Jane was too shocked to be able to say anything. Even though she had known there was a very real possibility of Mrs Burghley telling everyone what she had seen, Jane had always considered this outcome in an abstract way, like a puzzle needing to be solved. She had never allowed the emotion to overwhelm her, had never really allowed herself to think about all the consequences. Risking a glance at Tom, she took in the pallor of his complexion. He didn't look like a man happy to be considering his impending nuptials.

Of course, she had a choice. Tom would offer her marriage. He was a gentleman, but more than that, he was a man who had his own set of morals, and abandoning a friend in need would not be acceptable to him. Already he had told her he would offer marriage, but that didn't mean she would have to accept.

Jane knew most people would view her as a fool for even considering turning down Tom's proposal. He was an extremely eligible bachelor and a good man. He was

kind, easy to get along with and devastatingly handsome. In theory, there was nothing but positives.

Jane turned and looked out of the window, trying to
distract herself with the view of the streets of London
flashing past, but it was impossible. She was always
aware of Tom when he was in close proximity and now
the closeness felt overwhelming.

Digging the nails of one hand into the other, she relished the bite of discomfort for a second, finding the
pain the only way to take herself away from the decision. Then the carriage slowed, the Mountjoys' townhouse came into view and she knew she had no more
time for distractions. She needed to make a decision.

Chapter Twenty

'I need a moment,' Jane said as she leaped from the carriage when it had barely stopped moving. She rushed towards the house, brushing past the footman as he opened the door, and disappearing before Tom could even step down to the pavement.

Slowly he stepped out, turning round to help Mrs Weyman down as well. Together they walked up to the house. Lady Mountjoy came to greet them by the door, her expression serious.

'Come in,' she said, ushering them inside. 'Lucy, why don't you go and check on Jane—see if she needs anything. I need to talk to Mr Stewart.'

Mrs Weyman looked glad to be able to escape, although Tom had hoped he would be able to go after Jane himself. Perhaps it was better they both had a few more minutes before they committed to each other for the rest of their lives.

Lady Mountjoy led him through to the drawing room and closed the door firmly behind them. Tom waited for her to sit, and then almost collapsed into one of the comfortable arm chairs.

'How bad is it?' He knew Lady Mountjoy would have heard every piece of gossip there was to hear and would be fully apprised of the situation. She knew everyone, was a friend to many and was even respected by the few who were not part of her inner circle.

'It is bad, Mr Stewart, very bad indeed...' She paused, and then seemed to take pity on him, for her expression softened. 'But not unsalvageable.'

'What are they saying?'

'The rumours were started by Mrs Burghley—a friend of yours, I believe.'

'A short-lived acquaintance.'

'A woman scorned?'

Tom shook his head. 'We went to the theatre together once. I did not feel there was anything between us, but perhaps Mrs Burghley thought differently.'

'I do not know the woman well. I came across her a few times whilst her husband was still alive. She's beautiful and I assume she is used to getting the things she wants.'

'Undoubtedly.'

'And she couldn't have you.'

They both remained silent for a minute. Tom had regretted the decision to take Mrs Burghley to the theatre ever since that fateful night.

'What has she said?'

'She has told everyone that after your trip to the theatre she accompanied you and Miss Ashworth to a friend's house. Whilst there, you and Miss Ashworth sneaked off into the garden and she found you entwined and kissing in the darkness.'

Tom let his head fall into his hands. It was a very ac-
curate retelling of what had happened. She hadn't em-
bellished it at all, which made it all the more plausible.

'She hasn't said who the friends were, although I assume it was Lucy and her husband.'

Tom nodded. At least they hadn't been pulled into
it, branded as a couple with loose morals.

'It *could* be a disaster,' Lady Mountjoy said. 'If you
refused to marry Jane—but I think you will do the
right thing.'

'Of course,' he said stiffly.

'A quick wedding, and a show of being together in
wedded bliss, and the *ton* will soon find something
else to gossip about. In a couple of months, no one will
even remember the circumstances of your marriage.'
She scrutinised him for a moment. 'You do not look
convinced.'

'Of course I will marry Miss Ashworth,' Tom said
slowly. 'I respect her too much to do anything else. I
got us into this mess, and I will do the right thing and
get us out of it.'

'That sounds an awful lot of duty and not much ro-
mance,' Lady Mountjoy said with a sigh. 'I know you
care for her.'

Tom remembered all the times Jane had swooped
in and helped him with Edward. He remembered the
quiet, unassuming way she listened to him and made
him laugh when he didn't think there was anything to
laugh about. The way she'd looked at him before they
had kissed and the way he had felt that irresistible pull
towards her, that need to be with her.

'I care for her, but I cannot offer her the sort of marriage she wants. She will have my name as protection, she will have a comfortable lifestyle. She will want for nothing material.'

'What about affection?'

He sucked in a raspy breath. Of course he cared for her, but he couldn't offer her love. If their arrangement was more practical, it would be easier to keep the boundaries that kept her safe. He couldn't trust himself always to put her needs first—he had shown he couldn't be trusted when he had abandoned his sister. He would be better able to protect Jane if she knew the limits of their marriage.

'I cannot offer her love,' he said, supressing the part of him that was shouting protestations inside his head.

Lady Mountjoy smoothed her skirts. 'I do not pretend to be able to read minds, but I think I can see when one person cares for another, and you care for Jane.'

'That is why I cannot risk her heart,' Tom said softly. 'This way will be better. She will be my wife in name, and free to pursue whatever path she wants without me tying her down.' He shrugged, trying to brush off the weight that was pressing down on him, trying to suffocate him. 'We will both benefit. I will gain a mother figure for Edward, and she will avoid the scandal of the gossip that is circulating.'

'I do not believe your true feelings are so practical, Tom.'

He shook his head, refusing to let out the storm of emotion building inside him. It was better this way, better for both of them. There was no way of avoiding the marriage, but he could still protect Jane.

* * *

Jane was pacing up and down when Lucy knocked on the door and entered immediately.

'You look frantic, Jane,' Lucy said, catching her by the arms and forcing her to stop moving for a second. 'Take some deep breaths.'

Slowly Jane obeyed, feeling some of the nervous tension flow from her.

'This is a nightmare,' she said, clutching hold of Lucy and looking at her imploringly, as if there was something her friend could do to stop it.

'I agree it is hardly ideal,' Lucy said slowly. 'But is it really a nightmare?'

Jane looked at her as if she had grown a second head. 'Yes.'

'A scandal is not what any of us want, but all it really does is speed things along.'

'What do you mean?'

'It is obvious that you love Mr Stewart,' Lucy said, as if she hadn't just exposed Jane's biggest secret. 'And he loves you. All this gossip has done is speed up your engagement and wedding.'

Jane spluttered. 'I do not love Mr Stewart.'

'Of course you do. It is obvious in the way you look at him, the way you talk about him, the way you two share little jokes and intimate looks. You forget, I have been in love with William for a long time, Jane, much of it illicitly. I know how a woman acts when she is in love.'

'He does not love me.'

Lucy took her hands and squeezed them in her own. 'He loves you, Jane. He may not have admitted it to himself yet, but that man loves you.'

Jane bit her lip, wondering if there could be any truth in what Lucy was saying. Her friend was romantic, always sure that things were going to turn out for the best. She thought of their kisses, of the easy companionship they had together, the way they laughed and talked. For her, that all translated into the deep emotional connection she felt for this man—maybe it did for him too.

'I don't have to marry him,' she said quietly.

'Don't do anything rash.'

'I'm considering my options. I have a publisher interested in my books. I could go home to Somerset and write and draw and paint and support myself.'

'Is that what you want?'

For the first time, she let go of any of the little lies she'd told herself, of the doubts and boundaries holding her back.

'No,' she said eventually. 'I want to write and draw, but I want to do it with Tom.'

'You have your answer, then.'

It felt like a long walk downstairs, and Jane paused on the first floor landing before starting on the final steps that would take her to her future husband. The door to the drawing room had come open a crack, and she could hear Lady Mountjoy's voice, followed by Tom's. She wondered what they had discussed, and whether the older woman was angry at the idea of a scandal or elated at the thought of a wedding. Knowing Lady Mountjoy, probably the latter. The countess had never shied away from a brewing scandal in the time Jane had known her, and always seemed able to twist the situation so the young couple she was championing came out on top.

'This way will be better,' Tom was saying, his voice clear but with a dejected note. 'She will be my wife in name, and free to pursue whatever path she wants without me tying her down. We will both benefit. I will gain a mother figure for Edward, and she will avoid the scandal of the gossip that is circulating.'

It was as though someone had reached into her chest and ripped her heart in two. Here she was, convincing herself that Tom loved her, and all he could do was think about the practical reasons it would not be so bad to have her as his wife. Suddenly, she felt foolish and naïve. A vision of a marriage of convenience to Tom burst into her mind, with her stuck at home, pining after the husband she secretly loved whilst he continued to seek his life of pleasure.

She let out a little sob, angry with herself for almost falling for the fantasy, and devastated that she would not get the happy ending she had conjured in her mind. Clamping her hand over her mouth, she realised they must have heard her inside the drawing room. She ran, not even taking the time to grab her coat, and burst out into the street as if she were being chased by hungry wolves.

Somewhere behind her she heard Tom calling her name, but nothing would have enticed her to return in that moment. Not caring where she ended up, Jane ran, darting down streets and dodging people out for a stroll now the snow had melted. She ran until the tears had stopped falling and the sobs had left her body empty and aching. Finally, she sank down onto a bench, gasping for breath, wondering when she had let herself get so vulnerable.

Chapter Twenty-One

'You are in a foul mood,' Western said as he eyed Tom up and down. 'And you look a state.'

'Don't be afraid to speak your mind there, Western.'

'I'm only saying what I am seeing.'

Tom grunted and went to set up the line of plates thirty paces away. They were out in the country, an hour's ride from central London, and so far they hadn't seen another soul since having arrived at the spot. It was a favourite retreat of theirs, somewhere they came every few months to shoot pistols without being disturbed. Sometimes they would even talk, although Tom hoped this time they could just shoot and ruminate on their problems in silence.

He walked the thirty paces back and picked up the pistol Western had left in the case. It was a beautiful weapon, shiny and well maintained. Tom had inherited it from his father and, as much as he'd hated the old man, he had to admit he had good taste in pistols. This pair not only looked good but shot straight and were reliable, everything you wanted from a weapon.

When he was satisfied the pistol was in good working order, he loaded it and then took up his position. Western stood next to him, the other pistol in his hand, his stance identical to Tom's.

Tom fired first, pleased to see one of the plates shatter, the pottery exploding outwards and tinkling to the ground. Western fired a moment later, also hitting a plate at the other end of the row.

'Nice shot,' Western commented. 'It looked to be right in the centre of the plate. Did you know you always have the best aim when you're angry?'

'I'm not angry.'

Western scoffed. 'I've known you a long time, Stewart. I know when you're angry.'

Tom bent over his pistol, concentrating on reloading it. He *was* angry. Angry at himself for how he had handled the situation with Jane, angry with Jane for not granting him a few minutes to explain himself, angry with Mrs Burghley for forcing his hand and starting the gossip that was going to destroy Jane's reputation.

He turned and aimed again, taking his time and shooting as he exhaled, feeling a surge of triumph as another plate shattered.

'I can guess, if you would prefer it,' Western said.

'You can be annoying as hell, Western, did you know that?'

'My wife tells me on a daily basis.'

Tom sighed and put down the pistol, knowing Western wasn't going to stop until he had the whole story from him.

'I've messed up,' Tom said quietly.

'With the woman you were telling me about?'

'Jane, yes.'

Western took another shot, smashing one of the plates, and then motioned for Tom to go on.

'Mrs Burghley told a few people about having seen us kiss,' he said, still unable to comprehend how he was in this situation when a couple of days ago he had been sure he would marry Jane. 'The rumours spread quickly.'

'Were you forced to propose?'

'I had told Jane I would—I promised her I wouldn't abandon her. Even so, when we heard the rumours it was a bit of a shock. I think part of me thought Mrs Burghley might do the kind thing and keep quiet.'

'Did you react poorly?'

Tom thought back, wondering if Jane had seen it as so. He hadn't jumped for joy when he'd realised her reputation had been destroyed in one swoop, but he didn't think he had reacted particularly poorly.

'I wasn't ecstatic,' he said slowly. 'But I accepted what had to happen. We were out when we heard the rumours and hurried to get back to Lady Mountjoy's house.'

Western nodded, starting to reload his pistol, handing it to Tom before picking up the one Tom had abandoned. Tom aimed and fired, finding it easier to think when part of his brain was distracted by shooting the pistol.

'Jane went upstairs to take a minute and I spoke to Lady Mountjoy.' He paused, trying to remember the exact words he had said. 'I told Lady Mountjoy it couldn't be a marriage fuelled by love, but that it would suit both of us perfectly well. Jane would keep her reputation and I would gain a mother figure for Edward.'

Western looked at him with an expression of surprise.

'I thought you were meant to be good with the ladies. I take it she heard this?'

'Yes, unfortunately she did.'

'Is she in love with you?'

Tom was about to say no, but then he stopped himself and considered. Jane was always practical, always sensible, but he knew there was a layer of deeper feeling there. When they had kissed, he'd seen it burning in her eyes, and even when they were together innocently, strolling through the park or dancing in the ballroom, he felt a warmth from her.

'I think maybe she is.'

'Then your words would be devastating to her. She probably harboured hopes that you loved her as she loved you.'

Tom tamped down the little voice that declared he did love her, trying to brush it away.

'I didn't even get the chance to talk to her about it,' he said quietly, shaking his head. 'She ran away, and I searched and searched, but couldn't find her. Later that day, she went home, but has refused to see me since.'

'I'm not surprised.'

'This will ruin her life, Western. *I* have ruined her life.'

Tom began to reload the pistol, taking his time to combat the shaking of his hands.

'Her reputation,' Western corrected softly. 'Not necessarily her life.'

'She will become a pariah in social circles.'

'But from what you've told me she doesn't sound the sort to really care.'

'Even some of her friends will turn her away.'

'Not true friends.'

Taking a few deep breaths to steady his hand, Tom aimed again, cursing when the shot went wide. Lowering the pistol, he considered Western's words and realised his friend was right. All this time Tom had been treating her like an ordinary young woman, a normal debutante, but Jane was nothing of the sort. She was fiercely independent and knew what she wanted from her future.

She might not be welcome in polite circles in London with a ruined reputation, but he didn't doubt her family would welcome her back. Jane had always spoken fondly of them, even if she was lost a little in amongst so many children. She had somewhere to go and, with the likelihood that Mr Hambly was going to publish her books, she had something that would occupy her time and hopefully bring her an income.

'She doesn't have to marry me,' he murmured. All this time he had assumed she needed him, that the only way for her to survive this was to marry him. It had meant he hadn't really thought about what was best for her.

Tom felt a coldness spread through him as he realised he had probably lost her for good.

'I don't want to lose her,' he said quietly.

'Why?' Western asked, the question sounding harsh. 'You only want to marry her to give Edward a mother figure.'

Tom knew his friend was deliberately provoking him, but he couldn't help but react all the same.

'That's not true.'

'Do you want to marry her?'

Tom didn't speak for a long moment, allowing the memories of the last few weeks to flood into his mind.

'Yes.'

'Why do you want to marry her?'

'I love her.' He blinked, surprising himself at the answer. Western clapped him on the back, throwing his head back and giving out a whoop of joy.

'In all the years that I've known you, nothing has been so hard as getting you to confess that.'

'I love her,' Tom repeated, realising it was true. He loved the way she smiled and the way she was always so direct. He loved the sparkle she got in her eyes when she wanted to be kissed and the enthusiastic way she tried anything new. He loved that she didn't care what people thought of her, forging her own path, even if people stared and whispered.

Shaking his head, he knew this realisation didn't solve all his problems.

'That only makes things worse,' he said quietly.

Western regarded him for a long time and then turned away to take his shot.

'You've never put into words what it is that stops you from allowing yourself to be happy,' he said quietly. 'But you do not fool me with this carefree act of yours. You have too big a heart to keep it locked away, pretending that you would rather have purely superficial relationships.'

Tom opened his mouth to make a flippant remark

but nothing would come out. He thought of all the years keeping people at arm's length. Western was the only one who truly knew him and that was because they'd been through hell on the battlefield together. No one else had come close in his adult life, and Tom knew that was because he was an expert at knowing the exact moment to step away.

Until Jane. Somehow she had slipped under his defences, she had clung on when he had attempted to keep his distance and their friendship had bloomed alongside the desire that burned between them.

'You don't have to tell me,' Western said, lining up another shot and smiling in satisfaction as the penultimate plate broke a second after the pistol shot rang out. 'But ask yourself if it is truly worth your happiness. Sometimes the ideas we create in our youth, we hang on to for far too long.'

He handed Tom the pistol with the final shot and took a step back. With his thoughts racing, Tom took his position, knowing if he didn't concentrate the shot would go wide again. He cleared his mind, pushing all the irrelevant noise to one side, and aimed, pulling the trigger with one lone thought left in his head: *I love her.*

The plate shattered and Tom felt a momentary thrill of triumph. Western took the pistol from him and went to start clearing up the shards of pottery from their makeshift targets.

Tom sat down, half-collapsing to the ground. He looked up at the clear sky above, trying to find answers that weren't there.

I need to see her, he realised. Perhaps everything would become clearer if he could see Jane, if he could tell her how he felt. It might not change anything for her, but it would mean they were both making decisions without hiding anything from one another.

'I've been going about this all wrong,' he murmured to himself. Not that he hadn't tried to see Jane since she had fled into the street and disappeared, but each time he'd been denied. Lady Mountjoy had been sympathetic, inviting him to wait in the drawing room on each occasion he had called, but each time she had returned downstairs, shaking her head and telling him Jane would not come out to see him today.

He'd given up too easily, sometimes secretly relieved, as he had not known what he wanted to say to her. There was an urgency inside him, pushing him to make things right, but he had been unable to work out how.

'You get back to the city,' Western said as he returned with all the pieces of broken pottery. 'I'll tidy up here. I'll clean the pistols and drop them off in a day or two.'

Without a word of argument, Tom nodded, already striding over to where his horse was loosely tied to a fence post. It was an hour's ride back to central London. If he went straight to Lady Mountjoy's, he could confess how he felt to Jane by three o'clock. They would still have much to work out, and she still might refuse his offer of marriage, but it was better than standing around here, feeling wretched and not acting on anything.

'I'm going to miss you so much,' Jane said, squeezing Lucy hard as they embraced.

'I will be coming to visit before you know it.' Lucy had tears in her eyes and suddenly they spilled over onto her cheeks.

'Promise you'll write to me every week. I want to know every little snippet of news.'

'I promise.'

They hugged again, neither wanting to be the first one to let go.

'If we are to make the coach to Bath, we really should leave now,' Lady Mountjoy said, her tone gentle.

Jane nodded, looking around at the plush drawing room, sad that her time in London had come to an end like this.

'Thank you for your hospitality,' Jane said to Lord Mountjoy.

'You are welcome to stay with us any time,' he said magnanimously. 'I do hope you get all the happiness you deserve, Miss Ashworth.'

Jane took one last look around and then allowed Lady Mountjoy to lead her out to the waiting carriage. There was a coach leaving London at noon to start the first leg of the journey to Bath. Lady Mountjoy had offered to accompany Jane, to give her the use of the family carriage, but Jane felt that she needed some time alone before she was swept back into family life. Perhaps a few days on the road would be enough time for her to learn to hide her heartbreak.

They stepped up into Lady Mountjoy's carriage that would take them to the coach and Jane caught a glimpse of all the luggage strapped to the back. It was much more than she had brought to London, and it reminded her of her hostess' generosity during her stay.

'I want to thank you too,' Jane said as they settled on their seats.

'Don't thank me,' the countess said. 'I've made such a mess of all this for you. I deserve to be condemned.'

'No. You are the kindest person I know. You saw what it would mean to take five girls like us and show us the world of the debutante. Even I, who was determined not to enjoy myself at first, have had the most incredible experience these last six months.'

'That's kind of you to say, my dear,' Lady Mountjoy said, leaning forward and placing her hand over Jane's. 'I worry that my motivation was selfish, that I missed escorting my daughters to the balls of the Season so much, I tried to recreate those times I loved without acknowledging enough that you are all your own people with your own aims and goals.'

'You have nothing to reproach yourself for. Everything you have done for us has been wonderful.'

'Are you sure you wish to leave, my dear?'

Jane nodded. Over the last few days, she had thought about little else. After she had heard Tom declaring their marriage would be nothing but a practical arrangement, she had felt her heart crack and crumble. In that moment, she'd realised quite how much she had been hoping for the fantasy. Even though she had tried to hide it from herself, she loved Tom and had desperately wanted his love in return.

'It is your decision,' Lady Mountjoy said, leaning back in her seat. 'And it may be the right one, as long as you are sure.'

'I can't stay here, not knowing I will have to face Tom at some point.'

'No, I can see that would be difficult.'

'I know the mature thing would be to talk to him, but

I just can't do it. I can't listen to him tell me all the reasons we should get married when I know he wishes it weren't so.'

Lady Mountjoy bit her lip and looked as though she wanted to say something.

'I want to run away and get swallowed up by the noise and chaos at home so I do not have to think about Tom or the scandal or my ruined reputation.'

'The gossip may follow you.'

'I know,' Jane said with a sigh. 'But what harm can it really do me in my tiny Somerset village where people have known me all my life? They won't believe it. I'm steadfast Jane, sensible Jane.' She scoffed. At least her reputation as being dull and undesirable was good for something. 'There may be rumours, but I doubt anything will stick, and it is not as if I am trying to land myself a husband.'

'And what of Tom?'

Jane felt a piercing pain slice through her heart every time she thought of the man she loved. 'I suppose I won't see him again.' At least the scandal wouldn't hurt him. If anything, it would enhance his reputation as a rake, and mean he escaped the machinations of society debutantes and their mothers.

'This is all wrong!' Lady Mountjoy burst out suddenly. 'He loves you. I know he loves you.'

Jane shook her head sadly. She had hoped he did, even convinced herself he did. She remembered the heat in his kisses, the affection in his eyes when he'd looked at her. They had talked to one another like old friends and she knew marriage with him, the right sort of marriage, would have been easy.

'I know he has reasons why he thinks he should not marry,' Jane said, unsure how much Lady Mountjoy knew about Tom's sister and how he blamed himself for leaving her behind. 'But if he loved me, truly loved me, then none of that would matter—not enough to keep us apart.'

'Sometimes he can be so stubborn,' the countess murmured, then fell silent, staring out of the window.

Jane tried not to think about it, tried not to think about what their lives could have been like if she had said yes to him, tried not to wonder if she was making a mistake in refusing to marry him even if he was only offering her a match of convenience.

'If you change your mind, do remember you are always welcome to stay with us, here or in Somerset. No matter what you decide, you are family now, and if you need anything at all I want you to ask.'

Jane nodded, realising she was going to miss Lady Mountjoy as much as she would miss Lucy. The rest of the debutantes had fallen one by one, finding their husbands and their happiness. Jane longed to catch up with Charlotte, who had stayed in Somerset with her husband, and with Eliza, who was on her honeymoon. Perhaps soon they could all reunite. She tried to dampen down the tears that threatened to come when she realised she was the only one of the five debutantes who had not ended the trip to London with the man she loved. Love and marriage had never been her aim. She should be proud she had achieved what she had set out to do and had garnered the interest of a publisher for her stories.

The carriage rolled to a stop and the driver set about

arranging the transfer of her trunk and bags across to the coach to Bath. Jane felt a wrench of emotion and sprung forward in her seat, embracing the older woman who had given her so much.

'I will miss you,' she said, her voice muffled by Lady Mountjoy's dress.

'And I you, Jane. Do write and let me know you have reached home safely, and I will pay you a visit when we return to Somerset in a couple of months.'

It felt as though the walk to the coach were a mile rather than a mere twenty feet and Jane couldn't bear to look back, getting on and taking her seat whilst desperately trying to stop herself from breaking down.

Slowly the coach filled up, the space quickly becoming hot despite the freezing temperatures outside. Everyone had on multiple layers, thick dresses or jackets layered over with coats and gloves, and it took a while for people to shed some of those layers to get comfortable. As a result, Jane felt crushed in the corner of the coach, pressed up against the side by a large middle-aged woman, and barely able to move her legs, as they were precariously placed so as not to touch those of the tall man opposite her. It was going to be a long few days.

Chapter Twenty-Two

Having ridden as fast as was possible on the busyroads back into the centre of London, Tom now paused for a minute outside the Mountjoys' townhouse. Whilst riding, he had mulled over the right way to phrase things a hundred times, but now he was standing here he did not have a clue what he actually wanted to say.

'Stop delaying,' he muttered to himself and forced his feet to move.

The door opened immediately, and Tom was surprised to find Lady Mountjoy standing there, her eyes red-rimmed.

'Is something amiss?'

'Come in, come in,' the countess said, ushering him inside. 'Foolish boy, asking me if something is amiss.'

'What has happened? Is it Jane? Is she unwell?' He had an awful sinking sensation in his stomach and almost pushed past Lady Mountjoy, determined to climb the stairs and check for himself that Jane was unharmed.

Lady Mountjoy turned and walked away, motioning for him to follow her through to the drawing room.

'Jane's health is as robust as always. On that front you do not have to fear.'

'I really need to speak to her.'

'That won't be possible…'

'I know she has refused the last few days, but I am adamant I will succeed today.'

'It isn't possible, Tom, because she has left.'

Tom felt the world shift under his feet.

'She can't have left.'

'I assure you, she has. Three hours ago I waved her off on the coach to Bath.'

'No.' He staggered backwards and sat down. This wasn't how this afternoon was meant to go. As he had been riding over, he had thought and thought about what he was going to say to Jane. He knew he had to tell her he loved her, that the scandal and his desire for a happy family for Edward were not the only reasons he knew marriage to her was the right thing. He had hoped when they were together, when he could hold her hands and look into her eyes, the words would come naturally and she would be able to see what lay in his heart.

'She decided to return to Somerset.' Lady Mountjoy looked at him with a dejected expression. 'She is convinced you do not love her.'

Tom closed his eyes and shook his head. 'Of course I love her. How could I not?'

'Then whatever has been stopping you from telling that poor girl you feel the same way she does?'

'I need to find her. The coach left three hours ago, you say?'

'Yes. It will be on the road out of London now.'

He took his pocket watch out of his jacket and checked

the time. Nightfall was only a few hours away and it would be treacherous to ride in the dark on the poorly maintained roads. Conditions were worse the further you got out of London and, as much as he wanted to reach Jane as quickly as possible, he knew he couldn't risk his horse's safety to do so.

'I will bring her back,' he said, standing abruptly.

'Be careful.'

He bowed and then strode from the house. Even though he wanted to set off immediately, he knew charging out into the darkness unprepared was beyond foolish. Tonight he would ready his horse and ensure his affairs were in order and tomorrow he would leave at dawn. Even with the head start, the coach would make slow progress, and he would likely catch up with it tomorrow evening before it stopped for the night.

Rationally, he knew twenty-four hours was hardly any time to wait, but it felt like an eternity. He had a sense of urgency, a need to tell Jane how he felt now he had worked it out for himself.

Twenty-four hours later, Tom was wet and cold, cursing the English weather and wondering whether the warmer days of spring would ever arrive. A steady drizzle had plagued him all day, slowly soaking through his coat and penetrating his clothes layer by layer. He was now so stiff he doubted he would be able to straighten up if he dismounted and he had ceased being able to feel the ends of his fingers about an hour ago.

The light was fading fast and, although a local had assured him it was only another few minutes to the coaching inn, he was beginning to doubt whether this stage of his journey would ever end.

Time and time again throughout the day he had been splattered by thick mud as coaches rolled past, and for one of the only times in his life he wished he had been sensible enough to travel in the comfort of his own carriage rather than on horseback.

Sending up a silent prayer of thanks, he murmured a few words of encouragement to Rupert as he spotted the faint glow of an oil lamp ahead. Slowly the coaching inn came into view, a long, squat building that looked as if it had stood in the same position for hundreds of years. The yard was large and well maintained and Tom was thankful when a stable boy ran out to greet him as he entered through the gate.

'Give him a good brush down for me,' Tom said, passing a couple of coins to the young boy.

'Yes, sir. I'll make sure he is fed and watered too.'

'Thank you.'

Tom peered around him, noting the two carriages stationary on one side of the yard. It was highly likely that one of the coaches was the one headed to Bath, the one Jane was travelling on. Unless they had made extraordinarily good progress, they couldn't have reached much further before the light had begun to fail, and Tom knew there wasn't another coaching inn for ten miles.

Looking down at himself, he grimaced. He was hardly the suave and charming man the gossips liked to paint him, splattered top-to toe in mud and grunting at the stiffness in his muscles. All the same, he moved as quickly as he could towards the entrance, wonder-

ing if Jane would be sitting in the dining area or if she
would have already retired to her room.

'Filthy weather still, I see, sir.' An older man with a
friendly smile greeted him as he entered.

'Indeed.'

'Will you be wanting a room?'

'Yes.' He hoped they had something available as,
now he had dismounted, he doubted he would be able
to get back on his horse.

'I will show you up in a moment, sir. Would you like
a drink or something to eat first?'

There was an enticing smell coming from the dining room and Tom knew his body would appreciate a
good meal and a spot by a roaring fire.

'Later, perhaps, but first I need to know—has the
coach to Bath stopped here?'

'Yes, sir. Filled most of our rooms.'

'Good. I've been riding all day to catch up with it. I
am looking for a Miss Jane Ashworth.'

The innkeeper's eyes narrowed and Tom glanced
down, realising in his current state he didn't look particularly trustworthy.

'My sister,' he said in explanation. 'She is returning to our home in Bath but I have some sad news of
a relative.'

'I see, sir. I can deliver a message to the young lady
and see if she wishes to meet with you. Excuse the caution, but you can't be too careful these days. There are
so many ne'er do wells about.'

'Thank you. Perhaps you could arrange for some hot
water so I can clean up before dinner.'

'Of course, sir.'

The innkeeper disappeared for a moment, shouting instructions to a weary-looking maid before reappearing with a bunch of keys. He led Tom upstairs and down a narrow corridor to the room at the end.

'I only have our most expensive room left,' he said as he opened the door.

'That is fine.'

It was a good-sized room with a four-poster bed and an arm chair in front of the fire. There was no blaze burning in the grate but the wood was piled high, ready to be lit.

'I will send Sally up to light the fire and bring you some hot water.'

'Thank you.'

Tom waited for the innkeeper to leave before sinking into the chair and kicking off his boots. He felt restless, as if he wanted to pound on every door, shouting for Jane, but knew he needed to be patient. In a few minutes the innkeeper would deliver his message and Jane would agree to meet him. After chasing her for a day, he could wait another half hour.

Glad of the warmth when the maid arrived and started the fire, he unpacked the small bag he had travelled with. It contained only a single change of clothes. He hadn't expected the weather to be quite so foul, and in his haste he hadn't thought ahead to what would happen if he didn't catch up with Jane in one day.

Soon the maid reappeared with a steaming bowl of water and he set to work, peeling off his wet clothes and hanging them up to dry. When he had stripped down to just his breeches, he took a moment to stand in front of the fire, feeling the heat seep through his skin and start to warm his core.

The hot water was bliss and he was grateful to be able to wash away the grime and mud from the day. As he stood in front of the mirror combing his hair, there was a soft knock on the door. Thinking it would be the maid or the innkeeper, he called for them to come in, not bothering to reach for a shirt.

'Oh, you're naked.' Jane's voice was shocked, but he barely even registered the tone, so glad was he to see her.

'Hardly,' he said, indicating the breeches.

She coughed and then slowly raised her eyes to meet his.

'Perhaps I should come back later.'

'You are not going anywhere,' he said, adamant now he had found her he was not going to let her out of his sight until he had said all he had come to say.

Striding over to the door, he ushered her inside and closed it firmly behind her, turning the key in the lock so no one could burst in on them.

'What are you doing here, Tom?'

'You ran away.'

'I didn't run away. I decided to go home.'

'Without telling me.'

'It is no longer any of your concern what I do.'

There was a flare of defiance in her voice but he could see she was sad too.

'Of course it is,' he said, and then forced himself to breath slowly. There were so many things he needed to say to her and it was vital he did it in the right way. 'Will you sit down? I would like to talk to you, properly, without rushing.'

She hesitated and then went and perched on the edge of the arm chair by the fire. Tom took a moment to look her over. Her eyes were red-rimmed, and he wondered if she had been crying, but apart from that she looked well. He didn't know what he had expected—perhaps that she wouldn't cope without him, as he felt he hadn't coped without her, but at first glance she seemed to be fine.

He took a step towards the bed and then sat down, wishing he was closer but knowing Jane needed to hear his words before he reached for her hand.

'I am sorry for what you heard me say to Lady Mountjoy,' he said quietly. 'I was panicked and worried about the future.'

'That is understandable,' Jane said, her face impassive. 'Thank you for the apology, but it really wasn't necessary for you to race all this way to say you were sorry how things ended.'

She stood and turned to leave and for a moment Tom was stunned. Recovering as quickly as he could, he leaped from the bed and grasped hold of her by the arms.

'That was not all I came to say.'

Jane looked down, swallowing as her eyes skimmed across his naked chest and arms.

'Please put on a shirt,' she said, her voice low, and he could see there was a flicker of desire in her eyes when she looked back up at him.

Tom complied, taking a moment to pull on the clean shirt he had hung up a few minutes earlier. When he turned back to Jane, she looked as though she wanted to flee.

'I've been beyond foolish,' he said, realising if she left

now he might never get a chance to say what he needed to. 'It took losing you to make me realise what we had, what we could have in the future.'

'I don't understand.'

Reaching down, he took both her hands in his own.

'I love you, Jane.'

She looked up at him as if he had just declared he was off to live on the moon.

'No, you don't.'

He laughed, loving how certain she was about everything, even now.

'I do. I didn't realise it at first. I think I tried not to admit it to myself because it would mean confronting things I have tried to hide from for a long time.'

'You love me?'

'Yes. I love you. I love *everything* about you. When I pictured my life without you, it made me so miserable. It was a life without laughter and happiness and love.'

Shaking her head, she pulled away. 'How have you gone from thinking our marriage would be a convenient arrangement, something done to preserve my reputation with the added benefit of providing a stable family for Edward, to this?'

'I think I knew I loved you even then. I just couldn't admit it.'

'Because loving me is so shameful.'

'No,' he said firmly. 'You are worth the love of a hundred men. It was my problems, my stubbornness, that stopped me from being able to accept what my heart was trying to tell me.'

Jane fell quiet, her head bowed and her eyes darting back and forth across the floor.

'I need some time,' she said abruptly, turning to leave.

'Jane,' he said, softly now. 'All I am asking for is some time to explain.' He was asking for a lot more than that—they both knew it—but first they needed to sit down and talk.

She nodded. 'I'm not going to run again,' she said with a half-smile. 'But I just need a few minutes.'

'Have you eaten?'

'No.'

'Shall I ask the maid to bring something up and we can talk over dinner?'

'That sounds like a nice idea. Perhaps in half an hour.'

Without waiting for his answer, she left, walking away quickly so he couldn't try to stop her. Normally he was good at reading people, at knowing what they were thinking or what they were going to do, but at this moment he had no idea what was going through Jane's head.

Jane burst out of the double doors into the courtyard, gasping for breath. She felt as though she were suffocating and tried to suck in great lungfuls of air. The cool raindrops that landed on her face were a shock to her body and this seemed to help her, to ground her a little, and slowly she felt some semblance of normality returning.

Glancing up, she was grateful to see there were hardly any windows looking out over the courtyard. The last thing she needed was for Tom to witness her panic and come rushing down.

Leaning back against the wall, she tried to empty

her mind of everything but the air going in and out of her chest. It took a few minutes but after some time she felt much calmer.

He loves me. Jane knew if he had told her this a week ago she would have been dancing with joy, planning out their lives together. Now everything was different. She did believe him. Tom wasn't cruel. He wouldn't tell her he loved her if he didn't. Despite everything that had happened between them, she still knew he was a good man, a man who would never intentionally go out of his way to hurt her.

He loves me. Part of her wished she could ignore everything else—ignore the fact he didn't want the responsibility for someone else, that if he had the choice they wouldn't be getting married—but this was her life, her future, and she refused to go into it blindly.

Jane knew she had to listen, to hear what he had to say, and then she could consider whether they would be better together or apart.

'I love you, Tom Stewart,' she murmured, wondering if love was going to be enough.

Half an hour later, there was a delicious aroma wafting out of Tom's room as Jane approached. Quietly she knocked on the door, not wanting to announce to all the other guests at the inn that she was going in to have dinner alone with a man, unchaperoned.

'Come in,' Tom said as he opened the door. He was dressed properly now, in a shirt and jacket. They were a little crumpled but fresh. As usual, he looked devastatingly handsome.

Someone had set up a small table and brought in another chair, placing it so it faced the arm chair that was already in the room. On the table were two steaming bowls of stew—the delicious smell she had detected on walking along the corridor. There was also a plate of bread and a selection of meats and cheese. Jane had taken some bread and an apple for her lunch from the inn she had stayed at the night before, but apart from that she hadn't eaten since breakfast, and suddenly she realised quite how hungry she was.

'That smells wonderful.'

'I know. I had a hard time not eating both portions before you arrived and pretending they only brought bread and cheese.'

'I applaud your restraint. Shall we eat?'

The stew was delicious, warm, flavoursome and filling, just what Jane needed after a long day being rocked in the uncomfortable and crowded coach. She felt herself relaxing and didn't object when Tom started to talk about everyday things. He told her of his time in Italy and the skirmishes he and his friend Western had got into in the army. It felt good to listen, to not worry about the future for a little while.

Once the meal was finished, they placed the plates outside the door and Tom took her hand, leading her to the bed.

'Sit with me,' he said, his eyes holding hers. 'Sit with me while we talk.' Hesitantly, she nodded. There was a knot of nerves in her stomach, swirling and squirming. In the next few minutes, they would decide what their entire futures looked like.

'I meant what I said earlier,' Tom said quietly. 'I love you. I didn't allow myself to admit it, because it would mean confronting all the demons from my past, but it is the truth.'

'I believe you.' She hesitated, wondering how she could make him see it wasn't his love she was questioning. 'I know the heartache you went through with your sister. I know you still blame yourself for leaving her behind. I understand that is why you have never wanted a relationship where the other person becomes reliant on you, but if we marry that will happen.' She paused and looked him directly in the eye. 'If we marry, I will be your wife.'

'I know.'

'And the last thing I want to do is make you feel trapped or as if you have been forced into this.'

Tom reached out and took her hand. 'I have been doing a lot of thinking over the last few days and I realised something you said to me a few days ago was true. I was a young man when I left for the army, a young man who had experienced nothing but cruelty and disdain from my father. If could turn back the clock and have my time again, I wouldn't leave my sister there, but that is said with hindsight and growth.'

Jane felt a surge of hope begin to build inside her. This was exactly what Tom needed to see, needed to realise, but she hadn't thought it possible, given how long he had been holding on to his guilt.

'If placed in that situation again, I know I would act differently,' he said, looking at her with affection in his eyes. 'So I have to believe the same is true for my life with you and with Edward.'

'I know you would always put that boy first and do your best by him.'

'I would. I still feel guilty about leaving my sister behind, but I need to move forward in my life as the man I am now, not the boy I was then.' He paused and then took her hand. 'I am sorry it took me nearly losing you to realise this. For so long, I've felt so guilty. Any time the subject has come up, I've hurried to suppress it. I didn't want to examine what had happened and that meant I was stuck in a perpetual loop of guilt and regret.'

'I think everything you've said is true,' she said, knowing it meant they might be able to share a future.

'I want it all, Jane. I want you and I want love and I want us to be a family with Edward. I stand by part of what you overheard me say to Lady Mountjoy— Edward's life will be much better with you in it. So will mine. We would be lucky to have you. *I* would be lucky to have you.'

'I would be lucky to have you too,' Jane said quietly.

Tom raised his head a little so his eyes held hers.

'You mean that?'

'Yes. I love you, Tom. I've loved you for longer than I could admit to myself. I want nothing more than to make a life with you.'

'I would never take away your independence.'

'I know. It is one of the many things I love about you.'

With a gentle hand, Tom reached up and cupped her cheek, and Jane felt the inevitable pull between them. His fingers caressed her skin, sending little shocks through her body and making her want to collapse into him.

'I have something very important to ask you, Jane,' he said, his voice low. 'Will you marry me?'

'Yes.'

He kissed her, his lips brushing over hers, teasing her exquisitely until she couldn't help but tangle her fingers in his hair and pull him closer. She moaned as he pulled away and then started trailing kisses down from her earlobe and onto her neck. Somehow they had collapsed backwards on the bed and Jane felt the wonderful anticipation of what was to come.

'I propose we don't have a long engagement,' he murmured as he ran a hand over her body, catching the bottom of her skirts and lifting them to expose the bare skin of her legs beneath.

'Six months?' she offered.

'You are ridiculous,' he said, a hand climbing up higher on her leg, passing her knee and making her gasp in anticipation.

'Four months?'

'If you think you can keep our nightly visits secret for four months, then you are deluded,' he whispered in her ear.

'Two months?'

'Still far too long.' His hand was midway up her thigh now and he paused, making her almost cry out with frustration. 'How about I make you an offer?'

'Go on, then.'

'Tomorrow morning I ride back to London and petition the archbishop for a special licence. He will not refuse. Then you become my wife within the week.'

'People will think we have something to hide.'

'We do,' he said, his hand tracing circles upwards. 'We have so much to hide.'

He kissed her again, long and deep, and in that moment Jane would have agreed to anything.

'One week,' she murmured as he pulled away.

'One week. Then we can do this every single night.'

Jane was surprised when he pulled her to her feet and spun her so she faced the door. For a second, she felt a crushing disappointment, thinking he was going to send her on her way, then she felt his fingers on the back of her dress, unfastening the ties that kept it in place.

He worked quickly, loosening it off until it was ready to fall past her hips and pool on the floor. Underneath she had on a chemise, stays and a long petticoat, so she was not yet naked, but she could feel his eyes raking over her body all the same.

'You're beautiful, Jane,' he said as he unlaced her stays and threw the piece of clothing to the floor.

She shook her head. It was inconceivable to her that he should find her this attractive, that he could desire her the way she desired him.

The petticoat was next, falling around her ankles, leaving her with only her chemise to cover her body.

Jane let out a little gasp as he gripped the hem of her chemise, even though she knew this was coming. With one swift movement he lifted it off over her head and Jane felt the chill of the air prickle her skin.

'Look at me,' he instructed her. 'You are beautiful. I cannot resist you. I don't know what you have done to me, but I am enchanted, bewitched.'

Again she shook her head.

'You're beautiful, Jane, and I will tell you so every day of our lives until you see it for yourself.'

He moved in closer and kissed her, this time his

hands running across the bare skin of her shoulders. It felt exquisite, like nothing Jane had ever felt before, and she leaned into him, wanting to hold him closer. Although Tom had dressed for dinner, he had already shrugged off his jacket and loosened his cravat, so it was quick work to pull free his shirt from his trousers and manoeuvre it over his head. Jane felt clumsy and inexperienced, fumbling a little, but as she ran her hands down his naked chest all her doubts and uncertainties went away.

As they kissed Tom tumbled her back onto the bed, his body over hers. His fingers danced over her skin, caressing and building up a wonderful tension inside her. Instinctively she felt her hips rise to meet his, her body arch to enjoy his touch.

Tom trailed kisses down her neck and along the length of her collar bone. There was a wonderful moment of anticipation as he paused, before dipping lower and kissing her breasts, circling her nipples until she couldn't bear it any longer, and pressed his head into her. He grinned up at her and then ever so slowly took one of her nipples into his mouth. Jane almost screamed at the jolts of pleasure that shot through her body, hoping he would never stop, whilst also wondering how long she could bear the exquisite sensation.

At the same time his hand moved lower until his fingers touched her most private place. Jane gasped, throwing her head back on the pillow and wondering why anyone ever left the bedroom if this was what it could feel like. Slowly, ever so slowly, he began to move his fingers, caressing and stroking, as Jane felt a ball of tension start to build in her belly. Even as she writhed underneath him, he didn't stop, coming up to kiss her lips as she felt every muscle in her body tense and then glorious waves of pleasure spread out from her very core.

She felt as though she were floating and it took a while for the sensation to subside. Her breath was coming in short gasps and for a minute she could do nothing but enjoy the feeling of pure ecstasy.

As she opened her eyes, she saw Tom pushing down the waistband of his trousers, a question in his eyes.

'We can stop if you want?'

'No,' she said, pulling him to her. 'Don't stop.'

She reached out and touched him, loving the way he threw his head back as she grasped hold of him, feeling the silky softness over his hardness. She felt a moment of panic as he positioned himself but that was soon replaced by a wonderful anticipation.

'I'll go slow,' he said, seeing the expression in her eyes.

He pushed into her and Jane felt a fullness like nothing she had ever experienced before. He moved slowly, as he had promised, even though Jane could see it was taking great effort on his part. Little by little she started to raise her hips to meet his, marvelling at how wonderful it felt. She let her head fall back on the pillow and abandoned herself to the moment, moaning as Tom started to move faster and faster until she felt the waves of pleasure crash through her again as they climaxed together.

After a moment, Tom collapsed down on the bed next to her, pulling her into his arms, and they lay like that for a long time, neither able to speak.

Once she felt a little recovered, Jane turned over

so she was facing him, and Tom pulled at the sheets, covering her body so she didn't get cold. His hand was resting on her waist, the position so intimate Jane felt a swell of happiness.

'Is it always like that?' she asked.

'I have heard,' Tom said slowly, choosing his words, 'That making love is best when you are actually in love. I expect that was why it was so good.'

'You truly love me?'

'With all my heart.'

Jane snuggled down under the bed clothes, feeling a wonderful contentment wash over her. This was not how she had expected this day to end, but she would take the happiness over the heartbreak she'd felt this morning any day.

Chapter Twenty-Three

Tom jolted awake, his reflexes quick enough to stop himself from hitting the floor as he toppled off the chair. He checked his pocket watch as he stood, eyes widening as he realised the time. Ever since Edward had come to live with him, the little boy had struggled to get to sleep, then would awake about midnight, crying for his mother. Tom often stayed up working or reading in his study until he heard the young boy stir and then headed upstairs to comfort him.

Quickly he took the stairs two at a time until he reached Edward's bedroom on the first floor. It was looking more like a child's room than when he had first arrived, with Edward's pride and joy, a wooden rocking horse, in one corner.

Edward was sleeping peacefully in his bed, cheeks rosy and hair tousled on the pillow.

Leaning over the slumbering boy, Tom kissed him gently on the cheek. He felt an overwhelming love for him. Although he knew one night without the nightmares and tears Edward shed for his mother was only a start, it felt like a new chapter was dawning where some of the pain could be soothed.

'Is it morning?' Edward muttered as Tom retreated to the door.

'Not yet. You keep sleeping. Today is a big day.'

Tom debated whether to bother going to bed. It was five o'clock and already he felt the rush of anticipation for the day. He wished Jane were here, waiting for him in his room. He wanted to tell her about Edward sleeping through, about his hopes that they had seen the last of the night terrors and sobbing from the little boy. There was still a long way to go, but he felt optimistic that this was the first step of many.

'I'm so excited!' Edward shouted as he bounded up the stairs and into Jane's room, throwing his arms around her to cuddle her. Jane pulled the boy into a tight embrace, not caring that he was wrinkling the silk of her new dress. She would take a cuddle from Edward over a pristine appearance any day.

'I'm sorry, miss,' the harried-looking nanny said as she rushed into the room. 'I couldn't keep up.'

The agency had sent the nanny a week earlier and she had been worth the wait. Young and energetic, she was a welcome addition to the household. Edward seemed to like her, although would often sneak off to find the company of Jane or his uncle.

'You are just the person I wanted to see,' Jane said, crouching down to face the boy. 'Your uncle and I have been talking about a honeymoon. Not yet—perhaps in a few months.'

She saw the little boy's face drop. 'I don't want you to go.'

'We wouldn't ever go anywhere without you, Edward.'

'You mean I could come?'

'Yes. We were thinking of taking a trip to Italy, and I wondered if perhaps you would like to go back to where you lived with your mother and see all your friends?'

He nodded, his eyes wide.

'Good. That is settled, then. After the wedding, you can help us plan the trip.'

'Come now, Edward, Miss Ashworth has much to do this morning, I'm sure.'

There was a clatter of feet outside, and as Edward left the room Lucy entered, arm-in-arm with Lady Mountjoy.

'This may be the second happiest day of my life,' Lucy said as she started fussing around Jane, straightening her skirt and smoothing out the creases in the fabric.

'It certainly is one of the happiest of mine,' said Lady Mountjoy. The older woman waited for Lucy to finish and then stepped forward, holding out a small package. 'This is for you, Jane, my final debutante. I always knew you were destined for a great match.' She swiped at her eyes, trying to get rid of the tears that were forming. 'And there is no greater match than one made out of true love.'

The countess embraced her and then handed over the package. Jane opened it, gasping at the beautiful earrings inside. They were elegant and simple, the sparkling diamonds at the centre of the earring resplendent enough that they didn't need any extra adornments.

'Thank you, they're beautiful. It is too generous, Lady Mountjoy.'

'Nonsense. You have given me a wonderful gift this year, all of you debutantes who came to join me. It has been one of the most eventful but fantastic years I have ever known. I feel privileged to have been even a small part of your journey.'

'None of this would have been possible without you,' Jane said, trying not to cry herself.

Lady Mountjoy took her leave, making her way downstairs for the ceremony, leaving Jane and Lucy alone.

'Charlotte has just arrived,' Lucy said as she helped put the finishing touches to Jane's hair. 'She is so happy to be here.' Charlotte was another of the debutantes selected by Lady Mountjoy for her long trip to London. She had never made it to the capital, though, having fallen in love during the few weeks they had spent on the Mountjoy estate prior to leaving for London, and marrying Lady Mountjoy's nephew.

'I'm glad she's made it.'

Eliza was the only one missing from their little friendship group. Jane had written, but Eliza had set off on her honeymoon a few weeks earlier, and she doubted the letter would reach her friend before the wedding happened.

'I think it is almost time,' Lucy said, giving Jane's arm an excited squeeze. 'Do you need a moment?'

'No.' Jane shook her head. She didn't feel nervous, not really. Ever since the night in the coaching inn, she was convinced she and Tom were perfect for each other. It had been an agonising few weeks whilst he had arranged the special licence and all she wanted now was to become Mrs Stewart.

Together they walked downstairs, Lucy handing her a bunch of flowers before she walked into the richly decorated drawing room. They had both wanted a quiet, small wedding and had agreed Tom's drawing room was the perfect place for their nuptials. Jane had never been to a wedding outside of a church before, but as she surveyed the guests in the familiar room she knew this had been the right decision. On one side of the room sat Lord and Lady Mountjoy, Lucy and Captain Weyman and Charlotte and her husband, Lord Overby.

On the other side was Edward, his nanny and Mr and Mrs Western, who Jane had met a few times now, soon realising what an important part of her husband's life they were.

Jane's whole family hadn't been able to make the journey, but her father sat at the front of the room, beaming proudly, and Jane had assured her mother she and Tom would come and visit very soon.

Jane's eyes took everyone in as they swept over the room and then settled on the man standing at the front. Mr Thomas Stewart, former rake, current charmer and soon to be her husband.

He turned at that moment and smiled at her and Jane felt overwhelmed by love. This wasn't what she had expected from her time in London, and certainly not how she'd thought they would end up when she had first suggested to Tom they feign interest in one another to save her from having to socialise with other eligible bachelors.

'You look beautiful, my love,' Tom murmured as she reached him.

As the ceremony was about to start, she felt a light tug on her free hand and glanced down. Edward had joined them in front of everyone else and was now holding her hand. She beamed down at him and then up at her very-soon-to-be husband as she repeated her marriage vows.

Epilogue

Two years later

Jane sat back in her chair, sipping a glass of orange juice and enjoying the heat of the sun on her face. Somewhere in the distance she could hear an excited whoop and laughter coming from Edward as he ran rings round his uncle and the three other men who had happily agreed to teach the young boy cricket.

'Tell us about your books, Jane,' Lucy said, leaning forward as far as she could in her seat, but floundering as her bump got in the way. It was a surprise to no one that Lucy was pregnant with her third child so soon after having had twins a year earlier. She was a natural mother and bloomed into the role, happily declaring she wanted a dozen children. The twins were sleeping peacefully in a bassinet in the shade and Jane felt a maternal tug as she glanced over at them.

'The first three have been published and Mr Hambly tells me they've been a terrific success. The first editions sold out within a few weeks and he had to get busy printing more.'

'That is amazing,' Eliza said, shaking her head in disbelief. 'I can't believe you were working towards this all the time we were together and none of us knew.'

'You were a little preoccupied with the delightful Lord Thannock,' Lucy teased.

'As were you, with the dashing Captain Weyman.'

'And Charlotte was busy smuggling pigs into country estates and bewitching the man she protested she could not stand,' Jane added.

They all laughed as they remembered that first summer together. It had been two years since Lady Mountjoy had brought them together at her big country estate with the proposal she select a debutante to take to London for the winter months and the spring Season. It had been an eventful two years, with four marriages, four honeymoons and three babies, and Jane felt grateful they were all here together to sit down and enjoy one another's company for a few days.

Lady Mountjoy had invited them all back for a house party, and they had been so eager to come together they had rearranged any other engagements to make sure it happened.

'How are my favourite debutantes?' Lady Mountjoy said as she stepped out onto the terrace to join them.

'Hardly debutantes any more,' Charlotte said, cradling her one-year-old in her arms. 'I am relegated to sit with the matrons at any events we attend now.'

'It's worth it, though, isn't it?' Lady Mountjoy said in a loud whisper, indicating the little girl in Charlotte's arms. 'It's worth it to be a mother.'

Jane found her hand travelling to her belly. She wasn't as far gone as Lucy, but she would soon be adding to their family. Already she felt so lucky to have Edward, who she loved as though he were her own. Another child would be an extra blessing.

'Are you still writing and illustrating more books?' Eliza asked her, fascinated by the process. Eliza had returned from her honeymoon to find Lucy and Jane both married and happily settled, and Jane a published author. She had grumbled about things moving too quickly whilst she'd been away, but Jane had seen by her expression she was delighted by all the news.

'Yes, Mr Hambly has told me he will publish whatever I can write. It is a different feeling. For so long I wrote and illustrated the stories, not knowing whether anyone but me would ever see them. Now I get a rush of nervousness thinking everything will be studied and judged.'

'You have nothing to worry about,' Eliza declared with her characteristic confidence. 'I've bought all three already published and they are nothing short of perfect.'

Jane beamed at her friend, her smile growing even wider as Edward ran back to the table for a drink, followed by Tom and the other husbands.

'I think a toast is needed,' Lady Mountjoy said, waiting until everyone had assembled and found a glass. 'Two years ago we embarked on a fantastic journey. I was lucky enough to meet you fabulous ladies and grow to know and love you like you are family.' She paused, smiling as Lord Mountjoy stepped out of the drawing room and looped an arm around her waist.

'For years, I've been telling every young debutante I meet, every eligible bachelor—anyone who will listen, really—the importance of marrying for love. You spend more time with your spouse than anyone else, and that time can be the happiest if you choose your partner correctly.'

She paused for a moment, looking round at the group of young women and their husbands. 'I am delighted you have all chosen so well. To spend a life with the person you love is a life well spent,' Lady Mountjoy concluded. Lord Mountjoy beamed behind her and leaned round to give his wife a kiss on the cheek.

She raised her glass in a toast. 'To love and friendship.'

That was a toast Jane could agree with, and it seemed apt, given she was surrounded by people she loved and wonderful friends.

'Love and friendship,' she said, feeling her heart soar as Tom leaned in and kissed her.

* * * * *

THE KISS THAT MADE HER COUNTESS

To my boys, everything is so much more fun with you

Chapter One

Northumberland, Midsummer's Eve, 1816

Not for the first time that evening Alice felt ridiculous. She glanced down at the borrowed dress, the hem splattered with mud, and the delicate shoes. If they ever made it to Lady Salisbury's ball she would trail dirt all over the ballroom floor.

'Come, Alice. We can't stop now,' Lydia called over her shoulder before vaulting over a wooden fence. Alice followed a little more slowly, wondering how she had been dragged into this madcap plan. 'We're almost there. I swear I can hear the music.'

With as much grace and elegance as she could muster, Alice climbed over the fence, closing her eyes in horror as the material of her dress snagged on a protruding nail. There was the sickening sound of ripping fabric as she lost her balance and the dress was tugged free.

'Lydia, wait,' Alice shouted, looking up to see her friend plunging head first through a hedge. She had no choice but to follow, grimacing as she spotted the ripped area near the hem of her dress. Hopefully she would be able to mend it and clean it before her cousin even noticed the dress was missing.

She paused before the hedge, wondering how Lydia had made her way through the dense foliage, and then a hand shot out and gripped her wrist. Lydia was giggling as Alice emerged, an expression of surprise on her face, and soon Alice was laughing too.

'Just think, in a few minutes we will be whirling across the ballroom in the arms of the most handsome bachelors in all of Northumberland,' Lydia said as she gripped Alice's hand. 'Maybe there will be a dashing duke or an eligible earl to sweep you off your feet.'

For a moment Alice closed her eyes and contemplated the possibilities. It was highly unlikely she would meet anyone at the ball that could save her from the impending match that made her heart sink every time she thought of her future.

'My last night of freedom,' she murmured.

Lydia scoffed. 'You make it sound as if you are on your way to the gallows.'

'That is exactly what it feels like.'

'Surely he is not that bad.'

Alice screwed up her face and gave a little shudder. 'I am well aware I have lived a sheltered life so have not come across the scoundrels and the criminals of this country, but Cousin Cecil is by far the worst person I have ever met.'

'Perhaps your parents will not make you marry him.'

'I doubt they will save me from that fate.' Tomorrow Alice's second cousin, Cecil Billington, was coming to stay for a week with the single purpose of finalising an agreement of marriage between him and Alice. As yet he had not proposed, but Alice was aware of the negotiations going on in the background with her father. She hadn't dared enquire as to the specifics; even just the idea of Cecil made her feel sick.

'Then, tonight will have to make up for the next forty years of putting up with Cecil.'

Lydia grabbed her by the hand and began pulling her over the grass again. The house was in view now, the terrace at the back lit up with dozens of lamps positioned at equal intervals along the stone balustrade. Music drifted out from the open doors, and there was the swell of voices as those escaping the heat of the ballroom strolled along the terrace.

'Someone will see us,' Alice said, feeling suddenly exposed. There was only about thirty feet separating them and the house now, but it was all open lawn, and by the time they reached the steps leading up to the terrace it would be a miracle if they made it even halfway unobserved.

'Then, let us act like we belong. We more than look the part. If we stroll serenely arm-in-arm, I wager no one will pay us any attention. We are just two invited guests having a wonderful time at the Midsummer's Eve ball.'

Alice considered for a moment and then nodded. 'You are right. If we try to creep in, it will be obvious immediately. The only way we have half a chance is by pretending we are meant to be here.'

Instantly she straightened her back and lifted her chin, trying to mimic the poise and confidence of Lady Salisbury, the hostess of the sumptuous masked ball. Sometimes Alice would catch a glimpse of the viscountess stepping out of her carriage or taking a stroll through the extensive grounds of Salisbury Hall. She looked regal in her posture and elegant in her movements, and Alice tried to copy how she held herself and how she walked.

'Wait,' Lydia called and slipped a mask into Alice's hand. It was delicate in design, only meant to fit over the upper part of the wearer's face. White in colour, it had an intricate silver pattern painted onto it, a collection of swirls and dots that glimmered in the moonlight. Alice put it on, securing the mask with the silver ribbon tied into a bow at the back of her head. She looked over to Lydia to see her friend had a similar mask now obscuring the top half of her face.

Lydia slipped her arm through Alice's, and together they strolled slowly across the lawn. Despite her urge to run, Alice knew this ruse would work best if they moved at a sedate pace. No one blinked as they ascended the stairs onto the terrace, and Alice heard her friend suppress a little squeal of excitement as they reached the doors to the ballroom.

Neither girl had ever been to a ball like this before. On occasion they would attend the dances at the local Assembly Rooms, but even those were few and far between. Once Alice had begged her parents to allow her and her sister to stay with some friends in Newcastle to enjoy the delights of the social calendar there, but worried about their daughters' reputations, her parents had refused.

'This is magical,' Alice whispered, pausing on the threshold to take everything in. The room was large and richly decorated. The walls were covered in the finest cream wallpaper. At set intervals there were large, gold-framed mirrors, positioned to reflect the guests on the dance floor and make the ballroom seem as if it were even bigger than it was. From the ceiling hung two magnificent chandeliers, each with at least a hundred candles burning bright and illuminating the room. In between the mirrors on the walls there were yet more candles, flickering and reflecting off the glass and making the whole ballroom shimmer and shine.

The assembled guests added to the vision of opulence, the men in finely tailored tailcoats with silk cravats and the women in beautiful dresses of silk and satin. The theme of this masked ball was the Midsummer celebrations, and many of the guests had dressed with a nod to this in mind. Some women had freshly picked flowers woven into their hair or pinned to their dresses as they normally would a brooch.

'I have never seen anything like this,' Lydia said, her mouth open in awe.

'Thank you,' Alice said, squeezing her friend's hand. 'For making me come tonight. You're right. I deserve one last night of happiness before a lifetime of being married to vile Cousin Cecil.'

Lydia leaned in close and held Alice's eye. 'Enjoy it to the utmost. Dance with every man that asks, sip sparkling wine like it is water, admire all the marvellous women in their beautiful dresses.'

'I will.'

For a moment Alice felt a little overwhelmed. This was not her world, not where she belonged, and she was aware she didn't know how to talk to these people. It felt as though someone might come and pluck her out of the crowd and announce *Alice James, you do not belong here.*

A young gentleman, no older than Alice and Lydia, approached, swallowing nervously. He smiled at them both, showing a line of crooked teeth, and then directed his focus on Lydia.

'I know we have not been introduced, but may I have the pleasure of the next dance?'

Alice watched as her friend blushed under her mask. Lydia was bold and confident on the outside, but sometimes she would stutter and stammer amongst people she did not know.

'I would be delighted,' Lydia said, giving Alice a backwards glance as her partner led her off to the edge of the dance floor to wait for the next dance to be called.

Suddenly alone Alice felt very exposed, and she shrank back, aghast when she brushed against a large pot filled with a leafy plant with brightly coloured flowers. It wobbled on its table, threatening to crash to the ground. She lunged, trying to steady it, and as her hands reached around the ceramic she had an awful vision of the container crashing to the floor and the whole ballroom turning to her in the silence that followed, realising she shouldn't be there.

'Steady,' a deep voice said right in her ear, making her jump and almost sending the pot flying again. An arm brushed past her waist, reaching quickly to stop the plant from toppling.

For a long moment Alice did not move, only turning when she was certain there was going to be no terrible accident with the plant in front of her. When she did finally turn she inhaled sharply. Standing right behind her, just the right distance away so as not to attract any disapproving stares, was the most handsome man she had ever laid eyes on. He wasn't wearing a mask, and Alice reasoned there was no point. Everyone in the room would know who he was just by looking at his eyes. They were blue, but not the same pale blue of her own eyes but bright and vibrant, piercing in their intensity. He had that attractive combination of blue eyes and dark hair that was uncommon in itself but that, added to the perfect proportions of the rest of his facial features, meant he was easily the most desirable man in the room.

'Thank you,' she said, her heart still pounding in her chest from the worry that she was about to cause a scene with the crashing décor. 'That could have been a disaster.'

Simon smiled blandly at the pretty young woman in front of him and turned to leave, not wanting to get caught up in conversation with someone he should probably know. There were hundreds of young ladies in Northumberland he'd been introduced to, and he could never remember their names. It was one of the tribulations of being an earl: everyone knew you, everyone recognised you, and most expected you to remember them.

His brother had been good at that sort of thing, remembering every face and name, making connections between members of the same families. When out on the estate or visiting the local village Robert would stop and talk to almost everyone he met, enquiring after the health of various ailing relatives or newborn babies. Robert had been loved by their tenants and staff in a way that was impossible to follow, especially when Simon had trouble remembering even a fraction of the names of the people he encountered in the local area.

As he turned he spotted his sister-in-law entering the ballroom. He had a lot of time and respect for Maria, the dowager countess, but right now he did not want to see her. Recently she had been urging him to marry and settle down, which was the furthest thing from what he had planned for his life. Tonight no doubt she would have a list of eligible young ladies lined up for him to dance with, all perfectly nice and decent young ladies, but there was no point in him seeking a connection with anyone, not now, not ever.

Not wanting to get caught by Maria and her list of accomplished young ladies, he hastily turned back to the woman in front of him.

'I don't think we've been introduced,' he said.

'Miss Alice James,' she said, bobbing into a little curtsy. She looked up at him expectantly, and he realised she was waiting for him to introduce himself.

'Lord Westcroft,' he said, seeing her eyes widen. Unless she was a consummate actress it would seem she hadn't known who he was. He didn't like to view himself as conceited, but generally most people *did* recognise him when he entered a room. It was one of the disadvantages of being an earl.

'A pleasure to meet you, my Lord.'

'The dancing is about to begin, Miss James. I wonder if I might have the pleasure of this dance?'

'You want to dance with me?' She sounded incredulous, and he had to suppress a smile at her honest reaction.

'If that is agreeable to you?'

She nodded, and he held out his arm to her, escorting

her to the dance floor just as the musicians played the first note of the music for a country dance.

He had been dancing all his life, and over the years been to hundreds of balls and danced countless dances. Before his brother had died he had quite enjoyed socialising, but everything had lost its shine after Robert's death. Miss James stood opposite him and beamed, looking around her in delight. She was young, but not so young that this could be her first ball, and he wondered if she approached everything with such irrepressible happiness.

The dance was fast-paced, and as it was their turn to progress down the line of other dancers, Miss James looked up at him and smiled with such unbridled joy that for a moment he froze. Thankfully he recovered before she noticed, and they continued the dance without him missing a step, but as they took their place at the end of the line he found he could not take his eyes off her. Even with her mask on he could see she was pretty. She had thick auburn hair that was pinned back in the current fashion, but a few strands had slipped loose and curled around her neck. Her eyes were a pale blue that shimmered in the candlelight, but the part of her he felt himself drawn to was her lips. She smiled all the time, her expression varying between a closed-lip, small smile of contentment to a wider smile of pleasure at various points throughout the dance. When she got a step wrong, she didn't flush with embarrassment as many young ladies would, but instead giggled at her own mistake. Simon realised he hadn't met anyone in a long time who was completely and utterly living in the moment and, in that moment, happy.

As the music finished he bowed to his partner and then surprised himself by offering her his arm.

'Shall we get some air, Miss James?'

She looked up at him, cheeks flushed from the exertion, and nodded.

'That would be most welcome.'

Simon saw his sister-in-law's eyes on him as he escorted Miss James from the dance floor to the edge of the ballroom, stopping to pick up two glasses of punch on the way. The ballroom was hot now, with the press of bodies, and it was a relief to step outside into the cool air.

'I think Midsummer might be my new favourite time of year,' Miss James said as they chose a spot by the stone balustrade. She leaned on it, looking out at the garden and the night sky beyond.

'What has it displaced?' Simon asked.

'I do love Christmas. There is something rather magical about crackling wood on the fire whilst it snows outside and you are all snug inside. But I will never forget this wonderful Midsummer night.'

'Forgive me, Miss James, but have we met before?'

'No.'

'You seem very certain.'

She smiled at him. There was no guile in her expression, and he realised that she had no expectation from him. Most young women he was introduced to looked at him as something to be conquered. Their ultimate aim was to impress him so they might have a chance at becoming his countess. It was tiresome and meant he had started to avoid situations where he was likely to be pushed into small talk with unmarried young women. Miss James had no calculating aspect to her; she was not trying to impress him. It was refreshing to talk to someone and realise they wanted nothing from you.

'I think I would remember, my Lord.'

'You are from Northumberland?'

'Yes, my family live only a few miles away.'

'Then, our paths must have crossed at a ball or a dinner party, surely.'

He saw her eyes widen and a look of panic on her face. He wondered for a moment if she might try to flee, but instead she fiddled with her glass and then took a great gulp of punch.

'I have a little confession,' she said, leaning in closer so only he could hear her words. 'This is my first ball.'

'Your first?'

'Yes.'

He looked at her closer, wondering if he had been wrong in assessing her age. He'd placed her at around twenty or twenty-one. Young still, but certainly old enough to have been out in society for a good few years. It was hard to tell with the mask covering her eyes, but he did not think he had got his estimation wrong.

'I have been to dances,' she said quickly. 'Just not to any balls like this.'

'How can that be, Miss James?'

She bit her lip and flicked him a nervous glance.

'If I tell you, you might have me escorted out.'

It was his turn to smile.

'I doubt it, Miss James. Unless you tell me you sneaked in with the sole purpose to sabotage Lady Salisbury's ball or steal her silverware.'

Miss James pressed her lips together and then leaned in even closer, her shoulders almost touching his.

'You are half-right,' she said, her voice low so only he could hear.

'You plan to steal Lady Salisbury's silverware.'

She flicked him an amused glance. 'No, I am no criminal, but I did sneak in.' As soon as she said the words, she clapped her hands over her mouth in horror. 'I can't believe I just told you that. It was the one thing I was meant to keep secret tonight, and it is the first thing I tell you.'

Simon felt a swell of mirth rise up inside him, and he realised for the first time in a long time he was having fun. Fun had seemed a foreign concept these last few years. In a short space of time he had lost his brother, inherited a title he had never wanted and been forced to confront the issue of his own mortality. He'd been forced into making monumental decisions over the last few weeks, everything serious and fraught with emotion.

'You sneaked in?'

She nodded, eyes wide with horror.

'Are you going to tell anyone?'

'I am not sure yet,' he said, suppressing a smile of his own.

'Lydia is going to be furious,' Miss James murmured.

'There are two of you?'

She closed her eyes and shook her head. 'I need to stop talking.'

'Please don't, Miss James. This is the most fun I've had for months.'

'Now you're mocking me.'

'Not at all.'

'You're an earl. This cannot be the most fun you've had. Your life must be full of luxury and entertainment.'

'I find it is mainly full of accounts and responsibilities,' he said. 'That is unfair and very… I am well aware of the privileged life I lead. It is full of luxury and extravagance, as you say, but not fun.'

'That is sad,' Alice said, and she touched him on the hand. It was a fleeting contact, but it made his skin tingle, and he looked up quickly. There was no guile in her eyes, and he realised the furthest thing from her mind was seduction—whether because she had a young man she fancied herself in love with or because their backgrounds were so far apart she knew there could never be anything between them.

'It is sad,' he said quietly. 'So tonight I charge you with lifting this grumpy man's spirits.'

'And in exchange you will not expose my deception.'

'We have a deal. Tell me, Miss James, how did you manage to sneak in without one of the dozens of footmen seeing you?'

She motioned out at the garden beyond the terrace. Only the terrace was lit, the grass and the formal garden beyond in darkness.

'We crept through the garden.'

He glanced down and laughed. 'I can see there was a little mud.'

'I was terrified when we arrived that I might have foliage in my hair. We had to squeeze through a hedge to get into the right part of the garden.'

'That is commitment to your cause. What made you so keen to come here tonight?'

She sighed and looked out into the darkness.

'I doubt you know the feeling of helplessness, of not being in control of your own future,' she said with a hint of melancholy. She was wrong in her assumption, but now was not the time to correct her. 'Soon I will not be able to choose anything more thrilling than what curtains to hang or what to serve for dinner.'

'You are to be married.'

The expression on her face told him she was not happy about the prospect.

She straightened and turned to face him. 'I am to marry my second cousin, vile Cecil.'

'Vile Cecil?'

'It is an apt description of him.'

'I already feel sorry for you. What makes him so vile?'

Miss James exhaled, puffing out her cheeks in a way that made him smile. He didn't know her exact background, but by the way she spoke and held herself he would guess she was from a family of the minor gentry. Perhaps a landowner father or even a vicar. She knew how to conduct herself but hadn't been subject to the scrutiny many of the women of the *ton* had to endure, so the odd shrug of the shoulders or theatrical sigh hadn't been trained out of her.

'Where to start? Imagine you are a young lady,' she said, and he adopted his most serious expression.

'I am imagining.'

'Good. You are introduced to a distant relative about fifteen years older than you,' she said and held up a finger. 'The age gap is not an issue you must understand. I am aware women are of higher value to society when they are young and beautiful and men when they are older and richer.'

'I did not think you would be such a cynic, Miss James.' Simon was surprised to find he was enjoying himself immensely. There was something freeing talking to this woman who was a total stranger and had no expectations of him at all.

'Is it cynical to observe the truth?' She pushed on. 'This distant relative is unfortunate-looking, with a lazy eye, yellowed teeth and rapidly thinning hair that he arranges in a way he hopes will hide the fact he hasn't much left. But you have been raised to appreciate no one can help how they look so you push aside all thoughts of their physical appearance.'

Simon pressed his lips together. Miss James had an amusing way of telling a story, and he urged her to continue. 'I am channelling those very thoughts,' he said.

'Good. Then he reaches out and with a sweaty palm lays a hand on your shoulder. A fleeting touch you could forgive, but the hand lingers far too long, and all the while his eyes do not move from your chest.'

'He is not sounding very enticing.'

'Then throughout the evening he makes his horrible opinions known on everything from how the poor should be punished for the awful situations they find themselves in to slavery to how it is God's plan for the lower levels of society to be decimated by illness that spreads more when people live in close conditions.'

'I am beginning to see why he is vile.'

'And he does all this whilst trying to squeeze your knee under the table.'

'Your parents are happy for you to marry him?'

Miss James sighed. 'Last year my sister…' She bit her lip again, drawing his gaze for a moment. 'I probably shouldn't tell you this.' Then she shrugged and continued. 'Yet our paths are never going to cross again.'

'What if I add in the extra layer of security by swearing I will never breathe a word of this to anyone.'

'You are a man of your word?'

'I never break an oath.'

'Last year my sister was caught up in a bit of a scandal. Rumours of late-night liaisons with a married gentleman. For a month she and I were forbidden to leave the house, and my parents thought we might even have to leave Bamburgh and move elsewhere. Thankfully a friend of my father's stepped in and proposed marriage to my sister to save her and the rest of our family from scandal.'

'Did it work?'

'Yes, although there are still a few people who cross the street to avoid my mother and me if we are out shopping. My sister is happy as mistress of her own home, living down in Devon, and she has a baby on the way. All things for a short while we thought she might never have.'

'This has pushed your parents to make an unwise match for you?'

'I think they are panicked. They are aware the taint of scandal can linger for a long time, and they keep reminding me I am already one and twenty. There are no local unmarried young men of the right social class so they decided they would arrange the only match that was assured.'

'Could you not refuse?'

Miss James laughed, but there was no bitterness in her tone, just pure amusement.

'We live in very different worlds, my Lord. I have no money of my own, no income, no way of supporting myself. I cannot even boast of a very good education so I doubt anyone would employ me as a governess. My value comes in marrying someone who can support me and any future children and remove that burden from my parents.'

'Vile Cecil is wealthy?'

'Moderately so. Enough to satisfy my parents. He is eager to be married and comes tomorrow to stay to discuss our engagement.'

'He has not asked you yet?'

'No, but that part is a mere formality.' She closed her eyes. 'So you see, this is my one last chance to dance at a ball with whoever I choose, to get a little tipsy with punch and to take ill-advised strolls along the terrace with mysterious gentlemen.'

'Then, we must ensure you have the best night of your life.'

Chapter Two

Alice felt a little giddy with recklessness. She should never have spoken of the things she had told Lord Westcroft, but it had been liberating to talk so freely. She could be confident that after tonight her path would never cross with the earl's again. In a few weeks she would be Mrs Cecil Billington, living a life of misery in some rural part of Suffolk where she knew no one except her odious husband.

'I think we need more punch,' Lord Westcroft said, bowing to her and disappearing inside before she could object. She had only drunk alcohol a few times before, small sips of wine with dinner, and she didn't know what was in the punch, but she was already feeling the wonderful warmth spreading out from her stomach around her body.

He returned with two more glasses and handed her one. As he walked back to her Alice was aware of all the curious stares they received from the other guests. No doubt everyone knew who Lord Westcroft was, and they would probably be wondering who he was spending all this time with. Alice tried to shrink into herself, feeling suddenly self-conscious.

'A toast, to one final night of freedom before you are condemned to a life with vile Cecil.'

Alice smiled, raising her glass and then putting it to her lips. She had never met an earl before, but she had not expected one to be like Lord Westcroft. He was surprisingly easy to talk to and had a laid-back manner that reminded her more of the young lads in the village than what she pictured an aristocrat would be like.

'How about you?' she said after she had drained half her glass. 'I've told you my deepest secrets. It is only fair I hear one of yours.'

For a moment she wondered if she had gone too far as his expression darkened, but after a second he placed his glass on the balustrade and leaned forward, looking out into the darkness of the garden.

'Shall I tell you something I have told no one else yet?' There was a sudden serious note in his voice.

Alice nodded, feeling her pulse quicken.

'I have never danced a waltz in the open air before.' He grinned at her and then held out his hand.

'I thought you were going to confess something serious,' she said, unable to stop herself from grinning at him in relief.

'You are keeping me waiting, Miss James. May I have this dance?'

'Everyone will stare at us.'

'That is true.'

'I am trying not to draw attention to myself.'

'It is far too late to be worried about that. Everyone is staring already.'

'How do you stand all the interest in you?'

'You grow accustomed to it.'

He held out his hand, and Alice took it despite the sensible part of her cautioning against it.

Inside, the first few notes of the waltz had started, and there were a dozen couples on the dance floor, twirling and stepping in time to the music.

She felt a thrill of pleasure as Lord Westcroft placed a hand in the small of her back and, exerting a gentle pressure, began to guide her into her first spin. He was an excellent dancer; he made it look effortless, and once Alice had got her confidence she was able to lift her eyes to meet his and just enjoy the dance knowing he would not let her slip.

For a few minutes she forgot there were other people at the ball: it was just her and Lord Westcroft, dancing under the stars. Every time they spun she felt her body sway a little closer to his, and once or twice his legs brushed hers. As the music swelled and then faded, she felt suddenly bereft and had to chide herself for the romantic thoughts that were trying to push to the fore in her mind.

'Thank you for the dance, Miss James,' Lord Westcroft said, bowing to her, his lips hovering over her hand.

She thought he might leave her then. They had spent well over half an hour together, dancing and talking and sipping punch in the moonlight, and it was not advisable for a gentleman to spend too much time with any one young lady or rumours would begin to circulate. The sensible thing for Lord Westcroft to do would be to bid her farewell and go dance with another young lady.

For a moment she saw him contemplate doing just that. He glanced over his shoulder, looking at the ballroom with an expression of trepidation. Then he turned back to her with a smile.

'Would you like to go for a stroll?'

'A stroll?'

'Only along the terrace and back. Perhaps a few dozen times. I find myself reluctant to let you go just yet, Miss James. I have this fear you will disappear as soon as I look away for an instant.'

'You wouldn't prefer to go and dance with someone else?'

'No,' he said simply.

'Then, I would enjoy a stroll very much.'

He offered her his arm, and she slipped her hand through and rested it in the crook of his elbow. They had only taken a few steps when they were cut off by a statuesque woman in a beautiful green and gold dress. Even with her mask on, Alice recognised Lady Salisbury. There was an expression of concerned curiosity on her face as she positioned herself directly in their path.

'Lord Westcroft, I hope you are enjoying the ball.'

'I am, thank you, Lady Salisbury.'

The viscountess turned to Alice, and Alice felt something shrivel inside her. There was coldness in the older woman's expression that hadn't been there when she had been looking at Lord Westcroft.

'I do not think we have been introduced, Miss...' Lady Salisbury said with a smile that did not reach her eyes.

Alice felt her mouth go instantly dry and her tongue stick to the roof.

'You must forgive me,' Lord Westcroft said before Alice could summon any words. 'I have a little confession to make.'

'Oh?' Lady Salisbury said, not taking her eyes off Alice.

'This is Miss James, a distant relative on my mother's side. She has been staying with my mother these past few weeks. When my mother heard I was attending your ball, she requested I ask you if Miss James could come as my guest, but I completely forgot. When Miss James appeared at my door in my mother's carriage tonight, I panicked and pretended you had agreed to her coming. I have to admit I hoped no one would notice and no word would get back to my mother about my oversight.'

Lady Salisbury looked from Lord Westcroft to Alice and back again for a moment and then broke out into a smile.

'Lord Westcroft, you should have just brought Miss James to me when you arrived. You know I can never deny you anything. He is charming, is he not, Miss James?'

'He is,' Alice agreed.

'I beg your forgiveness,' Lord Westcroft said and then leaned in closer to Lady Salisbury and spoke in a conspiratorial manner. 'And I beg you do not tell my mother of my error.'

'My lips are sealed, Lord Westcroft.'

'Now, Miss James, we cannot have the earl monopolising your time and attention at the ball tonight. I am sure there are many other gentlemen you wish to have the chance to dance with.'

'I have been selfish,' Lord Westcroft said, smiling indulgently at Alice as a distant relative might. 'I promise, once we have finished our stroll, to deliver Miss James to the ballroom where she can enjoy the attentions of all the gentlemen here tonight, clamouring to fill her dance-card.'

Lady Salisbury inclined her head and took her leave, glancing over her shoulder at them before she reentered the ballroom. Alice waited until she was sure the older woman was out of earshot to exhale loudly.

'I cannot breathe,' she said, trying to suck in large gasps of air.

'Be calm, Miss James. Lady Salisbury's suspicions are averted for now.'

'I thought she was going to rip my mask from my face and declare me an intruder, then command her footmen to escort me off her property.'

'I would not put it past her. She does not have the most forgiving of natures.'

'I need to leave,' Alice said desperately.

'That is the last thing you should do.'

She looked up at him, incredulous. He was remarkably calm, but she supposed if his lie was found out, it wouldn't really affect him. Lady Salisbury would forgive the earl, it would be Alice who would be thrown out in disgrace.

'Right now Lady Salisbury is watching you closely. If she sees you scurrying away she will know you were not meant to be here.'

'What do you suggest, then?'

'We stroll along the terrace as we had planned, and then you return to the ballroom and dance with a few different gentlemen before slipping away unnoticed.'

'I do not know if my nerves can stand it.'

He leaned in a little closer, his breath tickling her ear as he spoke. 'I'll be with you.'

* * *

Simon knew he was acting recklessly, but he could not find it in himself to care. No one knew who Miss James was or where she came from, so he did not have to worry as much as he normally would when spending time with a young lady. If he were honest, this evening was the first time he'd enjoyed himself quite so much in a long time, and it was because of Miss James.

In two weeks he would have left England, never to return, so for once he did not have to worry if he were upsetting anyone. There was no requirement for him to nod politely whilst an elderly acquaintance regaled him with a tiresome tale or an eager social climber thrust her daughter in his direction. Tonight he could do whatever he wanted safe in the knowledge that he would never see most of these people ever again. All he had to do was ensure he did not ruin Miss James in the process.

He watched her as they strolled along the terrace, reaching the end in less than a minute despite walking sedately. As they walked, some of the tension seeped from her shoulders, and before they turned back to head in the other direction she was smiling again.

'This is by far the most reckless thing I have ever done,' she said, leaning in so no one else could hear her words. 'I expect you do wild things all the time.'

'Once...' he said, almost wistfully. A few years ago his life had been charmed, although he hadn't been aware of it at the time. He'd lost his father when he was just twelve years old, and for a long time the grief had affected him, but five years ago things had been good. He had been surrounded by people who loved him—his mother, his older brother, his sister-in-law and his lovely nieces—and he'd had the freedom to do whatever he chose. As the second son, the title and the responsibility were never meant to be his. Robert was fair and loving and had ensured Simon had a home of his own and enough income to live a comfortable life. He'd relished his freedom then, the ability to go off at a moment's notice, to follow his desires on a whim.

They reached the end of the terrace again and turned, Simon glancing into the ballroom. Lady Salisbury was still watching them as she spoke to an elderly couple. Her eyes were narrowed slightly, and Simon realised she was still suspicious of his companion.

'Perhaps we should get you out of here,' he murmured, glancing at the steps that led to the garden.

'Surely Lady Salisbury would notice. I can feel her eyes on me.'

'You're right,' he said, feeling a little disappointed. There was something appealing about slipping into the darkened gardens in the company of Miss James. 'Let us go into the ballroom.'

'I feel so sick I might be sick over the shoes of whatever gentleman I am meant to dance with.'

'Don't do that,' he said with a smile. 'That is a sure way to get yourself noticed.'

He led her inside, his eyes dancing over the groups of people before resting on the person he was looking for.

'Forrester, good to see you,' he said, clapping a man of around his age on the back.

'Northumberland,' Forrester said with a grin. He leaned in closer, giving Miss James an appraising look. 'How do you manage to always end up with the most beautiful woman in the room on your arm?'

'Forrester, meet Miss James. Miss James, this is a good friend of mine from my schooldays, Mr Nicholas Forrester.'

Forrester bent over Alice's hand, giving her his most charming smile.

'We need a favour,' Simon said quickly. 'Will you dance the next dance with Miss James? Keep her away from Lady Salisbury. If our hostess asks who she is, tell her she's a distant relative of my mother's.'

'Is that the truth?'

'No.'

Forrester looked intrigued. 'You haven't smuggled one of your mistresses into this society affair, have you, Northumberland?'

Next to him he saw Miss James blush, and he quickly shook his head. 'No, Miss James is completely respectable. Will you dance with her as a favour?'

'No favour needed. Would you do me the honour, Miss James?'

She inclined her head, and Simon watched as Forrester lead her to the dance floor. They had a few minutes before the next dance was called, and he realised he felt a spark of jealousy as Forrester bent his head close to Miss James's to discuss something over the hum of conversation in the room.

He should move on, find some débutante to talk to, so if Lady Salisbury glanced in his direction she would see nothing suspicious, only an unmarried gentleman talking to a woman with a sizeable dowry. Simon cast his eyes around the room, but after a few seconds he found he was drawn back to where Miss James stood with Forrester. They were both smiling now, and he felt a prickle of unease. He hoped she hadn't told Forrester of her true identity.

With his eyes locked on the couple, he watched as they took their places for a quadrille. Miss James danced well for someone who had only been to a few dances at the local Assembly Rooms. Her steps were graceful, and her body swayed in time to the music. His eyes glided over her body, taking in the curve of her hips and her slender, pinched-in waist. For the first time in a long time he felt a surge of desire.

Shaking his head ruefully he forced himself to focus on something else. Desire had no place in his life now, but he would not punish himself for merely appreciating a beautiful woman.

'You're prowling,' Maria said as she approached, her voice low and filled with mirth.

'Prowling? You make me sound like an animal.'

'You *look* like an animal. Perhaps a wolf or a grumpy bear.'

'Just what every man wishes to be compared to,' he murmured.

'If you do not wish to be called a grumpy bear, perhaps do not frown so. Balls are meant to be fun.'

He plastered an exaggerated smile on his face and watched as Maria recoiled.

'For the love of everything that is holy, please stop,' she said. 'How old are you?'

'Thirty-two.'

'Then, why must you act as if you were five?'

'Only for you, my dearest sister.'

Maria was only a few years older than him. She had married his older brother, Robert, when she was nineteen and Robert twenty-three. Simon had been thirteen at the time and reeling from his father's sudden death. Maria had seen a boy struggling with the world and given him the kindness that no one else in his family could at that moment, grieving as they all were, and Simon would never forget it. Over the years their relationship had grown and changed with each new stage of life, but now he was blessed with a sister-in-law who he loved as if she were his own flesh and blood.

'She is pretty,' Maria said, motioning to where Miss James twirled on the dance floor.

'Mmm...' Simon responded. Maria didn't know of his plans to leave England yet. He hadn't told her of the passage he had booked to Europe or his expectation he would never be back. His sister-in-law had suffered so much over the last few years, he knew his departure would devastate her. He would tell her: he wasn't so much of a brute as to leave without saying goodbye, but he didn't want there to be too much time between his revelation and his departure. If anyone could get him to change his mind, it would be Maria.

'Do you know her from somewhere?'

'No,' Simon said, and then glanced over his shoulder. 'But if Lady Salisbury asks, she's a distant relative of my mother's.'

Maria raised an eyebrow. 'What are you doing, Simon?' Then her face lit up with pure joy. 'Are you courting her?'

'Good Lord, no,' he said, pulling Maria to one side, looking round to check no one else had heard her words. He was considered a highly eligible bachelor, with his title, wealth and single status despite being into his thirties. *Everyone* was waiting for him to declare he was finally ready to start looking for a wife. He didn't need any flames being added to that fire.

'Then, who is she?'

'A pleasant young woman I met about an hour ago.'

'Why are you watching her so closely?'

'I'm not,' he said, realising his eyes were on her again. With an effort he looked away and focussed on his sister-in-law.

'Whatever you are doing, be careful,' Maria cautioned him. She flitted between the role of a protective older sister and an excitable friend. There were many people he was going to miss when he left, and Maria was close to the top of that list.

The music swelled and the dance finished, and Simon watched as Forrester bowed to Miss James. They lingered for a moment, talking quietly, before Forrester escorted Miss James to the edge of the dance floor.

'Excuse me,' Simon said, hoping Maria did not follow him, moving quickly to scoop Miss James up before anyone else could. Lady Salisbury was on the other side of the room now and seemed to momentarily have lost interest in the young woman. It would be a good opportunity to sneak Miss James back out the way she had come.

'Thank you for the dance, Miss James,' Forrester said as Simon approached. 'I think Northumberland would run me through with a sword if I asked you to dance again, but I do hope you have an enjoyable evening.'

Once Forrester had left, Simon leaned in as close as he dared and said quietly, 'Lady Salisbury is otherwise occupied. I wonder if it would be best to sneak you out of here now.'

Chapter Three

With her heart hammering in her chest Alice tried to act nonchalant as she followed Lord Westcroft from the ballroom. She looked all around for Lydia but could not see her anywhere and wondered if Lady Salisbury had recognised her as an interloper as well. It was more likely Lydia had realised Lady Salisbury was watching her and slipped away herself. Her friend was highly excitable but astute and observant. Hopefully she was halfway back to the village by now.

'We stand here, pretending to talk, until no one is looking, then we quickly walk down the steps into the darkness of the garden.'

'What if someone sees us?'

'They won't.'

'Would it be safer for me to go by myself?'

She saw him grimace and then shake his head. 'We do not know if anyone is roaming the gardens. There could be all sorts of dangers out there.'

'You make it sound as though wild animals prowl through the flower beds.'

'The truth is much more dangerous. There are unscrupulous people in this world.'

Before Alice could protest any further, he grabbed her by the hand and pulled her down the steps into the shadows of one of the alcoves set below the terrace. They were completely hidden here, out of view from anyone on the terrace above or the ballroom beyond. Someone would have to come all the way down the stairs for them to be seen.

'We'll wait here for a moment and then make a run for it across the lawn,' Lord Westcroft said. His expression was serious, but Alice had a suspicion that he was enjoying himself. They stood quietly for a few minutes, Alice's hand tucked into Lord Westcroft's, and then he nodded to her, and together they set off across the lawn. All the time they were running, Alice felt exposed and was certain there would be a shout from the terrace, perhaps the pattering of feet as people descended the steps into the garden to identify them. Only once they were secreted behind a hedge did she allow herself to breathe normally.

She glanced back towards the house and was relieved to see no one was paying any particular attention to the garden. Hopefully they had made it across unnoticed. Lord Westcroft was also looking back, but after a moment his eyes lowered to meet hers.

Alice felt a spark of attraction between them. She knew much of it was from the excitement of the last few minutes, but she had the irrepressible urge to reach up and trail her fingers over Lord Westcroft's face. She was horrified to find her hand halfway up to his cheek and felt a wave of mortification as he caught it in his own.

'We should get you home, Miss James,' he murmured, holding onto her hand and making no move to leave.

She nodded, her eyes fixed on his.

Alice was never normally reckless. Never before tonight had she sneaked into anyplace she shouldn't be. She obeyed her parents' rules and conducted herself in a manner that was expected of an unmarried young woman. Yet she didn't pull away. She didn't turn her head or break eye contact.

Despite the worry of the last half an hour it had been a magical evening. For a few hours she had been able to pretend she was someone else, swept away in the glamour and opulence of the masquerade ball. For a time she had been able to forget the impending engagement she was about to be pushed into and dance and laugh as if she were free to do whatever she pleased.

Lord Westcroft's thumb caressed the back of her hand, and then before she could stop herself, she pushed up on her tiptoes and kissed him. It was a momentary brush of her lips against his, but as they came together something primal tightened deep inside her, and she realised she wanted so much more.

'Miss James,' he murmured as she pulled away, desire burning bright in his eyes. She thought he might reprimand her. All evening he had been a perfect gentleman, despite the attraction that crackled between them. For a long moment he did nothing, his body so close she could feel the heat of him, and then he gripped her around the waist and kissed her again.

This kiss was deep and passionate and made Alice forget where she was. His lips were soft against hers, and she could taste the sweetness of the punch they had both had. His scent was something entirely different, and she had to fight the urge to bury herself in his neck.

Alice felt her body sink into his, and in that moment all she could think about were his lips on hers. There were no thoughts of consequences, no thoughts of being sensible or respectable. It was just Lord Westcroft and his kiss.

They both stiffened and pulled apart at exactly the same moment. Somewhere to her left, coming from the direction of the house, was a rustling noise. For an instant Alice wondered if it could be an animal, and then the sound came again and she knew for certain it was another person. Whether it was a couple who had slipped into the gardens for some privacy, or one of the servants patrolling to ensure no one was sneaking in after Lady Salisbury's suspicions had been roused, it didn't matter. Someone else was there in the gardens, and if they were caught there would be a horrific scandal.

Alice felt a cold shudder run through her. It would be a repeat of what had happened with her sister, only worse. At least Margaret had a gentleman who had been happy to marry her and save her from the scandal. She doubted even vile Cecil would take her if she got caught kissing the earl in the garden whilst attending a party she had not been invited to.

'I have to go,' she said, pulling away sharply.

'Wait,' Lord Westcroft whispered, catching her hand. 'It might not be safe.'

'I have to go,' she repeated.

This time she wrenched her hand from his and set off at a run across the gardens. She had an advantage, following the route she had crept through with Lydia only a few hours earlier. She weaved around flower beds, squeezed through hedges and pushed herself over fences.

At first she fancied she heard footsteps behind her and thought Lord Westcroft was following her, but somewhere after she had squeezed through the second hedge she lost him.

Only once she was on the road that led back to the village did she slow, her chest heaving, to catch her breath. She desperately hoped Lydia had found her way home already and wasn't trapped somewhere by Lady Salisbury and her suspicions.

Despite the fear of being found out and the frantic dash back through the gardens, Alice could not find it in herself to regret the evening. She had been more reckless than she ever had before, or ever would be again, but for a few hours she had felt alive.

Chapter Four

Simon groaned as he rested his head in his hands, leaning forward onto the desk. He rubbed his temples, trying to alleviate the pounding. Headaches were part of his daily life now, horrible, pulsating episodes of pain that stopped him whatever he was doing and forced him to seek out the relief of a darkened room. For the last year he had been unable to deny that they were happening more frequently and getting worse.

Today however, his headache was a little different. It was the heavy fog caused by drinking too much alcohol, and it was completely self-inflicted.

There was a knock on the door, and he quickly straightened as his butler entered.

'The dowager countess is here, my Lord.'

'Show her in,' he said, hoping he didn't look too terrible.

Maria breezed in, stopping to regard him and shake her head like a fussy mother hen. 'You look terrible, Simon.'

'You look lovely.'

She tutted at his glib reply and sank down into a chair

across from him. 'I have never seen you drink as much as you did last night.'

After Miss James had fled through the gardens, he had followed her, only to lose her a few minutes later. For someone running in highly impractical satin shoes, she had moved fast. He was unsure if they had been spotted and had returned to the ball half expecting someone to come up and make some lewd remarks. As the evening had worn on without anyone saying anything, his relief had led him to the card room, and he had spent far too long playing cards and drinking whisky, trying to forget how good it had been to lose himself for a few minutes in Miss James's kiss.

'We have something very serious to discuss, Simon,' Maria said, her expression grave. For a moment he wondered if she had worked out he was suffering from the headaches. Maria was astute, and if anyone was going to uncover his secret it would be his sister-in-law. 'Last night, in the gardens, someone saw you.'

It took a moment for the words to sink in, and he cleared his throat.

'Who saw what?'

'I had a visit this morning from Miss Elizabeth Cheevers and her mother. It was unannounced and horribly awkward. It would seem they were in the village to shop for some material for a new dress, and when they stopped at the haberdasher's they overheard something disturbing.'

Simon sat a little straighter, his stomach sinking.

'Go on.'

'You were seen in the garden last night, kissing a young woman. By the description, it sounds like Miss

James, but they did not have a name to attach to the rumours as yet.'

Simon felt the world tilt and judder around him for a second, and he had to grip the arms of his chair to steady himself.

'This is bad, Simon,' Maria said, biting her lip. 'It is the talk of the village already, which means by tomorrow the whole county will likely know.'

'They will not know who Miss James is. She kept her mask on the whole time.'

'There are people out there who will make it their whole purpose in life to identify the young woman you were seen kissing. They will think it their moral duty.'

Simon stood and paced to the door and back, trying to order his thoughts. It would be easier if his head weren't pounding so much. For him the consequences were minimal. At worst he would get some snide remarks and a few people avoiding him when he went out and about, but he was an earl and there was only a limited number of people who would dare be rude to him. Added to that, with his plans to leave England in a few weeks, it would hardly affect him.

Miss James was another matter entirely. There was a small hope that she would not be identified. As she was not an invited guest, she would not be the first person to be suspected, but with her distinctive red hair and pretty blue eyes he doubted she would stay hidden for long. He cursed his own stupidity of giving Lady Salisbury her real name, but last night in the moment of their hostess's questioning he had not thought her name would matter.

He closed his eyes. This was the last thing he needed

right now. His plans to leave England could not be disrupted.

'Do not be so selfish,' he muttered to himself, then turned to Maria. 'Please excuse me. I have to try to put this right.'

'You're going to see her?'

'I have to.'

'People will be watching what you do and where you go.'

'I can be discreet.'

'I do not doubt it, but please be careful. I did not speak to Miss James for long, but she seemed a sweet young woman.'

Simon inclined his head and then strode from the room. There was no time to waste. He needed to get to Miss James before the gossip started circling.

Alice sat demurely, her hands folded in her lap and a serene expression fixed on her face, all the while trying not to burst into tears. Across the room her mother sat beaming at her and their new guest. Cecil Billington had been placed beside her on the sofa and had gradually inched closer until his knees were almost touching hers.

'I think you would like Ensley, Miss James,' Cecil said, smiling at her with his mouth full of crooked, yellow teeth. He reached out and boldly stroked the back of her hand as he spoke, and Alice had to use all her self-control to stop herself from pulling away abruptly.

'It is a pleasant village?'

'On the whole, yes. There are plenty of like-minded people to socialise with and a few decent shops. There are more poor people than I would like, but I am working with the other local landlords to raise the rents so we only get a certain class of people in the village. You cannot eliminate the lower classes entirely—we need somewhere for our servants and the people who provide the essential services for the village to live—but I have proposed a system to limit the numbers.'

'Where will the people go who do not make the cut?' Alice asked coldly.

Cecil shrugged. 'That is not my concern. You understand the idea is to make the village a more agreeable place. A place where children can skip freely down the streets and women can walk without fear in the evenings.'

'I thought you said it was a pleasant place already,' Alice said and tried to ignore the warning look she received from her mother.

'Let us not talk of Ensley,' Cecil said, shifting ever closer. 'I am very much looking forward to my stay here, Miss James. I hope you will allow me to accompany you on your daily business.'

'Alice would like that very much,' Mrs James said quickly.

Alice smiled sweetly. 'Today I am going to take a basket of food to Mrs Willow and her children. Mr Willow died last year of consumption, and I understand two of the children have been unwell.'

Alice's mother inhaled loudly and as Alice glanced over gave her a stern look. Cecil looked appalled as she had known he would and shifted uncomfortably.

'Surely you cannot mean to visit a family where there is illness, Miss James? You have to think of yourself.'

'I promised Mrs Willow I would go. She struggles with six children now she is all by herself.'

Cecil curled his lip and flexed his fingers where they rested on her hand.

'Even in the summer months we must be vigilant against disease,' he said.

'Perhaps you could postpone the visit for a few days, Alice,' Mrs James said firmly. 'I am sure Mr Billington would appreciate your time being spent to show him a little of the village and the surrounding area. It is a glorious day. You might even take a stroll on the beach.'

'A promise is a promise, Mother,' Alice said quickly. 'I am sure Mr Billington would not want me to brush off my commitments so readily. It is not an attractive quality in a woman to be unreliable.'

She was saved from further argument by the door opening and their maid slipping into the room. They were not a grand household. Her father's income could only provide enough for one maid and a young lad who helped both inside the house and in the garden. Milly helped Alice's mother in the kitchen and did some of the housework duties around the house, but Alice was expected to do her fair share. All of which had increased significantly since her sister had left home.

'There is a gentleman to see Miss James,' Milly said, turning over a small card in her fingers. She looked in awe of the little piece of embossed card.

'A gentleman?' Mrs James said, standing and casting an apologetic look at Cecil.

'Yes, ma'am,' Milly lowered her voice. 'He says he's the Earl of Northumberland.'

Mrs James's eyes widened, and she took a step forward before turning to Alice.

'Alice James, if this is one of your friends being silly, I will not be impressed.'

In any other circumstance Alice would have had to suppress a smile. It *was* the sort of thing Lydia would do, press an unsuspecting male friend or relative into giving Milly a card with a false name upon it. However, today Alice knew it was no trick.

She felt her mouth go dry and her pulse quicken. There was no good reason for him to be here. Last night had been magical, but Alice was well aware it had been an interlude in her otherwise normal life, nothing more. Lord Westcroft had no place in her small drawing room in their modest home in Bamburgh, just as she had no place in the lofty halls of his grand country house.

'Shall I show him in?' Milly asked, her hand hovering on the door-handle.

'Yes, you had better,' Mrs James said, glancing at Alice again. 'Do you know him?'

Before Alice could answer the door opened again, and Lord Westcroft stepped into the room. He looked out of place in the drab drawing room, and Alice suddenly felt self-conscious. In the cold light of day he would see her dress was made of inferior material, her hands dry and reddened by the manual labour she had to undertake. Normally these things did not bother her, but in front of him she felt a fraud, an imposter. Last night she had soared with all the wealthy ladies, the candlelight allowing her to pass as one of them. It would be painfully clear today she did not fit with the women he was accustomed to.

As he entered the room Alice thought back to the perfect kiss they had shared in the garden before she had fled through the night. It had been magical, everything a young woman could dream of for her first kiss. She found her eyes flicking to his lips now and had to force herself to look away, to focus on the floor as she bobbed into an unsteady little curtsy.

'It is an honour to have you in our home, my Lord,' Mrs James said, bustling over and pausing in front of the earl.

'I am sorry to call unannounced. I hope you can forgive me for dropping in like this.'

'You know an earl?' Cecil muttered out of the corner of his mouth, spittle gathering in the corners in a little frothy bubble.

'A little,' Alice said warily. Lord Westcroft had seemed a sensible man last night and had been aware of the damage that could be done to her reputation by the wrong association. She knew he would not be here if it weren't important. She thought of the rustle in the bushes the night before as they had shared their kiss, the feeling that someone had spotted them, that eyes were watching them, and she shuddered.

'Miss James,' Lord Westcroft said, turning to her with a dazzling smile, 'it is delightful to see you again.'

'And you, my Lord,' Alice said, trying to read his expression.

'And this must be your dear cousin you were telling me about,' Lord Westcroft said, directing his gaze onto Cecil. Alice caught the mischief in the earl's eye and pressed her lips together giving a miniscule shake of her head.

'Billington, Cecil Billington, at your service, my Lord,' Cecil said, stretching out a hand to shake Lord Westcroft's.

'Forgive me, my Lord. I was not aware you were acquainted with my daughter.'

'Our acquaintance has not been a lengthy one,' Lord Westcroft said, allowing Mrs James to usher him into the room. The room was not large, and alongside a low table there was only the armchair Mrs James had been sitting in and the long sofa where Alice and Cecil were. Lord Westcroft seemed unperturbed and took a place next to Alice on the other side.

As they sat his leg brushed hers, and she glanced up at him. For a moment it seemed like they were the only two people in the room; everyone else had faded into the background. Then Cecil cleared his throat, and Alice was pulled right back to reality, sandwiched between the man who could ruin her future and the man she desperately wished she did not have to spend a lifetime tied to.

For one heady moment she wondered if Lord Westcroft had decided to come and rescue her, to declare himself in love after their one evening spent together. Then she looked at his serious expression and knew that wasn't the case.

'Miss James and I met through the course of some of her charitable works,' Lord Westcroft said smoothly. Alice nodded a little too eagerly at the lie and had to tell herself to calm down. Her mother would think it suspicious she had not mentioned meeting a man of his status, although she was hardly going to contradict the earl to his face.

Alice had told Lord Westcroft the evening before of her scheme to pair some of the wealthier families in the village with some of the poorer ones, to provide support over the harsher winters, little parcels of firewood or baskets of food. By joining families one on one, she hoped the wealthier ones would start to feel a little responsibility to their less fortunate counterparts. It would make it harder to distance themselves from the tribulations and struggles of the people they could help.

'I am very keen to get involved with your endeavours, Miss James. I wondered if you might be able to spare me some time to discuss things this morning.'

Alice searched his face, trying to work out what had prompted this visit, but his expression was impassive, a bland smile that was meant to alleviate the concerns of the other people in the room.

'Miss James and I were planning on going for a walk over the dunes,' Cecil said, leaning forward to insert himself into the conversation. 'I understand Miss James's friend is going to make herself available to chaperon.'

'Excellent,' Lord Westcroft said. 'I apologise, Mr Billington, for interrupting your plans like this, but I will not forget your generosity in giving up your time with Miss James for me.'

Cecil opened his mouth and closed it again a few times. It was clear he had meant to accompany Lord Westcroft and Alice on the walk, inserting himself into whatever business they were about to discuss, but Lord Westcroft had quickly outmanoeuvred him.

'Perhaps we should go now, Miss James. I have an appointment this afternoon I wish to keep.'

'Lydia is planning on meeting you?' Mrs James said quickly. Lord Westcroft might be an earl, but the rules of polite society still applied. Even though no one would ever think he could be interested in the likes of Alice, they still had to safeguard her reputation.

'Yes, Mama. She is going to meet us on the beach in twenty minutes.'

'Wonderful,' Lord Westcroft said, rising to his feet. 'It was a pleasure to meet you, Mrs James, and you, Mr Billington.' He bowed to the older woman and shook Cecil's outstretched hand, surreptitiously wiping his hand on his jacket after doing so. Then before anyone could think of any objections, he offered Alice his arm, and quickly they left the room together.

'Let me get my bonnet,' Alice said, running upstairs to fetch it and tie it securely under her chin. It was a glorious day out, but the wind was strong, whipping off the sea with a ferocity that was not common for this time of year. Her skin was so pale it only took a few minutes in the sunlight to turn pink and then burn, but with the wind it was even worse, and she didn't doubt she would have red cheeks later despite her precautions.

They left the house quickly, and Alice was pleased to find they were, so far, unobserved. Her home was on the outskirts of Bamburgh village, at the bottom past the castle that stood proud on the rocky hill. It meant the beach was in easy reach, and they would not have to walk along the high street to get there.

For a few minutes they walked in silence, both looking around all the time to see if they were being watched. Only when they got to the edge of the dunes did Alice feel herself relax.

Waiting as she had promised was Lydia, her eyes alight with intrigue and excitement. As she saw Alice approach on Lord Westcroft's arm she frowned, standing a little straighter.

'This cannot be vile Cecil,' Lydia said quietly as they

approached, clapping her hands over her mouth as soon as the words were out in a bid to claw them back in. Her eyes narrowed, and she shook her head. 'I recognise you.' Five seconds passed and then ten, and then realisation dawned on her.

'Lydia, please,' Alice said quickly. 'Do not make a fuss.'

'This is Lord Westcroft, Earl of Northumberland,' she said, jabbing a finger in his direction. 'The most eligible bachelor in all of England. Last seen at Lady Salisbury's ball last night with a mystery woman in blue.' Lydia turned to her. 'I saw you dancing with him. Although, I didn't know who he was at the time. You're the mystery woman people are talking about.'

Alice felt her heart sink. She had hoped Lord Westcroft was here for some other reason, but deep down she supposed she had known that it was as a consequence of their actions the night before.

'Everyone is saying he was spotted kissing some unknown guest at Lady Salisbury's ball in the gardens.'

Lord Westcroft groaned.

'We were seen?' Alice asked, turning to him.

'It would appear so. I understand gossip and speculation is rampaging through the county.'

Alice felt the world around her tilt, and she clutched a little tighter at Lord Westcroft's arm.

'That is why I thought it imperative to come this morning.'

'Do people know it was me?'

'Not yet,' Lord Westcroft said, stopping and waiting until Alice looked up at him, 'but I think it is inevitable.'

Chapter Five

Alice felt her legs almost give way underneath her, and she was glad of Lord Westcroft's arm supporting her own.

'Perhaps we could take a walk along the beach, Miss James,' Lord Westcroft said, his voice calm. 'We have much to talk about.'

'Everyone will know,' Alice said, shaking her head. She felt sick and hot and as if her whole life were about to implode around her.

'Please, Miss James. I implore you to remain calm,' Lord Westcroft said, his voice silky smooth, and Alice felt some of the panic recede. Perhaps he had a plan, some way of diverting suspicion from her.

In front of her Lydia stood, eyes wide, hardly able to believe what was happening.

'You should do what Lord Westcroft asks, Alice,' Lydia said, motioning for them to go ahead of her across the sand dunes. 'I am sure you have much to discuss.'

Thankfully the wind had kept most people away from the beach, and there were only a few couples in the far distance strolling along the damp sand. Alice picked a path through the dune and onto the beach itself, having to hitch up her skirt as she traversed the soft sand. The climb up the dunes was strenuous even though they were not high along this part of the coast, but the sand was powdery soft, and if you didn't put your feet in exactly the right place you slipped down again. Once at the top she paused for a second to catch her breath and check Lord Westcroft was following her, thinking he might find the unfamiliar terrain difficult, but he was directly behind her, traversing the dunes like a steady-footed mountain goat.

She slipped and slid down the other side, stopping at the bottom to wait for Lord Westcroft and Lydia.

'I'll walk behind,' Lydia said, giving Alice's arm a reassuring squeeze. 'Close enough to count as a chaperon but far enough to give you some privacy.'

'Thank you,' Alice said. She knew how lucky she was to have Lydia as a friend. Not only was the young woman full of spirit and the joys of life, she was loyal and kind too. One of her greatest fears about leaving Bamburgh and starting her life anew, apart from the horror of being married to vile Cousin Cecil, was leaving Lydia behind. She desperately wanted to know how Lydia had fared at the ball the evening before but pushed her questions to the back of her mind. There would be plenty of time for her to catch up with her friend later.

'Come, Miss James. Our time together is short, and we have much to discuss.'

Lord Westcroft led her across the sand. They walked just below the high-tide mark, the sand still damp under their feet. The beach was beautifully clean, the sea clear, with hardly any seaweed deposited on the sand. Alice adjusted her bonnet as they walked, pulling it down a little lower to protect her from the sun.

'My sister-in-law came to see me earlier this morning,' Lord Westcroft said, wasting no time now they were alone. 'She tells me last night we were seen in the garden.' He paused and glanced at her before returning his gaze to the horizon. 'Kissing.'

'Someone actually saw us kiss?' Alice asked, horrified. It would have been ruinous to be merely seen sneaking off into the gardens unchaperoned with the earl, but if someone had seen them kiss, it was impossible to argue there was some innocent explanation for their presence in the garden.

'They did,' Lord Westcroft said. He was looking straight ahead, his posture stiff, and Alice realised he must have come straight to seek her out after he had been informed they had been seen. She felt a swell of gratitude for this man who had shown her kindness the night before and for a short while had made her dream of something other than the future that she was destined for. He could have brushed away the gossip; it would hardly have touched him. A few people might whisper behind their hands when they saw him, but being subject to such gossip would hardly affect his life at all. There were no consequences for men of his social status, not like there were for women of hers. Yet he had still hurried to her, seeking to reach her before the gossips identified her as the mystery woman and ruined her life.

'There is a chance no one will find out who you are,' Lord Westcroft said, glancing at her and grimacing. 'Although, you do have quite distinctive hair. I doubt there is anyone else in all of Northumberland with hair the same shade as yours. Now I think of it I am sure it is why Lady Salisbury was so suspicious at the ball.'

'So the likelihood I remain unidentified is small,' Alice said quietly. She could see her whole life crashing down around her. The devastation it would cause her parents, the end of her life as she knew it. Even Cousin Cecil would declare her too damaged for marriage. She wondered if her sister might take her in: surely the scandal wouldn't reach all the way to Devon. It would be a horrible existence, though, always wondering if someone might know someone who had told them of her infamy.

'Yes. I think you have to prepare yourself for the very real possibility that you will be identified. Of course, there is no proof. You could decide to bluster the whole affair out, especially if you can get your parents on your side. If they swear you did not leave home last night, then I am sure no one will come out and call them liars directly.'

Alice considered the suggestion. 'You mean let people gossip and speculate but deny everything and hope with time things settle down.'

'It might work, and it would mean you could continue your normal life.' He stopped walking for a moment, turning to her and running a hand through his hair. 'I haven't even said I'm sorry, Miss James,' he said and gave her a sad smile. 'I am, from the bottom of my heart. I'm sorry. I shouldn't have kissed you. I have been playing society's game for long enough. I should have been more careful.' He shook his head. 'I pride myself on being a practical person, yet I let myself get carried away.'

'It was not all your fault,' Alice said. 'I kissed you first.'

'I think we were both caught up in the magic of the moment,' he said, his eyes flicking to her lips for a fraction of a second. Alice felt a bolt of anticipation run through her, and she wondered if he felt it too, for he turned away abruptly, offering her his arm again.

For a minute neither of them spoke, and Alice got the sense Lord Westcroft was building up to something. She looked out to sea, trying to imagine her life with the shadow of this kiss hanging over it. She realised, despite what was to come, she couldn't bring herself to regret the evening entirely. She wished she had been more careful, that no one had seen their moment of intimacy in the garden, but she could not wish she had never gone. It had been the first time she had abandoned caution and allowed herself to enjoy the moment, and it had been wonderful from start to finish.

'Vile Cecil arrived as planned I see,' Lord Westcroft said, surprising Alice with his change of direction.

'Yes. I understand he stayed over in Belford last night so he could ride the last few miles this morning. I thought I might have a few more hours before he descended upon us, but it was not to be.'

'Has he proposed yet?'

Alice shook her head. 'No.' She bit her lip and felt her heart sink. 'You think I should press him to before any of the rumours reach him.'

'No,' Lord Westcroft said quickly. 'I would not wish that on anyone, not unless that is what you want.' He paused and then looked at her intently again. 'I just want you to realise what options you have. All is not lost. There is the possibility to live a normal life.'

Alice felt a sudden spark of anger. It felt as though he

were doing his very best to come up with a solution that did not involve him. If he were any sort of gentleman, he would at least mention the idea of marrying her. Alice was not so naïve to think an earl would ever actually end up with a young woman like her, but it would be courteous to at least pretend he would consider it.

She was about to say something to that effect when he stopped walking and waited for her to turn to face him.

'There is another possibility, Miss James,' he said quietly, 'but I need you to really listen as I tell you what I can offer you and what I cannot.'

Alice felt her pulse quicken, and she suddenly wished there was somewhere to sit down, but the only place was the damp sand, and she didn't want to have to explain a wet, sandy dress to her mother.

'In two weeks I leave England,' he said, his expression completely serious with a hint of sadness. 'I plan to travel to the Continent and find somewhere quiet to make my home for the next few months. I have been preparing for this trip for a long time, and I cannot postpone it. There are factors outside my control to consider.'

Alice remained silent, waiting for him to tell her more. It was clear he was not suggesting she accompany him.

'When I leave the country, I do not envisage ever coming back,' he said slowly, his words quiet but clear, and he regarded her intently as if needing to see she understood the gravity of what he was saying. 'Are you aware of my family's history at all?'

She shook her head.

'I was never meant to be earl. My father died when he should still have had a good number of years of life left. He was youthful and healthy, yet one day he just dropped down dead.' Lord Westcroft looked away for a moment, and Alice saw the glint of tears in his eyes. 'For the six months before he died he suffered from debilitating headaches, terrible daily pains that worsened week by week. Then one day he called out in pain, his face a picture of agony, and a few seconds later he collapsed on the floor, dead.'

Alice closed her eyes for a second, wanting to reach out and take Lord Westcroft's hand. He looked devastated, and she realised he must have witnessed his father's death.

'My brother, Robert, became the earl. He was ten years older than me, and for a while he looked out for me like a father. You met my sister-in-law last night. They married just after the mourning period for my father was complete and had three beautiful daughters. There was no reason to think they wouldn't have more children, that they wouldn't have a son who would inherit. I settled into my role as younger brother to the earl.'

Behind them Lydia had stopped too, just out of earshot, and Alice was pleased to see the beach remained almost empty. Horrible as his revelations so far had been, she felt like Lord Westcroft had worse to tell her.

'Then five years ago Robert started to get headaches. Every day he would wake up, and they would be worse than the last.'

Alice's hand went to her mouth. She knew Lord Westcroft's brother was dead, and she could now see where this story was headed. It was terrible.

'One day he dropped dead. He had been out for a ride with his wife and had just dismounted and then collapsed with no warning. The doctor said he was dead before he hit the ground.'

Reaching out Alice laid a hand on Lord Westcroft's arm. To lose one close relative in such a way was horrific, but two would be completely devastating.

He looked at her with haunted eyes and then spoke ever so quietly. 'A year ago I began experiencing headaches. Mild at first, and not every day, but over the last six months they have built in intensity. Every day they build and build until I am forced to lie down in a darkened room.'

'You think…' She couldn't bring herself to say the words.

'I have consulted doctors. They tell me there is nothing to be done and no way of telling when I might be struck down.'

Alice shook her head, unable to comprehend what living with such knowledge would do to you. Every moment he must live in fear of it being his last.

'I am sorry, my Lord. That is no way to live,' Alice said quietly.

'I have made my peace with it, but I have decided I do not want someone I love to witness my death. My mother has suffered enough, my sister-in-law too,' he said grimacing. 'And if I were to die in front of one of my nieces…' He shook his head. 'It is an intolerable thought.'

'This is why you are leaving the country?'

'Yes. I am going to find somewhere peaceful to rent a house, employ someone to cook and clean, pay them well for their services and inform them one day they might walk in to find me dead on the floor.'

Alice shook her head. 'Surely it would be better to

be amongst the people that love you, to spend however long you have with your family.'

Lord Westcroft spoke softly, but there was a steely determination in his voice that Alice realised was born from adversity. 'Every night when I go to sleep, when my thoughts are drifting and I no longer have conscious control of them, I see my father in the moment of his death. I relive the feelings of grief and devastation and shock over and over. I will not inflict that on anyone I love.'

He fell silent, and Alice pressed her lips together. He had lived with this burden for years and had had to face the question of his own mortality for a long time as well. It was not for her to question everything he had been through and the decisions he was making now as a consequence.

'I am sorry for everything you have been through,' Alice said, waiting until he looked at her and then holding his eye. 'It is more than any person should have to bear.'

'I have accepted this as my lot in life. I have had more than thirty years of living in comfort with a family who love me and a very privileged position in society. There are many who have much less than me.' He reached out and took her hand. It was an intimate gesture as Alice felt her heart quicken in her chest. 'I do not normally burden people with the whole story, but I think it is important for you to understand it all, to know exactly what it is I can offer you and what I cannot.'

The wind whipped around them as they stood together on the beach, blowing Alice's skirt against Lord Westcroft's legs, but he hardly seemed to notice.

'We find ourselves chased by scandal, Miss James,

and I think it inevitable your name will be associated with the kiss we shared, even if no one can prove it was you in that garden. I can offer you marriage, a protection of sorts, but it will not be the sort of marriage you expected for yourself.' He paused, checking she was following his words. 'If it is what you choose, I will marry you. It will save you from scandal, and once you become countess no one will care how we were a little careless. You will have my name and title as protection.'

Alice felt her head swim. Even from their short acquaintance she had known Lord Westcroft was an honourable man, but she had not expected this offer from him.

'I would obtain a special licence, and we would marry within the next few weeks. Then I would continue with my plan to leave the country.'

Alice's eyes flicked up to meet his, and she realised the importance of what he was saying and why he had told her exactly what had happened to his father and brother.

'You would be free to use whichever of my houses you wished, and I would ensure there was a good amount of money available for you. You would have a comfortable life, Miss James, but it would be a life spent on your own, at least at first.'

She opened her mouth to speak, but he pushed on quickly.

'Hear the last of my proposition,' he urged her. 'After we are married, you will not see me again. We will not consummate our union, and you will never bear me children. You will live as my wife in name until I die, and then you will be my widow.'

Alice took a step back, unable to take it all in. It was a generous proposition in so many ways, but she wasn't so naïve to think it the perfect solution to her problems. She would become a countess, an elevation in social status most women could only dream of, but Lord Westcroft had made it clear it would not be a normal marriage where their union would be celebrated. Alice tried to imagine her life if she did decide to marry Lord Westcroft. She would be mistress of her own home, finally in control of her own life, but it would be a lonely existence.

'There are some terms that I would ask you to abide by, if you did decide to accept my offer,' Lord Westcroft said slowly. She could see he wasn't sure if he had lost her to her racing thoughts.

'What terms?' It was best to know everything now, to have all the facts in her possession so she could make the best decision.

'I would ask you not to take a lover whilst I was alive.' He pressed his lips together and looked over her shoulder into the distance. 'It would complicate the matter of inheritance if you were to get pregnant.' She nodded, understanding his reasoning, and he quickly continued. 'I would leave you a generous settlement in my will. Enough to allow you to live as a wealthy widow for the rest of your life if you so desired, or to provide a generous dowry to take to your next marriage.'

His offer was kind, his tone calm but firm, and Alice realised he had thought about this a lot on his way to see her. What he was prepared to offer and what he wasn't. It showed how sure he was in his decisions and how convinced he was that he would likely go the same way as his father and his brother soon.

He fell silent and looked at her with those bright blue eyes, and she felt a pang of sadness that there was no desire in them now. What he was proposing was purely an arrangement made to safeguard her reputation and fulfil his obligation. He owed her nothing, but chivalry demanded he take responsibility for his part in tarnishing her reputation.

Alice turned away, desperately trying to weigh up what he was offering her. If she accepted his proposition she would be a countess, mistress of her own home and finally in charge of her own life. Yet she would live alone, with no prospect of love until Lord Westcroft died abroad and released her from the marriage.

She wanted children, a home filled with love, and this would give her none of that, but it would likely mean postponing that part of her life, not forgoing it.

The alternative was Cecil, if he would have her. After this scandal her parents would be more keen than ever to marry her off quickly and quietly, and she would be stuck with Cecil and his pawing hands and horrible views on society for the rest of her life.

'I could come with you,' she offered, turning back quickly. 'If you would prefer someone to look after you.'

'No,' he said sharply and then made an effort to soften his tone. 'I need to be alone. I can offer you my name and my protection, but no more, Miss James, not under any circumstance.'

'I understand,' she said. She would not build this into a fantasy of something that could never be. The decision had to be made on what he was offering, weighing that up with the alternative.

'I do not wish to rush you in your decision, but if we

are going to do this, it has to be quick for a couple of reasons. The first, as I said, I plan to be on a boat leaving London in two weeks, and the second is that rumours will spread fast. If we announce our engagement it will stop any malicious gossip in its tracks. You will be protected by your new title, but that only works if we preempt the majority of the speculation.'

'Your offer is very generous, Lord Westcroft,' Alice said, raising her eyes to meet his. 'I do not want you to feel obligated to do this. I never set out to trap you. I never thought this would be the culmination of last night.'

He smiled grimly. 'I know, Miss James. Perhaps we were both a little naïve thinking we could get away with such a deception. Please do not concern yourself with worrying that I might think you did this on purpose. I pride myself on being a good judge of character, and I like yours. If we had met in other circumstances, perhaps we would even have been friends.' He took her hand in his, and Alice inhaled sharply at the contact. 'I would not propose to a woman who I thought would bring my family's name into disrepute. I cannot make this decision for you, but please do not think I am insincere in what I am offering.'

Alice closed her eyes and let the two possible lives wash over her. The first was marriage to Cecil, a man she despised. The second was less conventional, perhaps a little lonely, but contained the chance of happiness along the way. She knew she had to be brave and reach out and grab what was being offered.

'Thank you, Lord Westcroft. I accept.'

Chapter Six

Simon adjusted his cravat and looked in the mirror. On the outside he looked composed and together, but inside he was less certain about what he was about to do. It was his wedding day, a day he had thought might never happen, yet here he was twelve days after proposing to Miss James, ready to get married.

It had been an odd couple of weeks. He had paused his preparations for leaving England, instead spending all his time preparing for his coming nuptials. Obtaining the special licence that allowed them to marry in haste had taken much time and a small fortune. Simon had called on friends throughout the country to exert their considerable influence and get one issued so quickly. It was a relief to know he would not have to change his plans after the wedding.

There was a knock on his door, and he glanced at the clock. There was still fifteen minutes until the ceremony, but he expected the vicar was already downstairs, preparing for the hurried nuptials.

'Come in,' he called, turning to face the door.

The door opened, and Sylvia, his youngest niece, slipped inside. She was six years old, a confident, happy child who managed to hold the whole family in her thrall despite her young age. She had only been one when her father died, and it saddened Simon that she would have no recollection of him at all.

'Good afternoon, little minx.'

She skipped into the room and threw herself down on the bed dramatically.

'Do you have to get married, Uncle?' she asked, clutching her doll to her chest. 'I don't want you to.'

'I have to get married,' Simon said, stopping what he was doing and coming to sit beside her. 'I would not be a very good person if I did not.'

'I wouldn't tell anyone you had been bad.'

'You might not tell anyone, but I would know.'

'What is she like? I probably won't like her.'

'Nonsense, Sylvia. I think you will like her very much.' He hid a grimace. He at least hoped so. Miss James seemed decent and kind, but he barely knew her. In the course of the last twelve days since he'd proposed, he had spent at most an hour in her company, the very minimum he could get away with. The truth was he didn't want to get to know Miss James. He didn't want to know her hopes and fears, her likes and dislikes. It would make leaving harder. This way Miss James remained a stranger, even if they would be married in an hour.

'Is she very pretty, like a princess?'

Simon considered. 'Yes, she is, although not as pretty as you, of course.'

Sylvia giggled and rolled her eyes. 'You have to say that. You're my uncle. Will you come and live with us, now you are to be married?' At present his sister-in-law and nieces lived in one of the many houses that made up the Westcroft estate. It was modest in size, plenty big enough for the growing children, but small enough to feel homely. Simon had offered Westcroft Hall to Maria and her children, insisting they need not move out of the home they had shared when Robert was alive, but his sister-in-law had refused, saying she could not bear to wake up in the bed she had shared with Robert every day, knowing she would never see his smile or feel his arms around her again. It meant Simon reluctantly had moved into Westcroft Hall, feeling as though he were stealing more of his brother's life from him.

'No, little minx,' he said with a sad smile. Of all the things he would miss about England, his nieces were at the top of the list. He loved the time he spent with them, the fun and laughter they brought to his life. They were one of the main reasons he had decided to go too. It was much better he fade from their memory, dead in a distant land, than they witness him expiring in front of them. That sort of thing scarred a person for life.

'I wish you would. I like it most of all when you are there, and I suppose I would learn to like Miss James.'

'Things will change these next few weeks, Sylvia,' he said, his tone serious. He hadn't told anyone of his plans yet, only Miss James who had been sworn to secrecy. Tomorrow he would bid farewell to his mother, his sister-in-law and his nieces before starting his journey south.

'I don't want things to change,' Sylvia said, her voice quiet, and he wondered if she had sensed something big was about to happen, something more than this sudden marriage to Miss James.

'I know it can be hard when things change, but you

must remember that you are surrounded by people who love you.'

Sylvia looked at him with her big eyes and nodded sadly, perhaps sensing there was more than what Simon was saying, more that would unsettle her.

'Sylvia, stop bothering your uncle,' Maria said as she bustled into the room. 'He has a wedding to prepare for.'

'I'm not bothering him. He likes my company,' Sylvia said, smiling cheekily at her mother.

'Go and find your sisters, Sylvia. I need to speak to your uncle in private.'

Sylvia pulled a face but slipped off the bed and left the room. Maria poked her head out the door after a few seconds to check she wasn't listening outside.

'Everything is ready downstairs,' she said, looking at him with concern. Everyone had been treating him like he had gone a little mad the last couple of weeks. The marriage they could understand, even if it was not ideal. He had been caught compromising the reputation of a young lady. Anyone who knew him would understand that he could not let the young woman in question suffer the consequences of their indiscretion alone, but it was the speed of the wedding that was a shock to his family. After delicate enquiries—which he quickly suppressed—as to whether Miss James was expecting a child, his friends and family had started to give him concerned looks all the time. He knew he could fix things by telling them of his plans, but he couldn't bear the burden it would place on them, knowing he too could follow in the path of his father and brother and expire any day.

'Are you sure you want to go through with this?' Maria asked, hovering near the door. 'There would be no shame in a longer engagement. It would allow you to get to know Miss James a little more. Surely that can only be a good thing.'

'Everything is arranged, Maria. The vicar is downstairs. This marriage needs to happen. What is the sense in delaying things?'

Maria bit her lip and stepped closer, laying a hand on his arm. 'If you told me you loved her, that you could not bear to spend a single moment apart from her, then I could understand the rush, but I do not think that is the case. You speak of Miss James with respect but not love.' She studied his face, and Simon felt as though she were looking into his soul. 'There is something more, isn't there?'

He swallowed, knowing if anyone was able to work out that he had been suffering with his headaches it would be Maria. She had watched her husband go through much the same, and he was worried she could see the same patterns emerging in him.

'Let us just enjoy the day,' he said, giving her a smile that he knew didn't reach his eyes.

Maria sighed but nodded, turning to leave.

'I wish you every happiness, Simon,' she said softly at the door. 'I know you think you do not deserve it, but you do.'

He stalled for a few more minutes before heading downstairs, a heavy weight in his stomach. Even though he didn't plan on sticking around to be part of this marriage he was entering into, it was still another person he was taking responsibility for. With one final check in the mirror, he tried to ignore the dark circles under his eyes and walked from his room.

* * *

Alice shifted nervously, wishing her mother would stop fussing and leave her alone. Her parents were understandably delighted by the turn of events; their daughter marrying an earl was beyond their wildest dreams.

It hadn't been all pleasant when she had first told them: they had been furious that she had allowed her reputation to be compromised, and only a visit from Lord Westcroft to assure Mr and Mrs James his intentions were now honourable could quieten their fears Alice would end up deserted and ruined.

Mrs James stepped back and admired her handiwork, tutted and then reached out to fiddle with Alice's hair again. They had been given one of the many bedrooms in Westcroft Hall for her to get ready in, and now Alice stood in the new dress that had been delivered a few days earlier, a gift from Lord Westcroft for their wedding day.

There was a soft knock on the door, and a moment later it opened and the dowager countess, Lord Westcroft's sister-in-law, entered the room.

'Mrs James, I think everything is almost ready downstairs. Perhaps you would like to take a seat with your husband.'

Mrs James flushed and curtsied clumsily, gave Alice a final look-over and then left the room.

The dowager countess smiled at Alice, her expression warm.

'How are you, my dear?'

'I feel as though I have a hundred frogs jumping inside my stomach,' Alice said and then flushed. It was probably too honest an answer.

'I remember my wedding day. I felt much the same. It

was a small affair in the local church, yet I felt as though the whole world was watching me.' She paused and then stepped closer. 'I know this has been thrust upon you both, but Lord Westcroft is a good man. He will do his duty by you and so much more.'

Alice looked away. Lord Westcroft's family were not aware of the nature of their impending marriage. They thought Alice and Lord Westcroft would live together as man and wife, not go their separate ways after the wedding, never to see one another again.

'You are kind, Lady Westcroft.'

She waved a hand. 'You must call me Maria. After today there will be three Lady Westcrofts. Simon's mother, me and now you. Let everyone else tie themselves up in knots working out who they are talking about, but we will be family and can be much more familiar.'

Alice felt the tears prick her eyes. These last few weeks she had felt bereft and uncertain in her decision. Her parents had been focussed on her elevation in status and what that meant for them. Lord Westcroft had been notably absent, sending her notes to update her on the progress of their impending wedding but only spending at most an hour with her in the last few weeks. It was comforting to have a friendly face, someone to make her think she might be welcomed into this family even if Lord Westcroft was not around to help her find her place.

'You will call me Alice?'

'I would be delighted to, Alice. Now, I do not know where you and Simon are planning on setting up your main residence, but whilst you are here in Northumberland we will take tea together at least once a week and go for long walks about the estate. I know how apprehensive you can feel, marrying into such a wealthy and influential family, and if there is anything I can do to help ease your path, you must tell me.'

'That is very kind, Maria.'

She smiled with a mischievous twinkle in her eye. 'Although, of course, I would not dream of interrupting you during the honeymoon period. Simon did not say if you were going away, but I expect he will at least take you on a tour of the residences he owns around the country.'

Alice dropped her gaze. Maria was a perceptive woman, and Alice sensed her future sister-in-law could tell there was something out of the ordinary about this marriage.

After a moment Maria let out an almost imperceptible sigh and then shrugged. 'I think it is time, Alice. Shall we make our way to the drawing room?'

Alice nodded and followed Maria out of the room, her eyes flitting over the dozens of portraits that lined the upstairs hallway. The house was old, with oak panelling in the main parts, with various wings and rooms added on at different points. It meant it had a haphazard charm and a mishmash of different styles throughout. They were in the oldest part here, built in Tudor times with sloping floorboards and walls that leaned first inward then outward. The walk felt as though it took for ever, even though it must have been less than thirty seconds between Alice leaving her room to getting downstairs.

They paused outside the drawing room, with Maria giving her one last squeeze of the hand before she slipped inside. For a moment Alice was left alone. She wondered if she was making a huge mistake. Lord Westcroft was a good man—she could tell that from the little time they had spent together—but she was not going to see him after they had sorted the practicalities of the next few days. She would be a countess, but a lonely one.

Alice squared her shoulders. She had chosen this path, and now she would follow it. The alternative had been worse, and now she had to find a way to make the life she had opted for bearable.

She ran her hands over the gold silk of the wedding dress, swallowing hard as she pushed open the door of the drawing room to see her future husband standing inside.

Chapter Seven

Ten months later

The house was quiet and dark as he approached, and he wondered if all the staff were in bed. It was late, much later than he had planned to arrive, but his ship had been delayed, and he had spent some time wandering the streets, trying to clear his head after the long and stormy voyage.

The last four days it had rained incessantly, a foreboding welcome back to England after nearly a year's absence. He had taken a boat from Italy, a journey that should have taken a little over two weeks, but because of the weather it had been much longer, and at one point he'd thought the captain was going to declare the trip a lost cause and turn around to seek shelter in one of the French ports.

Finally he had arrived home, uncertain how he felt to be back in London after his self-imposed exile.

He looked up at his townhouse and felt a wave of familiarity wash over him. His father had bought this house when Simon was a young boy, and he could remember visiting it for the first time, enthralled by all the sights and smells of London. His father had taken him by the hand and led him up the steps to the front door, then given him a tour of the house room by room, finishing up in the nursery at the very top. He'd pointed out the view over the square, the rooftops of London beyond, and Simon could remember feeling happy.

He'd spent much time there over the years, first with his parents when they travelled to London for the season, then when he was a young man Robert had given him free use of the house whenever he was in London. Since becoming the earl, Simon had been here even more, with his responsibilities often meaning he had to spend months at a time in London rather than in the wilds of Northumberland.

Before his departure to the Continent he had spent a long time ensuring there was enough supervision and funds to run all of his households without his oversight. He had not wanted to burden his mother or sister-in-law with the day-to-day questions that arose from owning a number of properties and employing the staff needed to keep everything running smoothly, so he had made sure there were senior household servants in each house he owned who were happy to take responsibility without the oversight of a master or mistress. He also employed a land steward and his assistant to collect rents and sort any queries from tenants and make decisions on the wider estate business.

Miss Stick was his trusted housekeeper of the London townhouse. Employed by the family for decades, she was a stiff and proper woman in her fifties with a good head for household accounts and just the right mix of authoritarian discipline and warmth to mean servants under her command were fiercely loyal and hardworking. No doubt, at half past midnight Miss Stick and the small complement of servants in the house were long asleep.

He had not sent word he was returning to England. Throughout his journey back he kept telling himself he would write to his mother, to Maria, to his steward to alert them of his plans to return to the country, but he never had. If he searched his soul he knew it was because he had wanted the chance to change his mind, even up until the boat docked and his feet touched English soil.

'Home,' he murmured as he touched the railing outside his house for the first time in many months. It was a strange feeling: for so long he had thought he would never see home again, convinced he would go to die in some foreign country surrounded by strangers. It was surreal to be back, and for much of the last few weeks he had felt as though he were floating through a dream.

He contemplated knocking at the door and decided against it, instead slipping round the side of the house and going through the gate into the small back garden. There were stairs here that led to the kitchen at basement level, and unless things had changed drastically he knew where Miss Stick hid the spare key.

A smile formed on his lips as he reached up to the lip above the door, his fingers closing around the cool metal of the key to the back door. He put it in the lock, turned it and slipped into the house.

Tomorrow it would be a surprise for the housekeeper to find him returned, but tonight at least the servants could sleep. There would be one bedroom at least kept ready for guests, for he was not the only person to use the house. Maria would often make the trip to London to

visit friends and family, and less often his mother would
too. He knew they weren't here now, though, for he had
received a letter from his mother just before he had left
Italy telling him that Maria and the children had just returned from London for the summer and that she was
pleased to have them back in Northumberland.

Quickly he secured the door behind him and made his
way through the kitchen and upstairs to the main part of
the house. In the darkness everything looked the same
as it always had, and he felt a sense of familiarity and
comfort wash over him.

Upstairs he paused outside the bedroom door. There
was a chance that his bedroom was not made up ready
for someone to sleep in, but if that were the case he could
check the others and choose one where the sheets were
fresh to lie down on for the night.

He opened the door, surprised to find the room fresh
and cool, a slight breeze blowing in through the open
window. It was only open a crack, just enough to air the
room and keep it at decent temperature despite the hu-
midity outside. It was unlike Miss Stick to allow a window to stay open all night. She would normally cite the
crime rate in this part of the city, figures Simon would
not be able to refute but which seemed much higher than
he would have imagined.

The curtains in the room billowed slightly with the
breeze, and it took his eyes a moment to adjust to the
darkness of the room. Outside, the moon was obscured
by the heavy clouds that still threatened rain despite the
days of downpours, and it was hard to see anything beyond the outline of the furniture. He took a few steps
towards the large bed and felt the covers, relieved to

find bed-sheets under his fingers. Quietly he closed the door and began to undress. His luggage would follow, and he was too weary to go digging through drawers to find any nightclothes so instead he stripped naked to the waist, throwing his clothes onto the chair that sat in the corner of the room, then gripped the bed-sheets and climbed into bed.

As soon as his body slipped between the sheets he knew something was wrong. There was a warmth there that shouldn't have been, the sort of warmth that can only come from a body. Tentatively he reached out, and his hand brushed against warm skin. For a moment he lingered, too shocked to move, and then he felt the person in his bed rolling over. Quickly he scrambled back, but it was too late. A hand shot out and grabbed hold of his wrist, and in the darkness he saw two wide eyes shining in an otherwise pitch-black room.

The woman screamed. It was the loudest sound he had ever heard, a scream filled with terror. He could not imagine anything more petrifying than finding someone else climbing into bed with you at night when you thought you were safe and alone in your room, so he did not blame her, but the sound pierced through him and made it impossible to reassure her.

From somewhere above he heard clattering as servants leaped out of their beds and rushed towards the stairs that would lead them here.

'I mean you no harm,' he said as calmly as he could muster. 'I am sorry.'

His words took a moment to penetrate the noise, but after a few seconds the screaming stopped and was replaced by a quiet whimpering.

'Miss James, is that you?'

'Yes,' she replied after a moment, scrambling to pull the bed-sheets up around her.

'My sincerest apologies. I did not know you would be in London.'

'No,' she murmured, 'I don't suppose you did.' There was a pause as she tried to compose herself, and then she said with more authority, 'It is not Miss James anymore, my Lord. You may have forgotten our marriage, but by law I am still Lady Westcroft.'

Her voice was cool, almost cold, and if the servants hadn't arrived at that very moment he thought she might go on to say more.

'My apologies, Lady Westcroft,' he said quietly.

'What is happening?' Miss Stick said as she rushed into the room, dressing gown billowing around her, cotton mob cap on her head. 'Lord Westcroft?'

Another servant, a maid he did not recognise, came rushing in behind Miss Stick followed by a young footman. The maid was holding a candle, and finally there was light in the room.

He surveyed the scene, a sinking feeling in his stomach. This was not how he had hoped his homecoming would unfold. He'd wanted to slip in, largely unobserved, and make quiet enquiries to bring himself up to date with the world he had left behind before everyone found out he was home. Instead probably every house on the square would know of his midnight return by the morning, no matter how firmly he pressed his servants on the need for discretion.

Simon breathed deeply and then adopted his most commanding tone.

'I am sorry to have disturbed you all. I thought to re-turn without waking the whole household but was not aware Lady Westcroft was in residence.' Momentarily his eyes met his wife's, and then she looked away. 'Please return to your beds and go back to sleep.'

The maid and the footman turned immediately, but Miss Stick called out to stop them.

'The candle, Mary. You cannot expect Lord and Lady Westcroft to be left in the dark.'

The maid blushed and quickly placed the candle on the mantelpiece before curtsying and hurrying from the room.

Miss Stick waited until they had left and lowered her voice.

'The green room is also made up, my Lord, should you need it,' Miss Stick spoke with the practised discretion of a valued servant, making no assumptions, just letting him know the options available.

'Thank you, Miss Stick.'

'Do you need anything, my Lord? My Lady?'

'No, thank you,' he said, watching as the housekeeper turned to his wife. He was amazed to see her normally stern expression soften a little as Lady Westcroft smiled at her.

'No, thank you, Miss Stick. You have been wonderful as usual.'

The housekeeper's lips twitched, and he was surprised to realise she was almost smiling. Then she left the room, closing the door softly behind her.

For a long moment there was nothing but silence between them. The woman in front of him was a stranger, and he could see how invasive it was to have him climb half-naked into her bed. Yet he felt a flicker of irritation along with the regret at not checking the room was empty.

'It is late, Lord Westcroft,' she said, quietly but firmly. She was dressed in a cotton nightgown, and although it was not made of the most substantial material, it had a high neck and long sleeves that covered her modesty, yet she wrapped her arms about her in a way that made him realise she felt uncomfortable. He glanced down at his bare chest and hastily reached for his shirt, discarded on the chair.

'I will leave you to sleep, Lady Westcroft,' he said, gathering the rest of his clothes. 'My apologies again.' It felt strange to be leaving his bedroom, yet he would not think of throwing her out in the middle of the night. Instead he made a hasty retreat, closing the door on the stranger who was his wife.

Chapter Eight

Alice clasped her hands together to stop them from shaking as she paused outside the door to the dining room. Breakfast was normally one of her favourite times of the day. She loved taking her time over the first meal of the day, savouring her toast and eggs whilst she sipped on a steaming cup of delicious coffee. Miss Stick always ensured there was a newspaper ready and available for her to read, alternating between the more serious publications, which ensured she was informed about political and worldly matters, and the gossip sheets that meant she was never behind when it came to the intrigue of the *ton*. Since moving to London eight months previously, she had followed the same routine. Coffee, breakfast and half an hour with the newspaper before she was ready to face the day. It had been peaceful, but now her peace was shattered.

Straightening her back and lifting her chin, she pushed open the door and walked into the room, clenching her jaw as she saw Lord Westcroft was sitting in her favourite seat. It was the one at the head of the table, traditionally the master of the house's spot, but Alice had lived this past year with no husband and no master, and when she had decided to move her breakfast spot to the head of the table, there had been no one to object. That place was set in front of the large window and caught the best of the morning light.

Telling herself not to be so petty she forced a smile onto her face as Lord Westcroft looked up. He was holding her newspaper, the pages slightly crumpled in his hands.

'Good morning, Lady Westcroft. I hope you managed to sleep again after I disturbed you last night. My apologies again.'

'I did, thank you,' she lied. For hours she had lain in bed wondering what this sudden, unexpected return meant for her. Lord Westcroft hadn't deceived her when he had offered her marriage. He had been clear that he would not be there by her side as her husband, but she had not expected his departure to be so sudden, or so complete. One day after their wedding, he had left. Alice had known he had made plans to sail to the Continent but she had assumed he would escort her to her new home first, perhaps introduce her to the servants, be there as she got to know his mother and sister-in-law. A week, perhaps two—it wouldn't have needed long, but instead he had left without doing any of that. He had also made it clear his journey was one way and that she should not expect him back.

She took a seat at the dining table, looking up when Miss Stick came into the room, a frown on her face when she saw Lord Westcroft sitting in Alice's accustomed place, reading her newspaper. Alice felt a rush of warmth for the housekeeper. She had been terrified of her when she had first arrived in London and almost made the decision to flee back to Northumberland, but slowly she had won the housekeeper round, making an ally out of the older woman.

'Good morning, Lady Westcroft. I will tell Cook to make you a fresh cup of coffee and get started on your eggs. Is there anything else you need this morning?'

'No, thank you, Miss Stick. Join me in the drawing room after breakfast, and we can discuss the meals for the week.'

Miss Stick inclined her head and left the room. Alice felt her husband's eyes on her and turned to him.

'If you would be so kind as to inform me of your plans, Lord Westcroft, insofar as planning the meals and social calendar for the week goes, I would appreciate it.'

He looked at her as if she had grown a second head.

'Social calendar?' he murmured.

She held up a hand and counted off on her fingers, 'I have a number of events planned this week. Afternoon tea with the London Ladies' Benevolent Society, dinner parties with the Hampshires and the Dunns, and a fund-raising event at the end of the week. It would be helpful to know if you will be here or not.'

'You live here?' he asked, puzzlement on his face.

'Yes,' she said, slowly.

'In London?'

'Yes.'

'In this house?'

'Where would you prefer I live, my Lord?'

He rallied, and she silently chided herself for her frosty tone, but the situation was impossible. She had made a life for herself here. It had been far from easy, and it had taken months to build the social circle she had now, but it had been worth it. Now that Lord West-croft was back, his purpose as yet undeclared, she felt as though he might suddenly pull it all away from her.

'I thought you were in Northumberland.'

'I spent a few months in Northumberland after we married, then I moved to London.'

'No one said, in their letters.'

Alice looked away, glad when the maid bustled in with a plate of eggs and toast and a steaming pot of coffee.

She hadn't written to Lord Westcroft: there had hardly seemed a point. Her husband was a stranger, a man she had spent very little time with before they were married and even less after. She knew his mother had written detailed letters telling him about the family and the estate, and so had Maria, but she had asked both not to include her in their letters. They had complied, seeing her discomfort of her new position and wanting to do anything to help her feel accepted and settled.

Lord Westcroft waited until they were alone again and then fixed her with an unwavering stare. 'I know it must be a shock, my turning up like this with no warning.'

'It is,' Alice said, buttering her toast a little more vigorously than she normally would. 'But it is your home. I do not know why I am surprised.'

'Perhaps because I told you I was leaving and never coming back,' he said gently.

Alice put down her knife. She could feel the tension in every muscle of her body. For twenty-one years she had not been in control of her own life. She had lived by her parents' rules, tied to the fate they determined for her, and then suddenly she had been granted her freedom. Lord Westcroft had given her a great gift, she knew that, and her coolness towards him now was only because she feared she might lose that freedom. She exhaled slowly, suppressing the uncertainty and the fear, and turned to her husband.

'How are you?' she said, studying him properly. 'It is good to see you looking so well.'

Simon felt the weight of her scrutiny. Her eyes took their time as she looked over his face and body. He knew what she would see, something entirely unexpected: a man who had gone away to die looking healthier and stronger than ever before.

'I am well,' he said quietly. 'At least, I think I am.'

'You think…?'

He sighed heavily and glanced out the window to where the sunshine was reflecting off the puddles that lay on the street. It had been a difficult truth to come to terms with, almost as difficult as thinking he was dying.

'I told you of my father and brother, their headaches, their sudden deaths,' he said, hoping he would not have to go through the painful history again.

'Yes, I remember, and your mother told me a little more after we were married, after you left.'

'Yes, she suffered terribly. First her husband, then her eldest son. Both struck down in their prime when they had young families to care for.'

'When you left you were getting awful headaches,' Lady Westcroft prompted gently. 'It was the reason you were so keen to leave so quickly.'

'I'd been having them for some time on a daily basis. I'd consulted two reputable doctors, and after listening to the story of my father and brother they both told me the same thing.' He paused, remembering the first time a doctor had looked him in the eye and told him he was going to die. 'They told me in all likelihood I would be dead before the year was out.'

'They couldn't have known that,' she murmured, shaking her head.

'They spoke of a malformation of the vessels in the brain, a condition that runs in families. Apparently it has been seen in cadavers when they have undergone dissection for medical training. Evidence of a catastrophic bleed in the brain and a story of headaches before death.'

She looked away, her fork pushing the egg around on her plate before she laid it down and picked up her cup of coffee, cradling it with both hands.

'They told you that was what would happen to you?'

'Yes.'

'That's terrible.'

'At the time I felt like it only confirmed my suspicions.'

She took a sip of coffee and then looked over at him. 'Yet you're still here and look as healthy as a man in his prime.'

'When I left I was having daily headaches, but over the next few months they gradually dwindled.'

He had been unable to believe it at first, thinking it was perhaps just a short reprieve, but as he had travelled farther from England, his headaches had become fewer. He'd settled in a remote part of Italy, high in the Tuscan hills. It was beautiful there, and for the first time in a long time he had felt at peace.

'When I had been in Italy for two months I sought the advice of an eminent physician in Florence. I explained my symptoms and what had happened to my father and my brother. He told me it was not yet my time to die.'

Lady Westcroft's eyes widened, and she had a look of incredulity on her face. 'Did he explain the headaches?'

Simon shifted uncomfortably. 'He said they were likely caused by the huge amount of stress I was under, imagining myself dying.' For some reason it felt uncomfortable to admit it, that he had brought the headaches on himself. 'He told me it was self-perpetuating. The first time I got a headache I thought it must be the start of the same condition they had died from. The stress of that thought meant I woke every day with a headache that would not relent.'

'It is easy to see how that could happen,' Lady Westcroft said. Now she had lost her frostiness towards him, she seemed more like the reasonable young woman he had proposed to. He watched her as she sipped her coffee. He was ashamed to admit he had not thought much about her this past year. His guilt had been over leaving his mother and sister-in-law behind, along with his young nieces. They had been the reason he had returned, not the wife he had almost forgotten about.

It was only a year ago he had left, a little less, yet he realised Lady Westcroft *had* changed. Not physically, at least not at first glance, but there was something about her manner, a poise and confidence that she hadn't had before. When they had married she had seemed overwhelmed by the wealth and status of the family she was marrying into, yet now she sat in this dining room confident in her role as mistress of the house. He even thought he'd seen her eyeing his chair at the head of the table when she'd entered.

'I am truly glad you are not dying, Lord Westcroft,' she said softly.

'Thank you. So am I.' He paused, deciding to be entirely candid with her. 'The doctor in Italy said there was a good possibility I had the same condition as my father and brother, that he could not guarantee I would not be plagued by the headaches that were the harbinger of a sudden death, but he urged me to resume my life and said it might happen in a year or in forty years.'

'So here you are,' Lady Westcroft said.

'Here I am.'

She glanced at the clock on the mantelpiece and put down her cup of coffee. Her breakfast lay barely touched on her plate.

'I am sure you are still finalising your plans, my Lord,' she said, standing and dropping into a formal little curtsy. 'When you have decided what you will be doing and where you will be staying, please let me know. Now I must leave you. I have an engagement I forgot about.'

Before he had a chance to answer, she turned and hurried out the room. He had the sense she was escaping him, running away from having to interact with him anymore. Leaning back in his chair he laced his fingers together in front of his chest. At least he had begun the conversation between them. Throughout his voyage home he had avoided thinking too much of his accidental wife. In his mind she was living quietly in one of his properties in Northumberland, taking long country walks and occupying herself with needlework or watercolours. He'd thought he would have time before he told her the circumstances of their marriage had changed, that she was no longer wife to an absent husband. He'd imagined arranging a time to meet as they discussed how their lives would continue now he was home. With a groan he remembered instead how he had climbed into bed with her after a year of no contact whatsoever. Never would he be able to rid himself of the terrified look on her face or the awful scream as she saw him in the darkness.

He sighed. It was a lot for her to take in, yet all he wanted was to reassure her. In the main her life need not change. There was no requirement for them to live as husband and wife, even if he were in the country. She could stay at one property, he another. Lady Westcroft was a sensible woman; he may have only known her for a short time, but he had been able to tell that from their acquaintance before their marriage. She was sensible, and he was sure with a little time she would see their arrangement could continue without too much disruption.

For a second he thought back to the kiss they had shared in the garden of Lady Salisbury's party on Midsummer's Eve the year before. It had been a magical moment, and for a few minutes he had allowed himself to imagine a different future.

Quickly he shook his head. It wasn't to be. He had decided long ago he was never going to marry or have children. He had broken his first vow when his hand had been forced after meeting the now Lady Westcroft that fateful Midsummer's Eve, but that didn't mean he had to change his whole life's philosophy.

Chapter Nine

Alice looked round the room in satisfaction. There was a low hum of chatter and everyone was smiling and seeming to have a good time. The London Ladies' Benevolent Society had been established long before she had arrived in London, but she had found them a lacklustre group of four elderly women of the upper-middle class who had good intentions but not much idea as to how to implement them. In the last six months, since she had taken the helm of the society, it had gone from strength to strength. They now had regular monthly meetings, the location of which rotated between the homes of the more influential members, and held fundraising activities every couple of months too. Alice was well aware that initially many of the ladies had only agreed to be part of it so they could get the measure of her, the mysterious new countess that no one knew anything about, but she hoped that now they saw the benefits of a well-run society that could help them focus their philanthropic efforts.

She took a sip of tea and tried to focus on what Lady Kennington was saying as she rapped earnestly on the arm of the sofa with her fan.

'It just is not good enough. These poor orphans are dressed in rags, given gruel to eat and not even taught their letters or numbers, then society acts surprised when they go on to be the next generation of beggars and criminals. There needs to be better provision for them.'

'There is not endless money, though, Lady Kennington,' Mrs Taylor said. She was a wealthy widow who donated both her time and money generously. Alice was pleased at how she had chipped away at the hierarchical structure these last few months. She'd wanted all members to feel they had a voice, an opinion, whether they be duchess or doctor's wife.

'No, there is not. Yet I wonder whether the conditions the poor orphans find themselves in isn't at least a little deliberate. There is a large proportion of society who think people should stay within their own social status. We have all seen how the self-made man is snubbed at society events, even when he is the wealthiest in the room.'

'Do you have a solution, Lady Kennington?' Alice asked. A few months ago she would have worried that there was an unspoken agenda when there was talk of people staying within their own social class, but she had learned it was best to act oblivious to people's opinions. If they never saw you react, they soon got bored and started talking about someone else.

'St Benedict's Home for Orphaned Children,' Lady Kennington announced with a triumphant smile. 'A small orphanage near the slums of St Giles. I think they have beds for twelve girls and twelve boys. At the moment it is in the poorest part of the city, and the children are lucky to reach their fourteenth birthday, when they are thrown back out on the streets.'

'I think I know the one you mean,' Alice said, thinking of the dilapidated building that looked as though it would collapse with the slightest gust of wind.

'We cannot intervene everywhere, but I propose we invest some of our funds there. Make a difference for those twenty-four children and use them as a study to present to Parliament to show the benefits to all society if we look after the poorest amongst us.'

Alice felt a shiver run through her at the idea. More than anything she wanted to make a difference for children. It had been hard coming to terms over the last year with the fact that she would not have children of her own, at least not anytime soon. She had begun to build a relationship with her beautiful nieces, the three children her sister-in-law had gracefully helped her bond with, and she had also recently returned from a short trip to see her own sister and little nephew. She could surround herself with children to love even if she could have none of her own yet, but she also wanted to make a difference to some of the orphaned and destitute children of London. The unwavering support of someone as influential as Lady Kennington would mean projects like St Benedict's Orphanage were much more likely to become success stories.

She was surprised when the door opened and Lord Westcroft walked into the room. He in turn looked stunned by two dozen women crowded into his drawing room, and Alice saw him stiffen and then glance over his shoulder, but it was too late. He had been spotted.

'Lord Westcroft,' Lady Kennington called, beaming at

him. 'You have returned from your travels.' She turned to Alice and said admonishingly, 'You should have told us, my dear. This is exciting news.'

No one else noticed the fraction of a second's hesitation before Lord Westcroft smiled indulgingly and stepped into the room as if he had always planned to spare a few minutes of his time with the ladies. He moved between groups of people smoothly, greeting old acquaintances and bowing to new ones, and Alice watched in wonder as he left each group beaming with pleasure at the small snippet of attention he bestowed upon them. He went round the room before approaching Alice and her little group, greeting Lady Kennington and speaking warmly to Mrs Taylor.

'This is quite the gathering, Lady Westcroft,' he said, looking around.

'Hard to believe six months ago the London Ladies' Benevolent Society was four elderly women and a small pot of donations,' Lady Kennington said, patting Alice on the hand. 'Lady Westcroft has done a marvellous job at getting everyone so interested and invested in the society.'

Lord Westcroft smiled politely and then turned to Alice. 'I hate to take you away from your gathering, but there are one or two things we need to discuss quickly. Shall we step outside?'

Lady Kennington chuckled under her breath and leaned into Mrs Taylor. 'I remember that first blush of love. Only back a day and already he's finding excuses to pull his wife aside.'

Alice didn't respond but stood, smoothing her skirt, and followed Lord Westcroft from the room.

The London house was a good size for a townhouse, but it wasn't large compared to Lord Westcroft's other residences. Downstairs there was the drawing room, the dining room, another small, cosier reception room and Lord Westcroft's study. The study was the only room in the house she had never made herself at home in. It had felt too personal somehow, even though until yesterday she had been under the impression Lord Westcroft was never going to return.

He led her into the study now, closing the door quietly behind him.

'There are a lot of women in our drawing room,' he said.

'I think I mentioned the meeting of the London Ladies' Benevolent Society.'

'I expected something...different.' He leaned against the edge of the desk, his posture relaxed, and the expression on his face one of curiosity rather than annoyance. She had been well aware that he would be surprised by the invasion of his home by twenty-four benevolently minded women and hadn't known how he would take it. She was pleasantly surprised to find he wasn't angry or ordering everyone out, merely curious. 'You came to London less than a year ago for the first time ever?'

'Yes.'

'You knew no one?'

She shook her head.

'Yet here you are, with some of the wealthiest women in England taking tea in our drawing room.'

'You left, my Lord,' Alice said, holding up a hand to stall the interruption she knew was coming. 'I am not placing any blame. You told me exactly what would happen once we were married, but I do not think I had truly understood. I was alone, completely alone. Independent, wealthy, no longer obliged to do what my parents wanted of me. Yet I was lost.'

He shifted, and for a moment Alice thought he might reach out and take her hand. She chided herself at the surge of anticipation she felt at the idea, especially when he merely crossed one leg over the other and rested his hand back on the edge of the desk.

'I could either sit in one of your houses in Northumberland, waiting for you to die so my life could start again, or I could choose to build something for myself now. The first option was just too depressing so I chose the second.'

There was silence for a moment, and she glanced up at his face, relieved to see he was smiling, albeit sadly. 'I left you with quite the dilemma. Please do not misconstrue my intentions in speaking with you now. I am impressed, not annoyed. I think it is a miracle you have managed to get society to accept you so readily, let alone chair a benevolent charity.'

'You do not mind the twenty-four women sitting in your drawing room?'

He grimaced and then shrugged. 'It is not what I would have chosen for my first day back in London, but I acknowledge I did not give you any notice of my return so it would be unreasonable for you to keep the house quiet and not have social plans.' Lord Westcroft paused, looking at her intently before continuing. 'I am keen to discuss our situation and how we will manage things going forward, though.'

Alice felt a bubble of nerves deep inside. She wondered if he would expect her to remove herself to the countryside. So far since returning, he had been polite but distant. She was fast realising that she was still an afterthought in his life. Whatever his reasons for coming back to England, she was not one of them. Alice tried not to be hurt by the realisation she was once again close to the bottom of his list of priorities. She prided herself on being a rational woman and knew Lord Westcroft had given her so much when he married her to protect her reputation, so it felt ungrateful to want him to think more of her, yet it hurt when she felt like a problem to be solved.

She turned away, needing a moment to compose herself. When she turned back it was with steely determination. This might be Lord Westcroft's house, but she had worked hard this last year to find her footing in London, and she wasn't going to scurry back to Northumberland just because it made his life a little more convenient and allowed him to forget he had a wife. If he found it too uncomfortable to be here with her, then he could leave, but she was not going to quietly give up everything she had built for herself these last few months.

'I shall look at my calendar, my Lord,' she said, ensuring her tone was polite and courteous. 'Now, if you will excuse me, I must return to my guests.'

She didn't wait for his response, turning and leaving the study quickly and closing the door behind her. As she walked back through the hall she realised her hands were shaking, and she paused for a moment before re-entering the drawing room, fixing her face into a warm and happy expression that she didn't quite feel.

'Good Lord, Westcroft, you leave the country to die and come back looking healthier than the rest of us put together,' William Wetherby said as he clapped Simon on the back. Wetherby was an old friend, their friendship forged in the difficult days when they had both been sent away to school. Wetherby had been a scrawny lad from a once-wealthy family that had fallen on hard times. He'd had his place at Eton paid for by a generous aunt but had been mercilessly teased about his old clothes and lack of funds to spend in the local town.

Now Wetherby had grown into a giant of a man, broad across the chest with a thick dark beard and a muscular build. He was no longer poor either, having spent the last decade building up a thriving importing business.

Simon smiled, a little surprised at how pleased he felt to see his old friend. When he had left England he had thought it would be the last time he saw anyone he knew. At the time, he had told himself he'd made his peace with that, but now he realised that wasn't the case.

'It is good to see you, Wetherby,' Simon said, accepting the embrace his old friend pulled him into. Wetherby had always been effusive, and the years hadn't changed him in that respect.

There were a few other men gathered nearby who greeted him and shook his hand. London society was made up of a relatively small number of people, and even the men he did not know well he was acquainted with. After a minute Wetherby guided Simon to a corner table and motioned for a couple of drinks to be brought over.

In his youth Simon had not enjoyed the atmosphere in the exclusive gentlemen's club that his father and brother had attended and his membership was expected, but as he had grown older he had come to appreciate the quiet, luxurious atmosphere the club afforded. It was a place to escape many of the demands made on his time, and when he needed it to, it allowed him to spend an hour or so alone with his thoughts.

'I find myself fearful to enquire after your health,' Wetherby said as they sat facing each other.

Not many people knew of the terrible headaches Simon had suffered before he left England, nor the fear he had harboured that the headaches were a sign he would soon die, but he had taken Wetherby into his confidence when he sought his help with obtaining the special licence for his marriage almost a year earlier. Wetherby had worked tirelessly, calling in favours from various friends and acquaintances, to make sure Simon could marry before he left England.

'The headaches have all but gone. A doctor in Florence tells me it is not my time to leave this earth just yet.'

'That is a relief.' Wetherby eyed him cautiously. 'So you are back for good?'

For a long moment Simon didn't answer. It was a question he had put off thinking about throughout his trip home. When it became apparent his headaches were abating, he had been left unsure what to do. The doctor in Florence had been clear he wasn't giving Simon the reassurance that he wouldn't one day succumb to the same condition that had killed his father and brother, just the likelihood that it wouldn't be yet. For a few months after this news, Simon had stalled, trying to enjoy the solitude in his remote Tuscan villa, but all the while, home had been calling.

He had wanted to see his mother and sister-in-law, to receive the bear hugs he loved so much from his nieces and see how they had grown. He felt a deep unease at abandoning his responsibilities and the need to remove the burden he had placed on so many when he had left. More than all of that, to his surprise, was this burning desire to be home. Italy was beautiful and peaceful, but he felt the pull of the familiar.

Yet now he was back, he needed to decide what the future would look like. The likelihood that one day he would die suddenly and violently hadn't changed, it was merely the time frame that had been altered in his mind. He still didn't want anyone he loved to witness his death, and that would mean keeping his distance, yet his heart called for the opposite.

He shifted uncomfortably in his chair. Then there was the question of his wife. He pushed the thought aside. Lady Westcroft made an already complicated situation even more difficult to untangle.

'At least for a while. I will head to Northumberland soon. I wanted to reacclimatise myself to life in England before heading back home, but I should see the family soon.'

'I expect you wanted to see your wife too,' Wetherby said, his eyes flicking up to examine Simon's expression.

'In truth I did not realise she was in London.'

'She has been here for quite a time now. Lady Westcroft has made a significant impression on London society.'

Simon raised an eyebrow. It was clear what his friend said was true: his wife had a busy social calendar and chaired a benevolent society despite arriving in London a mere eight months earlier with no friends and no connections.

'You have met her?'

'Of course. I invited her to share my box at the opera just last week,' Wetherby said as he leaned forward. 'She is your countess, Westcroft, although I hasten to give her credit for the impression she has made. People gave her a chance because you married her, but she has grasped hold of that chance and charmed everyone at every opportunity.'

'It does seem as though she has been busy.' He thought back to the wide-eyed, uncertain girl he had met at the masquerade ball. No one could deny the change in his wife since then, and perhaps it was to be expected. He had left her to fend for herself, and she had thrived. He was pleased for her—the last thing he wanted was for her to be unhappy—but he felt a little uncomfortable too, although if he was asked to articulate why, he would have found it difficult.

'You will take her back to Northumberland with you?'

'I will ask, but I get the impression Lady Westcroft has a full social calendar these next few weeks.'

Wetherby laughed. 'I expect she does. Her company is very much in demand.'

Simon felt a flicker of guilt. There was a lot to feel guilty about with respect to his wife. He'd married her and then abandoned her, and even though he had been completely honest with her before their marriage, he had known that she wouldn't have quite understood the realities of the change in her circumstance. Now he had this horrible feeling that he had trapped her. The deal he had promised her was a short marriage to save her reputation, followed by the freedom of widowhood. She would be wealthy enough to make her own decisions and, after a short period of mourning, could either cultivate a life as a wealthy widow or start to look for a second husband, someone she could share a full and proper marriage with.

He swallowed hard, covering the movement by raising his glass to his lips. He had the sense that he had stolen her life away from her and as yet she wasn't quite aware of it. If he lived for another forty years she would be trapped in this union, never experiencing a love match, never getting to have children of her own. It was not what he had promised her.

He took another gulp of his drink before setting the glass down on the table. Somehow they would find a way through this mess, but he had an overwhelming feeling that he had deceived Lady Westcroft. Never had he pressed her to marry him, only laid it out as an option, but he wasn't sure she would have accepted if she had known it would mean being tied to him for an indeterminate amount of time, unable to move on with a life of her own.

'How are you, Wetherby?' Simon asked, wanting to change the subject, needing the distraction of talking about something else for a while.

'I am well, thank you. I leave in a few weeks for a trip to Africa. I hear the earth is littered with diamonds in places, and I want to see for myself whether this is true.'

Simon grinned. His friend had always had difficulty staying in one place for too long, and every few years would announce a new voyage. Wetherby had shaken off the bad luck that had made him an easy victim during their schooldays and seemed to find success in each of his ventures. Even if the ground wasn't littered with diamonds, no doubt there would be some opportunity his friend would spot and bend to his advantage.

'I must leave you,' Wetherby said, standing and clapping him on the shoulder. 'We should talk properly, perhaps when you are back from Northumberland, but today I have a prior engagement with an architect.' He leaned in closer. 'The chap is a genius, and I'm trying to persuade him to take time away from his other projects to build me a nice little house in the Sussex countryside.'

'I wish you luck,' Simon said, rising and shaking Wetherby's hand.

He was left alone with his thoughts, wondering how to make things right with Lady Westcroft, but aware that short of dying there was no way of delivering the life he had promised her.

Chapter Ten

Simon had risen early, keen to busy himself with some of the many things he had neglected in the time he had been away. He had spent much of the morning going over correspondence that had been kept for him whilst he was in Italy and then around lunchtime had met with his solicitor to discuss some minor legal issues that needed his input. Although he had not consciously sought to avoid Lady Westcroft, he was aware that he had organised his morning so their paths were unlikely to cross.

Now that he was walking home he had a sinking feeling in his stomach. It wasn't that he disliked his wife—far from it. Despite hardly knowing her he felt certain she was good and kind, a sweet young woman who had thrived in difficult circumstances. In a way, that made what he was doing to her even worse. His return had once again thrown her life into turmoil.

Simon slowed as he approached the Serpentine. He had decided to take the longer route through the park back to his townhouse, enjoying the warmth of the early-summer afternoon and also feeling a need to delay his return when he might have to sit and have a serious discussion with his wife about their futures.

As he paused to look at the water, a group of about a dozen ladies seated on the grass a little way from its edge caught his eye. They were finely dressed and as he looked closer he realised he recognised one or two, his eyes sweeping over the group until they settled on the pretty, petite form of his wife. She was dressed in dark blue, a colour that served to accentuate the red in her hair and the beautiful porcelain paleness of her skin. She looked relaxed, leaning back on her hands as she turned her head to talk to the woman next to her.

None of the ladies had spotted him, and so for a moment he just watched Lady Westcroft. She was mesmerising. It was undeniable she was pretty, but that quality became enchanting when she smiled. The smile was natural and easy on her lips, and Simon felt himself drawn to her as he had been on the night of the masquerade ball. He wanted to stride over and pull her into his arms, tracing the softness of her face with his fingers, making it so her smile was directed at only him.

It was an unsettling feeling, and quickly he tried to dampen it. The last thing he needed now was to feel attraction towards his wife. He needed a clear head in the negotiations that were to come about their future, and feeling desire for the woman whose life he was ruining would not help.

As he watched, two young children ran up to the group, talking excitedly to the woman who sat beside Lady Westcroft. The boy had a model boat in his hand and was gesticulating at the Serpentine. Their mother laughed indulgently, but it was Lady Westcroft who stood and took the boy's hand, allowing him to lead her down to the water. She crouched down in between the little boy and girl, listening intently to what they said and then helped them set the boat on the water. On the first attempt it wobbled and nearly capsized, and he found himself smiling as Lady Westcroft threw her head back and laughed alongside the children. The second attempt was more successful, and they stayed watching the boat as it bobbed along in the water.

Simon felt a pang of sadness, both for himself and his wife. He could see by this simple interaction how good Lady Westcroft was with children. Despite not spending the time to get to know her hopes and dreams for the future, he could remember her talking of the idea of children fondly and this being the main concern when weighing up whether she should accept his proposal for the marriage to save her reputation.

At the time, the offer he had made called for her to postpone her desire for a family, but now, with the question of his mortality very much unclear, it might be that Lady Westcroft would never have children of her own.

Simon was about to turn away when his wife glanced up, looking directly at him. For a moment she did not move and then she stood, inclining her head in an invitation for him to join her.

With a sinking heart he walked over slowly. In all this mess he could not deny his own disappointment, even though he felt guilty for even considering trying to live a normal life. Once, long before he had lost his brother, he had assumed he would marry and have a family of his own. Now he knew that would never happen, and even though he'd had years to get used to the idea, sometimes he yearned for a normal life. Then he felt guilty for being so selfish when he was lucky to be alive while his brother was not.

'Lord Westcroft, I did not expect to see you here in the park,' Lady Westcroft said. She spoke warmly although addressed him formally. He was once again impressed at how much she had learned these last few months in London. Not only had she gained the support of the most influential in society, she had quickly refined her country manners that might make her stand out as different.

'I had an appointment with my solicitor and thought I would take the scenic route home. It is a beautiful afternoon.'

'It is indeed. We were meant to meet at Mrs Lattimer's for tea, but no one could resist when she suggested an outing to the park instead.' Lady Westcroft motioned behind her to the woman she had been sitting next to.

Simon looked round, nodding in greeting to the ladies he was acquainted with. They were watching him with open curiosity, no doubt keen to see how he interacted with the wife he had left behind after a single day of marriage.

'I do not want to disturb you.'

She looked up at him with a half-smile on her face. When he had left ten months earlier, she had seemed young and innocent; now there was an air of experience in her poised demeanour, and Simon knew he was responsible for forcing her to grow up.

'It is good to see you, my Lord. I have hardly set eyes on you since you returned to England.'

Simon attempted to smile but struggled to produce more than a twitch of his lips, surprised again at how forgiving his wife seemed. He'd abandoned her in a world she did not know, and now he was threatening to rock the life she had made for herself again.

'Shall we take a little stroll? I am sure Sebastian and Lilith will not mind.' With natural ease Lady Westcroft crouched down and swept the model boat from the water, handing it back to Sebastian. 'We do not want it to sail out into the middle of the lake. I do not relish the idea of wading out to fetch it.'

Sebastian giggled and then wrapped his chubby arms around her neck. Simon watched as his wife's face flushed with joy. Lady Westcroft waited until the two children were safely back in the care of their nanny before she turned her attention back to Simon.

'They are sweet children,' she said with a smile as she followed his gaze before lowering her voice. 'Sometimes I find myself envious of their nanny. I am sure behind closed doors they are sometimes a terror, but you would not believe it when you see them in public.'

'Have you had a pleasant day?'

'Yes, thank you. I spent some time going through the household accounts with Miss Stick this morning. A mere formality, as she is the most organised of house-keepers I have ever met, but I like to learn how to do these things, and she is a good teacher. Then this after-noon has been spent in the sunshine with friends.'

'It does sound a nice way to spend an afternoon,' Simon murmured.

She looked at him curiously. 'I do have a good life, my Lord. I am aware how lucky I am.'

So much hung unsaid between them, and Simon knew they would have to address it soon, but he didn't want to do that here with everyone watching them. What he had to say would be better received in private where Lady Westcroft would have the freedom to react without having to think of who was watching.

They walked a little farther along the path, arm-in-arm. Half her face was in shadow from the bonnet that was tied firmly under her chin, and it made it difficult to work out what she might be thinking.

Simon wished for a moment that this was their life, an easy happiness where all they had to worry about was which social invitations to accept and which to refuse. Quickly he pushed the thought away. The idea of a conventional marriage to Lady Westcroft was tempting as he walked beside her. She was kind and sensible and pleasant to be around. He couldn't deny the flicker of desire he felt every time she looked at him with those blue eyes or the way something clenched deep inside him when she smiled. Yet it was a temptation he could never give in to. It would be unfair, with his future so uncertain. It would be better to offer her a deal where they both led separate but contented lives, only occasionally meeting.

As if sensing his thoughts, she turned to face him again, her eyes rising to meet his. 'You seem troubled, my Lord.'

He cleared his throat but couldn't find the words.

'Is something amiss?'

'I watched you for a moment with those children. You were very good with them.'

'I like children.'

'I know.'

She held his gaze, something defiant in her eyes as if pushing him to confront the big issue that stood between them.

'Would you like children, Lady Westcroft?' The question came out much more directly than he meant it to, but with her standing so close he felt as if his thoughts were all scrambled.

It took her a moment to reply, and when she did her tone was much more formal. 'I understand the limits of our marriage, Lord Westcroft, and I am not a naïve girl any more. I understand a marriage has to be consummated for there to be children.' Her cheeks flushed as she spoke, and he felt like a cad.

'Forgive me, I did not meant to cause you pain. I…' He was unsure how to put into words the turmoil he felt inside. It was impossible to know how to tell Lady Westcroft that because of his mistake in making the assumption that he was dying, he had stolen from her the future he had promised.

She turned away, but before she did, he saw the tears glistening in her eyes.

'I must return to my friends, my Lord,' she said, already beginning to move away. 'Perhaps I shall see you at home later this evening.'

He inclined his head, watching her as she walked back to the group of ladies a little distance away. As he turned to leave he felt a wave of guilt almost consume him. He needed space and time, some way to come up with a plan where no one suffered too much. Here in London, he felt as though everything was pressing in, threatening to crush him.

It was growing dark outside when Alice sat down to see to her mound of correspondence. She had a letter from each of her nieces to reply to, each of different lengths dependent on their ages, and one from Maria as well. She wondered if her sister-in-law knew of Lord Westcroft's return and realised she shouldn't be the one to tell her. No doubt her husband would contact his family soon, if he hadn't already. Gossip travelled at an unbelievable pace, and he had been seen by half the wealthy women in London that afternoon when he had stumbled upon Alice and her friends in Hyde Park. It might be hundreds of miles to the Westcroft estate in Northumberland, but the news of his return would be up there before the month was out.

She enjoyed the ritual of letter-writing and took her time selecting her pen and positioning the paper, ensuring she had good candlelight so as not to strain her eyes.

As she was about to put pen to paper she paused, hearing footsteps in the hallway outside and then a knock on the door. She turned to see Miss Stick entering, holding something in her hand.

'Lord Westcroft asked me to give this to you, my Lady,' Miss Stick said. The older woman was always polite and formal, but Alice had gone to great efforts to get to know the housekeeper in recent months. She could see something was wrong and took the letter in trepidation.

She was puzzled to see her husband's seal on the back and glanced up at Miss Stick briefly.

'I am sorry, my Lady. He left about an hour ago.'

With a sinking feeling she opened the note and let her eyes skim over the words. It was brief, only a couple of sentences, explaining he needed to go and see his family, to tell them he was back before the gossip reached them. There was no indication of when he might come back to London, just an apology for leaving so soon.

For a second she slumped, feeling rejected once again, then forced herself to rally.

'Lord Westcroft has gone,' she said to Miss Stick. 'There is no word as to when he will return. I expect he will stay in Northumberland for some time.'

Miss Stick's expression softened slightly, and then she nodded and held Alice's eye. 'There will be no change to your plans then, my Lady? Everything will continue as normal?'

'Everything will continue as normal,' Alice confirmed.

Once she was alone Alice allowed her control to slip and slumped in her chair. He hadn't even bothered to say goodbye. She could justify his behaviour all she liked, but that was hard to bear. She understood he would have been keen to return to his family, to be the one to tell them he was back in the country so they weren't surprised by the information from someone else, yet it would only have taken a few minutes to bid her farewell.

She thought back to their conversation that afternoon and knew it had likely played a part in why he was so quick to rush away. They were two strangers thrown together by a foolish kiss almost a year earlier. Now he had returned, it would be difficult to unpick the tangled strands of their lives and find a way to live comfortably with one another, whether that meant together or apart. She could see he was struggling with that, but it didn't mean his leaving so abruptly was painless.

Alice looked at the note again. It was short, only a couple of sentences, informing her he was leaving immediately to travel north and see his family.

'There's nothing wrong with that,' she murmured, trying to convince herself. She took a deep breath and pressed her hands down on the little writing desk, refusing to let this latest development throw her off course.

Loudly she exhaled and stood, pacing back and forth across the room. She had known before they married that she would not have a conventional union. But he had told her that her life would be one way, and now it had completely changed. Of course she was pleased he was not going to die alone, far away from family, but she would like a little acknowledgement that his return affected her as well as him.

With an effort she paused by the window, setting her shoulders and lifting her chin. This was a good lesson to learn. Her husband might be back, but he was not ever going to see her as anything more than the woman he married to save her from ruin. She could not expect affection from or companionship with him, instead she would have to continue as she had been, building a life she was content in, even if she were alone.

Chapter Eleven

The house was quiet as he approached on horseback, each window in darkness despite it being only a little past nine o'clock. This time he had made sure he sent word of his return to London from Northumberland, allowing both his wife and the servants to prepare for his arrival. He wondered if Lady Westcroft had moved from the master bedroom or if she would expect him to sleep elsewhere now she had claimed it as her own this past year. In truth he did not really mind; he'd woken up in many different bedrooms over his lifetime, and another change would not unsettle him. What it did do was highlight one of the many issues they would have to sort out now he had returned to London.

The door opened quickly, and Frank Smith, the young footman, hurried out to hold the reins of his horse to lead it to the back of the house where there was a small stable. Both Simon's father and brother had been keen horsemen, as was he, and his father had added a stable large enough for three horses on the patch of land behind the house. It meant the garden was smaller than it could be, but the horses did not have to be stabled elsewhere whilst he was in residence.

Inside the house was quiet, but Miss Stick came to greet him in the hall and take his hat and gloves.

'Where is Lady Westcroft?' He had spent the journey mentally cataloguing all the issues they needed to discuss now he was back in England, from where they would both live to how they should handle enquiries into their personal lives.

'At the Livingstone ball tonight, my Lord. I doubt she will be back until the early hours of the morning. She tells me it is one of the biggest events of the year, even if half of London has left for their country residences already.'

He frowned. He hadn't considered the possibility his wife would not be at home. He had to admit he had not thought of Lady Westcroft much this past year, but when he had, he'd never thought she would be out enjoying the balls and dinner parties of a London season. Of course he did not begrudge her a little fun, but he was keen to discuss their plans for the future, and after spending the best part of a week on the road to get back to London, he did not want to delay any longer. He'd been a mess when he had left London so abruptly a few weeks earlier, and he regretted fleeing without properly taking his leave of his wife. He wanted to apologise and to begin to discuss the future that they inevitably shared.

'The Livingstone ball?'

'Yes, my Lord. They live just off Grosvenor Square, I believe.'

He checked the time and then nodded decisively. He would go to the ball. Although he had not responded to any invitation, he would not be turned away, and if Lady

Westcroft was there already there would be some expectation that he be in attendance too.

'I need to freshen up and change, then I will go to the ball at the Livingstones' house.'

'Very good, my Lord. We do not have anyone employed as your valet at the moment, but I will send young Smith up with everything you need just as soon as he hands over your horse to the stable-boy.

'Thank you.'

'You're in the green bedroom,' Miss Stick said, watching him carefully. Many men would refuse to let their wives have the master bedroom, but Simon merely nodded his head and made his way up the stairs.

Ninety minutes later he was standing on the threshold of Mr and Mrs Livingstone's house, wondering if he had made a terrible mistake. Mr Livingstone was obscenely wealthy, having made his money in importing luxury fabrics. It was said even Queen Charlotte waited excitedly for Mr Livingstone's shipments to arrive at the docks and would get first refusal on anything new and exotic. The house was illuminated by hundreds of candles, and even from the doorstep he could hear the loud hum of conversation over the music. If he stepped into the ballroom he would be seen by half the *ton* within seconds, and news of his second return to London would spread quickly.

After a moment he pushed aside the doubts, telling himself he had to return to society at some point. Over the next few months he would need to step up and ensure everything for his tenants was running smoothly and see if there was any work that needed doing to his properties, but he would also have to take up his role as earl again in more public ways. In October he would be expected to return to Parliament, and there were always obligations throughout the social season.

The door opened, and he was welcomed into the house. Thankfully the ball was well underway with a dozen couples dancing in the middle of the ballroom whilst everyone else watched from the sides, talking in little huddles.

'Lord Westcroft, we were not expecting you,' Mrs Livingstone said, hurrying over as soon as she spotted him. 'How delightful to have you back in society after your year of travels.'

'It is wonderful to see you again, Mrs Livingstone.' He craned his neck a little, trying to see if he could spot his wife amongst the guests that lined the ballroom.

'You are looking for Lady Westcroft, no doubt,' Mrs Livingstone said with an indulgent smile. 'She is—'

'On the dance floor,' he murmured before she could finish.

For a moment it felt as though time slowed as his eyes followed Lady Westcroft around the ballroom. She stepped gracefully, with none of the hesitation he had felt from her when they had first danced together at the Midsummer's Eve ball. She looked beautiful in a dress of dark green, the material shimmering as she moved, and the skirt swished around her ankles. It complemented her pale skin and red hair to perfection, and Simon could not take his eyes off her.

She smiled then, and he felt a stab of disappointment that it wasn't at him, watching as she dropped her head back and laughed at something her dance partner had said.

He bowed absently to Mrs Livingstone and made his

way through the crowd of people, murmuring greetings as he went. He could not tear his eyes away from his wife, and as the music swelled and then quietened, he was standing at the front of the small crowd at the edge of the dance floor.

At first she did not notice him standing there, but as she turned to face him and her eyes met his, he saw a shadow cross her face. It was momentary, and if he hadn't been watching her so intently he would have missed it, but he felt a sadness that he could be the one to ruin her evening when she otherwise looked as though she were having a wonderful time.

'You're back, my Lord,' she said, excusing herself from her companion.

'I'm back.'

It wouldn't be a complete shock this time. He had ensured he had written before leaving Northumberland and sent the message by fast rider so she would not be taken by surprise at his arrival, but the good conditions on the roads meant he had made fast progress and was in London a couple of days before he was expected.

'Are you well?'

'Yes, thank you. And you?'

She inclined her head, and for the first time he felt regret at how formal their interaction was. It was entirely his fault, he knew that. He'd married a complete stranger and then disappeared for a year. Of course their conversation was going to be stilted and awkward: they barely knew one another.

'How are Maria and the girls? And your mother?' she asked, warmth flaring in her eyes.

'They are well. The girls have grown and changed a

lot in a year, but they are happy and healthy and have progressed well with their schooling.'

'Are they still terrorising that poor governess?'

'Miss Pickles? Yes, she threatened to leave, and Maria had me intervene to ask her to stay. She doesn't think she'll last more than another month.'

Lady Westcroft smiled indulgently, and he marvelled at how she had managed to build a relationship with his family despite not knowing them at all when he had married her. His sister-in-law spoke of his wife so warmly you would have thought they had been best friends their entire lives, and his mother had chided him for not making Lady Westcroft's life easier this past year. It had forced him to acknowledge the guilt he felt at leaving her so soon after their marriage and not even thinking to write to her throughout the year.

'The girls are well-behaved when they are on their own, but when they are all together, they lose the ability to control that naughty streak,' Lady Westcroft said, her voice filled with love. 'Maria spoke of separating them for their lessons if the governess could not cope with all three of them at once. It will be a shame, but perhaps it is the best solution.'

'They put a frog on the poor woman's dinner plate, slipped it in amongst her vegetables when she wasn't looking. Apparently it hopped onto her fork and looked at her.'

'Was that the event that pushed her towards threatening to leave?'

'One of many, I think,' Simon said. He felt himself begin to relax and was reminded again of how reasonable Lady Westcroft was. It boded well for their marriage of convenience, and he hoped they would be able to come to some arrangement about how to live that would suit both of them.

The music started again, the musicians returned from their short break, refreshments in hand, and Simon recognised a waltz, the music they had danced to on the terrace of the Midsummer's Eve ball almost a year ago.

Without thinking he held out his hand. 'Would you care to dance?'

For a second he saw a flicker of hesitation in her eyes, and then she nodded.

'It would be my pleasure.'

Simon felt the eyes of the room on them as they took their place on the dance floor.

'Why does it feel like everyone is watching us?' Lady Westcroft said, leaning in close to whisper in his ear.

'They are. We haven't been seen in public together before, and no one can work out the truth of our marriage. I am sure they are fascinated by it and want to see if they can pick up any clues as to whether we despise each other or can't keep our hands from one another.'

She smiled then, with a hint of sadness. 'Whereas the truth is much more mundane.'

He placed a hand in the small of her back and adjusted his stance so he was holding her close. It would be a positioning that would be frowned upon at any other time, but they were still considered newly-weds, and there was a certain indulgence for reckless behaviour. As the waltz began he remembered the magic of their first dance together and how she had laughed as she missed a step. He got a sense she was on edge now, but not because she thought she would forget the steps. It was incredible how much she had learned in a year, not least how to fit in at these society events.

'You're grinning,' she whispered.

'I'm remembering our first waltz.'

This made her smile too. 'It was a magical evening.'

'An evening that changed our lives.'

As he twirled her she looked up at him, her face now serious. 'I do appreciate what you did for me. Often I think of what my life would be like married to Cecil.'

'Vile Cousin Cecil,' he said, shaking his head. 'Do you know I had almost forgotten about him.'

'He was outraged when he heard I was going to marry you. He came to my parents' house, stood outside and called me all number of horrible names.'

'I did not realise.'

'My mother counselled me not to tell you. She did not want anything to cause any discord. I think until we were actually standing in front of the vicar she was worried you might change your mind, and she would have two disgraced daughters.' She paused and gave a little shrug of her shoulders even whilst they were dancing. 'I hear from my mother that Cecil is still searching for a wife.'

'I pity the young woman who accepts him.'

'So do I.'

They danced in silence for a minute, and Simon wondered if his wife had taken dance lessons in the time he had been away. She stepped with such confidence now, with the ease of someone who was certain they would not forget the steps. He did not want to insult her by implying she had once not been so graceful and intuitive in her movements, but he was intrigued.

'Please do not take this the wrong way, Lady Westcroft, but you dance beautifully now…' He trailed off as she laughed.

'You mean compared to when we last twirled around a ballroom?'

'I very much enjoyed our dances at the masquerade ball.'

She looked up at him, her expression suddenly serious. 'Your sister-in-law was ever so kind to me after you left. I was like a ship adrift, unsure of what was expected of me or even how to act. She took me in, cocooned me in love, gave me a safe space to grow and discover myself and then urged me to fly once I was ready.'

'Maria is a good woman.'

'The very best,' Lady Westcroft said, strong emotion in her voice. 'When I said I would like to come to London, to look at doing some charitable work and step into society, she ensured I would not make a fool of myself. She taught me how to address people and how to walk into a room with confidence, and we spent many hours twirling round the drawing room, practising dancing, trying not to trip over one of the girls.'

Simon felt a stab of guilt. He should have been the one who guided his new wife through her début in London society; instead, he hadn't even considered it might be somewhere she would want to be.

'I can just imagine it,' he said and to his relief found she was smiling.

'It has been quite the strangest year of my life,' she said quietly, 'but I have learned so much and met so many interesting people.'

'I am glad. Tell me, Lady Westcroft, how did you manage to get these people to accept you?'

'With my rough edges and crude country manners?'

He quickly started to deny that was what he meant and then saw the sparkle of amusement in her eyes.

'You are different to what the ladies of the *ton* are used to.'

'You are not wrong. Did you know when I came to London I got a summons from the palace? The Queen Charlotte herself wanted to cast her eye over me and see what sort of woman you had chosen to be your countess.'

'That cannot have been easy.'

'I almost turned tail and ran all the way back to Northumberland to hide in my childhood bedroom.'

'Yet you stayed. You faced the queen and claimed your place in society.'

'I think her approval helped me greatly. Once she had declared me a darling of the *ton*, everyone wanted to get to know the surprise countess.' She gave a little shake of her head as if remembering the day she had been called to the palace. 'That is not to say that I was confident when I was led down the long corridors to meet the queen. My knees actually knocked together whilst I waited outside to be summoned into her presence.'

'She is a formidable lady,' Simon murmured. 'I am impressed, Lady Westcroft.'

His wife pulled a face and leaned in closer, allowing him to catch a hint of an alluring scent, a mixture of lavender and something else he couldn't quite put his finger on.

'I know there is a great expectation that we address one another formally, but at least in private might you call me Alice? There are three Lady Westcrofts in your family at present, and it gets a little tedious for ever trying to work out who everyone is referring to.'

'Alice,' he said, pleased to be rid of the formality. 'And you should call me Simon.'

'Thank you.'

The music swelled and died away, and they came to a stop in the middle of the dance floor. He bowed and she curtsied, and for a long moment he stared into her eyes. There was something mesmerising about the blue of her eyes, and the spell was only broken when she looked away. He had been going to suggest they take a little refreshment together, perhaps step out of the ballroom into one of the quieter areas so they could spend a little bit of the evening talking, but Alice touched his arm fleetingly and then excused herself, murmuring something about a full dance-card. She disappeared into the press of people around the perimeter of the ballroom before he could protest, leaving him standing alone.

Alice was pleased with the fast pace of the next three dances. It meant she was out of breath towards the end, but also none of her partners expected more than minor snippets of conversation in between the bursts of vigorous footwork. Her partners were all pleasant gentlemen who she had danced with before, mainly husbands of the women she knew socially or through the London Ladies' Benevolent Society.

Out of the corner of her eye she could see her husband prowling around the room. It had been quite a surprise, his turning up this evening. She had expected him back in London in the next few days but had thought they would meet behind closed doors at the townhouse, not at the Livingstones' ball in front of everyone.

After they had shared a waltz, Alice had been eager to get away, hoping that if she kept herself busy and unavailable, her husband might decide to go home or, at the very least, retire to the card tables. Instead he'd watched her constantly, brushing away the attempts by other guests at engaging him in conversation. It was unnerving, and she was sure people were beginning to notice.

She wondered if she could slip away. A carriage waited somewhere outside to take her home once the evening had concluded, but the way Simon was watching her, he would follow her out and suggest they share the carriage home. He was eager to talk, to discuss their future, she could tell by the nervous energy about him, but she needed a little time to compose herself first.

He caught her eye for a second, and she felt a spark travel through her before she quickly looked away. *This* was the problem. Simon had returned to London eager to work out how they would live their lives married but very much separate. It was what she wanted too, to continue to build the success of her charitable work, to find her place in society and enjoy her life in a way she had never been allowed to before this past year. Yet when he stepped close to her, when he looked at her with those brilliant blue eyes, all she could think of was kissing him. It was as if she were swept back to the Midsummer's Eve ball all over again and they were recklessly running through the garden hand in hand. Whenever he came close she felt her heart hammer in her chest, and she got an overwhelming urge to kiss him.

It was highly inconvenient for many reasons, not least because he clearly didn't think of her as anything more than a relative he was responsible for, someone a little troublesome who had been foisted upon him.

She broke eye contact, quickly looking away and trying to work out if there was a way to escape without him seeing her. She hesitated for just a moment too long, and as she stepped away from the dance floor her husband was at her side.

'I do not think there is any more dancing for a while,' he said.

'That is a shame,' she murmured and caught his raised eyebrow. She had to remind herself her husband was an intelligent man and probably had worked out she was trying to avoid him.

'Perhaps we can find somewhere quieter to talk, even if just for a few minutes.'

Alice sighed and then nodded. 'I am fatigued. Unless you wish to stay, shall we share a carriage home?'

He looked relieved, and Alice realised with surprise that he wasn't used to society events. Although he hadn't written to her over the last year, he had sent a couple of short notes to Maria and his mother, and they had shared a little of what his life had been like. From what she could gather he had lived quietly, opting for a villa in a rural location with his closest neighbours some miles away. He had not looked to socialise in his new community, and although his journey back to England would have involved travelling by ship with others, he would not have encountered a situation like this for a long time. Even if he had been attending balls and social gatherings since early adulthood, it would still be quite an adjustment for him to make from his recent experiences.

She felt a little guilty for avoiding him for so long. There were many things he could have done better in their relationship, but wanting to discuss the practicalities of their arrangement now wasn't one of them.

'Should we say goodnight to Mr and Mrs Livingstone?' Alice said as he led her rapidly towards the door.

Simon leaned in, and Alice felt herself shiver as his breath tickled her ear. 'They will not mind if we slip away. They will tell themselves it is only to be expected when two newly-weds are reunited after time apart.'

He placed a hand on the small of her back to guide her, and Alice had to suppress a little groan of frustration. He seemed entirely unaffected by her: it was as if to him the kiss on Midsummer's Eve had never happened.

It took a few minutes to find their carriage amongst the dozens standing outside. Theirs was tucked down a side street, and the driver was sitting on top enjoying the evening air as they approached.

Alice remained silent once they had climbed inside, and Simon instructed the driver to take them home.

It was dark in the carriage as they sat across from one another. Alice could only see the contours of her husband's face and the glint of his eyes in the moonlight, but nothing to help her anticipate how the conversation would begin.

'You looked happy tonight,' Simon said after a minute. 'It was lovely to see.'

His words were not what she expected, and it took her a moment to compose herself enough to answer. 'I am happy,' she said eventually.

'Are you? I worried quite a lot before we married that you were choosing an option that would not give you the life you wanted. You were stuck between a marriage to Cecil and a life that was not the future you had once imagined.'

She was touched that he had considered her feelings in such depth when he'd had so much else to occupy his mind. She chose her words carefully now, not wanting to give him the wrong impression.

'This isn't the life I imagined or the life I hoped for when I was a young girl, yet these last few months I have been content. I cannot lie to you and say I do not sometimes wish for children, for a husband who loves me and a house filled with family, but I am slowly learning there are other ways to seek contentment in life.'

'You are refreshing, Alice,' Simon said, his voice low and serious, a note of wonder about it. 'You always speak your mind even if it makes you vulnerable.'

'I do not think there is any point in lying about one's feelings. If I told you I was blissfully happy and never thought of a different life, then it might influence what we decide on for our future. It is important you know how I really feel. This past year I have not had anyone to hide behind. I've had to assert my own views, to make decisions and bear the consequences.'

'I am sorry you have been so alone.'

'It has not been entirely a bad thing,' she said quietly. 'I have learned a lot about myself and how much more capable I am than I ever realised.'

'I suppose you never had the chance to step out into the world alone before. Young gentlemen often have that taste of independence when they leave home to attend university or go to seek their fortune through work or the military. Yet young women stay under their father's control until they marry.'

'I will always be grateful for the past year. It has shown me I can achieve so much more than I ever thought.'

They fell silent for a moment, and Alice glanced out of the window to see they were already slowing to a stop in front of the townhouse. Their conversation hadn't delved very deep, and she knew soon they would have to sit down across a table from one another and decide what their lives would look like.

Simon helped her from the carriage, and they walked arm-in-arm up the steps to the front door. She felt torn, simultaneously wanting to rip herself away from Simon so he wouldn't have a chance to hurt her and strike up a conversation so he would have to linger.

In the end she bid him goodnight in the hallway and hurried upstairs, feeling her heart pound in her chest as Simon called after her.

'Tomorrow we should talk properly,' Simon said, his voice quiet but clear. She nodded, hoping she would sleep well before the negotiation for her future began.

Chapter Twelve

'Your note was a little cryptic,' Alice said as she strolled into the park, parasol in hand to shield her from the warmth of the sun.

He had been up early, unable to settle. Throughout the night he had been plagued by indecision and by thoughts of his wife that were not helpful in assisting him to come to a sensible conclusion about how he wanted their future to look. He'd risen early and, when there had been no sign of Alice at an early breakfast, had decided to leave her a note to meet him in Hyde Park, dressed in her riding habit.

When he had first arrived in the park it had been quiet, with only a few other early-risers out for a brisk morning walk or for a ride. On his trip back to Northumberland he had picked up his beautiful horse, Socrates, and this morning had enjoyed a long ride without the pressures of travelling on the dusty roads. Before Alice's arrival he had also hired a horse for her to ride. There was something about having the breeze on your face and the thought of freedom to gallop off towards the horizon that helped to clear the mind. It would also ensure their conversation didn't become too heated or intense. Alice was an immensely pragmatic woman—he had seen that in how she had reacted to impossible situations this past year—but they were talking about her entire future.

He saw her eye with uncertainty the horses he was holding by the reins.

'You wish for us to ride?'

'I find I do my best thinking on horseback.' He paused as she regarded the horses with trepidation, realising he did not even know if his wife could ride. 'You have ridden before?'

She nodded slowly. 'Twice. Both unmitigated disasters.' For a long moment she would not meet his eye, and then she sighed. 'But I suppose I could try again.'

'What went wrong before?'

'Do you remember my friend Lydia?'

'The young lady you sneaked into the Midsummer's Eve ball with?'

'Yes. When we were younger she persuaded me to ride her father's horse with her. We thought it would be easy, but as soon as we were seated the horse got spooked and reared up, and Lydia tumbled to the ground. The horse took off along the high street, and I could do nothing but close my eyes, cling onto its neck and hope I did not die.'

'How old were you?'

'Eight or nine. The horse ran for three miles before it calmed.'

'You managed to stay on its back?'

'Somehow I did.'

'That is impressive.'

'I thought I would die if I fell. We got into so much

trouble I wasn't allowed to see Lydia for a month, and my father took a cane to my hands, whipping them so badly they bled.' She turned over her hands and looked down at them. Simon had the urge to reach out and run his fingers over the skin of her palms but stopped himself just in time.

'What about the second time?'

'That was a little less dramatic, and less illicit. My sister had a suitor in the days before—' She glanced up at him quickly.

Alice had told him of her sister's near disgrace, the weeks of turmoil as the whole family thought there was no way to save Margaret's reputation. Then a surprise proposal had materialised, followed by a quick marriage.

'Before her marriage,' he finished diplomatically.

'Yes. They would go walking over the fields, and I used to have to accompany them to chaperon. One day he brought his horse and suggested I ride. I was nervous, but Margaret was keen as it would give her a little more privacy with this man she thought she might want to marry. I agreed reluctantly, and after I got over my nerves it was quite a pleasant experience, riding through the fields in the sunshine.'

'Did something happen?'

'There was a man out with his dog. The dog got excited and spooked the horse. The horse ran, and at first I managed to hang on, but the path took us under a low hanging branch, and I did not duck in time.'

'That must have hurt.'

'I was lucky I was not seriously injured.'

'I did not know,' Simon murmured quietly, frowning. There was so much he did not know about his wife.

All these little stories from her childhood, her likes and dislikes. It wasn't surprising as he had spent no time with her, but despite his plan to keep a good amount of distance between them, he felt a flicker of sadness. His brother, Robert, had shared everything with Maria, and over the course of their marriage they had learned all those little stories, all the childhood anecdotes that build to mould a person into their adult form. 'We can walk if you prefer.'

Alice inhaled deeply and then shook her head. 'No, I wish to be able to ride. A sedate half an hour around Hyde Park will be a good way to get me over my fear.'

'Only if you are sure.'

She nodded and approached the smaller of the two horses, a docile mare that regarded her with hooded eyes. She took her time, stroking the horse's nose and then neck, talking softly to the animal. Alice might not have ridden for a long time, but she knew how to approach an animal to ensure the encounter was a calm one.

After a few minutes she looked around. 'I am not sure I am strong enough to pull myself onto her back.'

'I will help you.' He looped Socrates's reins over a fence-post and came up behind Alice, guiding her hands to the correct spot on her horse's back to help her to pull herself up. 'Put a foot in my hand, and I will lift you. Once you are high enough, you need to twist around and find a comfortable position in the saddle.'

As he moved closer he caught a hint of her scent and had to resist the urge to lean in farther. It was tantalising, a subtle mix of lavender and rosewater, and he had the sudden desire to press his lips against the soft skin of her neck. There was a spot just behind and below her ear that looked perfect for his lips, and he had to stop himself quickly as he realised he had almost leaned in to kiss it.

His body brushed against hers as she lifted her foot into his hand, and he quickly boosted her into the air. With his help she twisted lithely and was quickly seated in the saddle. He took a minute to help her position her feet and showed her how best to hold the reins, all while trying to ignore the urge to pull her out of the saddle and back into his arms.

He tried to reason it was only natural, this attraction he felt. He had been starved of companionship for a long time, and Alice was an attractive young woman. Never before had he dallied with a respectable unmarried woman, but on the night of the Midsummer's Eve ball nearly a year earlier, he had been unable to resist kissing her, even though he'd known better. That attraction, that deep desire, had not faded in the time he was away, although now it was even more imperative that he did not do anything to jeopardize the delicate balance of their relationship.

Once Alice was settled he pulled himself away and mounted his horse, glancing over to check his wife was not looking too nervous.

'Shall we start with a gentle walk down to the Serpentine?'

'That would be pleasant.'

He urged Socrates on gently and was pleased to see Alice doing the same to her horse, and after a minute he was able to fall into step beside her. They had to wind along a couple of tree-lined paths to get to the wide-open space of the more central area of Hyde Park, but before long they were side by side, riding towards the water.

'How are you finding it?'

'I am a little nervous,' Alice confessed with a self-deprecating smile, 'but I think I am beginning to enjoy it.'

'I am glad. We can stop at any time.'

They rode in silence for a few minutes, and each time he glanced across at Alice he could see she was deep in thought. He realised he knew so little of her hopes and her wants that he had no idea what she would be amenable to when they discussed their future. It was clear she understood they would not have a conventional marriage, even now that he had returned to England, yet it was hard to fathom whether she wished to continue her life completely separate from his or if she wanted companionship from him.

As they approached the sparkling blue water, he slowed and her horse followed his lead, and for a moment they took in the view without saying anything. It was a glorious day, and the park was wonderfully empty despite the pleasant weather.

'Is there somewhere we can go that is a little more private?' Alice said, leaning towards him slightly. 'I do not wish what we discuss to become gossip by this afternoon.'

'Of course. The park is vast. If you are happy to continue with our ride, we can find somewhere we will not be overheard.'

'Thank you.'

He led them away from the lake, pleased to see with every passing minute Alice's confidence was growing, the reins now held loosely in her hands as they allowed the horses to pick the pace. After ten minutes they were away from the people strolling by the water, and it felt as though they had this part of the park to themselves.

As he watched, Alice straightened in her seat as if gearing herself up for battle. He felt a stab of regret that they needed to have this discussion but also knew that once their expectations and preferences were out in the open, they could move away from the uncertainty that surrounded them both.

'You wished to discuss our future, Simon,' Alice said, glancing over at him but not holding his eye. He could sense her trepidation of the subject but was pleased she had initiated the conversation.

'I think we both need to know where we stand.'

'Do you wish to divorce me?' she said, her voice low. Simon was an experienced rider, but in his shock he almost fell out of his saddle.

'Divorce you? Whatever gave you that idea?'

She looked at him incredulously for almost a minute before replying. 'You married me thinking you would be dead within a few months, so that our union was an act of duty that would not really affect you. Now that you have been told you are not imminently going to be struck down, in fact you may never be in the way your brother and your father were, I expect you wish to return to your normal life to a certain degree.'

'I am not going to divorce you, Alice. That would ruin us both.'

'I would not try to stop you,' she said softly.

'Do you want me to divorce you?' he asked, unable to fathom how divorce had even entered her mind. Divorce was a messy and protracted affair, and he had only seen it occur a couple of times, and on each occasion neither party had come out unscathed. He found he was upset at even the idea of divorcing Alice.

'No,' she said quickly. 'Far from it. From the whispered conversations I have heard about when Lord Southerhay divorced his wife eight years ago, I can see it is a catastrophic course of events with both parties completely humiliated by the discussion of their private business in front of Parliament itself. I am aware if you divorced me my life as I know it would be over. I doubt I would ever marry again, and I wouldn't have children, a family. My own family would disown me. It would be the worst possible outcome.' She paused and then looked over at him, holding his eye. 'But I do understand if that is the path you wish to take. I am not what you had planned for your life, and if you now want to find a wife you actually want to marry, I will understand.'

'I am not that heartless, Alice,' he said, his voice low. He felt a flicker of anger that she would think so little of him and had to remind himself she had only known neglect and desertion from him. Divorce was a fate worse than death to many and happened only once in a generation in their social class. Yet surely she would understand they had entered into this marriage to save her from ruin, and he wouldn't callously abandon her now.

'Not divorce, then,' she said, nodding with relief.

'Not divorce, we can agree on that.' He paused, wondering how he was going to say what he had to. Despite not knowing Alice well, he did know she wanted a family one day. She had spoken of being surrounded by children, of a happy family life with a husband who loved her. He remembered how she had been with the two children in Hyde Park, sailing the model boat on the

Serpentine. At that image he felt the words stick in his throat. That was not the life he could give her.

'I may have been told by the doctors the headaches were not a harbinger of imminent death, but I still cannot know what the future might hold,' he said slowly, watching Alice's reaction. 'I may suffer the same fate as my father and my brother, and it could happen at any time. It has meant addressing my mortality each and every day, knowing this could be my last. I was eager to return to England to see my family and to take up my responsibilities once again, but it does not change the fact that one day in a few months or years I may have to leave suddenly again, or I may die without any warning.'

'That could be said for any of us,' Alice said softly. 'I do not mean to take away from the seriousness of your situation—of course your risk is greater—but none of us know what the future will hold. I may catch consumption from one of the children at the orphanage tomorrow and wither away within the next six months, or I could be thrown from this horse and crack my skull this afternoon.'

'You are not wrong. I know it is foolish to live one's life always thinking about whether today is the day you die, but I find it is not a thought I can change just by intention.'

Alice nodded slowly. 'I understand that,' she said, giving him a sad smile. 'Although, I wish it were not so.'

'It also means that I will not have children. I refuse to bring a child into this world who might suffer the same.'

He could see Alice had more to say, perhaps more to argue on this subject, but after a moment she pressed her lips together and nodded. 'I understand,' she said simply.

Looking at her intently he spoke a little softer. 'I know this is not the life I promised you. I offered a year or two of comfort with your reputation intact, and then perhaps a few months of mourning before you could start looking for a husband of your own choice. A man you wanted to marry and who would give you your family.'

Alice looked away, but before she did, he thought he saw tears in her eyes. He felt like a cad, ripping away her hopes for the future like this.

'I do not begrudge you being alive, Simon,' she said softly. 'Whatever that means for my future.'

They were kind words from a kind young woman, and for a moment he wanted to pull her into his arms, hold her close to him and tell her he would give her whatever she wanted, yet he couldn't do it. Their lives were destined to go in very different directions, and as much as he liked Alice, as much as he desired her and could see himself being happy with her if they lived a conventional life as husband and wife, it wasn't a path he could take.

He couldn't bring himself to voice the other reason he couldn't build a true relationship with her—it was buried too deep inside and he didn't like to examine it too closely—but there was a part of him that felt as though he were stealing his brother's life. He had the title, the properties, the place in Parliament, all the things his brother should be enjoying still. If he allowed himself to have a normal life with Alice, to treat her as his true wife, to have children with her, that would be a step too far in assuming the life that should have been his brother's.

Alice took a deep breath and seemed to brace herself for what she had to say next.

'I understand you do not want to have children, that you are concerned about passing to them whatever it is your father and brother were afflicted by. I also understand that means we cannot have an intimate relationship as is normal between husband and wife.'

He hadn't expected she would be so direct, but he was pleased that there was no ambiguity in her words. The last thing they wanted was to speak in metaphors and then both leave with a different understanding of what the future would hold.

'I am not sure what it is you do want, Simon. Do you wish for us to lead completely separate lives? For me to reside in Northumberland whilst you are in London, and then when you travel north we cross on the road when I am heading for London? Or do you want us to have a closer relationship, a friendship, a companionship? It is very hard to know what to suggest when I have no idea what it is you would be comfortable with.'

Up until he had arrived back in England, he would have said the first of her suggestions was the one that made the most sense, but now, even after spending just a few scattered hours with Alice, he wasn't sure he wanted to move around the country like ships passing in the night, barely acknowledging she existed. Whilst he was in Italy, his marriage had seemed an abstract concept, something that was very easy to put out of his mind, but now that he had returned it was far harder to ignore her, and he realised he didn't wish to.

'I propose a friendship, perhaps with time, even a companionship. We do not need to be tied to one another, if you wish to stay in London when I go to Northumberland, then there is no issue. If I wish to visit friends, then I will inform you, but there is no expectation that we conduct every aspect of our lives together.'

'That sounds agreeable,' Alice said. 'So we shall endeavour to at least keep the other person informed of our plans.'

'Yes,' he murmured. 'I know I left rather abruptly a few weeks ago when I travelled to Northumberland. I should have informed you in person. I was overwhelmed by my return home, but it is no excuse for leaving without bidding you farewell. I am sorry.'

'Thank you.'

They had ridden some way across the open grass now and were in a deserted part of the park. There was a good view over the green space up here, and for a moment Simon paused to take it all in. He felt a roil of emotion as he let his eyes take in the rooftops of London beyond the park. When he'd left England eleven months ago, he had thought he would never look upon this view, nor see his beloved Northumberland again either. His homecoming had proved more emotional than he had imagined.

'I have brought some refreshment. Shall we pause here and toast our marriage with a glass of lemonade?'

'That sounds lovely.' Alice smiled at him, and for an instant he had the urge to throw away every caution and pull her into his arms, to hell with the consequences. Quickly he pushed the thought away: he had given in to his desire once with Alice, and that had upended both their lives. He must control himself better around his pretty wife.

Chapter Thirteen

Alice tried to push away the desire she felt as Simon wrapped his hands around her waist to help her from her saddle. It was an impossible situation, and she had to do everything in her power not to make it worse.

She considered his offer of friendship, companionship perhaps, and realised it was better than she had feared but not what she had secretly hoped for. It was ridiculous to even think about, but deep down she knew she wished Simon had come racing back to London because he had suddenly realised he could not live without her. It was so far from the truth of the matter it was almost laughable. He did not want to live with her as most men wanted to live with their wives. He would treat her as a spinster relative, with kindness and perhaps even a little platonic affection, but there would be no intimacy, no love.

Alice pushed away the disappointment. This way was better. She could continue with her life here in London, travel to Northumberland to see Maria and the children as planned later in the summer, take her trips to visit her own sister. Sometimes Simon would be at home when she returned, sometimes he would not. Her life would not change substantially, and perhaps with a little time she would grow to enjoy this new phase.

She was determined not to become reliant on Simon's company, though. He had shown how quickly he could disappear and how little importance he placed on including her in his plans. She would have to conduct her life with this in mind, always wary that he could disappear at any moment.

With his hands around her waist, Simon steadied Alice as she slid to the ground. They ended up standing close, and Alice could not resist the urge to raise a hand and place it on his chest. Even through the layers of clothing, she could feel his heart beating, slow and steady underneath the subtle rise and fall as he inhaled and exhaled. She glanced up at him and saw him regarding her strangely, with an almost hungry look in his eyes, and she realised that desire for her he had shown on the night of the Midsummer's Eve ball had not disappeared completely. He was holding himself tight, coiled like a deadly snake ready to spring out at its prey, and she realised with a rush of satisfaction she was making him feel on edge.

She was pleased not at his discomfort but that she was not the only one struggling to deny she felt something more than a desire for friendship between them.

Alice allowed her hand to linger for another few seconds and then withdrew, stepping to the side to move around him, trying to pretend nothing had happened. Despite being a married woman of eleven months, she was still very much an innocent in the ways of seduction. However, people assumed she had at least had her wedding night with her husband, and it meant she was no longer shielded from some of the more delicate conversations held between married women.

She had no plans to try to seduce Simon: not only would she have no idea how to go about it but also it wouldn't be fair. She might not agree with his reasons for deciding not to have children, but it *was* his decision, and she would not trick him into any intimacy in the hopes that she might have the family she dreamed of. Instead she would work on making the life she did have as fulfilling as possible, and perhaps dreaming of her husband's lips on hers last thing at night when they went to bed.

Simon lingered by the horses for a moment and when he turned to face her, he looked composed with no hint of the desire that had flashed in his eyes when she'd stood close.

He took a blanket from the saddlebag on his horse and spread it on the grass, indicating for her to have a seat. She lowered herself to the ground, making herself comfortable on the soft wool of the blanket. From the saddlebag he also produced a large bottle of lemonade and a parcel that she suspected contained some of Cook's delicious biscuits.

He brought them over, indicating the lemonade. 'I forgot glasses,' he said with a shrug. 'We will have to drink from the bottle.'

'I do not mind. When I was young my parents would sometimes take us for picnics on the beach in the summer when it was a particularly hot day. We would walk across the dunes and find a quiet spot, spread out a blanket and enjoy our lunch with the sea lapping at the shore in the distance. My mother never remembered to pack glasses, and Margaret and I always shared lemonade straight from the bottle.'

'It sounds idyllic.'

Alice wobbled her head from side to side. She couldn't complain about her childhood, not when she compared it to the awful circumstances the children in the London orphanages and on the streets lived in, yet it had not been happy. There had been happy times, long summer days spent playing with Lydia and her sister, paddling in the sea and coming home soaked through with seawater, the winter storms where she and Margaret would creep to the empty attic room and watch the thunder and lightning light up the village and the sand dunes beyond. She had some fond memories, but there had always been an uneasiness in their house. Her father was strict, even more so than most parents she knew. He would bring out his cane if he thought she or Margaret had committed any more substantial infractions of his rules. Often the girls would be unable to eat their dinner because their punishment had split the skin on their hands.

Their mother had not been so coldly cruel, but she had expected quiet obedience from her two daughters and was quick to anger if they did not obey. It had not been a happy childhood, but she had been clothed and housed in comfort, with decent meals on the table.

'You have happy memories?'

'I used to enjoy the times I had playing on the beach with my sister,' Alice said, deciding not to mention the difficult feelings she had towards her parents.

'That is a well-practised answer. You are skilled at diplomacy, Alice.' He regarded her as he sat down. 'Am I to take it your childhood wasn't idyllic?'

She puffed her cheeks out and then blew out the air before shaking her head.

'It wasn't idyllic,' she said slowly. 'It wasn't terrible, but my parents were distant and cold, and I was always one step away from punishment. I cannot complain when I see what some children have to endure, but it is not the way I would want to bring my children up.' She glanced at him quickly before adding, 'If ever I have them.'

'It is perhaps why you are so interested in the work with children on the streets and in orphanages that the London Ladies' Benevolent Society does.'

'I think you may be right,' she said, taking the bottle of lemonade after he had popped out the cork for her. It felt strange to swig from a bottle in front of this man she barely knew, but she was thirsty, and after a moment she pushed away her reticence and took a delicate sip. The lemonade was delicious and refreshing, and she decided to forget about what she looked like or what Simon thought of her and took a long gulp of the beverage. 'Since I have taken over the helm I have steered the society towards projects that help women and children. We do a lot of fundraising and donate to many good causes, but there has been a definite shift to help the most vulnerable in society with our efforts.'

'I have been making enquiries,' Simon said as he sat beside her. The blanket wasn't huge, and he sat close without his position being scandalous. They were a married couple and there was nothing wrong with them sharing some refreshment whilst seated together in a public park, yet somehow when his hand brushed hers it felt as though they were doing something illicit.

'Enquiries?'

'Into your society. I am impressed. What you have managed to do in a year is nothing short of extraordinary.'

A subtle warmth diffused through her body, making her skin tingle at his compliment.

'It has taken up much of my time these last few months, but I feel like we are finally making a difference where it is most needed.'

She glanced at him and decided she would share a little more. He looked engaged and interested, and although she had vowed she would continue her life in the knowledge he might leave it at any moment, she did not have to petulantly shut him out of her world.

'Lady Kennington has identified a small orphanage close to the slums of St Giles that she thinks would benefit immensely from our patronage. Apparently it is a dilapidated building that takes from the poorest areas. I am planning on visiting later today to see whether we will be able to help.'

'I am sure any donations will be thankfully received.'

'I hope we might be able to offer more than that. Many of the ladies from the Benevolent Society are keen to do more than just fundraise. We have a mix of backgrounds and a wealth of expertise at our disposal. It will depend on who runs the orphanage, but I am hopeful we might be able to provide more than just money.'

'What do you mean?' He leaned forward, looking intrigued, and Alice felt a rush of satisfaction at his interest.

'One of the main limitations of many of the orphanages is the lack of support as the children get to the age when they are no longer eligible for a bed and a hot meal from the establishment. They may have rudimentary reading and writing skills, perhaps very basic arithmetic, and they will be trained to do a number of menial household jobs, but often it is not enough. People see they are from the orphanage and will not give them a chance, except in the very lowest paid positions.'

'I cannot argue with the truth of that.'

'I am not sure exactly what the answer is yet. Perhaps better schooling, perhaps a focus on certain trades and skills for when they leave the orphanage. I am hoping with a small establishment like St Benedict's we may be able to foster a system where some of our benefactors look to take in the young boys and girls when they reach fourteen and help to train them as maids and footmen. It may take a little patience, but I believe with the right people it could make the world of difference.'

'A little like your scheme to match the wealthier families with the poorer to provide support over the winter in Bamburgh.'

She felt her cheeks flush, finding that she was pleased he had remembered.

'It is an admirable idea, but it would be a big adjustment, asking these children to abide by the rules of a wealthy and prominent household.'

Alice shook her head vehemently. 'It is the perfect time to do it. They have been used to strict rules for years, being told exactly what they can do and when by the master or matron of the orphanage. It is better to take them from that environment, before there have been too many other corrupting influences.' She cocked her head to one side. 'You have borne witness to this scheme in action.'

He looked at her in surprise. 'I have?'

'Yes, in the young footman, Frank Smith.'

'He is a lad from an orphanage?'

'Yes. I had a long discussion with Miss Stick about whether she would be supportive of the idea of bringing him in to train up.'

'She was happy to do it?'

'Very happy. Miss Stick has a hard demeanour but a very good soul,' Alice said affectionately. 'We visited the orphanage together to talk to Frank and to check he would be a good fit, then he joined the household five months ago.'

'Five months ago he was an orphanage boy?'

'He was.'

Simon let out a low whistle. 'I would not have guessed.'

'Three times a week he spends an hour with either myself or Miss Stick to develop his reading and writing and arithmetic skills, and once he is secure in basic knowledge, we will discuss what he wishes to do with his life and hopefully be able to guide him in that direction.'

'That is an ambitious plan, Alice,' Simon said, looking at her in wonder. 'You think this will work?'

She shrugged. 'I think with Frank it will. He is a determined young man who has seen the worst of life at a very young age, and he is motivated not to end the same way his own parents did, in poverty, unable to support their family. I am not saying it is the answer for everyone, but perhaps it is enough to help a few.'

'Once Frank has gained the skills he needs to get a job elsewhere, you will repeat the process I assume?'

'That is the plan, whilst gently advocating for others to do the same.'

'What if it goes wrong?'

She put her hands a little behind her bottom and leaned back, tilting her face up to the sun underneath the rim of her bonnet. Her skin would burn if she stayed this way for too long, but a couple of minutes would not matter, and it felt so glorious to have the warmth of the sun on her face.

'You mean what if one of the children from the orphanage steals all the silver or brings the household into disrepute?' She shrugged again. 'It is the risk you take when you hire any servant. References can be forged, recommendations coerced. At least this way you know the person's background, and you can learn what they have been through.'

For a minute Simon remained silent, and then he nodded thoughtfully. 'I think the scheme has merit. It will be interesting to see what comes of it.' It was the first time he had spoken of being interested in something shared in the future, and Alice wondered if he would really stick around to see the results of her plans or if in a few months he would disappear again, his only correspondence a short note telling her he was gone.

'I am visiting St Benedict's Orphanage this afternoon. I will keep you updated on my progress.'

Simon frowned. 'I hope you do not plan to go alone. It is not in a salubrious part of the city.'

'I am meeting the matron of the orphanage. I hardly think my life will be in danger.'

'You should take someone with you.'

'Are you volunteering?' It was said in jest, but she saw Simon tilt his head to one side as he considered.

'I am. I have no plans this afternoon. I would be happy to accompany you.'

For a moment she didn't know what to say. Part of her felt unsettled: it was strange enough having her husband back in her life, sharing her home, but she had not expected him to have any involvement with the charity work she did too.

'Thank you,' she said eventually.

'As pleasant as this has been, we should head back home soon,' Simon said, rising to his feet and holding out a hand to help her up. She stood, her body bumping lightly against his, and for a moment she felt as though time stood still. The sensible part of her mind screamed for her to step away, to put some distance between them, but her body just would not obey. She wished she didn't feel this attraction towards her husband. He had made it perfectly clear there would be no intimacy between them, yet she yearned for him to kiss her, to trail his fingers over her skin and make her feel truly alive.

With great effort she stepped away, turning her back for a moment to compose herself. By the time she turned back, Simon had moved and was busying himself with the horses, seemingly unperturbed by their moment of closeness.

Chapter Fourteen

St Benedict's Orphanage was based in a run-down building that had been built on the very edge of the slums of St Giles. It was tucked between two equally rickety buildings, one of which leaned forward over the street as if threatening to collapse any moment. When they had stepped out of the carriage, Simon had looked up and down the street dubiously, wondering how likely it was that the whole row would collapse and crush everyone inside. Such tragedies were not unheard of in these areas where the buildings were poorly constructed in the first place and decades of hard use had chipped away at any structural integrity that might have once been present.

The inside of the orphanage was not much better. There were sloping wooden floors, small windows and a staircase that creaked ominously whenever anyone climbed it. The rooms were dark and draughty, and the accommodation consisted of one long, thin room for the boys and another of similar proportions for the girls. Downstairs there was a communal area set with tables where the orphans both ate and did their lessons.

Despite the grim conditions the children lived in, Simon had been pleasantly surprised when he met Mrs

Phillips, the kindly woman appointed matron of the orphanage by the board of governors. There were twenty-four children under her care, all thin and pale, but neatly turned-out with faces scrubbed and hair cut short to guard against lice.

She had spoken passionately about the work she did in measured tones but with an accent that made Simon think she had grown up locally, perhaps even a child of the slum herself once. She certainly was a good advocate for the orphanage.

They were now sitting at the back of the room whilst the children were finishing their lessons. All twenty-four were taught together, despite them ranging in ages from two to fourteen. They sat, boys on one side of the room, girls on the other, the youngest at the front and the oldest at the back. At the front of the room the teacher pointed to letters and phrases written out, and the children had to read out in unison what they said.

'Look,' Alice whispered, motioning to a few children in the middle of the room. As well as reading the words they were also copying them onto slate tablets. 'I think they only have four slate tablets between twenty-four children.' She shifted a little, leaning forward to see a little better. 'That is something we could easily donate funds for.'

As she sat back, her arm brushed against his, a fleeting contact, but it made him stiffen all the same. He realised he liked this version of his wife. Here at the orphanage, the naïve country girl he had married was long gone; instead, there was an idealistic woman who was determined to make a difference in the world. When she conversed with the matron, she spoke with conviction and confidence, a woman who was used to being listened to.

After a few more minutes the lessons finished and the children filed out of the classroom, some into the kitchen beyond to get started on helping to prepare the evening meal, others upstairs where no doubt some other work waited for them. They moved quietly, a little subdued, and Simon felt a pang of pity for those who had lost their families and now lived in this dull, monotonous life, although he supposed it was better than the alternative that waited for them on the streets.

'Thank you for your visit, Lady Westcroft,' Mrs Phillips said as she ushered the last of the children upstairs and came to stand with them. 'We are most honoured in your interest in our small orphanage.'

'I am grateful for your hospitality and your honesty,' Alice said warmly. Mrs Phillips had a positive outlook, but she had not glossed over the shortcomings of the small orphanage, letting them see the bad alongside the good. 'We have our next meeting of the London Ladies' Benevolent Society in two weeks. I will report back to our members, and I am hopeful we will be able to offer some monetary and practical support.' Alice paused, looking at the matron with an assessing gaze, then nodded as if making a decision. 'I am conscious of your years of experience, Mrs Phillips, and I am wary of charging in and suggesting changes that may not be helpful, despite our best intentions. I wonder if you might take some time to write down what you think might be helpful so I can present your thoughts to the other members, or consider if you were willing to even come and talk to the ladies yourself.' Alice held up her hands and smiled at the matron. 'I know you are terribly busy, but give it some thought, and let me know what you can manage.'

'I will, Lady Westcroft.' Mrs Phillips turned to Simon. 'It is a pleasure to meet you, Lord Westcroft.'

'And you, Mrs Phillips.' He inclined his head and then offered Alice his arm as the matron showed them out.

Their carriage was waiting outside, surrounded by a gaggle of curious children. Simon was about to gently shoo them away when Alice gripped his arm.

'Thank you,' she said, looking up at him with her pale blue eyes. She had a contented smile on her face, and Simon felt a desire to keep that smile on her lips for ever.

'What for?'

'I admit I have only had the one husband,' she said with a mischievous glance at him, 'and that husband only for a few days, but I have seen how other men treat their wives. They disregard their views, silence their opinions. Many other men would have insisted on taking the lead with Mrs Phillips, even if it were not their cause to lead on. You did not. You stepped back and allowed me to be the one to ask questions and be in control, even for that short amount of time.'

'Most men are fools,' he murmured. 'They do not listen long enough to their wives to realise what they have to offer the world.' He smiled at her, feeling a unfamiliar satisfaction. This past year he had lived a lonely life, and he realised with a jolt that spending time with Alice, with her kind manner and lively conversation, were just what he needed. Despite the urge he felt to stand on the street corner staring into his wife's eyes, he motioned to the carriage. 'Shall we return home before we become targets for every cutpurse in London?'

Alice inclined her head, but as they stepped from the kerb to cross the road to their carriage, a group of beggar children broke off from the main gaggle and surrounded them, clamouring for money.

There were a couple of older boys in the group, but most of the children were no more than seven. Out of the corner of his eye, Simon saw a man leaning against the wall of a building on the other side of the street, and suddenly he felt a cold chill run through him. The man was resolutely not looking at them despite them being in his direct line of sight. It was suspicious, and without saying anything Simon reached out to grip hold of Alice's arm, wanting to pull her closer to him.

He'd had a privileged upbringing with most of his childhood spent on the estate in Northumberland, but his time travelling had taught him to be vigilant and trust his instincts. He believed the human mind was very good at working out when there was something wrong: it was why people talked of following their gut. Right now his gut was telling him to get his wife out of this situation as quickly as possible.

Alice looked at him in shock as he wrapped an arm around her waist and propelled her through the crowd of children, into the carriage. They had almost made it to the door when one of the younger boys stepped in front of them and with lightning-fast speed whipped out a knife. He held it low so it was hidden from any casual onlooker by the press of bodies around them. Simon saw the boy's hand was shaking, the knife weaving from side to side. He was a pale, scrawny lad, his face grimy and his feet bare on the cobbles. He looked pitiful rather than threatening, and as Simon watched the knife he realised it was likely a distraction. Whilst their eyes were fixed on the blade someone else would be trying to pick his pocket or relieve Alice of anything valuable.

He spun, reaching out to grab the thin wrist of an even younger boy whose hand had slipped inside Simon's jacket. The boy cried out in fear, and after a second the crowd of beggars that surrounded them disappeared, the children scarpering in different directions, diving into alleyways or dashing around corners. Simon looked up, past the carriage, to see the man who had been observing them calmly walking away too.

Only he, Alice and the little pickpocket remained.

The boy struggled, wriggling and tugging at his wrist, desperation on his face as he realised there was no escaping this predicament.

'Stop it,' Simon said, his voice firm but not cruel. The boy looked only five or six, although it was hard to tell as he was clearly malnourished, his growth no doubt stunted by a poor diet.

The boy stilled, looking up at Simon for the first time with big brown eyes.

Next to him he felt Alice shift, but he dared not take his attention from the boy in front of him.

'I don't want to hang,' the boy said after a minute, tears forming in his eyes and rolling onto his cheeks, making tracks through the dirt.

'You're not going to hang,' Simon said, moderating his tone. 'How old are you?'

The boy sniffed. 'Seven.'

Simon grimaced. If he handed this lad to a magistrate

and insisted he be punished for attempting to steal his purse, the child could end up taking a trip to the gallows. Some judges were more lenient towards the younger children that appeared before them, but others looked to set an example to thousands of children who committed crimes each year just looking to fill their hungry bellies.

'What is your name?'

The boy pressed his lips together and shook his head. Alice crouched down, seeming not to notice as the hem of her dress brushed against the dirt of the cobbles.

'What is your name?' she asked this time, her voice soft as if she were talking to one of their nieces.

'Peter, miss.' The boy looked at Alice, and then the tears started to flow from his eyes like a river after a winter storm. 'I don't want to hang, miss. Please don't let him hang me.'

'You're not going to hang,' Simon said firmly. 'There was a man watching us. Tall, dark hair, green coat. Was he with you?'

The boy nodded miserably.

'He told you what to do?'

Again the boy nodded.

'What is his name?'

'I can't tell you. He'll gut me if I do, and that's even worse than hanging.'

'Is he your father?' Alice asked.

'No, my father's dead.'

'What about your mother?'

The boy's eyes darted to the side, and he shrugged.

'Your mother is alive?' Simon said, waiting for the boy to look at him again. He still held the lad by the wrist, knowing as soon as he loosened his grip, the young boy would disappear into the warren of streets that made up St Giles.

Peter nodded glumly.

'Do you live near here?'

Again the boy nodded.

Simon turned to the driver of the carriage who had hopped down from his seat to join them.

'Drummond, take my wife home. Ensure she is escorted safely all the way to the front door.'

Simon turned to Alice to see her frowning.

'You mean to send me back alone?'

'You will be quite safe with Drummond, in the carriage.'

'It is not my safety I fear for.'

He looked at his wife for a moment, realisation dawning. 'You wish to see where this boy lives too?'

'He is only seven, Simon, and clearly he was under the influence of that man who was watching us. I do not want to see him punished.'

'You think I do not mean it when I say I do not want to see him hanged?'

Alice didn't say anything, but her lack of denial hurt more than he thought possible. He might not plan to be a true husband to his wife, but to realise how little she trusted him was difficult to accept.

'I merely want to take this boy home to his family and have a quiet word with his mother. She may be pragmatic, she may not, but I cannot merely let the boy go,' Simon said, his voice low. 'He will be off through the streets and back into the arms of the gang that pressed him to pick my pocket.' He spoke sharply and saw Alice recoil slightly, but she did not retreat.

'I shall come with you, then.'

'Lead the way, Peter,' Simon said brusquely.

Sullenly the young boy led them through a maze of streets to a set of rickety steps that led up to a wooden platform.

'Up there,' Peter said, motioning with his head. The streets were busy and they were drawing curious looks, and Simon found he wanted to get this over with, deliver the boy back to his mother and get Alice home to safety.

They climbed the stairs, and Simon knocked on the door, hearing the sound of a crying baby inside before the murmur of a low voice. After a minute the door opened, and a young woman peered out. She was in her twenties, but already her face was lined and her skin sallow. She held a baby in her arms and was bobbing up and down to soothe it. Her eyes widened as she saw Peter, and she looked up at Simon fearfully.

'What has he done?' she said, her voice cracking.

'You are Peter's mother?'

'Yes. What trouble has he found now?'

'He was in the company of a number of other children and a man who seemed to be directing them to pick people's pockets.'

The woman's face paled, and she reached out for her son, a protective look on her face.

'Don't blame my Peter, please, sir. He's only seven, only a young boy. He's hungry, that's all. We haven't been able to afford much food these last few months, not since his father died. Please don't report him. They'll make an example of him, I know they will.'

To his surprise Alice stepped forward and laid a hand on the woman's arm.

'We are not going to report him. We just wanted to be sure he got home to you safely.'

'And to let you know he is running with a group of pickpockets. If he continues with them, the next time he gets caught, whoever catches him may not be so lenient.'

'You're not going to report him?'

'No.' Simon let go of Peter's wrist, and the boy slipped into the darkness of the room behind his mother, peering out from behind her with a stunned look on his face.

'Thank you, sir. I will make sure he doesn't do anything like this again.'

Simon nodded and then took a step back. There was nothing more they could do here. In all likelihood Peter would be back with the gang of pickpockets first thing tomorrow, choosing to risk his neck rather than endure the relentless hunger he must feel each and every day. It was an awful situation, but now the boy was home safe he had to hand responsibility over to his mother.

He gestured to Alice that they should leave, and she gave Peter's mother one final reassuring smile before they climbed back down the rickety steps.

They walked in silence for a few minutes, navigating the maze of streets until they stepped back out to where the carriage was waiting.

Once inside Simon settled back on his seat and watched the orphanage disappear from view as the carriage rolled away. He was still hurt by Alice's mistrust of him, and he knew he needed to address it lest it eat away at him.

Before he could speak Alice leaned forward and placed her hand on his. It wasn't an overly intimate gesture, at least not for a wife to a husband in normal circumstances, but even the most innocent of touches seemed to ignite something inside him and made it impossible to focus.

'Thank you,' she said, looking across at him and giving him a soft smile.

'You did not trust I would not hand the boy over to a magistrate,' Simon said, watching as Alice stiffened and then nodded slowly.

'You are right,' she said eventually, then let out a deep sigh. 'We do not really know one another at all, do we, Simon?'

'Have I ever done anything to make you think I am an unreasonable man?'

'No,' she said quickly. 'You have always done exactly what you said you would.'

'Then, why doubt me?'

'Do you know how many hours we have spent in one another's company?'

He shook his head.

'Eight. Eight hours. Three at the Midsummer's Eve ball a year ago, one in the weeks before our wedding and one hour after we were married, then three in the days since you have returned. I have spent more time with my hatmaker in the last year, and I absolutely loathe hats.' She was speaking fast now, and he saw the pent-up frustration in her eyes. Their ride through Hyde Park earlier had been pleasant and their discussion reasonable, but he realised much of that was because Alice had been holding back the hurt she was feeling at how he had abandoned her. 'How am I meant to know how you will react to a certain situation? How am I meant to trust your word? We are two strangers tiptoeing around one another, neither sure how the other will react.' She sniffed and turned her head away, blinking furiously. After a moment she turned back. 'I *know* it has to be this way, Simon. I can understand your reasons and I accept them, but it does not mean you can have it both ways. Either you stay distant, living your life without the complication of another's feelings or you allow me close, but if you choose the former you must understand you cannot have the perks without the drawbacks.' She sat back, her chest heaving and her cheeks flushed with colour.

'I thought we had come to an understanding in the park.'

'Friendship?'

'Yes. A decision we would both live our lives independently, but with consideration of the other person.'

She looked at him then, a fierce intensity burning in her eyes, and for a moment he thought he saw a flash of desire, but then she pressed her lips together and inhaled sharply.

'You chide me for not trusting you, yet trust must be built, as must a friendship. I thought that was what you were doing, accompanying me to the orphanage, trying to build some common ground between us, but perhaps I was wrong.'

'You were not wrong, Alice,' he said, sitting back and running a hand through his hair. 'God's blood, I'm trying. This is difficult for me as well.'

She snorted and shook her head, and he felt a swell of anger rise inside him.

'I grant you it is more difficult for you, to have me return alive when I had promised you your freedom, but I too am trying to navigate an impossible situation.'

She leaned forward, jabbing a finger in his direction. 'Do not imply I want you dead.'

'It would be far simpler for you if I were.'

'You think I am that cruel?'

Simon felt the momentary anger simmer and then die away inside him, and he lowered his voice.

'No,' he said quietly. 'Of course not. Forgive me, that was unacceptable.'

Alice looked at him, her eyes narrowed. 'Just because you do not think you deserve to be alive doesn't mean I would ever agree with you. I went into this marriage with my eyes open, and although it may not be exactly what you promised, I would never, ever wish you were dead so that I could have my freedom.' She paused to draw in a ragged breath. '*You* are not a victim here, Simon. You get to dictate how our lives continue. You have the position of power. You say we cannot have a normal marriage,' she said and snapped her fingers, 'so we do not have a normal marriage. You say we cannot have children—' another snap of the fingers '—no children. You say we will work towards a friendship.' The third snap seemed to pierce his very soul. 'Friendship it is.'

Her words cut through him, and he gripped the seat, trying to anchor himself as the world spun around him.

For a long time they were silent, and the carriage was travelling through familiar streets before Simon was able to speak again.

'What do you mean, I do not think I deserve to be alive?'

'It is true, is it not?'

He shook his head, but even to him the movement was unconvincing.

'When you left, your mother and your sister-in-law

were devastated. It was as though they were in mourning, and for two women who had lost so much already, it nearly broke them.'

Simon closed his eyes for a moment, knowing this was going to be hard to hear. He had known his departure to Italy would be painful for those who loved him, but at the time he had thought it would ultimately protect them.

'Your mother couldn't get out of bed for a week.' She held up a hand. 'I do not tell you this to punish you, to make you feel guilty, but I think it is important you realise the impact of your actions on those who love you.'

'I knew it would be hard for them, but I thought it better than the alternative.'

'When your mother was up to having visitors, I went and sat with her every day, and she told me all about you and your family. She told me of how you idolised your father, how he was a wonderful man who both you and your brother looked up to. She told me of how his death had ripped you apart. A boy of twelve needs his father, and you lost yours in one of the worst ways imaginable.'

The carriage was beginning to slow as they approached the house, but Simon knocked loudly on the roof and stuck his head out the window, telling the driver to loop around until he was instructed otherwise.

'You mourned him deeply, but you still had your brother. Your mother told me you loved Robert more than anyone else.'

'He was the best of men.'

'And she said you slowly were able to put your father's death behind you.'

'With Robert's help.'

'Robert, with the beautiful wife and the incredible daughters. The earl, the beloved landlord.'

Simon nodded. His brother had been the perfect earl, the right mix of family man and imposing figure of authority.

'Then he died, and you were thrust back into mourning again, but this time there was no beloved brother to pull you out of it, and what was more you were expected to step into his shoes, to take his place.'

'I could never take his place.'

'But you were forced to. You became the earl, you took his seat in Parliament, you inherited all his properties, you were made to live the life which, only a few months before, your brother had.' Alice's voice softened, and she reached out and took his hand. 'Your mother thinks it was too much for you to bear, the idea that you were taking the life that should have been Robert's.'

'It was his life.'

'And she believes somewhere deep down you don't think you deserve to be alive when two great men, your father and your brother, were snatched away from this earth so early.'

Simon didn't say anything. It felt as though his heart were being squeezed inside his chest, and with every passing second the pain became more intense.

'It is why you will not even countenance a traditional marriage with me,' Alice said, her voice so low it was barely more than a whisper. 'You think that is a step too far. You have no choice but to be the earl and to take your seat in Parliament and to be the landlord to your tenants, but you can choose not to allow yourself any happiness, not to take that final part of Robert's life, the role of husband and father.'

'You have clearly thought about this a lot,' he murmured.

'I have thought of little else this past year. Your family have been struck by such tragedy, it is impossible to fathom the sorrow you must feel, yet I pity you not just for the loss of your father and brother but for your resolution that you do not deserve the happiness that they once had just because only you now survive.'

'I do not want your pity.'

Her fingers danced over the back of his hand, and he glanced up involuntarily. Alice looked agitated, as if she were about to burst into tears, but he did not have the emotional reserve to even think about comforting her right now.

With an air of desolate determination, she blinked back the tears. 'You do not want anything from anyone, Simon. You want to walk through this world without your troubles touching anyone else, but we do not live in isolation. Every time you push people away, every time you run away from your problems, you are hurting someone else besides yourself. I don't want you to suffer, Simon, but I also want you to see that when you suffer so do the rest of us, each and every person who cares about you.'

Ever since his father's death, he had not wanted to be a burden. He had seen how the bereavement had devastated his mother, how much more responsibility his brother had had to shoulder. He had wanted to make their lives easier, and here was Alice showing him he had done the complete opposite. He knew she was right, that whilst he had tried to push away his own pain, he had inadvertently made things harder for the very people he was trying to protect.

Quickly he thumped on the roof of the carriage again, waiting for it to slow before he threw open the door and jumped out. It had not completely stopped, and he startled a couple who were strolling arm-in-arm down the street, but he found he could not bring himself to care. He slammed the carriage door shut and without another word strode off, desperate to put as much distance between himself and Alice as possible.

His head was spinning, and he drew in deep ragged breaths, wondering how she had so thoroughly summed up everything he felt about his brother's death and the life he now lived.

Chapter Fifteen

Alice hated the silence in the house as she paced the floor of the drawing room. She had not meant to upset Simon, but once she had started trying to make him see what he was doing to himself she had been unable to stop.

Now it was eight hours later and Simon was still not home.

'You've probably made him run all the way back to Italy,' she muttered to herself.

Alice wished she had held her tongue. Simon was still grief-stricken from the death of his father and brother and reeling from the uncertainty of whether he suffered from the same condition that might strike him down at any moment. What she had said in the carriage was like sticking a knife in an already-wounded man. She was not proud of her actions, even though her words had been true.

She groaned. It had come from a selfish place, a need to lash out, as she had realised that Simon was never going to see her as anything more than a burden. Perhaps one he could develop a friendship with, but a burden all the same. When he had been quietly supportive in the orphanage, she had understood how much she yearned for a deeper relationship with this man. As much as she could tell herself she wished to safeguard her independence and protect herself from him hurting her by disappearing again, deep down she knew she wanted more.

'You are a fool,' she chided herself. Her outburst had only served to push him away and hurt him.

There was a noise from outside, and Alice stopped her pacing immediately. She had sent the servants to bed long ago, resolving to wait up herself to see if Simon returned. It was past two o'clock in the morning, and she had almost given up hope.

Alice rushed to the front door and opened it, jumping back as Simon half stumbled, half fell inside. He twisted as he fell and landed on his bottom, looking up at her and giving her a lopsided smile.

For a moment Alice didn't move, too stunned to do anything more than stare.

'Good evening, my beautiful wife,' Simon said, slurring his words.

'You're drunk.'

'I may have had one or two little glasses of whisky.' He tried to stand, but his feet got tangled, and he ended up where he had started on the floor.

'I have been so worried about you.' She took a deep breath, knowing she would have to apologise again in the morning when he was sober, but needing to get the words out now as well. 'I'm so sorry for what I said, Simon. It was unforgiveable.'

He tried to stand again, and this time managed to get to his feet, stumbling slightly as he moved. Alice reached out and steadied him, and he wrapped an arm around her shoulder.

'You smell nice,' he said, burying his face in her hair and inhaling deeply. 'You always smell nice.'

'I think we had better get you to bed,' she said as he reached up and plucked a pin out of her hair.

'You have such beautiful hair.' With clumsy fingers he pulled out a couple more pins, allowing the soft waves to cascade over her shoulders. 'You should wear it loose all the time. You look like a goddess.'

'You are very effusive when you are drunk.'

He grinned at her. 'Truthful. I'm truthful when I'm drunk.'

'Do you think you can manage the stairs?'

'Of course,' he said, almost tripping over his own feet and looking up at her guiltily. 'Perhaps with your help.'

Slowly they climbed the stairs, pausing halfway up for Simon to rest his head on her shoulder and declare she had the prettiest shoulders in the world.

Once upstairs they started along the hallway, passing the door to the master bedroom that was still Alice's. Simon reached out for the door-handle and opened it, pulling her in that direction.

'You don't sleep here,' she said, trying to pull him back into the hall, but her small stature put her at a disadvantage.

'We should sleep together,' he murmured. 'We are married. There is nothing wrong with it.'

'Do not jest, Simon.'

'I am completely serious,' he slurred, looking at her intently. 'What man wouldn't want to fall asleep with you in his arms?'

He had pulled her farther into the room now, and Alice looked back dubiously at the door.

'You can sleep here tonight. I will take your bedroom.'

'Stay with me, Miss James.'

'Alice,' she corrected him.

She stumbled back and sat down on the edge of the bed, almost sliding off onto the floor. Twice he reached down to try to pull his boots off, and twice he missed.

'Let me,' she said, placing a hand on his chest to stop him from bending down again. He caught hold of her wrist, his fingers caressing the delicate skin. For a moment she did not move, allowing herself to enjoy the caress. These last few days she had found thoughts of her husband touching her had crept into her mind unbidden far more than she would like to admit. It was typical that it took far too many glasses of whisky for her fantasy to become reality.

Brusquely she shrugged him off and bent down to pull off his boots.

'Thank you,' he murmured, lying back on the bed.

'No, no, no,' Alice said quickly, knowing if he fell asleep like this he would be uncomfortable and his clothes almost certainly ruined. 'We need to get you out of your jacket and cravat at the very least.'

'You want to see me naked, Alice,' he murmured, a smile on his face but his eyes closed.

She remained silent, putting her energy into helping him sit back up and then manoeuvring the jacket from his shoulders. His movements were uncoordinated, and it took far longer than it should, but eventually he was just in his shirt and trousers.

'Let's get you into bed,' she said, figuring he could sleep comfortably enough in the remaining clothes.

'I'm not undressed,' he murmured, and as she watched, he pulled his shirt over his head revealing the toned torso underneath. Although she had only ever seen him clothed, Alice knew he had a lean, muscled physique. Even through the layers of his shirt and jacket, the few times they had danced she had been able to feel the power he held in his body. Now, though, with his upper body bared in moonlight, she paused, her eyes raking over his half-naked form.

Alice felt something stir inside her, and she had to resist the urge to reach out and trail her fingers across his skin. In the state he was in, he would invite her in, forgetting about all the reasons he did not want to be intimate with her, but she would not do that to him, no matter how much she craved his touch.

'Let's get you into bed,' she said again, adopting her best schoolmistress voice and trying to pretend she was completely unaffected by him.

Somehow she managed to get him standing so she could pull back the sheets and then help him climb into bed. As she leaned over to ensure the pillows were comfortable under his head, his arm reach out and caught her around the waist.

'Don't leave me, Alice,' he said, his touch gentle but firm.

'I'll just be along the hall.'

'Stay with me tonight. You are my wife.'

'In name only,' she said, regretting the sharpness of her words immediately, but thankfully Simon did not seem to notice.

'There's space for you right here,' he said, and with a firm pull he tumbled her into bed beside him.

Alice let out a low cry of surprise and was about to sit up when Simon rolled over and flung his arm across her, pinning her in place. His face nuzzled into her neck, his lips brushing against her skin.

'Have I told you that you smell delicious?' he mumbled.

'You did mention it on the stairs.'

He murmured something incomprehensible, and then with his lips against her skin and his arm thrown possessively over her body, his breathing deepened.

'Simon,' Alice whispered, wriggling from side to side, unable to believe he had fallen asleep so quickly.

There was no response. She stilled, considering her predicament. The right thing to do would be to slip out from under his arm and leave him to sleep alone. She could spend the night in his bed; his room was comfortable and his bed made up and inviting. Yet something made her want to stay. Alice knew Simon was only being affectionate because he was in his cups. Tomorrow in the cold light of day, he would probably regret his actions, but tonight he had wanted her. This past year she had craved affection, craved the touch of another person, especially whilst she was in London. At least in Northumberland she received the occasional embrace from her sister-in-law or nieces, but here she was the lady of the house and so far above everyone else in social status there was no contact whatsoever.

Alice closed her eyes for a moment and wondered if she were being completely foolish, but it was merely a cuddle, one warm body pressed against another, nothing more. Tomorrow she could tell Simon she had been trapped by his arm over her waist, and it wouldn't be entirely untrue.

Deciding she would allow herself to have this one chaste night with her husband in their marital bed, Alice closed her eyes and tried to quieten her racing thoughts.

In all his thirty-three years, Simon had only been blindingly drunk a handful of times, normally after celebrations where drink after drink had been on offer and his spirits high. He thought back to the night after his graduation, surrounded by friends, toasting the end of their time at university. The memory gave him a momentary warm feeling, and he luxuriated in it for a few seconds before returning to the matter in hand.

'You're not a young pup anymore,' he muttered to himself. Ten years ago he could have drunk twice as much and not felt the room tilt around him the next day, but now his body was protesting, and he would probably pay for his excesses the entire day, or at the very least until he could get a strong cup of coffee inside him.

As he lay in bed, eyes firmly closed to guard against the room spinning, he realised he was not alone. There was a warm body in the bed next to him, soft and smooth, and he was pressed at least partially against her.

His eyes shot open, and he took in the red hair spread across the pillow and the peaceful face of his wife as she slept. She looked contented, happy even, and as he watched, she burrowed farther down into the pillow, her body shifting and pressing against him.

For a moment Simon was too shocked to move. She was in a sensible cotton nightgown with a dressing gown overtop, but at some point in the night the material had ridden up to reveal her legs and, above them, the hint of her buttocks. Up higher his hand rested across her waist, fingers splayed, the tips brushing against her breast.

Simon felt a surge of desire almost overwhelm him. He had always found his wife attractive, but lying in bed next to her, her warm body pressed against his, was unbearable. He wanted to lower his lips to hers and kiss her until she woke, and then strip the sensible nightdress from her body and enjoy every inch of her.

A sensible man would move away, but Simon could not bring himself to roll over. With a great effort he thought back to the night before. Alice did not look like she had been ravaged, her nightclothes were not torn or discarded, and she slept peacefully beside him.

Slowly the events of the previous evening came back to him. He retraced his steps from his gentlemen's club where he had spent half the afternoon trying to drown out the echo of Alice's words with a bottle of whisky. Later he had moved on to less salubrious establishments and had continued drinking where no one knew him.

He remembered stumbling home and Alice waiting for him, the rest of the house in darkness, and finally he remembered her helping him upstairs to bed.

Gently he pressed a kiss against the back of her head. She couldn't know how much he desired her, how every day he dreamed about scooping her into his arms and making her into his true wife. It was torture being so close and being unable to act on the desire that surged through him.

She was right in her assessment of him the day before, although her delivery of the stinging truths had left a lot to be desired. He wouldn't allow them to become close for two reasons. The first was as he had told her when he'd returned: he did not know when he might suddenly die, killed by the same affliction that had suddenly taken his father and his brother. He did not want to build a relationship with Alice only to pull it all away from her when his inevitable death came.

The second reason was something he thought had remained hidden deep inside, this feeling that he had stepped into Robert's life. He had the title, the seat in Parliament, the estate and all the properties, the responsibility of being the earl. All the things Robert had relished and enjoyed. It would be too much if Simon had a happy marriage and children too, those things that his brother had cherished the most.

'Not so hidden,' he murmured quietly. It would seem his mother had guessed what stopped him from settling down as an earl was expected to, what drove him away from a conventional marriage to live a life of loneliness.

He wished it wasn't the case, and he knew Robert would never begrudge him happiness, but he couldn't help feeling as though he had stolen his brother's life.

Next to him Alice shifted and pressed herself even closer against him, giving a little sigh of contentment. He knew she wanted more from their marriage, that despite having built a life for herself here with her charities and position in society, she craved human touch and affection. He had seen the way she glanced at him, the desire in her eyes, and part of him responded in the same way.

With his free hand he reached out and gently stroked her hair, allowing himself to imagine for a moment a life where he gave in to his desire. Long mornings spent in bed together, snatched kisses in public, walking hand in hand through Hyde Park. Skipping dinner in favour of returning to the bedroom and trying to quench the insatiable desire they felt.

It was a tempting picture, and with her warm body pressed against him he almost gave in, but nothing had changed, not really. Alice might know of the pain and turmoil that raged inside him, but that did not lessen it.

She let out a soft sigh and then wriggled a little, and as he watched, her eyelids flickered open. She gave him a sleepy smile, not really registering she was pressed against her husband in bed, but after a few seconds her eyes widened, and she scrabbled to sit up, pulling the bedcovers around her.

He hair was loosed down her back, and he vaguely remembered leaning in and plucking some of the pins out the night before, yet he certainly wouldn't have had the dexterity to remove them all. That meant she had taken some out herself. Equally, even if he had been the one to pull her into bed, she would not have remained trapped indefinitely. At some point she had decided to stay, decided to spend the night with her husband, removed the rest of the pins from her hair and fallen asleep in his arms.

'Good morning,' he said, speaking softly, aware that soon his head would begin pounding from the aftereffects of the alcohol.

'Good morning,' Alice said eventually.

'Thank you for helping me to bed last night.'

She inclined her head, unable to meet his eye for a second. 'How do you feel?'

'Like I drank far too much whisky yesterday,' he said with a half-smile. 'Unsurprisingly.'

She looked at him, biting her lip and screwing up the bed-sheets in her hands.

'I'm so sorry,' she blurted out, a look of anguish on her face. 'What I said to you yesterday was unforgiveable. I should have kept my thoughts to myself. It is none of my business why you do not wish to have a conventional wife or a family. It should be enough that you tell me that you don't.'

'Nonsense,' he said softly. 'The way we entered into this marriage might have been unorthodox, but I cannot continue pretending I do not have a wife.' He reached out and placed his hand next to hers so their fingers were touching. 'If anyone has the right to talk to me of these things it is you.'

'I went about it the wrong way.'

'That I will not deny,' he said, softening the reproof with a smile, 'but I do not believe your intention was malicious. Indeed, I think it came from a place of affection, which is remarkable, given how I have held you at arm's-length since I returned.' He looked down now to where their arms touched and wished he could reach out and take her hand in his own, but despite the desire he felt, despite the affection and respect, he still could not rid himself of the belief that he did not deserve the happiness that such a union would bring.

Alice looked at him sadly. 'You do deserve happiness, Simon. I know it doesn't mean much coming from me, a near stranger, but I have listened to what your family have said about you this past year. I have heard of your devotion to your nieces and how you coaxed Sylvia from a very dark place after her father died. I have heard how you supported Maria and ensured she didn't have to think of the practicalities when she was left widowed with three young children.' She paused, looking at him almost pleadingly before pressing on. 'Then, there are your actions when it comes to me. We were both foolish at the Midsummer's Eve ball, but you would not have suffered the consequences, especially with your plans already made to leave England. Yet despite having an easy way out, you did not hesitate to upend your decision to ensure I was protected. You gave me your name and a life of comfort and opportunity. Do you know how few men would do that for a woman they barely knew?' She shook her head, not waiting for an answer. 'You swooped in and rescued me, Simon, from a life of shame and scandal, when my best hope was that a man I hated would consent to marry me. How could I not fall a little in love with you?'

This made him look up sharply, and Alice held up a placating hand.

'Do not fear, I do not deny over the past year I have dreamed of you returning from Italy, telling me you could not bear to be away from me, but since your return you have made it clear there will be no intimacy between us. We shall live our lives like two spinster siblings, chaste with a moderate affection. I have heard what you have told me over and over again.'

'I have been a little blunt, haven't I?'

She smiled at that. 'Perhaps I have needed the bluntness.'

'I cannot change how I feel about Robert,' Simon said.

'I know.' Her expression was sad but not surprised. He

felt a sudden surge of anger, directed towards himself. Here he was in bed beside a beautiful woman, a woman he had could not stop thinking about kissing, and all he had done these past few days was make her miserable.

'If you think you could allow yourself to be happy with someone else, I would understand,' Alice said softly. 'I know I was not the woman you would have chosen for a wife, and if you wish to take a mistress I will not object.'

'You doubt my attraction to you,' he said, his voice low.

She looked at him in surprise, and Simon felt something shift inside him. If he were to reach out and pull her to him, there would be nothing illicit about it. They were husband and wife, and Alice could not hide the fact that she was attracted to him. The only person standing in the way of the desire they both felt was him.

He felt the familiar guilt he was hit with every time he contemplated something enjoyable, but this time he pushed it down. He wasn't proposing he live a normal, full life with Alice, not like Robert had experienced with his wife, just that he and Alice enjoy the occasional bit of affection.

'Do not doubt my attraction to you.'

He looped a firm arm around her waist, feeling the warmth of her skin through the layers of her nightclothes. Alice's body was stiff for a second, and then she let out a little moan and relaxed against him.

Before he could talk himself out of it, Simon kissed her, a kiss filled with all the pent-up desire and passion that had been surging through him since his return. He gripped Alice gently, and manoeuvred her into his lap, loving the way she felt as she wrapped her legs around him.

Her lips were soft and sweet, and he kissed her deeply, as if searching for something he had lost long ago.

'You do not know how many times I have dreamed of doing this,' he said, pulling away for a second to kiss the soft skin of her neck. She shivered at the touch of his lips on her skin and pulled him closer.

He wanted to take his time and enjoy her, to show her pleasure in so many different ways, yet he also felt a frantic need to do this quickly in case the rational part of his mind took over at any point.

'Simon,' she whispered, invoking his name like he was a demigod. He kissed her again, long and deep, his hands caressing her back.

'This needs to come off,' he said, gripping the thin material of her nightgown. Without protest Alice slipped an arm from her dressing gown and then wriggled out of it completely. Now there was only her nightgown separating their bodies. She shifted on his lap, brushing against his hardness as she lifted herself up and he caught hold of the hem of the garment. Before either of them could come to their senses, he lifted the nightdress over her head and threw it on the floor beside the bed.

For a moment they both stilled, Alice with a look of apprehension in her eyes that reminded him that she might be a married woman in the eyes of society, but that she was still very much an innocent.

Slowly he lifted a hand and trailed a finger from the notch between her collarbones down between her breasts.

'You are beautiful, Alice,' he said.

Her instinct was to cover herself with her arms, wrapping them round her body, and he cursed himself for his part in making her feel unattractive or unwanted. Nothing could be further from the truth. Right now he could not understand how he had allowed himself to be apart from her for so long.

Gently he pressed her arms back to her sides and trailed his fingers over her chest again, loving the way her breath caught in her throat as his hand brushed against her breast.

'You're teasing me,' she said, a note of accusation in her voice.

'I am building the anticipation,' he said, smiling.

'Another way of saying *teasing*.'

'Would you prefer it if I just dove straight in?' he said, leaning forward and taking her nipple into his mouth, making her gasp with pleasure and shock.

Alice let out an incomprehensible moan, and he felt her body stiffen underneath him before slowly she relaxed, letting her head drop to his shoulder.

He pulled away, kissing her again and resuming his slow, gentle caress of her body.

'You have the softest skin I have ever felt,' he murmured, circling from the top of her chest around her breasts and back again. He repeated the movement again and again until he could feel the anticipation. Carefully he flipped her over so she was lying on her back on the bed, and he held himself above her, lowering his lips to meet her body. He took his time, trailing kisses across her breasts and over her abdomen as she writhed underneath him, the heat building between them.

He stroked her thighs as he kissed her, slowly coaxing her to relax.

'What are you doing to me?' Alice whispered as he

moved even lower, feeling her tense and push forwards involuntarily as he kissed her thighs.

He didn't answer her; instead, he trailed kisses up her thighs and then without any further warning kissed her in her most private place. Alice let out a shocked yelp, her hands scrabbling at his head.

'What are you doing, Simon?'

'I would have thought that obvious.'

'I did not know...'

'That you could be kissed there? No, I suppose you would not. Can I show you how good it can feel?'

With only a moment's hesitation she nodded, and Simon lowered his head, loving the way her hips came up to meet him. She was responsive to his every touch, and it wasn't long before he saw she was gripping the bed-sheets either side of her with her hands as if clinging on for her life.

Alice's breathing quickened and then she clamped her legs together, letting out a deep moan.

Simon raised himself up and pushed his trousers down, holding himself above Alice before he pressed against her. Slowly he entered her, feeling her body rise to meet his, and then he was fully buried inside her.

He held in place for a moment, his eyes meeting Alice's, and then he withdrew, knowing he had to go slow for her, but it took every ounce of his self-control. Gradually he increased the speed of his thrusts, lowering his lips to brush against hers and loving the way her fingers raked down his back. Beneath him he felt her tense and tighten and then let out a moan of pleasure as she climaxed, the look of ecstasy on her face and the tightness that engulfed him enough to push him over the edge.

Quickly he withdrew and finished on the sheets, even in the moment of passion in control enough to know he could not risk her getting pregnant.

He moved off Alice, coming in behind her and pulling her into an embrace. He couldn't see her face, but her body did not feel fully relaxed, and he wondered if she was already regretting their moment of intimacy.

Eventually she turned to face him, her eyes searching his for something he worried she would not find. Without a word she turned back, tucking her body close to his, and pulling his arm around her. She laced her fingers through his, and he held her tight.

Chapter Sixteen

Alice had been surprised that she'd slept again, a deep slumber that had not been disturbed by Simon rising at some point, and she was disappointed to find herself alone when she woke. She wondered if their intimacy had been enough to drive him away completely, out of London, perhaps even out of the country, she and glanced over at the little writing desk in the corner to see if she could spot a hastily scrawled note.

There was no note, and a few minutes later the door to the bedroom opened and Simon walked in carrying a tray of coffee and a couple of newspapers under one arm.

'You're awake,' he said with a smile.

Alice would never admit how much it pleased her that he was still here.

'What time is it?'

'After ten. I checked with Miss Stick, and she tells you have no engagements until your dinner party with the Hampshires this evening.'

Simon was fully dressed, and he showed no outward signs of his heavy night of drinking, although once he had poured the coffee he took a tentative sip before deciding to take a full cup.

'I brought you the papers,' he said. 'We are mentioned in the gossip rag.'

Alice's eyes widened. She had been featured many times before, but in recent months only small comments about what dress she had decided to wear or who she had danced with, nothing more interesting than that, but from Simon's tone she could tell today was different.

'Third paragraph down.'

She let her eyes drift over the first two paragraphs quickly, then read aloud.

'Lord Westcroft made a return to London this week, much to the surprise of society and to his wife. Lady Westcroft was left looking shocked at the Livingstones' ball when her husband waltzed in and swept her onto the dance floor. One has to wonder if the errant Lord Westcroft thinks of his wife at all—at the very least he does not seem to include her in his travel plans.'

She eyed Simon carefully. It was more a criticism of him than her, and not entirely untrue even if it was an unflattering view of the situation.

'They are not wrong. I did just waltz into the Livingstones' ball and surprise you. It must have been unsettling for you.'

Alice blinked, pulling the sheets up a little farther to cover her nakedness. *This* was what they were going to talk about now? After everything that had happened yesterday and this morning?

Pointedly she set the paper on the bed and looked at him expectantly. Simon sipped his coffee, pretending he didn't feel her eyes on him and then sighed.

'You wish to talk about this morning.'

'We *need* to talk about this morning.'

Simon cleared his throat and then for a long time did not say anything at all.

'Simon,' she prompted him eventually.

'I spent a long time thinking yesterday after our…discussion,' he said slowly. 'And I have to acknowledge that on many points you are correct. I do feel guilty about living the life my brother should have, and I shy away from following the same path as him in the parts that are not essential. I had vowed never to marry, but when we met we set into motion a chain of events that led us to the altar. It did not matter too much, for the marriage was not to be like Robert's, not a love match.'

Alice hugged her knees to her, wondering if she was strong enough to hear what he had to say.

'I am not trying to punish myself, or you, in any way, Alice. I know my father's and brother's deaths were not my fault, yet I cannot help the guilt I feel that I am still here whilst they are not.'

'I understand that can be quite common amongst people where one person survives a tragedy when others close to them have died.'

'It was hard hearing that everyone close to me had worked out what was going on in far better detail than I had,' he said quietly. 'I think that is why I was so upset yesterday. I thought what I was doing wasn't affecting other people too much, but I was wrong.'

Alice felt like they were reaching some ultimatum, some declaration of how he truly felt and what he wanted from his future.

'I cannot deny the desire I feel for you, Alice. I think that was obvious this morning.'

Alice felt her heart sink. As unlikely as it was, she

had hoped for a declaration of love, a suggestion that they make their marriage a conventional one where they enjoyed each other's company to the fullest. She chided herself for getting her hopes up once again. She was too naïve in the ways of the heart, and she needed to start protecting herself better.

'What do you propose we do?'

Simon sighed. 'I am not sure we can live in the same house and not end up in a similar situation as we did this morning.'

'You wish to leave?'

'No,' he said quickly. 'I do not. Yet I cannot offer you what a husband should in these circumstances.'

Love. He could not offer her love. Even if he stayed, he would be holding part of himself back, making sure he held her at arm's-length to deny himself the happiness they could have.

She pressed her lips together, wishing she could find the words to tell him how she felt, how it hurt to have him stand here and tell her that, despite the fact they were married and they both desired one another and cared for one another, he could not allow himself to build a mutually loving relationship with her. She should reject his unspoken proposal, but she thought of how her body craved his touch, of how happy she had felt in the moments of their lovemaking.

She had entered into this marriage after Simon had told her he would be dead within the year and she would be free to marry a man of her choosing, a man who could love her. That wasn't going to happen now, and if the doctors had got things wrong it might never be the case. She had forty years of marriage stretching out in front of her with a man who could not love her, and she could not seek that comfort elsewhere. At least if they had a physical relationship, she could slake some of her craving for intimacy with Simon's touch.

'We continue as before,' Alice said, decisively. 'Companionship, friendship, they are our focus, but with the added benefit of sharing a bed whenever we both choose.'

'You would be comfortable with that arrangement?'

'We are married. There is nothing wrong with it,' Alice said firmly. 'We are both adults with desires and needs, and I think it safe to say we both find the other attractive.'

'Indeed,' Simon murmured.

'Then, it is settled. I know not to expect a declaration of love from you, and you are happy to give me the freedom I have enjoyed for the last year to make my own decisions.'

'I feel as though we should shake hands,' Simon murmured.

'There is no need for that,' Alice said quickly. Despite the agreement she had just proposed, she felt as though she needed some privacy to pull apart what she had just agreed to. It was all very well telling Simon that she would not develop feelings for him, but if she were honest she was well past halfway to loving him already, flaws and all. 'Now, I need to wash and dress. Could you ring the bell for my lady's maid?'

Chapter Seventeen

It was growing dark when they stepped out of the carriage in front of Mr and Mrs Hampshire's house, Simon offering her his arm. Alice felt the spark that flowed between them as her body brushed against his and quickly tried to quell it. She'd spent the day trying to persuade herself she hadn't made the biggest mistake of her life, and now she was beginning to believe their decision might actually be for the best.

Simon had been attentive on the carriage ride to the Hampshires after a note had arrived that afternoon, inviting him to join the dinner party, and Alice was enjoying his company. For the past year she had always had to arrive alone at events like this, and it was pleasant to walk in on her husband's arm.

It was not to be a large affair, and in the drawing room Mrs Livingstone ensured they both had a drink before dinner. There were five other guests, all people Alice knew fairly well, including Lady Kennington and her husband, and a wealthy couple in their forties who had moved to London from Bath a year earlier with their eighteen-year-old daughter, Emma.

'Emma is going to play for us,' Mrs Hampshire announced, showing Alice and Simon to a small sofa to listen.

Emma Finn was a talented pianist, and she played a few pieces perfectly with no music in front of her. Alice found herself relaxing, sinking back into the cushions of the sofa and into her husband. Simon had an arm behind her, resting on the back of the sofa, but after a minute she felt his fingers gently caressing her neck. At first it was an occasional touch, a gentle stroke as she shifted in her seat, but as the other guests became focussed on Emma at the piano, his touch became bolder, and he began tracing circles on the soft skin of her neck, just below her ear.

Alice felt as though every inch of her skin was taut with anticipation, and as his touch intensified she could not follow the music. All she could think about was Simon's fingers dancing over her skin, imagining him dipping lower.

All too soon the music finished, and Alice had to shake herself from the daze she found herself in.

They were not seated next to each other at dinner, as was the custom, but Alice found it hard to concentrate on anything but the fleeting glances she shared with Simon across the table. He was directly opposite her, and she had to keep reminding herself it was not polite to just stare longingly at her husband all evening. She'd had her reservations about their new arrangement, but trying to bury her attraction for him would have been futile.

'What did you think of St Benedict's?' Lady Kennington asked her as the main courses were brought out. Alice started to answer and then felt Simon's foot tap her own under the table. She forced herself to concentrate.

'It is well-run. I liked Mrs Phillips, the matron. She seemed sensible and kind, and the children were polite and clean. But the orphanage was in a dire state, and I think they have very little funds available to them.'

'It is a good cause, is it not?'

'Very good. I have asked Mrs Phillips to put some thought into what she feels would be helpful from the London Ladies' Benevolent Society.' Alice was about to say more, but Simon was gently caressing her leg with his foot, and she was finding it difficult to concentrate.

'Are you feeling well, Lady Westcroft?' Lady Kennington enquired.

'A little warm, that is all,' Alice said quickly, resolutely not looking at her husband.

The rest of dinner followed in much the same way, with Alice trying to concentrate on the conversation around the table but being unable to think of anything but the man sitting across from her, imagining he was pushing her back onto the bed and making love to her. It felt like the meal went on for ages, and Alice was pleased when it was time to move back to the drawing room, with the men moving to another downstairs room for drinks and cards. After a minute of listening to Miss Finn on the piano, she quietly excused herself, muttering something about the ladies' retiring room. In truth she needed some time to herself.

There were candles lit in the hall, but it was dark compared to the drawing room, and as Alice made her way to the stairs she did not even think to look in the dark corners. She gasped as a figure stepped out from the shadows by the stairs, gripping her by the wrists and pressing her against the wall.

'Simon,' she whispered, her heart pounding.

'You mean to torture me,' he murmured in her ear.

'Torture you?'

'You look ravishing tonight, and all I can think about…' He kissed her neck, making Alice gasp. 'You bring me somewhere I cannot touch you. I cannot even sit next to you.'

His lips were hot on her skin, and she felt a shudder of pleasure run through her body. It didn't matter that they were standing in someone else's hall, it didn't matter that at any moment someone could come out of one of the rooms and see them: all she could think of was Simon and where he would kiss her next.

'All I could think about all dinner was stripping you naked and lying you down on the dinner table.'

Alice gasped, picturing the scene. 'Not with everyone watching.'

'They would scatter soon enough. Good Lord, how do you always smell so good?'

'Simon, not the hair,' she said as he reached for one of her pins. 'I have to go back in there.'

He ran a hand down her side, over her waist and around to her buttocks and then lowered his lips to the bare skin of her upper chest. For a moment she forgot where they were and let out a moan that seemed to echo around the grand entrance hall.

'We need to get home,' he said, lifting his lips for just a second. 'Or we will never be invited to a dinner party with the Hampshires again.'

Before she could answer, he kissed her deeply, one hand still pinning both of hers above her head. He was gentle, but there was no denying he was much stronger than her, and she loved the way he held her against the wall, the cool wallpaper against her back.

'I will make my excuses,' Alice said, allowing herself one last kiss before she pulled away.

She paused before reentering the drawing room, aware that her cheeks were flushed and her clothes probably a little dishevelled. Thankfully, Miss Finn was still playing another masterful piece on the piano, and Alice was able to sidle up to their hostess and speak to her discreetly.

'I am awfully sorry, Mrs Hampshire, but I feel a little unwell. I think it best I return home.'

Mrs Hampshire looked at Alice with concern. 'You do look pink, my dear. Yes, go home at once, and get that housekeeper of yours to make a tincture.'

'Thank you for a wonderful evening.'

'Do you wish for me to send someone to accompany you home?'

'No, I am sure Lord Westcroft will be happy to come with me.'

Mrs Livingstone smiled indulgently. 'Of course. I forget you are still like newly-weds. Come, let us go fetch your husband.'

It felt like an eternity before they had bid everyone goodnight and the carriage had been brought round to the front door, but after a final wave to their hosts, Alice and Simon were alone.

Before he stepped up into the carriage Simon had a quiet word with the driver and then they were underway, travelling at a good pace through the quiet streets.

'I have instructed Drummond to keep circling around London until I alert him we wish to go home,' Simon said.

Alice's eyes widened, but before she could say anything Simon gently pulled her onto his lap.

'Where were we?'

'I think you were kissing me here,' Alice said, indicating the spot on her neck just below her ear. When he kissed her there it sent little jolts of pleasure all the way through her body.

'And I think my hands were here,' Simon said, slipping his hands underneath her and giving her buttocks a squeeze as he gave her a mock lascivious raise of his eyebrows.

She leaned forward and kissed him, losing herself in desire. It felt as though she were falling head first into paradise, and she didn't want to ever stop.

They kissed for a long time, then Alice shifted, snaking her hands down in between them to push at the waistband of his trousers. He gathered her skirts up, and soon there was nothing between them. Alice positioned herself carefully, feeling the wonderful fullness as he entered her, and then she was lost as their bodies came together again and again until she cried out, and wave after wave of pleasure flooded through her.

Simon lifted her off him quickly before he, too, let out a low groan of pleasure.

For a long while neither of them spoke.

'You make me reckless,' she said eventually.

'I think it is the other way round,' Simon murmured. 'Take the Midsummer's Eve ball. I have spent the last ten years carefully avoiding any scandal that might tie me to a respectable young woman. A few hours in your company and I'm suggesting midnight dashes through the gardens and kissing you far too close to the house.'

Alice closed her eyes and remembered that night. It was the night that had changed the course of her life. When things got difficult, all she had to do was remind herself that she could have been unlucky enough to be married to vile Cousin Cecil. This arrangement with her husband was unusual and certainly not what she would have chosen for herself when she was a young girl dreaming of her perfect man, but it was better than a lifetime of repression as Cecil's wife.

'You look serious,' Simon said, leaning forward and stroking her forehead between her eyebrows. 'What are you thinking about?'

'How the course of my life changed completely in the space of one evening.'

'It did, didn't it?'

'I suppose none of us can know what life has in store for us.'

They lapsed into silence, and Alice wondered if Simon was thinking about all the uncertainty in his life. She wanted him to see that he was not the only one who did not know what would happen. He might have the same condition that had killed his father and his brother, but equally he might not. Even if he did, it might not strike him down for decades. There were so many dangers in life; people were caught up in unpredictable scenarios all the time. Simon had reason to be more worried than most, but it did not mean she agreed with his approach to hold everyone he loved at a distance in hope that they would not suffer as much when he did die.

She looked at him and bit her lip. Despite her stern words to herself and her best efforts, she knew she was falling in love with Simon. She felt more than desire, more than physical attraction. She wanted more than he could offer her. It was a sure way to get hurt, but it wasn't something under her conscious control.

Chapter Eighteen

The next week passed in a blur with one day running into the next. They spent a large proportion of their time in the bedroom. Simon could not keep his hands off Alice, wherever they were. He sought her out in the drawing room or at the breakfast table, and she was always as happy to kiss him as he was her. As the week progressed they stopped pretending to even try to do anything else and gave in to the pleasure of acting like newly-weds.

'I need to get dressed today,' Alice said on the morning of their eighth day together. 'Mrs Phillips from St Benedict's Orphanage sent a note yesterday saying she had spent some time thinking about what would be really helpful to the orphanage. She invited me to meet with her for an hour or so this afternoon.'

Simon frowned. 'I have an appointment with my solicitor that I cannot miss this afternoon, to go over a few land issues that have come up during my absence.'

Alice trailed her fingers over Simon's naked shoulder and then lowered her lips to kiss it absently. 'It does not matter. If Drummond takes me in the carriage I will be perfectly safe. I will ensure he drops me off right outside.'

'One of those street children had a knife.'

'I think that is probably true of many people in our beautiful city.'

'None of them have threatened you.'

'That is true.' She considered for a moment. 'How about I take Frank Smith with me? He is young and strong, and his background means he is used to the tricks and schemes of the street urchins.'

'I would prefer to come with you myself, but I suppose that is a fair compromise. With Drummond and Smith, you can hardly get into too much trouble.'

'I promise to go straight there and straight back,' Alice said, smiling. 'No matter how many pallid pickpockets I run into and feel sorry for.'

'No pallid pickpockets, and no diversions.'

She leaned in and kissed him, feeling a thrill of anticipation for the day ahead.

'I shall be back home around five, then we have dinner with the Dunns later.'

'Then, I have plenty of time to persuade you we should send our apologies and have dinner at home.'

'You would choose to stay home every night of the week,' Alice said as Simon's arm snaked around her waist.

'Tell me you'd rather spend the evening with dull old Mr Dunn droning on about the time he almost joined the navy or Mrs Dunn trying to pretend she has early knowledge of the fashions coming out of Paris, and I will admit defeat now.'

'You are being uncharitable,' she said as he pulled her down for a kiss.

'You have a choice. Either we can spend the evening

with the Dunns or we can cancel and I will count how many times I can kiss your body before you beg me for something more.'

'You are not playing fair, Simon,' Alice said, mock reproval in her voice. 'You get to persuade me with kisses. Mr Dunn only gets his tales about the navy.'

He kissed her again.

'When the stakes are this high, it is best not to play fair.'

Reluctantly Alice stood and moved over to the mirror. She needed to go to the modiste today too, after postponing her appointment for a fitting of a new dress earlier in the week.

'I will consider your proposition, but now I am going to have to insist you leave. I have neglected my errands for too long.'

Simon stood, picking up his crumpled shirt from the chair where she had thrown it the previous evening, and pulling it over his head.

'You wound me with the ease with which I am cast out, discarded,' Simon said, his hand on the door-handle. 'Until tonight, my sweet.'

The rest of Alice's day was productive, but she had the feeling of wanting to rush through everything so she could return home to Simon. It was a ridiculous idea, for he wouldn't be home from the solicitor until after she had finished at the orphanage.

At three o'clock she instructed Drummond to take her to St Benedict's. Frank Smith sat on the narrow bench at the front of the carriage beside Drummond, primed to step in if there were any trouble.

The journey through London was uneventful, and

before long the carriage stopped outside the orphanage. It was an overcast day, and the slums looked even less inviting with their narrow streets in shadow.

'I shall be about an hour. Keep vigilant,' Alice instructed Drummond and Smith before knocking on the door of the orphanage.

Mrs Phillips welcomed her in and showed her through to the small room at the back of the building that acted as the matron's bedroom and office. It was sparsely furnished, with bare floorboards and nothing on the walls. There was a single bed in the corner of the room and two straight-back chairs by a little table. At the foot of the bed was a small trunk, and on the back of the door a hook for a coat. Mrs Phillips might be matron of the establishment, but her accommodation wasn't much more comfortable than that of the children in her care.

Alice knew the woman's role carried huge responsibility but did not attract a large salary, especially in a small, poor establishment like St Benedict's. Mrs Phillips would eat the same food as the children and might even be restricted in when and why she could leave the premises.

One of the girls brought in a heavy teapot on a tray with two cups, and Mrs Phillips served Alice.

'Thank you for coming, Lady Westcroft. I have been thinking about what you suggested,' Mrs Phillips said as she handed a cup to Alice.

They talked for more than an hour, discussing all the issues Mrs Phillips had noted down, from small things like the purchase of more slate boards for the classroom to much larger concerns such as sanitation and access to clean water. By the end of their discussion, Alice felt exhausted but excited to share Mrs Phillips's ideas with the London Ladies' Benevolent Society.

At five o'clock, she bid Mrs Phillips farewell and stepped out into the warm late-afternoon air. Alice was preoccupied, wondering how best to present all the issues to the other ladies and she stepped out into the street without looking.

It was uncommon to see people on horseback in this part of the city. Most people travelled on foot, and those who had to pass through preferred the safety of a carriage. She looked up too late: the horse was almost upon her, and Alice saw the rider pull on the reins sharply, causing the horse to rear up in fright. Hooves thundered past her face, missing by mere inches as a firm hand on her shoulder pulled her backwards to safety.

The whole incident lasted less than a few seconds, but Alice felt as though she had been running for a whole hour. Her heart squeezed in her chest, and her breathing was ragged and uneven. The man on horseback called something incomprehensible and probably unkind and carried on along the street as if nothing had happened.

As she regained her composure Alice turned to the person who had pulled her back.

'Thank you—' she began, the words dying in her throat. Standing very close, a malicious glint in his eye, was the man who had watched them the time she and Simon had come to the orphanage.

'You're welcome, miss. Can't have a pretty lady like yourself trampled under a horse's hooves, brains splattered about the cobbles,' he said, his voice low so only she could hear.

Alice swallowed and glanced down, feeling a cold

chill spread through her as she caught the glint of metal in his hand. He was holding a small knife in the narrow space between their bodies, the tip pointed at her abdomen. The metal was dull and looked well-used, and Alice thought she saw a crust of blood around the hilt.

'Don't call out,' the man said calmly. 'Your best chance is if those two fools on top of the carriage do not come over to see what is happening.'

Glancing up, she saw Drummond's face. As yet he was not climbing down from the carriage, but he was looking over at her with an expression of puzzled concern on his face. Alice knew it would only be a matter of seconds until he was climbing down to investigate why she hadn't crossed the road and got into the safety of the carriage.

'Now, I did not have to save your life there, miss, but I am an upstanding citizen, and I think a good deed like that deserves a reward.'

Alice nodded, wishing she had brought her coin purse so she could have just handed it over without any delay.

'I do not carry money on my person,' she said truthfully. It was foolish to carry money in areas such as this where half the population were desperate enough to steal if the temptation were right.

'That is a shame, miss. I suppose we'll have to think of something else.' He looked her over, grunting as he saw she was not wearing a necklace or earrings. The only jewellery she had was the wedding band on her finger. 'You'd better start with that gold ring,' he said, motioning at it with his knife.

Alice looked down, reluctant to part with the ring Simon had given her on the day of their wedding. It was symbolic of so much, and she did not want to part with it, but she knew compliance was the best way to walk away unscathed from this situation.

She reached down with her right hand to try to pull the ring off, grimacing at the resistance. As she worked on pulling it over the knuckle, she saw Drummond and Smith finally realise there was something wrong. They moved fast for men trained as household servants, dashing across the road to come to her aid. The man who was stealing from her glanced up and saw them coming, reaching out to grab the ring from Alice. As he did so, Smith arrived and went to throw his whole body weight at the thief. The culprit ducked under Smith's arm and quickly struck out, clearing a path through the middle of them. To Alice's dismay he disappeared into the crowd within seconds.

'Thank you,' she said, turning to Drummond and Smith. They were both looking at her in horror. Slowly, not wanting to know what sight awaited her, she looked down. A bloom of blood was spreading across her pale blue dress, staining the material and seeping out around the blade of the knife that was still buried in her abdomen. 'There's a knife,' she said, feeling her whole body stagger to the left at the sight of the blood and the thought of the wound that must be underneath.

Instinctively her hand gripped the handle of the knife, thinking to pull it out, but Drummond reached out to stop her.

'Leave it,' he said forcefully. 'We need to get you back home and then a doctor can remove the knife. Do not even think about touching it.' Her abdomen was starting to throb and hurt, and she marvelled that she had not felt the knife slide into her flesh.

Drummond lowered his shoulder and half carried, half dragged Alice to the carriage. Carefully he helped her inside, instructing her to lie across the seats and avoid any unnecessary movement.

The journey back home seemed to take for ever, with Alice feeling every jolt of the carriage and every corner they rounded. Drummond was driving fast, aware Alice was inside the carriage bleeding, and no doubt eager to get her home before she lost so much blood she breathed her last breath. Frank sat opposite her, looking young and scared, his arm placed strategically to ensure she did not tumble from her seat.

As the carriage slowed, Alice saw Drummond jump down calling out as he did so, and the next thing she saw was Simon's anxious face.

'Alice, what happened?'

She tried to lift her head, but the world tilted and shifted under her, so instead she closed her eyes and let someone else tell him.

Outside she could hear Simon ordering someone to run for the doctor and also the barber-surgeon. Alice tried to protest: she had heard terrible stories about these barber-surgeons and the things they did in terms of professional interest. She did not want to endure an agonising procedure, her only comfort a little strong alcohol beforehand.

Tears began running down her cheeks as Simon carefully looked back into the carriage.

'Stay here with me, my love,' he said softly, reaching

out and taking her hand. Now half the front of her dress was bloodstained, and it hurt every time she moved.

Simon carefully climbed into the carriage and slipped his arms underneath her, lifting her ever so gently. He moved slowly, his eyes fixed on her face so he could see if there was any increase in pain as he carried her. The hardest part was getting out of the carriage, but once he extricated them, Simon could move more quickly. He carried her into the house and straight up the stairs to the bedroom they had shared this past week.

Miss Stick helped to position her in bed, pulling back the bed-sheets and then tucking them around Alice's legs, and then she hurried out to organise anything the doctor might need.

Simon stayed with her, kneeling by the side of the bed as if he were a child saying his prayers, his hand holding hers tight.

Alice closed her eyes, feeling suddenly weary despite the pain.

'Stay awake, my sweet,' Simon said softly but firmly. 'It is important you stay awake.'

With great effort she forced her eyes open. They felt like they had heavy weights attached to her eyelids, and all she wanted to do was surrender to the pull of sleep.

A few minutes later she heard the doctor arrive, and Simon quickly explained the situation. She had not met the man before, having been in good health since arriving in London, and was pleased to see a reassuring, sensible face looking down at her.

'We need to remove Lady Westcroft's clothing so I can see the wound fully before I attempt to take out the knife,' Dr Black said, motioning for Miss Stick to come forward from her position by the door. 'We need scissors, as sharp as possible, to cut away the material. I dare not try to lift her garments over her head.'

Miss Stick returned a few moments later with sharp scissors and leaned over Alice. Her normally composed demeanour had cracked, and Alice could see tears in the housekeeper's eyes.

'Let me, Miss Stick,' Simon said quietly, taking the scissors from the woman.

He worked slowly but steadily, instructing Miss Stick to hold the material of her dress taut as he cut it. The bodice part of her dress was thicker and Alice felt the scissors jolt and stop a few times, but after a minute the fabric was laid open to reveal her chemise and petticoats underneath.

Despite her predicament, Alice felt a little self-conscious. No doubt in the course of his job Dr Black was accustomed to seeing the naked form, but the only man who had ever seen her naked was her husband, and she suddenly had the urge to cover herself with her hands.

'Be still, Alice,' Simon murmured reassuringly as he gripped the hem of her chemise and began sliding the scissors along the material. 'There is only you and I and Miss Stick here with the doctor.'

Once Alice's chemise was cut, Miss Stick hurried forward and arranged a sheet over her chest to help preserve Alice's dignity, and then the doctor stepped forward to look at the wound.

The dagger was still embedded in her abdomen at the level of her navel, but far to the right in the space between the bottom of her ribs and the bones that marked the top of her pelvis. With every movement the wound stung and sent a jolt of pain through her body. The doctor took his time inspecting the wound and then moved away from the bed to talk to Simon.

'I wish to hear,' Alice called, surprised at how weak her voice sounded. The doctor looked over, a serious expression on his face, but Simon placed a hand on the man's elbow and guided him closer to the bed.

'It will be dangerous to remove the knife, but we must for the wound to begin to heal,' Dr Black said, his expression grave. 'I believe the blade has missed the major organs and vessels, but as we remove it we may reveal a bleed that has been plugged by the knife, or there could be damage to the bowel underneath.'

'Is there anything we can do to decrease the risk?' Simon asked, his face pale.

'You must stay completely still, Lady Westcroft. Even moving a fraction of an inch could be the difference between life and death.' The doctor looked between Simon and Alice. 'I will prepare the needle for stitching the wound after. It will be painful, but I have laudanum in my bag which should ease you.'

'I do not want laudanum,' Alice said, thinking back to when she had hit the tree as a girl on horseback and bruised her ribs. The doctor then had given her laudanum, and she had fought terrible hallucinations for days. The alternative was significant pain whilst her wound was stitched, but she would take that over the painkiller any day.

'Very well.'

The doctor moved away and spoke to Miss Stick in a low voice, instructing her on all the things he would need. Simon returned to Alice's side, crouching down by the bed and holding her hand.

'You are brave, my sweet,' he said, lowering his lips to her hand and kissing the skin.

'I do not think I have a choice,' Alice replied with a weak smile. 'It was that man, Simon, that horrible man we saw with the gang of pickpockets.'

'He targeted you on purpose?'

'I think he was waiting for me outside the orphanage. He held the knife to me, in between my body and his so Drummond and Smith could not see it, and he was demanding my valuables, but I did not take anything with me. He asked for my wedding ring, and I was going to give it to him, but Drummond grew suspicious as to why it was taking me so long to cross to the carriage, and he and Smith rushed over. He grabbed my ring.' Alice looked down at her fingers where the ring had been, tears pooling in her eyes. 'Then he pushed past me and ran away. He must have lashed out with the knife when he pushed past me.'

'Do not worry about any of that now,' Simon said, stroking her hair from her face. 'Let us focus on getting you better, and then we can worry about the scoundrel who did this to you.'

The doctor returned to the bedside, a small tray of items in his hand. Alice glanced down at it and then wished she hadn't. There was a long needle on it, thick thread trailing from behind, as well as a couple of small knives and a pair of scissors. Thankfully Miss Stick returned at the same time, and Alice forced herself to watch the housekeeper's preparations rather than the doctor's.

'Are you ready, Lady Westcroft?'

'I am,' Alice said, taking a deep breath and closing her eyes. She tried to think of all the things that made her happy. The dappled sun through the trees in the park, the sound of the sea crashing against the dunes in Bamburgh on stormy nights, the giggles of her nieces and, of course, Simon.

He held her hand firmly as the doctor anchored the skin around the knife and then in a smooth, slow motion pulled it out.

Alice let out a low, wounded cry and then against her better judgement looked down at the wound.

Fresh blood welled out of the gash in her side, and she felt the room spin around her. Darkness pulled at the periphery of her vision, and she gripped Simon's hand harder, but she was unable to cling to consciousness.

Alice woke to pain much worse than what she had already endured. The doctor was leaned over her, piercing her skin with the needle. That hurt in itself, but even worse was the pain as he pulled the thread through after. She felt every inch slide through the fresh hole in her skin.

'You must stay still, Lady Westcroft,' Dr Black said, his voice authoritative. He turned to Simon and instructed, 'Keep her still.'

Alice felt Simon stand and lean over her, kissing her on her forehead. 'Stay still, Alice. You are doing very well. This will not take long, and then you can rest.'

She clenched her teeth and endured the pain, tears rolling down her cheeks, and it was a great relief when the doctor stepped away.

'She must rest. The knife was small, but unfortunately it was not clean. I worry the wound might fester.' The doctor glanced over at her, pity in his eyes. 'If she does develop a fever, then send for me. Otherwise I will call tomorrow to check on the wound.'

'Thank you, Dr Black,' Simon said, shaking the man's hand.

Simon approached the bed with trepidation. Miss Stick had tried to shoo him out of the room whilst she and one of the maids changed the bloodstained sheets around Alice, as deftly as they could without jostling her. He had acknowledged he was in the way but had felt unable to retreat farther than the chair in the corner of the room whilst they worked. Now they were finished, he pulled his chair closer to the bed and took Alice's hand in his.

Her eyes flickered open, and she gave him a weak smile, but her face was ashen, and underneath her eyes were dark circles. She looked terribly unwell.

Gently he kissed her fingers where they entwined with his and then sat back in the chair and waited.

Alice slept fitfully, every so often trying to turn in her sleep to get into a more comfortable position. When this happened he would spring forward and press her shoulders gently, holding her on her back so she did not pull at the stitches or disturb the wound.

'Please do not die,' he whispered time and time again. It was strange to be sitting here next to his young and normally healthy wife. A year ago he had been convinced Alice would outlive him, but here he was the picture of health and she was suspended in that awful void between life and death.

Periodically Miss Stick would knock quietly at the door and enter the room, taking her time to straighten the sheets and ensure Alice was comfortable. He saw real affection and concern in the housekeeper's eyes. In her short time in London, Alice had made an impression on so many people.

The housekeeper would also bring Simon trays of tea and press him to drink and eat a little, pouring out the tea and handing it to him, not leaving the room until he had taken at least a few sips.

The hours seemed to drag as Simon found he could not rest, not whilst Alice's future was so uncertain. Every so often he would place a hand on her brow, dreading he would feel the heat that would indicate the wound was infected, pus accumulating under the stitches.

It was dark outside when he finally nodded off to sleep, dozing fitfully in the armchair, waking every few minutes to glance across at Alice and then his head dropping down onto his chest.

Miss Stick offered to sit with Alice so he could sleep, but Simon had an irrational fear that if he moved, if he left her bedside, something terrible would happen. He knew it was not true, but he could not help feeling that way.

As the first rays of sunshine filtered through the gap in the curtains, Alice stirred, her eyes flickering open as they had through the night, but this time she seemed to focus on him.

'How are you, my love?'

She smiled at him weakly and tried to push herself up in bed. Simon laid a restraining hand on her arm.

'Everything hurts,' she said, her face contorting into a frown.

'I can send for the doctor if you would like some opium, or perhaps just the laudanum he offered you yesterday.'

'No,' Alice said quickly. 'I just need to change position. Will you help me?'

'Of course.'

She was light and easy to manoeuvre, and slowly they managed to get her sitting up a little more. He regarded her with a frown. She was still terribly pale, but it was good to see her alert and able to focus on him.

'I am awfully thirsty.'

'Would you like water? Tea?'

'Just some water.' He poured her a glass from the jug in the corner of the room and held it to her lips as she took small sips. 'Have you been here all night?'

'Yes.'

'That is kind. Thank you.'

'I could not have been anywhere else,' he said, hearing the anguish in his own voice. He didn't want to examine what it meant. He didn't want to acknowledge the deep panic he felt at the idea of losing Alice. It was as though she had buried into his heart and become part of him.

'I feel better knowing you are here,' Alice said as she closed her eyes and drifted off to sleep again.

Chapter Nineteen

Alice spent an entire week in bed, and by the end she could quite happily have never seen another pillow or bed-sheet again in her life. Around day two the wound on her abdomen had reddened and grown tight, pulling at the stitches. Dr Black had visited, a grave expression on his face, asking to speak to Simon privately after he had examined the wound. Later Simon had told her of the doctor's concerns of infection and that if the redness and swelling did not settle, he might have to snip the stitches to let the accumulated pus out.

Thankfully the swelling had not worsened and after another day began to subside, and Alice did not succumb to a fever as they feared she might.

Dr Black was cautious and had insisted she stay in bed for the whole week, but today was her first day of freedom.

'I see that glint in your eyes,' Simon said, shaking his head. 'Do not think you are going to be running around this house just because you have been given permission to get out of bed.'

'If I stay in this room one day longer, I think I will go mad.'

'Dr Black said you could get up and sit in the chair, not go charging round the house like an excitable dog who has not seen his master for days.'

Alice sighed. She had hoped to make it downstairs. It would be wonderful to sit in the drawing room, perhaps in a chair by the window as she watched people on the street outside go about their lives.

'Let me help you,' he said, and he leaned down so Alice could slip an arm around his neck. He lifted her smoothly and then helped her to gently set her feet on the ground.

It felt strange to be standing again, and for a moment Alice's legs felt weak and wobbly, but Simon was there, as he had been this entire past week. Not once had he left her alone for more than an hour, using the time when she slept to bathe and change clothes and conduct the urgent bits of business that could not wait.

She had grown used to his constant attention, and his presence had made a difficult week much more bearable. They had read together, he had taught her to play chess, he had told her of his childhood, of the happy memories with his parents and his brother, and she had shared more of what her life had been like growing up in Bamburgh. She had thought at some point he would pull away, especially when it became more and more certain that she would make a full recovery, his duty done. Yet he had not. Each morning he was there in the chair beside her bed, and each evening he leaned over to kiss her, passion bubbling under the surface, barely restrained.

It was a stark contrast to the week they had spent prior to Alice's injury, unable to keep their hands from one another. Yet despite her injury Alice found she had enjoyed this second week together almost as much. She had a deeper understanding of her husband now, and she felt he had truly relaxed around her.

He settled her into the chair they had positioned by the window and took a seat beside her then closed his eyes and let out a jagged sigh.

'Is something amiss, Simon?'

He shook his head, but for a moment he did not look at her.

'You do not know how worried I have been,' he said quietly. 'When I saw you with that knife sticking out of you…' He shook his head.

'I know,' Alice said, biting her lip at the memory of the panic she had felt when she had looked down and seen the knife in her for the first time.

'I thought you were going to die. People who get stabbed do not often survive, especially if they are stabbed in the abdomen.'

'I am lucky, I know that.' She reached out and gripped his hand, waiting until he looked at her to continue. 'But the worst is over. Dr Black said so. The wound is healing well, and in a few days he will come and remove the stitches. I will have to avoid heavy lifting and strenuous activity for a while, but it will not be for ever.'

'I know you are recovering well, Alice,' Simon said. 'And I am so grateful for your strength.' He fell silent again.

Alice opened her mouth to speak, trying to find the right words to gently prompt to see if the issue were how their relationship had changed again. In the few weeks since his return, they had moved quickly from tiptoeing around each other to friendship and then being unable to keep their hands off one another. This past week had been another change again, with Simon caring for her as any true husband would care for his wife.

She felt a flicker of hope and wondered if this last week had made him realise what was important in his life. Not for the first time her mind started to fire pictures of their perfect future together at her. She imagined them strolling hand and hand through London before spending a few hours together raising money and awareness for the orphanage. Then at the end of the day they would return home together to retire to the bedroom and enjoy one another's company in a more intimate way. She even dared to dream of children, a little baby of their own, a house filled with happiness and love.

Alice hadn't even dared to dream about such a future, but Simon had changed this week. He had stopped trying to hold her at a distance and instead allowed her to see every part of him.

Before Alice could find the right words to ask if perhaps his feelings towards her and their future had changed, there was a gentle knock on the door, and a moment later Miss Stick entered.

'You have a visitor, Lady Westcroft.'

Simon frowned. They had kept visitors away this past week so she could focus on recovery, but the room was filled with flowers from well-wishers. Miss Stick had been wonderful at gently guiding friends and acquaintances away, suggesting they visit in a week or two when Alice was back on her feet.

'Hardly a visitor,' Maria said as she burst into the room. 'My darling Alice, I came the very second I heard the news. Let me look at you.' Maria swept over and knelt before Alice, regarding her carefully, then laid a hand on her heart and let out a choked sob. 'You're going to recover,' she said, tears dropping onto her cheeks. 'Forgive me, but for the entire journey here I feared you would have succumbed to infection, and I would be arriving to a house in mourning.'

Alice gripped Maria's hands, wishing she could pull her into an embrace but wary of the strain on her stitches.

Maria stood, turning to Simon and hugged him. 'You must be so relieved.'

'It has been a worrying week,' he admitted.

'But I am well on my way to recovery now. The doctor insisted I stay in bed for a whole week, but today, finally, I have been allowed up.'

'Sit down, Maria,' Simon said, indicating the chair next to Alice's. 'I will arrange some refreshment. You must be thirsty.'

'I am famished too. The coach set off before breakfast this morning, and in my rush to get here I have not stopped for it since.'

'I will organise food and tea.'

Simon strolled out of the room as Maria settled in the chair. Alice felt a great happiness at having her sister-in-law here. Out of everyone from her old family and new, Maria was the one she had leaned on the most this past year.

'You must tell me everything that happened. How did you get such an injury? Was it through your work with the orphanages?'

'Indirectly. I was visiting one of them near St Giles, and a man tried to rob me. He wanted my wedding ring, and as I was trying to take it off my finger, the driver and footman who had accompanied me realised something was wrong. They rushed over, and in the thief's desperation to get away he stabbed me.'

Maria's hand went to her mouth. 'You must have been so frightened, Alice.'

'It didn't feel real, not until we were back here and the doctor was talking about pulling the knife out and stitching me up.'

'The wound is healing? It has not festered?'

'No. There was a day or two where we thought it might go that way, but thankfully the redness subsided and it has since healed well.'

Maria leaned forward in her chair and lowered her voice. 'And what of Simon? I didn't expect the look of devotion he was giving you when I first arrived.'

'Simon has been wonderful,' Alice said carefully. She knew how invested Maria was in her brother-in-law's happiness and how much she wanted him to settle down and allow himself to experience the same sort of wedded bliss she had found with Robert. 'He has barely left my side.'

'He was always a kind boy, sensitive too, although that is hidden underneath the layers of grief and the hard shell of an exterior he has to project in his role as earl.'

'He is kind,' Alice said softly. He was so much more than that. She thought of the way he had kept her entertained during her recovery, which was wonderful in itself, but she knew he had done it to ensure her the best possible chance of getting better. If her mind was stimulated and he did not allow her to grow bored, then she was more likely to follow the doctor's orders and stay in bed.

'You have not found it too difficult, having him back?'

'I cannot lie. It was a shock at first, but I think we have found a happy equilibrium together.' She bit her lip, wondering what their relationship would look like when she was fully recovered. Her injury had put a stop to the physical intimacy they had shared in the week before she was stabbed, but their relationship had not faltered as she had been worried it might. Instead it had flourished.

'He has not mentioned leaving again?'

'No.' Alice felt her heart squeeze at the thought. She had told herself she would not become too used to Simon's company, but she knew if he left now she would be devastated. These past few weeks, she had tried her hardest to remember he did not want a deeper relationship, but slowly and surely she had fallen in love with her husband.

She pressed her lips together and glanced over her shoulder, wondering if she should confide in Maria, but before she could say anything Simon walked back into the room.

'Tea and toast and cake will be brought up shortly,' he said.

'Perhaps you might carry me downstairs, Simon. There is more room in the drawing room, and I would like a change of scenery.'

He considered for a moment and then nodded. 'If you are sure. Just for half an hour, though, then I will carry you back up to bed.'

Alice didn't argue, excited by the prospect of leaving her room for the first time in a week. Carefully Simon leaned down and positioned his arms underneath her, lifting her up smoothly from the chair. He walked slowly, ensuring his footsteps did not jar or jolt Alice as she held onto his neck.

They made it downstairs without incident, and Simon settled Alice in a comfortable armchair, ensuring she had just the right number of pillows behind her.

'Thank you,' Alice said, beaming up at him.

'You're welcome.' He dropped a kiss on the top of her head and then moved away. 'I will tell Miss Stick to take the opportunity to change your sheets now you are out of bed. I am sure it will feel good to have fresh ones.' He disappeared, and once again Alice was left alone with Maria.

Maria stared after him and then rose from her seat and softly closed the door behind her.

'Is something amiss?' Alice asked, confused at their need for privacy.

'You're in love with him,' Maria said, her eyes wide. 'It is obvious with every look, every touch.'

Alice started to shake her head and then stopped. It was impossible to hide such things from Maria: she was astute in all areas, but in particular she had a very well-developed emotional intelligence.

'We have grown close these last few weeks.'

'I can see that,' Maria said, studying Alice carefully. 'You have forgiven him for abandoning you?'

'Yes.'

Maria looked at Alice cautiously, as if aware her next question was delicate, especially for a woman who was up for the first time in days and shouldn't be upset.

'Have you spoken of your future together? Has he said he wants to settle down with you?'

'We have spoken many times,' Alice said, shaking

her head a little, recalling their conversations in Hyde Park and later in the carriage and the again in the bedroom. Each had resulted in a different plan, a different conclusion. 'But we have agreed on nothing long-term.'

'I do not wish you to get hurt, Alice.'

'I know. I do not wish for that either.' She lowered her voice further so it was barely more than a whisper. 'I have tried my very hardest not to fall in love with Simon these last few weeks, but I fear I have been unsuccessful. At first I tried to keep my distance, and then I told myself we could be close just as long as I remembered not to fall for him. I was very resolute at first, but he has a way of burrowing into your heart.'

'He is very loveable,' Maria said with a sigh. 'But so are you, and you deserve to be loved, Alice.'

'I cannot force him to love me,' she said quietly, wondering if she was mad to think that perhaps he did love her. Over the past week he had certainly been devoted to her care and recovery, and every time he came into the room he smiled broadly, a smile that told her he was pleased to see her. She thought maybe he did love her: he was just too stubborn to admit it, still ruled by the guilt of taking over every aspect of his late brother's life.

'He is a fool,' Maria said suddenly, anger flaring in her voice. 'I love you both dearly, but until I saw him with you today, I could not imagine how you would be together, yet you are perfect, you complement each other in exactly the right ways. It is an incredible turn of events, marrying a stranger and ending up with the one person you are destined for in this life, and if he squanders this chance of happiness, he is a complete and utter fool.'

'I think the problem is he feels he shouldn't be happy.'

'Silly boy,' Maria said, biting her lip and shaking her head at the same time. 'Do you want me to talk to him?'

'No,' Alice said quickly. She needed to step carefully with Simon; the last thing she wanted was to push him away. If he was made to confront his feelings for Alice too soon it might scare him away. It would be better to let things build, for him to see there was no point denying the love and happiness they brought to one another.

'If you are sure?'

'I am sure.'

'You two look deadly serious,' Simon said as he re-entered the room.

'We were discussing Alice's injury. It sounds horrific,' Maria turned to Alice and leaned over and squeezed her hand. 'You should return to Northumberland, where it is safe, as soon as you are well.'

Alice smiled. Maria had a motherly, protective instinct that sometimes went a little too far, but it came from a place of affection and love.

'I hardly think Alice need quit London for good,' Simon said quickly, 'just avoid certain areas.'

'I can't stay away from St Benedict's Orphanage for ever. The London Ladies' Benevolent Society has great plans for that place.'

'You are incorrigible,' Simon muttered. 'You were stabbed outside its doors, and still you will not give it up.'

'It is a worthy cause.'

Simon shrugged. 'I am going to invoke my privilege as husband and insist you do not go there ever again unless I am by your side.'

'I will agree without argument, as long as you make yourself available to me whenever I wish to visit.'

'I can see no problem with that,' Simon said softly.

* * *

Two hours later Alice was back in bed, resting. She had not wanted to admit she was fatigued by the short spell she had spent downstairs, but as Simon had carried her back up to the bedroom she had leaned in close to him and nuzzled her face into his neck.

'Was it too much for you, my dear?'

'No,' Alice said quickly, 'just enough. I am a little tired now, but I enjoyed seeing a different view of these four walls.'

Simon helped her to get comfortable in bed and then made to sit in the chair next to her.

'You should spend some time with Maria,' Alice said, trying to stifle a yawn. 'It will do you good to get some fresh air, and I can hardly accompany you out anytime soon.'

'What if you need anything?'

'I am sure Miss Stick will be more than happy to check on me at regular intervals, and I have a loud voice to call out if I need something desperately.'

A day ago he would have dismissed the idea immediately, but Alice's strength was returning quickly now, and he realised it would be good to get outside and enjoy some fresh air.

'If you are sure?'

'I am. In fact, I insist.'

Half an hour later he and Maria were on horseback, riding side by side towards the park. Maria was an excellent rider, confident and at ease around the horse he had chosen for her, even though she had never ridden it before. It made Simon think back to the pleasant ride he had shared with Alice a few weeks earlier. They had still been feeling their way through their relationship at that point, wondering if they could even live companionably in the same part of the country. Now the idea of living apart from her made him feel a little sick.

'Thank you for coming down. I know Alice enjoys your company immensely.'

'I packed my bags as soon as I received the news she had been hurt.' Maria paused before continuing mildly, not looking at him. 'I was worried she would be gravely wounded with no one who cared about her to look after her.'

'I am here,' Simon said quietly. He had known Maria a long time and knew she wasn't lashing out to hurt him and would get to her true point soon.

'Yes, you are, but when I last saw you we spoke of your wife who you had left in London after not bidding her farewell. You told me you did not know what you planned to do with her, but that you would try to accommodate her wishes, unless of course she wished to have a true and full marriage with you.'

'I was young and naïve.'

'It was four weeks ago, Simon.'

'A lot has happened in four weeks.'

'Evidently. I rush down here thinking Alice might be all alone, and I find you devoted to her comfort, the very picture of a loving husband.'

'Would you rather I abandoned her?'

'Good Lord, no. This is exactly what I have always hoped for you. Marriage is a wonderful gift if done right, and I think with Alice you have the chance to build something truly special.'

He remained silent. It was difficult to deny the feelings that had grown inside him over the past few weeks. He had always felt an attraction to Alice, but the more time he spent with her the more he realised he liked her too. She was kind and generous and entertaining to converse with. She had an opinion on most matters of politics or social dilemmas. Added to that was her natural warmth, the way she could get virtual strangers to trust her, to feel like treasured confidants.

'I do not know *exactly* what I feel for her,' Simon said, acknowledging how difficult this was for him. He had enjoyed the time spent in Alice's company, but with it had come guilt. Guilt that he was happy, living his life, whilst Robert was long gone.

'Perhaps you don't need to know. Perhaps it is enough to realise you make one another happier together than you are apart.'

Simon looked down at the reins in his hands, glad that there was the distraction of riding that meant he did not have to look Maria directly in the eye as they spoke.

'I cannot just banish what I feel about Robert,' he said eventually.

'I know. I doubt it will ever leave you completely, Simon, but you knew Robert better than anyone else. He loved you so much, and he wanted you to be happy. That would never have changed, and I know if he is looking down on us now he will be shouting for you to stop being so pigheaded and stubborn, to stop using his death as an excuse not to live your own life.'

'He was the best of brothers.'

'He was, and we were lucky enough to have time with him in this world.' Maria reached across the gap between them and grasped his wrist, waiting until he looked at her to continue. 'Honour his memory in the way he would have wanted it. Live your life as he would, being fair and kind and conscientious. Love with all your heart. That is a greater tribute to Robert than hiding away and never allowing yourself any happiness.'

For a long time they rode in silence, Maria content to sit quietly in her saddle to give Simon the space to think on what she had said. He knew in many ways Maria was right. Robert had only ever been thoughtful and generous; he would not begrudge Simon any happiness. The feeling of guilt—that he was stealing the life Robert should have had—had come directly from himself. It was a conviction that was difficult to shake.

Yet here he was considering an alternative. As they rode through the park Simon allowed himself to imagine what his life could be. Waking up to the woman he loved, taking long, leisurely strolls whilst they discussed anything from their families to what the latest law to pass in Parliament meant for the wider country. Then home to tumble into bed together. It was an enthralling glimpse into what the future could be.

'Lord Lathum and his wife have just had a baby,' Maria said suddenly.

Simon was pulled back to the present and looked at his sister-in-law in confusion. He barely knew Lord and Lady Lathum.

'I am pleased for them.'

'They are healthy. She is not yet eighteen, chosen for her childbearing potential and sizeable dowry, I am told,' Maria said, turning her horse around so they could start the walk back to the house. 'He is your age, certainly no older. There have been no problems in the family previously, but their child has been born with an unnaturally large head and an extra finger on his left hand.'

Simon blinked, wondering what point she was trying to make.

'You have lost me, Maria,' he said eventually.

'Let me speak plainly.'

'Please do,' he murmured.

Maria pressed on, ignoring him. 'I am hopeful that in the course of the next few weeks you will see the only sensible thing to do is to commit to a full and happy marriage with the sweet young woman you decided to marry last year. You will be blissfully happy, but for your wife at least there will be one thing missing from your union.'

'Children,' he said, his face darkening. He knew how much Alice loved children. She spoke of their nieces with such affection, and every time they passed a young child with their nanny or nursemaid in the street, her eyes lit up. She had a patient and caring nature, and instinctively Simon knew his wife would make a wonderful mother.

'Yes, children. Alice has never come out and said she wishes a house filled to the brim with children, but I can see it in her eyes.'

'That is one thing I will not be persuaded to change my mind on.'

'Lord and Lady Lathum should have had a healthy child. The odds were in their favour, yet they are devastated their firstborn son has not been born healthy.'

'I do not get your point, Maria,' Simon snapped.

Luckily Maria did not offend easily, and she ignored his abrupt tone.

'None of us know what the future may hold.'

'That is exactly what Alice says.'

'You may drop dead tomorrow or you might live until you are a crotchety old man of ninety. Take Alice as a wonderful example. She is young and healthy, but if that knife had been thrust in with a fraction more force or an inch higher, it would have hit her liver, and Alice would have bled out on the streets of St Giles.'

Simon grimaced.

'I have said enough,' Maria said and nodded in grim satisfaction. 'I know you do not wish to discuss it with me, but I owe it to Alice to at least try. I love her like a sister, and I would hate for her to find happiness with you only to realise that very happiness was stopping her from having the family she dreamed of.'

'It isn't as if she can choose not to be married to me. She cannot suddenly decide to go and make a future with another man, a man who does wish to have children.'

'Of course she can,' Maria said, shaking her head. 'Perhaps not within the social circles we move in, but there are plenty of women who reside with a man who is not their husband, someone who provides a home for them, love, children.'

'You go too far, Maria,' he said wearily. 'Alice would not do that.'

'No, she wouldn't,' his sister-in-law said quietly. 'You are right, but perhaps it serves to remind you that in saying you will never have children, you are also saying she will never have children. *You* are making a significant decision about Alice's future and expecting her to accept it without discussion.'

'We have discussed it.'

'Telling her you will never father a child and discussing the issue are not the same, Simon,' she chastised gently.

'I need some time to think,' Simon said, aware he sounded unforgivably rude, but his head was spinning, and he had the sudden urge to be alone. He needed time to work through everything Maria had said to him. The last thing he wanted was to make Alice unhappy.

'Of course. I will return home and check on Alice. You take all the time you need.'

It was almost dark by the time Simon dismounted outside the townhouse, handing Socrates's reins to the groom and looking up at the window of the room where Alice was recuperating. He was eager to return to her side. For the past week they had spent hardly any time apart, but he knew he would have to hold his tongue and perhaps even lie to her about what he and Maria had discussed that afternoon.

On his ride through Hyde Park after Maria had left him, he had turned over their conversation, examining it from each possible angle, until his head had started to throb. He had been unable to concentrate, so he had dismounted and sat on a bench overlooking the lake, trying to think of nothing but the ripples on the water in front of him.

As he sat, he had come to a realisation, one that he wished to share with Alice, but he knew she was not up to it yet. It might be weeks before she was strong enough to hear what he had to say, and the last thing he wanted to do was set her recovery back by any degree.

'I missed you,' Alice said as he knocked on the door and entered. Maria had been sitting by the bed, but she rose when Simon entered and murmured an excuse to go. Simon caught her by the hand as she walked past him, and Maria paused.

He smiled at her, squeezing her hand gently, and she searched his eyes for the answer to an unspoken question, and then she reached out and embraced him. Maria was the only person who could speak to him so freely and he would forgive in a heartbeat.

When they were alone, Alice looked at him curiously. 'What was that about?'

'Whilst we were out, Maria reminded me what a fool I was being.'

'A fool?'

'Yes.' He leaned down and kissed Alice on the forehead. 'It does not matter, my sweet. You rest, and I will tell you everything when you are recovered.'

Chapter Twenty

Three weeks later Alice stepped out of the door for the first time in a month. Her stitches had been removed by Dr Black, and she was declared fit to start building up to her normal levels of activity. To her dismay she had lost some muscle whilst invalided, and she knew it would not be an easy feat to get back to rushing around London, attending to her various commitments.

Alice was determined to make a good start and today had suggested she and Simon step out for a short walk around the local streets. It was early, only a little past nine o'clock in the morning. Alice had chosen this time deliberately for two reasons. The first was to avoid the jostling of people walking on the pavements later in the day. At nine o'clock most wealthy people were still at breakfast or readying themselves for the day, so the streets around Grosvenor Square were quiet. The second reason was that she did not wish to encounter any of her friends and acquaintances when she left the house for the first time. She was excited to get back to normal, but she did not particularly want to stop to reassure people she was recovering well multiple times on her walk.

'Are you ready?'

She breathed in deeply and then nodded. 'I am ready.'
'You will tell me if you start to tire?'
'I promise.'

They set off at a sedate pace, walking as you would if accompanying an elderly relative out and about, but after she had got used to moving outside again, Alice found she did not mind ambling along. She was pleasantly surprised to find her wound did not pull too much when she walked. Dr Black was right: the skin had knitted together beautifully, leaving her with a neat scar that he assured her would get smaller with time.

Simon was quiet as they walked ,and Alice wondered what he was thinking. He had been attentive these last few weeks, but sometimes she thought he was distracted, staring off into the distance for some time before focussing his attention in the room again. Once or twice she had panicked that he might be thinking about leaving again, finally fed up of life in London, life with her. Quickly she had pushed away the thought. Alice was trying to enjoy what time they did share and not think too much on the future, despite wishing Simon would fall to his knees, declare himself a fool and tell her he had loved her since their very first kiss.

They turned at the corner, planning on doing a small loop around the local streets before ending up back home. As they crossed the road to start on the second side of the square, a man in the distance called out.

Alice was horrified to find she stiffened, unable to move for a second. It was her first time out since the attack, and although physically she was more than ready, she did feel a little apprehensive.

The man in the distance called again, waving jovially.

'Northumberland,' the person shouted, taking his hat from his head and waving it.

'I take it you know that man?'

Simon frowned, looking hard at the man before shaking his head. 'It sounds like I should know him, but I do not recognise him.'

'He's coming over. Perhaps he will introduce himself to me.'

The man approached quickly, and then when he was five feet away he stood stock-still and looked at Simon strangely.

'My apologies, sir. I thought you were someone else.'

'We do not know each other?' Simon asked.

'No. I thought you were the Earl of Northumberland, an old friend of mine.'

'I am the earl,' Simon said, his voice dropping low.

'The Earl of Northumberland?'

'Yes. You must have known my father or my brother.'

'I knew Robert,' the man said, looking a little uncomfortable.

'My brother. He died a few years ago.'

'My deepest condolences. I apologise profusely for the misunderstanding. I have been out of the country some time, and I had not heard about your brother's death. You are very much like him in looks and countenance.'

Alice sucked in a sharp breath as she felt Simon sway almost imperceptibly beside her. She wanted to pull Simon away, to stop him from hearing the man's words. She knew he found it difficult to hear how similar he was to Robert. It brought to the fore the feelings that he had stepped into his brother's life, replacing him in every way.

'It is an easy mistake to make,' Simon said, nodding to the man before turning away.

'We can return home,' Alice suggested as they began to put space between them and the man.

'There is no need. I am perfectly fine.'

'It was an unsettling encounter. It is not weakness to admit you are a little upset.'

'I am not upset, I am not unsettled. I told you I am fine.'

Alice fell silent. Her husband was far from fine, no matter what he told her. He started walking a little quicker now, his head bent and his eyes darting from side to side. At first Alice tried to keep up, but as they walked faster the movement pulled at her scar, and after a couple of minutes she slipped her arm from his and stopped. Simon did not notice, at least not for a good few seconds, and when he did finally look up and around, it was with an air of barely suppressed irritation.

When he spotted her, he returned quickly.

'I think I want to return home,' she said, looking back over her shoulder at the way they had come.

'Of course.' He offered her his arm, but Alice waved it away, plastering a wide smile on her face. 'I am fine, Simon. I will walk home by myself. I am sure you have other things to do.'

For a moment she thought he would brush off her suggestion and escort her home, and they would return to their normal routine of the last few weeks, but instead he nodded, turning absently away from her.

Alice felt her heart squeeze and then shatter. Everything had been going so well, and then with one reminder of the brother whose place he had taken, Simon had completely regressed. Of course she did not mind if he showed emotion, if he leaned in and told her how difficult it was when he was mistaken for the brother he had loved so much: they could have shared that sadness. But instead he had blocked her out completely.

Quickly she turned, walking away before Simon could see how distressed she was.

The footman opened the door, surprise on his face that she had returned alone. Alice hurried in and struggled up the stairs to her room, forcing herself to remain calm. Simon had been upset, that was all, and she did not begrudge him some space to work through the emotions he felt at being mistaken for his brother. She would rather he talked to her about it, but she could not force that.

'Be calm,' she told herself, resisting the urge to pace over to the window and see if Simon had changed his mind and was returning.

For hours Simon walked, without sparing a thought for where he would end up or what direction he was travelling in. He thought he knew London well, but the streets passed in a blur, with the buildings getting smaller and closer together as he moved farther away from the centre of London to the poorer outskirts. At some point early on he must have crossed over the river, for when he stopped walking hours later he was well south of the Thames, but he did not have any recollection of doing so.

It was the fading light and lengthening shadows that brought him back to his senses. For a long time he had walked, head bent, trying to gain control of all the awful thoughts running through his mind, but he felt completely overwhelmed.

He took a moment to look around him, feeling as

though he had just come out of a trance. He was out of
the city proper, the roads widening and only a few scattered houses on either side. Vaguely he recalled travelling by this road on a few occasions: it was one of the few
that led out of London to the south, the route travellers
to Sussex would take to start their journey to the coast.

Now he had stopped he was aware of the ache in his
legs and feet. He was an active man, often walking for
hours in the Tuscan hills in the last year and enjoying
long, physically challenging rides on horseback as well,
but he realised he must have been walking for at least six
or seven hours. His mouth was dry, and he longed for
something to quench his thirst. In the distance he could
see the smartly painted swinging sign for one of the inns
that were dotted along the main routes out of London to
provide shelter and refreshments for weary travellers.

It only took him a couple of minutes to make his way
to the inn where he was welcomed by a middle-aged
woman with a smile and the offer of ale. He ordered and
was thankful when the drink arrived, downing half the
tankard as soon as he raised it to his lips.

Thankfully the inn was quiet, and Simon had found
a corner table to himself so he was able to nurse the rest
of the ale in peace, undisturbed by the few other patrons.

After a moment he closed his eyes, feeling awfully
weary. He could not quite believe he had been walking
for so long.

'Alice,' he murmured, thinking of how he had just
abandoned her in the middle of the street when he was
meant to be escorting her. It was inexcusable, yet he had
been unable to act in any other way. When the man had
approached them, mistaking Simon for his brother, he

had felt as though he had been shot through the heart. Every day he woke up wishing his brother were alive, feeling guilty that he got to continue with life when Robert did not. Ever since his talk with Maria, he had spent each day fighting so hard to push the feeling away, to convince himself he was something more than an imposter living the life his brother should have had. Then the feeling had come rushing back in an instant with one innocent little mistake.

For a minute Simon cradled his head in his hands, trying to unpick the tangled web of thoughts and mess of emotions jumbled inside him. It had been one of the reasons he had walked for so long: as soon as he stopped, the sorrow and despair threatened to overwhelm him, but he knew the answer wasn't running for ever.

He took another large gulp of ale and motioned for the barmaid to bring another over. He would only have the one more—the last thing he needed was to lose control of his senses.

Simon sat back in his chair and watched the other people in the room for a moment and then drained the last of the ale from his tankard. He knew he had to let his thoughts in, to acknowledge the pain he was feeling, the doubts, but part of him wanted to keep pushing it away.

'Here you are, sir,' the barmaid said, placing the ale down in front of him. 'Anything else I can get you?'

'No, thank you.' He tried to empty his mind as he stared into the full tankard of ale, but his thoughts were still racing. These last few weeks he had been pretending everything was all right, that he wasn't about to fall apart any moment. He had felt real happiness with

Alice, a sense of contentment that he now feared he did not deserve.

His mind brought forward an image that he often saw in those quiet moments when nothing else was happening. It was of Robert and Maria at their wedding, coming out of the church with their heads bent together. The image was as clear to Simon as if he were looking at a painting, even down to the blissful expressions on their faces.

He'd felt that same bliss when he'd been walking arm-in-arm with Alice, that same contentment. In his mind he had been planning what their future might be like, pushing aside the doubts that plagued him about how long he would live.

Deep in his chest he felt a throb of pain. For the last few weeks he had been lying to himself, pretending he was worthy of something he was not. If he pursued a relationship with Alice, he would be seeking that same happiness his brother had enjoyed, that same ideal of family life. If he followed his heart, he would be stepping into Robert's shoes completely, choosing a contented, domestic life.

'I can't be you,' he murmured, low enough not to attract any attention. 'I can't take your life.'

Morosely Simon stared into his ale, not knowing what was for the best. He couldn't just abandon Alice—that would be cruel—but he didn't know what he wanted from his life. He could either pursue happiness and lead a life plagued by guilt or accept that he couldn't be with Alice, despite falling for her these last few weeks.

Twenty-four hours later Simon was not back, and Alice's mild concern had turned to devastation and anger.

After everything they had been through, he had left again, disappeared without a word. She understood the strong emotions he felt around inheriting his brother's title, and if he had been here in the house she would have given him space to work through how he was feeling.

The problem was he wasn't in the house. He hadn't even sent a note to let her know where he was or how long he was planning on being absent. He could be half-way to France by now or boarding a boat for any part of the world he desired. The last time he had felt over-whelmed, he'd run away, fleeing the country. She wasn't entirely convinced he wouldn't do the same this time.

'I will not stay here, perpetually waiting,' Alice mur-mured, and decisively she crossed to the corner of the room and pulled the bell cord to summon the maid.

A minute later she appeared at Alice's door, bobbing into a little curtsy. 'What can I do, my Lady?'

'Ask Miss Stick to have my trunk brought up to my room and to get Drummond to ready the carriage and the horses.'

'Yes, my Lady.'

Alice began pulling her dresses out and quickly started to fold them. She did not care that they would be creased in the trunk, she could have them steamed when she arrived in Northumberland. All she cared about was getting away from London and away from Simon.

'Alice, the maid said you were packing to leave,' Maria said as she came into the room.

'I am planning on returning to Northumberland im-mediately.'

Maria raised an eyebrow in question.

'He's gone, Maria. Yesterday when we were out walk-ing, an old acquaintance of Robert's thought Simon was his older brother. It upset him, and he left almost immediately. I thought he would walk about for a while to think about things and then he would come home.'

'But he didn't return?'

Alice shook her head miserably. 'I have no idea where he is or if he is ever coming back.'

'Of course he is coming back, Alice. He loves you.'

'Does he? He has never told me so. He looks after me, treats me as an equal, but he has never been able to say that he loves me.'

Maria chewed on her lip. 'You are set on leaving?'

'I am, just as soon as I am packed.'

'Then, I will come with you. It would not be right for you to travel on your own after such an injury.'

'Are you sure?'

'Of course. I tire of London, especially as my girls are in Northumberland. I will return with you. Perhaps you can stay with me and the girls for a while. I do not think you should be on your own.'

'I would like that,' Alice said, suddenly feeling weary. She wanted to collapse on the bed and cry until she had no more tears to shed. She had allowed herself to believe Simon loved her, even if he could not bring himself to say it. She'd thought it was just because he found it difficult to acknowledge he was finally allowing himself to experience a little happiness.

'Come, Alice. I will make the arrangements. In a few days we will be back in Northumberland, and Simon will have to deal with an empty house here when he does emerge from wherever he has taken himself.'

Morosely Alice nodded and allowed herself to be cajoled and organised into getting everything she might possibly need for a summer spent in Northumberland.

Chapter Twenty-One

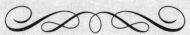

Simon climbed the last of the winding stairs, gripping the handrail as his foot struck the top one. He considered himself to be a fit and active man, yet even he was a little out of breath as he emerged into the cool late-afternoon air. It had been twenty years since he had last climbed the three hundred and eleven steps of the Monument, situated close to the magnificent St Paul's Cathedral. It had been one of his father's favourite places in London, and when he was young his father would often pay the entrance fee for him and Simon and then race his son up the stairs to the top. Once up there they would pick a spot on the narrow platform and stare out over London.

His father used to enjoy pointing out the magnificent buildings of the city, but for Simon it was the peace and the companionship he cherished the most. This was something that was his to share with his father, a sacred place where he could feel at peace.

Robert had offered to take him up the Monument once after their father had died, but Simon declined, wanting to keep his memories unsullied.

Now he stood alone, wishing his father and brother were by his side. There had been so much grief over the years, along with so much fear. It was hard to think about both. Despite his loving family, despite the best efforts of his mother and Maria, he had suppressed both his grief and his fear, pushing them deep down inside him where they had grown and got horribly out of control.

Up here, with the wind whipping at his face, he felt a moment of clarity after a difficult twenty-four hours. When he had been out walking with Alice and the man had called over to him, it had felt like his worst fear had come true, that someone had proved Simon had stolen Robert's life. Of course, now he looked at it rationally he could see that wasn't the case. It was merely an old acquaintance of his brother who had been momentarily confused by a family resemblance. Yet still he felt as though it had caused a monumental shift inside him, forcing him to confront his own fears and limitations. These last few weeks he had pushed aside his doubts about his happiness and his future, but they were still there, waiting to surface.

He closed his eyes, trying to empty his mind of everything but his doubts about the future, but as always it was the past that clung on, haunting him. The memory of his father came to him, but not the happy times, not the time spent exploring the countryside or strolling along the beach. Instead he was confronted by the terrible image of his father rising from his desk in his study, smiling as Simon hurried towards him, ready to impart some important fact about his day. Simon remembered how his father had stiffened, his face becoming a mask, then without any other warning he had dropped to the ground, dead before Simon could even utter a word.

Simon felt the sting of tears in his eyes. The moment of his father's death was crystal-clear in his mind: he could remember every expression, every miniscule movement, until there was nothing more. The period after was a blur, an overwhelming maelstrom of grief and shock that he had never properly recovered from.

Thoughts of his father's death led his mind to Alice and the panic he had felt when she had been stabbed. In the immediate aftermath, he had functioned by seeing to the practicalities, and as the days became weeks he suppressed the fear and desperation, trying to pretend the feelings weren't there. Yet he knew they bubbled under the surface, just waiting for an opportunity to get out. When he had seen the blood seeping through her dress he had felt a cold dread, a certainty that he would lose her just like he lost the other people most dear to him. The thought had plagued him for weeks, even as she recovered and it became clear she would not die from her wound.

'It is all such a mess,' he muttered to himself. He wished he were free to love without consequence, to live his life without fearing death but also in the shadow of the grief that had haunted him for years. He wanted to welcome in the love he felt for Alice, but he knew with that love there came the possibility she might one day be hurt, and one day he might lose her too.

'What would you do, Father?' Simon asked, gripping the railing. His father had always seemed so wise, contemplating Simon's questions and dilemmas with a serious demeanour, but always his answers would contain a little humour, something to show his son life was for enjoying as well as doing your duty.

He knew what his father would say. He could even

hear his deep, melodious voice as he urged Simon to live his life, to grab any chance at love, at happiness. Robert would tell him the same.

Simon felt the tears welling in his eyes. He did know how lucky he was to have been loved by two such incredible men. His father with his kindness and his patience, and Robert who had always been the sort of older brother everyone wished was their own.

He wondered how Robert would have coped if their lives were reversed, if Simon had been the one to die at a young age and Robert had survived. He knew the answer immediately. Robert would have gathered his family around him and ensured he made the most of every moment with his beautiful wife and children. He wouldn't have run away or spent his time wishing for things that could never be. He wouldn't have dwelt on questions he would never know the answer to or wasted his time worrying those he loved would be taken away.

'You have been a fool,' he murmured to himself, but even as he said the words he felt a flicker of rebellion inside him. For once he looked upon himself with kindness and compassion and reminded himself he had still been a boy when his father died, and although he was well into adulthood when Robert passed away, the sudden shock of his death would be enough to traumatise anyone.

Simon straightened, feeling a resolve like nothing he had experienced before. He knew it would not be a simple matter to start viewing himself with kindness, but he was going to try. There would be no more thoughts that he was less worthy than Robert, no more self-accusations that he was trying to step into his brother's life.

The first thing he had to do was make things right

with Alice. He had treated her terribly, unable to stop himself from showing her love and affection, but always holding back from telling her he loved her. It was cruel to keep her on edge and uncertain, and although that hadn't been his intention, it was no doubt the result. He could see now he had been holding part of himself back from her these last few weeks, not only because he felt guilty for feeling so happy but out of fear of giving his heart only to lose someone else he loved. It was understandable given his losses, but he hoped she could forgive him for pulling away when she needed him the most.

Taking in the view one last time, he turned and made his way back to the spiral staircase and then descended quickly, his feet clattering on the stone steps.

Back home the door was answered by a confused Frank Smith who looked at Simon as if he had grown an extra head.

'Where is Lady Westcroft?' Simon said, looking to the stairs and wondering if she was still resting from their trip out that had been cut short the day before.

'Lady Westcroft, my Lord?' Smith said, glancing over his shoulder.

'Yes, Smith. Where is my wife?'

'She left, my Lord. Her and the other Lady Westcroft.'

For a moment Simon could not move.

'Ah, you are home, my Lord,' Miss Stick said, emerging from the darkness of the stairs that led to the kitchen below. 'The Ladies Westcroft left a little earlier this morning. They took the carriage with Drummond and were heading for Northumberland.'

Simon reached out and steadied himself against

the wall. She'd gone. After everything he had put her through, she had finally had enough and left.

He did not blame her. He had behaved terribly yesterday, abandoning her when she was at such a low point. That would not be the worst part for Alice, though. Recently he had let her think that she could rely on him, and when she had started to trust he would not leave her again, he had disappeared without any regard for her.

'Will you pack for me, Miss Stick? I must follow my wife immediately. I will go and saddle Socrates.'

'Of course, my Lord.' Miss Stick hurried upstairs, and Simon made his way to the small stables. If he were quick, he would catch them on the road, although he would prefer privacy for what he needed to say to Alice.

It was a journey filled with peril and disaster. Only five miles out of London, Socrates threw a shoe. It was on a quiet stretch of road, a good mile out from the nearest village. Simon dismounted immediately and led Socrates by the reins to the village, hoping they had a farrier.

The farrier was able to fit Socrates with a new shoe, but the whole process took much longer than it should have. Simon wondered if the farrier was in league with the local tavern-keeper, for he delayed and delayed until it started to get dark, then suggested Simon rest Socrates overnight whilst he lodged in the tavern.

The next morning was no better with Simon coming upon an overturned carriage. The front wheel had splintered and flown off, and the carriage looked to have been dragged for some distance before the horses had been brought under control. Thankfully there were no fatalities, but one of the occupants, a young boy of eight, had fallen awkwardly on his arm, and the limb was bent at a strange angle.

Once he was satisfied no one else was badly injured, he put the boy on his horse and allowed him to ride to the next town where Simon sought out the local doctor and paid for his services. It meant he didn't begin his journey proper until after lunch and the distance he could cover before nightfall was limited.

When the third day of his journey dawned, he had only travelled fifty miles out of London and still had the prospect of many days ahead of him. It also meant the likelihood of catching up with Alice and Maria was very low, even though he could travel much quicker on horseback.

His third day of the journey was uneventful, but on the fourth disaster struck again as the inn where he was staying caught fire. He spent the morning stripped down to his shirtsleeves in a chain of men and women passing buckets of water from the river to throw on the blazing inn roof.

They were there for hours, and by the time the flames were under control the tavern had been decimated and half collapsed in on itself. Thankfully, due to the tireless efforts of everyone involved, the fire had not spread to any other buildings in the village.

Simon continued on his way much later that day, feeling as though his journey was cursed.

He arrived at Westcroft Hall in the early afternoon of a blustery, overcast day. There was a chance Alice had decided to go straight to one of the other properties he owned or to stay with Maria, but he felt she would have returned here first.

The door was opened by one of the young footmen who quickly took Simon's jacket and hat.

'Is my wife in residence?'

'She is, my Lord. She arrived yesterday.'

'Where is she?'

'I am here, Simon,' Alice said, her voice cool, with none of her usual affection.

He wanted to rush to her, to pull her into his arms and kiss her as if it were his last day on earth.

'I will ask Mrs Hemmings to prepare a bath.'

He looked down at his soot-stained clothes and grimaced. In his hurry to leave London he had packed light, but both his shirts had ended up grimy after the day spent fighting the tavern fire.

'Thank you.'

Alice nodded, holding his eye for just a second, and then she turned to leave.

'Alice,' he said, closing the space between them. 'Wait.'

As she spun to face him, he saw the sadness in her eyes and hated that he was the cause of it.

'Forgive me,' he said, his words quiet but clear. 'Please forgive me.'

There was a flare of something conciliatory in Alice's eyes, and then she looked away. 'I don't know if I can,' she said quietly. Without any fuss and without looking at him again, she walked away.

Chapter Twenty-Two

Alice had the urge to walk out of the house and keep walking. She wanted her face to be whipped by the wind, her hair flying loose about her shoulders and her skirt battering her legs. There was nothing quite like the wind as it hit the dunes on this part of the coast, and she felt the need to feel the cleansing sting as it brought colour to her cheeks.

She had not made any promises to listen to what Simon had to say, although she knew at some point they would need to discuss the future. They were still married: nothing could change that. It was only Alice's hopes and dreams and expectations that had changed.

Before she could change her mind, she grabbed her bonnet from its place close to the door, secured it tightly under her chin and then slipped out of the grand house. There was a path through the grounds that led to a narrow lane, and a twenty-minute brisk walk would bring her to the beach.

It had been a shock to see Simon so soon after she had arrived back in Northumberland, less than a day after she and Maria had pulled up in the carriage. Maria had reiterated her invitation to Alice to stay with her, but in the end Alice had decided she wanted a few days alone. She felt as though she were in mourning, experiencing a sadness for the loss of the dream she had woven around their lives.

Now with Simon back, she did not know what to think. He must have left London soon after they had and raced up here to speak to her, but that did not mean anything had changed—not really.

As Alice stepped onto the sand, she felt a powerful sense of being home. She loved London, loved the crowds and the sense that there was always something going on, but Northumberland was where she felt she belonged.

She climbed over the low dunes and walked along the beach a little, pleased to see she had the wide expanse of sand to herself. It was hardly weather for the beach, with the wind whipping up the sand every now and then so that she had to shield her eyes.

She chose a spot near the dunes where she was sheltered from the worst of the wind and made herself comfortable. What she loved most up here was the wide expanse of the sea. The water was always dark, the sand golden white, the sky changing with the seasons, yet one thing that never changed was the horizon. When she looked along the beach in either direction, as far as the eye could see was the flat line of the sea on the horizon, as if beckoning her to new adventures.

Alice sat for a long time, trying not to think of anything.

'I thought I might find you out here,' Simon said, surprising her. She hadn't thought he would follow her down to the beach.

He looked much fresher now after a bath, the soot washed from him and the grime scrubbed from his hair.

'I like the solitude on the beach, that sense that you are the only person in the whole world when you look out to sea.'

'It is beautiful.'

'Was your journey too strenuous?'

'It was not the most straightforward.'

'Was that soot on your clothing?'

'An inn I was staying at caught fire. I stayed to help put out the flames, but it was an old timber building, and the fire was relentless.'

Alice's eyes widened. 'Were you hurt?'

'No. Thankfully, no one was. The fire started when the innkeeper was cooking breakfast, so most of the guests were up, and there was time to rouse those who were not.'

'Did it spread to the rest of the village?'

'No.'

'That is something.' Alice shuddered. 'I always had such a fear of fire when I was a child. I used to fall asleep scared one of our neighbours would leave a candle burning and the whole row of houses would go up in flames.'

'I had never before seen a fire like this one. It was a destructive force, ripping through the building at such a speed you cannot imagine. It felt as though one minute there was a building with four walls and a roof, the next it was just a collection of timber supports left, sticking up from the ground with nothing to hold onto them.'

'I am glad you were not harmed,' Alice said, fixing her gaze again on the horizon.

He placed his hand on the sand next to hers, and Alice

felt the familiar spark travel through her as his finger brushed against hers.

'How are you? Has your wound completely healed?'

'It still pulls a little when I walk quickly, but apart from that it seems well healed.'

'I am glad.' He paused and then pressed on. 'I am sorry, Alice. Leaving you like that was unforgiveable.'

She shrugged, not meeting his eye. 'I should not be so upset. I should have expected it.'

'No,' he said sharply. 'I do not want you to expect such a thing.'

She turned to him, tears in her eyes. 'In London, after I had been injured, I thought that maybe something had changed between us, that maybe there was a chance that you could love me.'

There was pain in his eyes in response to her words, and he pressed his lips together so hard they went completely white. She realised how close he was to losing control and tentatively laid a hand over his. No matter how much she was hurting, she did not want to see Simon suffer like this. He had suffered enough in the last twenty years to last a lifetime.

'Can I tell you something? I know I have no right, but can I ask for your indulgence one last time before you decide what you are going to do?' He spoke quietly, but Alice could see he had control of himself again.

'Yes.'

'For twenty-one years I have been in mourning, but for the past five years I have felt as though I do not deserve to be here. I have hated every step I have had to take in Robert's shoes, every one of his duties I have had to shoulder. I have felt unworthy, and it has drained my very soul.'

Alice saw the anguish in his eyes and realised how much he had been suffering. She wanted to fold him in her arms and kiss him until he forgot the darkness, despite everything they had been through, but she knew he had to get this out in the open. Only then might he be able to begin to heal.

'Added to that is the fear that I will be struck down by the same condition that killed my father and my brother. I didn't want to die, didn't want my life to be over, but I felt like it was inevitable given how two good men, *better* men, had already been taken.'

'Not better,' Alice murmured.

'I have been hiding away, scared of dying but not feeling worthy of the life I had. The only way I knew how to cope was to push people away. Then I met you.' He flicked a glance at her, and she gave him an encouraging smile. 'That night at the Midsummer's Eve ball, when I met you I felt something shift. I was happy for the first time in a long time. It was as though you wakened something inside me.' He shook his head ruefully. 'Then I reverted back to my old ways and ran away, thinking I was sparing everyone the pain I felt, not realising I was only causing more of it.'

He turned to her, and Alice gave him an encouraging nod. She could feel the tears running down her cheeks as the wind whipped at them, but she didn't wipe them away.

'When I returned I did not know how we would live as husband and wife, but as soon as I saw you again I began falling in love. I fell hard and fast, even as I tried to pretend I felt nothing.'

Alice felt her eyes widen. She hadn't expected him to be able to say he loved her. For the first time since he had arrived in Northumberland, she allowed her mind to begin racing, to wonder if perhaps they had a chance at a future.

'You were like a magic potion, Alice. As you drew me in I started to realise little by little how terrible I had been feeling, how badly I had been treating myself, and how badly I had treated you. It was liberating to allow myself pleasure, to seek out enjoyment in things and re-alise that the guilt I was feeling for surviving when my brother had not was irrational. You did all of that. You showed me what it was to love and be loved.'

He reached out and stroked her cheek, and Alice felt a warmth flood through her body. She wanted to kiss him, to embrace him, but she knew it was important he say everything he needed to.

'When you were stabbed, I felt as though my world were ending. I didn't know how I would cope without you, even though I could not admit it to myself. I got so scared at the thought of losing someone else I loved. I tried to push everything down, to deny what I was feel-ing. Then when that man approached us in the street, mistaking me for Robert, it was as if every worry from the past came crashing back. I was overwhelmed. Sud-denly I felt like a fraud, as if all the progress I had made was not real.' He shook his head. 'I am so sorry for aban-doning you then, Alice. It was the worst possible thing I could have done.'

'Where did you go?'

'I walked the streets for hours, and then the next morning I went up the Monument. It was a place I used to visit with my father when I was young, and I realised I needed to properly clear my head, properly address what had happened.'

'That was when you came up with all of this?'

'It was the start. The journey here gave me a lot of time to think as well.'

Alice fell silent, her fingers drawing patterns in the sand by her sides.

'And now?' she asked eventually.

'Now I throw myself on your mercy, Alice. I love you with all my heart. Your smile lights up my world, and your laughter soothes my soul. I will do anything in my power to make you happy every day for the rest of our lives.'

'You want us to live as husband and wife?'

'Yes. More than anything.'

Alice felt her heart jump in her chest. Nothing was certain in life, but her main fear of giving her heart to Simon was that he would one day soon abandon her again. Now that he had acknowledged the reasons for his actions these past few years, she doubted he would act in the same way.

'I love you, Simon. I fell in love with you on the night of the Midsummer's Eve ball, and I have been pining for you ever since.'

'Do you think you can give me another chance?'

Alice closed her eyes and thought of all the reasons it might not work, then pushed them away. She loved him and he loved her. That was all they needed. Anything else they could work through together.

'Yes,' she said, leaning forward and kissing him.

'I have a question for you, one I hope you will say *yes* to.'

She frowned, puzzled.

Carefully he took something out of his jacket pocket and held it up so the light glinted off it. 'Alice, will you do me the honour of continuing to be my wife?'

'Is that my ring?'

'Yes.'

'How did you get it back?'

'The scoundrel who stabbed you was caught and brought before the magistrate a few days later. It seems he was wanted for a whole string of crimes. I talked to the magistrate, and they allowed me to search his possessions. He still had the ring on him when he was arrested.' He held it out. 'I will understand if you wish to have a different ring. We can choose one that does not have such memories associated with it.'

'No,' Alice said quickly. 'That is my wedding ring. That is the ring you placed on my finger when we married.'

Simon smiled and carefully slipped it onto the ring finger of her left hand.

'My beautiful wife,' he murmured and then leaned in and kissed her.

The wind whipped Alice's hair about her face, and the sand coated her skin, but Alice barely noticed. She was lost in the kiss of the man she loved, the man she had fallen for that very first night she had met him on a magical Midsummer's Eve.

Epilogue

Northumberland, Midsummer's Eve, 1818

Alice adjusted her mask, ensuring the ribbons were tied securely behind her head, and then she stepped out into the middle of the ballroom. The guests had been arriving for the last half an hour, and now Westcroft Hall was filled with chatter and laughter and music. Most people were wearing masks, delicate demimasks that barely concealed their identities, but it added to the sense of excitement.

'Good evening,' came a low voice from behind her, and Alice spun, a shiver running down her spine. Simon was standing there, dressed in a black jacket and gold cravat, easily the most handsome man in the room. 'May I have this dance?'

Alice inclined her head, and they walked to the dance floor to share the first dance of the evening.

Everyone was watching, but for Alice it felt as though they were the only two there, twirling around the ballroom as they did when they were the only two people in residence. For the duration of the dance she gazed into

Simon's eyes, and even as the music swelled and then died away, she found it hard to tear herself away.

'You're going to tell me I cannot have the next dance with you now, aren't you?' Simon said, a smile tugging at his lips.

Alice leaned in closer. 'If it were up to me, I would dance every single one with you, but we must fulfil our duties as host and hostess.'

'Can I tell you a secret?' Simon said, leaning in so his lips brushed against her ear.

Alice nodded.

'I would be willing to be labelled the worst host in the history of society balls if it meant I got to spend my evening only with you.'

'That is hardly a secret,' Alice said. She had the urge to kiss him and found her body swaying towards him.

'*Everyone* is watching,' Maria said as she glided over gracefully. 'If you ravish your wife here in the middle of the dance floor, you will never be able to show your faces in society again.'

'I would never,' Simon said, his eyes still locked on Alice's. 'A mere kiss, however…'

Alice felt helpless to resist and even began rising up on tiptoes until Maria gripped her arm.

'I am borrowing your wife, Simon. I'll give her back to you once you are no longer the centre of attention.'

Maria slipped her arm through Alice's and led her from the dance floor.

'This is marvellous, Alice. The most incredible ball I have ever been to.' Alice flushed with pleasure. It had been Simon's idea to host a ball on Midsummer's Eve, two years from the date they had first met, but Alice had been the one to remember all the details that had made the last ball so special and then to add in many more of her own.

The ballroom was beautifully decorated with fresh flowers spilling out of vases on tables and plinths around the room. Candles twinkled in the chandelier above their heads and in the sconces around the walls. It made the whole room look like a magical faerie glade, and their guests had embraced this theme with the women wearing floaty, flowery dresses and even some of the men tucking a rosebud or similar boutonnière.

The ballroom was not the only room that was decorated. They had decided on a woodland theme for each area, and it meant the entrance hall had garlands of leaves strung about it in a criss-cross pattern, making it look like their guests were entering the house under a canopy of trees. They had also opened up the drawing room as a quieter, cooler alternative to the ballroom, and for here Alice had sourced dozens of ferns that gave the room a calming atmosphere.

'The girls begged me to let them come and see the room decorated and everyone in their masks,' Maria said as they made their way through the crowd of people. 'I brought them down a little earlier, and I think Sylvia is convinced you are some sort of magical creature, placed in our family to bring us good luck.'

Alice flushed. The past year had flown by, and she and Simon had split their time between London and Northumberland, but by far her favourite part was spending time with their beautiful nieces.

She placed a hand on her swollen belly, looking down anxiously for a moment. They had discussed the subject of children of their own again and again in the early days after Simon's return. Simon worried about passing on whatever his father and brother had died from to any child of his, but as time passed he had also acknowledged that this was another unknown, something that might never come to pass, very much like his own risk of sudden death. They had agreed to put the subject to one side for a year or two and focus on the charity work Alice spent much of her time devoted to and touring the Westcroft properties to ensure everything was in order after Simon's long period away. They had continued to find it difficult to keep their hands off one another, but they took precautions. Fate had another idea, and a few months earlier Alice had realised she was pregnant.

In a way it had been better happening like this, the decision taken out of their hands. It was no one's fault, no one's decision, and as Alice's belly grew, their excitement for starting a family of their own did too.

They had returned to Northumberland a month earlier to prepare for the Midsummer's Eve ball and now planned to stay here until well after Alice had given birth. Alice wanted the reassurance of Maria's presence, and also she felt less nauseous when she could breathe in the fresh sea air rather than the heavy odours of London. Her own sister was planning on making the long journey up from Devon in a few months so she could also be on hand, which would also allow Alice to spend some precious time with Margaret and her little son.

They moved from group to group, exchanging pleasantries with their friends and neighbours, until Alice heard the first notes of a waltz and felt a hand on her shoulder.

'You promised me this dance, my love,' Simon said, his voice low and seductive.

This time he led her not to the dance floor but to the terrace beyond where there were lamps set along the stone balustrade and couples strolled arm-in-arm. They had been blessed with perfect weather for their ball. There was not a cloud in the sky, and hundreds of stars twinkled, helping to illuminate the terrace and the gardens beyond. Simon pulled her close, placing one had in the small of her back, and then they fell into step. Alice's heart soared as he twirled her and caught her and guided her across the terrace. When they danced like this, it always felt as though their bodies moved as one, perfectly synchronised like two swans gliding across a calm lake. As with the ball two years earlier, they had quite the audience by the time they had finished dancing, but everyone looked on indulgently, seeing nothing more than a young married couple enjoying the first flush of wedded bliss.

'This is the part where I should lead you into the garden,' Simon said, leaning close so his lips were almost touching hers.

'I think that might raise a few eyebrows.'

'You're right. Perhaps I should do this instead.'

He grinned at her and then closed the distance between them, brushing his lips against her own. The kiss was passionate but brief, even Simon knew he could not seduce his wife in front of sixty of the wealthiest and most influential people in Northumberland.

'This ball is perfect,' Alice said, rising up on her toes to whisper in his ear. 'But now I cannot wait for it to finish so we can retire upstairs.'

As Simon took her hand in his own, Alice rested her head against his shoulder and looked up at the stars, enjoying the perfect moment on a perfect night.

* * * * *